Dear Jolene & Marc

'ROUND A SQUARE TABLE

To my good
friends forever –
Love
Peg

11-2-07

'ROUND A SQUARE TABLE

PEGGY PALMORE SIMONS

To order additional copies of this book, contact:
Xlibris Corporation
1-888-795-4274
www.Xlibris.com
Orders@Xlibris.com
38198

CONTENTS

PROLOGUE

The reverie of a single flute filtered through the ceremony, harmonizing with haunting drumbeats. Kate understood most of the words the spiritual man spoke, words about love and partnership and equality. With his hand held over her head, the Medicine Man spoke in his native tongue, then repeated in English, "Kate, the Great Spirit walks with you to remind you that you are equal to men, all men, and that he shall guide you through life. When you see *du ni nv di*, you will become the healer of hearts."

A mysterious tingling ran through Kate. "Yes!" She'd known it all along. The burning inside her that yearned to nurse the sick. The Medicine Man had seen it in her, had known her soul's desire. And Flint, out of respect for his Cherokee heritage, would help and encourage her to become a nurse, a medicine woman, and eventually a doctor. She'd watch for *du ni nv di*, the Harvest Moon.

Kate glanced at Dr. Dora who stood smiling, holding a medical book in her arms. Kate would be Flint's equal, just as the Cherokee women were equal and greatly respected by their men.

The Medicine Man bowed his head and then made the same movements standing before Flint, adding a few words that she didn't understand. "Ah," Flint said, replying in his native tongue. The Medicine Man smiled and nodded. He placed a blanket around Kate and Flint's shoulders signifying them as one. Flint kissed Kate sweetly on the mouth. When he finally let Kate go, she laughed and cried at the same time then breathed deeply, full of rapturous joy.

No longer Katrina Lee Barnes, she was now Mrs. Flint Everson Powell. And the Cherokee Medicine Man's vision confirmed that which Kate already knew with all her heart. She would live the life of a healer. She need only watch for the Harvest Moon for her dream to come true.

When the ceremony was through, Dr. Dora handed her the Merck Medical book she had been holding as her wedding gift. "Follow your dreams," she said, giving Kate a quick hug, then waved good-bye, leaving the newly married couple alone.

Kate took Flint's hand and gripped it tightly. "What did the Medicine Man say to you?" she asked when they were alone.

"He said that you'd never be satisfied."

"And what did you say to him?" she asked frowning.

"That I'd give you many children to keep you busy." To that he laughed.

Kate pursed her lips but he merely took her hand and smiled.

Already she was feeling a twinge of dissatisfaction as they walked the dirt road to Mom and Pop's place. Like it or not, the prophesy was coming true. She pressed the medical book close to her chest. Now she must face her parents, but especially her mother to see if they would be welcome.

CHAPTER–1

CHANGE OF PLANS

March 1, 1929, Oklahoma Cherokee Village

Kate wrapped the afterbirth in a tow sack and handed it to Mary Red Bird's mother who left the cabin to dispose of the sack and contents. For the last several weeks, Mary had sipped infusions of Blue Cohosh root in warm water, promoting the rapid delivery that she had experienced this morning. While she waited for Mary's mother to return to the cabin, Kate carefully checked the baby for any abnormalities. She found none, a perfect papoose.

The young girl cooed to her baby. She smiled at him and touched his tousle of dark hair while he nursed at her breast. It would soon be time for Kate to leave Mary Red Bird alone with her infant.

At that thought, Kate took fresh water to the new mother's bedside, knowing how important water was to a nursing mother. With that done, she sat down on a poplar wood stool, the seat covered in deer hide. A hand-hewn white oak cradle sat next to the new mother's bed. The one-room cabin was sparsely furnished, much like Kate's small house.

For the next ten minutes, Kate and Mary sat in companionable silence, listening to the crackle of the fire in the wood stove. Then, Kate rose to her feet, stoked the small wood stove that sat in the corner of the cabin, and poked a few small limbs in the firebox. She closed the stove then picked the Merck medical book up from the table and held it, not wanting to forget it when she left.

The cabin door opened. A cool breeze swept in. Mary Red Bird's mother quickly closed the door behind her and returned to her daughter's side.

"I'll come back to see you in the morning, Mary," Kate said with a smile. She left the cabin brimming with gratification, taking along the medical book that Dr. Dora had given her after the wedding. The book was full of knowledge and wisdom. Kate carried the book with her nearly everywhere she went, even though she hardly needed it for midwifery.

Kate stopped to wrap her thin shawl around her shoulders. She stuck her book under her arm, and smiled toward the clear sky, stepping quickly with a proud sway, her breasts full and dripping. She headed toward Poteau where she would purchase medical supplies and meet up with her husband, Flint, before she walked back to her own home across from Mom and Pop's. Mom had agreed to care for her two children, Rob and Bo, while Kate was away for the day. Then Kate would need to get supper started, and Mom would be anxious to get back to her own house and to Pop.

Kate marveled at the miracle that she helped bring about with her own skill and wits. She must remember to write the event down in her journal . . . nurse Katrina, medicine woman, midwife.

A half-mile west of the Cherokee village, at the edge of Poteau, Kate veered south. Her boots kicked up dust on the narrow road where newly planted cotton patches straddled both sides. Most of the traffic at this end of town came from the Cherokee and Choctaw Reservations and Village, and from the workers and owners of several cotton fields along the way. Kate felt dizzy with inner joy by the time she reached town and stepped up on the boardwalk.

Looking around for Flint's Dodge, she didn't see it and figured that he'd walked the short distance from their house to town since the weather was spectacular this early spring day.

As she walked briskly along the boardwalk and headed for the apothecary, she recognized Pop's friend, a neighboring farmer, Leonard Schwartz, leaning against the wall outside the hardware store. Mr. Schwartz was no stranger to food and his barreled stomach showed it. Pasty white flesh around the pudgy man's eyes contrasted his farmer's tan. The town drunk, Willard Wilson, stood beside him. When Kate reached speaking distance, she slowed her steps, nodded and said, "Good day, Mr. Schwartz."

Wilson, as tall and skinny as Schwartz was short and stout, snickered, but it was Schwartz who spoke. "Well, well, if it ain't the half-breed's white squaw. And I thought you'd a' known better, too. Come girl. Why are you hauling a book around? Ya' can't read, can ya'?"

Shocked to realize that her father's friend hated the natives as many whites did, Kate decided to ignore him. She felt equally surprised that Schwartz treated her as poor white trash simply because Mom had pulled her out of school during her eighth grade to work along with her and Pop in the cotton fields.

Kate wrinkled her brow at Schwartz's insults and quickly stepped away from him. Pressing her book closer to her body, she breathed heavily, searching for a way to defend herself.

"How many half-breeds you all got out at the cotton patch, Kate?" Mr. Schwartz shouted after Kate as she continued to hurry away from him. He followed her closely, only a step or two behind her, as she passed in front of the hardware store. Suddenly, Schwartz reached out and grabbed her shawl-covered shoulder.

The door of the hardware store was blocked open during business hours, and Flint stepped through the threshold as Kate yanked away from Schwartz's grasp. Kate yelled, surprised but relieved to see her husband.

When Schwartz's hand fell from Kate, Flint reached for it, grabbed and bent it, forcing Schwartz off balance. Kate immediately stepped back in horror. "No, Flint!" she screamed.

. Schwartz's heavy body crashed against the hardware store, but with clinched teeth and a low growl, he bounced back, upright. Crouching like a wild cat, Flint sprang on Schwartz and flung him. For an instant, Schwartz plunged to the boardwalk. Then he slowly rose to his feet, sneered at Flint, and began swinging wildly.

To avoid more trouble, Kate rushed in to pull Flint away from the swine that insulted her, but Flint bumped into her and she stumbled backward. Wilson staggered precariously at the opposite edge of the fight.

The boardwalk squeaked and groaned, and Schwartz swung his fists in desperation toward Flint as Flint dodged his moves. An opening presented itself between Schwartz's frantic swings. Flint quickly pulled his fist back and punched the larger man. Kate stared in disbelief when Schwartz flung backward, heavy-bodied. With a sickening crack, Schwartz' head hit the edge of the boardwalk. Blood oozed from the gash that opened in Schwartz' head, staining the rough boards beneath him.

The ghastly sight petrified Kate. Frozen with fear, she stared down at the prone figure stretched out before her. Immediately, Schwartz's fists clenched in outstretched arms and his eyes clamped shut. Gurgles bubbled from his throat and white foam billowed out of his mouth. His palms opened when his head fell to the side, and he relaxed.

Kate pulled on Flint's arm, but he stood ghostly white in a trance. Suddenly, Flint held his stomach, bent forward, and groaned. Finally, he straightened up and grabbed Kate. They jumped from the boardwalk to the dusty street and headed down the road leading out of town.

"He's dead!" It was Wilson, bellowing toward the Sheriff's office. "Get the Sheriff, Billy."

It seemed to Kate that everything happened in slow motion, that no matter how hard she tried she could not run fast enough. But as she picked up speed beside Flint, she turned her head back to the dreadful scene in time to see Billy, the homely onlooker, whisk away in the direction of the Sheriff's office as if he had been horsewhipped.

Wasting no more time looking back, Kate ran swiftly with Flint, realizing they were both in dire trouble, likely to be hung if caught. A half-breed and a white woman stood no chance of real justice in this town.

Pregnant for at least three months, Kate couldn't run as fast as usual. Flint's crippling condition didn't help either. They'd be fortunate to keep ahead of the law.

Holding steadfastly to her book with her left hand, Kate clutched it to her body with her forearm. Flint held her other hand tightly, and grasped at her now and then. He helped her upright when she stumbled on the rough road leading out of the town of Poteau. Newly planted cotton flanked the road and offered them no place to hide. And if they ran through the cotton field now, their feet would sink into the soft soil, slowing them down. But soon they dodged stealthy into the woods where they raced out of sight.

Flint stopped to catch his breath. Bent over and panting, he said, "Katie, let's pack up the boys. We'll get Pop to help us before the law finds us."

"Flint! It was an accident. Why should we run?"

"They'd hang me Katie, just like . . . like any Indian."

Gulping air while making escape plans, they bounded through the woods, swerving trees and brush. They sprinted nearly a half-mile further before they came to their two-room house across from Mom and Pop's place.

When they reached the porch, Kate fell exhausted on the rough boards and Flint leaned against the porch railing, breathing heavily. Kate's breasts ached; her blouse was soaked with the milk. She realized that the thin shawl she wore over her shoulders when she left Mary Red Bird's had disappeared, but gratefully, her medical book appeared unharmed.

Glancing at Flint's grimaced face, Kate figured he was in great pain, but after a few seconds, he pushed himself from the railing to help her stand again. Together, they stumbled through the front door where Kate's mother sat at the square oak table. She had tended Rob and Bo in Kate's absence. Seeing them, she quickly raised herself from the table. Astonishment filled Mom's languid eyes and covered her round, flushed face.

Sitting cross-legged on the rough board floor in front of his Grandmother Annie Rose, Rob peered up from his picture book with inquisitive blue eyes directed toward Kate and Flint. A crib lined up against the wall next to a cot at the east end of the kitchen. Inside the crib Bo raised himself up and wailed. As if in response, milk flowed from Kate's breasts.

Without a word to his mother-in-law, Annie Rose, Flint stomped directly into the small bedroom off the west end of the kitchen and began rummaging around. "Where's the trunk, Kate?"

"At the end of the bed, under the stack of quilts."

Kate grabbed her mother's hand and led her to the front porch out of earshot of Rob and Bo.

"What's wrong, Kate?" Mom demanded, smoothing down the front of her neat calico dress.

"Mom, we're in trouble. We're leaving as soon as Pop can help us. Flint's killed . . . killed Mr. Schwartz." Kate wanted to explain everything, but there wasn't time. "Mom, stay with the boys, I'll get Pop."

"Leonard Schwartz?" She gasped. Mom flashed a hostile glance toward the house . . . toward the bedroom where Flint had gone.

Kate figured that her mother blamed Flint for the fray. She led her mother further out in the yard. "It was my fault, Mom. He was calling me names . . . grabbing at me."

Mom frowned, but nodded. She quickly turned from Kate and scurried back in to tend Rob and Bo while Kate ran toward her parent's house across the road to find her father. Kate glanced down the rough dirt road that led to Poteau. She saw no one, but she expected trouble from that direction any minute. Kate bounded up on the porch and opened the door.

"Pop," Kate called, whisking on through the house and out the back door.

Kate found her father digging in his garden. Pleasant surprise flooded his face when he looked her way. But then he cocked his head and walked to her.

"Kate, what are you doing here? Where's your . . . what's goin' on?"

Kate grabbed her father's shirtsleeve. "Pop, it was my fault. Your friend Schwartz grabbed me. Said Flint was a half-breed and I was his squaw. Flint hit him. Schwartz is bad off. I think he's dead. Oh, dear God."

Pop hurried Kate into the house where she stood in front of him and began to cry. She looked at her father with remorse. Pop patted her on her back. His tired shoulders slumped.

"We were planning to leave for California in a few days. Reckon you'd best gather up the boys, take our Model A, and head out down these back roads. Paul and your mother can help me pile some of our belongings in your Dodge truck and hightail it out of here come dark. We'll catch up with you all somewhere along the way."

"Oh, Pop. What about my midwifery?" The thought stung Kate and she kicked the rough wood floor with her boot. She hung her head, squinting back hot tears.

"I know Kate, I know, but this fray . . . killin' or not, will cause trouble for all the tribes around here. Best get Flint far away. Pop placed his hand on her shoulder, understanding her the way her mother never could. "We'll start over in California, away from these cotton fields and the likes of Leonard Schwartz. I knew he was a buzzard. No friend of mine, Kate. I'd a done the same as Flint."

"Can you take my oak table, Pop, and the boy's beds . . . and Rob's red wagon? You just made side racks for it. He's been hauling firewood for me Pop. We can't leave it!" Kate looked at her father in desperation. "How do you figure to take them? Ever'thing else I can shove down in the trunk." Kate's voice crackled. Her chin raised in question, tears hanging on the edge of her lids.

"No, can't leave the table, you're right there," Pop said, while he checked out the window for trouble. "It's family from way back. We'll heap it all in the truck bed. It'll haul plenty with those side racks Flint built. Your mom and brother and me, we'll get our stuff together and be ready to roll by dark. Hurry on now."

Pop was right. She and Flint and the boys would have to flee to California ahead of them. A cloud of dread and homesickness flowed over Kate as she looked around her folk's little house, nestled here under the gum tree, where she was born and where she grew up. Now she needed to weave new plans for her nursing career and for California.

But, oh how she had her heart set on nursing school and especially how she loved working with the Cherokee and Choctaw people.

The excitement and energy she felt earlier, delivering her first baby this morning all by herself, seemed like a dream now. Weeping softly, Kate left her father and hurried back across the road to her own little house. Wiping the tears from her face, Kate watched the road for signs of more trouble.

CHAPTER–2

CALIFORNIA

Kate, Flint, and the two boys crammed themselves in Pop's Model A and headed out the back road. They drove for many miles before dark and continued driving throughout the night before stretching their legs and gassing up somewhere off the main road. Kate and Flint sat wide-eyed and nervous, bobbling along in the crowded cab, while the boys snored softly.

Hours later, well into the next day, Pop, Mom and Paul caught up with the Model A. The families traded vehicles. Now Flint followed in the Dodge behind Pop and the Model A on the long, desolate road to California.

Once in California, Pop found a small truck farm in Bonita, an area inland from the Pacific coast in San Diego County, not far from the Mexican border. Seeing Pop so spirited and young again helped rid Kate of some of her disappointment.

One day, after settling down in the pastoral area of Bonita, Flint said, "Sure am glad I'm not working in them dirty oil fields anymore. But I'm even more glad that I escaped the noose for flattening Leonard Schwartz. Not likely that the Sheriff would follow us all the way to California," he said to Kate with assurance.

With midwifery no longer an option, Kate waited for the right moment to execute nursing school plans she'd been mulling over since she left Oklahoma. In the meantime, Flint applied for disability. No worry, he said, about the law in Poteau tracing him through his application for disability. When he'd joined the service many years before, his last name had been erroneously spelled as Prowell. It might take awhile, the Veteran's Welfare Bureau official letter indicated, but a monthly allowance for his partial disability should be forthcoming.

As the months of April and May passed, Kate grew more and more discontented that her plans had halted. She yearned for her own career in nursing, and she grew anxious for Flint to find her a home before the baby arrived at the end of summer. But, as she finished milking Bessie in the back yard stall, she heard Bo's hunger cry and her breasts filled instantly. She placed the milk bucket on the kitchen counter.

Kate started supper in her mother's kitchen where Mom sat tending the boys. Rob sat cross-legged on the floor playing with wooden blocks. Content for the time being, Kate leaned over and pecked a kiss on the top of his towhead. Then she rolled up her sleeves and scrubbed her hands and forearms in the kitchen sink. "Mom, there's a nursing school down in San Diego. Thought maybe Pop could give me a ride there to get information. Would you sit with the boys for a few hours next week while I'm gone?"

Seated at the worn table in the large open room where the kitchen and front room combined, Kate's mother uncrossed her legs and pursed her lips.

As Kate waited for her mother's dreaded response, she grabbed a clean flour-sack dishtowel off its peg and briskly dried her arms and hands.

"Mark my word, Kate. You won't have time for anything but caring for these children." Mom plinked the side of her empty coffee cup with her fingernails. "Why after your next baby gets here this summer, that's three mouths to feed, three to rock to sleep. Your eyes are bigger'n your belly," she said with sarcasm while her face flushed with a hint of self-righteousness.

Kate flung the dishtowel toward the wall where it miraculously met the peg and stayed put. She yanked her sleeves down while Mom ranted on.

"And Flint! He'll never let you run around to nurse the sick. You're his woman, Kate, and he's a storm a'brewin' if ever I smelt one. You can't see it, not that side of him. Well, enough said." Mom gave a final plink with her worn nails then eased up from the table. She brushed imaginary lint from her neat calico dress and walked out on her back porch, closing the door softly behind her.

Kate grimaced as she tied apron strings around her thick middle. Hoping to sooth the discomfort of her mother's reprimand, she pulled Bo to her breasts as she plopped down in the rocker that sat beside the kitchen wood stove. "The red-headed Irish are a testy lot."

Bo peeked at her from his meal and Rob peered up from his wooden blocks. They watched her as if they understood her every word. She tickled Bo's freckled nose with a wisp of her auburn hair that hung at the nape of her neck.

"Your Grandma Annie Rose never sees things the way I do. What's wrong with being a nurse?" Kate winced at Bo's ravenous slurping, and brushed his blondish-red hair back from his forehead with her fingertips. In a few minutes, Bo's mouth opened and his eyes closed. "Now that you've drained me dry, it won't be long before your daddy and Grandpop come in hungry for supper, Bo, so in the crib you go."

The spring months passed and heat and stickiness came right on time, just as hot and sticky as Oklahoma. The atmosphere outside her own heart and mind teamed with excitement wherever she went and with whomever she spoke. When Pop took Kate to the local market, she looked around at the people and their different skin colors. It appeared that they had come to California from every direction of the country. She heard Irish accents. Some darker skinned folks spoke Spanish, but mostly she heard southern accents just like her own. Kate sensed that Californians didn't care if others were red or black, Irish or Mexican, and that was at least one thing that felt right to Kate. She began to feel more comfortable in California.

But for Kate, one question lingered in the back of her mind . . . how to get to the nearest nursing school. She never learned how to drive and didn't know how she would get there without help. Surely Mom wouldn't allow Pop to help her even if he wanted to. Perhaps she needed a spirit guide to help her as her Cherokee friends did.

Finally, in June, while Mom held Bo on her knee, and Pop helped Rob in a chair beside him, Paul came in the door for supper. Kate served them as they sat around Mom's table. Flint usually didn't come home until everyone else had gone to bed.

But on this evening, while the family ate supper, Flint bustled in earlier than usual from his search for a home for his family. "Katie, Katie, I've found a paradise for you all." His deep voice quivered with excitement, as he stood with a hand on one hip and his pipe in the other, waving it toward the northeast. "Got the paper signed today on our homestead . . . Mt. McGinny to the east, maybe twenty miles from where you're sittin'." Flint turned around and knocked ashes from his pipe into the wood stove. "We'll park the Dodge at the old Irishman's place. Gus Hays is the closest neighbor I've found so far. Then we'll make tracks from there on up to the homestead first thing in the morning."

Kate rose from her plate of pinto beans and fried potatoes, and poured her husband a cup of coffee. "There's a house, Flint?"

Flint put his hand up, palm facing Kate, sign language he used to let her know that she needn't be bothered by trifles. He was in charge. She was of no account. Kate averted her eyes, hiding the anger that burned in them. She quickly dished a plate of food for her husband and plunked it down with the cup of coffee in front of the empty chair at the table.

"Land, Katie! Land with creeks! We'll camp there by the pond. As magnificent as any spot I've ever seen. There's a whole mountainside. Raise all the kids you want. And avocados." Flint stuck his pipe in his khaki shirt pocket, and then he sat down and forked potatoes in his mouth. He swallowed his food whole then continued in a dither. "This is avocado country, Katie. They're nearly a year-round crop, hey Jep?" Flint often showed his friendship by calling Kate's father, Jep, his nickname for Jefferson. Flint laughed in triumph of his find, and then slurped his coffee.

Pop nodded.

Filled with dread, Kate asked, "What about nursing school?"

"What do you need with school? You've got us . . . me and the kids. That right Annie?" he winked.

"That's right, Flint."

Kate detected a gleam in her mother's eyes and flinched. She felt the noose tightening, not around Flint's neck as she'd feared . . . but around her own.

CHAPTER—3

THE HOMESTEAD

Early the next morning and with her parents' home far behind, Kate sensed an animal watching her. With worried eyes, she searched the mountainside of sage and madrone but saw nothing to fear. She took a tentative step forward and saw a fleeting movement out of the corner of her eye. There, halfway up the hillside, a mountain lion crouched. Kate yelled.

"Flint, look! There on the side of the mountain, the flat rock!"

Flint turned toward her and squinted but did nothing to stop the animal. She hugged Bo closer to her swollen belly and waited on the trail for Rob. His short legs strained under the weight of the little red wagon.

"Sure seems further than a mile walk, Flint," Kate said, glancing up at the cloudless sky. "It's a scorcher, and the day is young." Squinting, she searched the sloping, rock-strewn trail ahead. Mountains loomed to the north and east shouldering rounded, house-sized rocks, some precariously perched upon others. Granite bits crunched beneath her feet. She glanced back at the flat rock. The big cat was gone. Relieved, she whisked in a quick breath of pungent air, but then the awful thought came to her that the mountain lion had probably sensed them or seen them and was on his way down.

"Is that Mt. McGinny, Flint?"

Flint kept pace a few feet ahead of Kate. "Yep, about half way up the side of that mountain and to the north. Southwest corner's right about where you see that big round boulder. One-hundred-sixty-acres. These mountains are part of the Cuyamaca Mountain Range. Mountain lions roam everywhere, Gus says."

Kate smiled at the thought of Gus, the old Irishman with sparkling green eyes. She met him at his place to park the Dodge before they started on their trek up the mountain. She was glad to have one neighbor at least.

Flint motioned toward the rock where the cat had been. He clutched a Winchester 44 rifle in his right hand. "We'll just leave him alone. No need to fear him. If he does get too close, the rifle's loaded, and that would be all she wrote, for him . . . or rattlers.

Kate knew how capable Flint was, especially in the wild. He knew the way of the Indian. She needn't worry. "Flint, do these mountain lions attack people?" she asked, recalling horror stories from Oklahoma.

Flint stopped and turned to answer her. "Oh, sometimes a deer, but mostly rodents. Those yellow cats avoid people, but I suppose if they're big, like that one." Flint motioned with his head toward the rock and again looked at Kate. "He might snatch a child. Back home Grover's baby was drug off. Why, I've seen those cats big as they get. Bigger than a man. This one looked near six feet to me. Couple hundred pounds. A male, I'd guess. He's not likely to come after us." Flint turned and walked on.

Mountain lion, rattlesnake, the sweltering heat . . . no matter how dismal life seemed, they were in Southern California and Kate determined to make the best of it. No mountain lion was going to make things any worse for her. She blew air to her face hoping to cool the sweat that poured from her, but without effect.

"We can't leave these youngsters anywhere without us or a good dog near. I don't like to think about Grover's baby. Well, I reckon we best put the past behind us, huh, Flint?"

Flint merely grunted in response. At least she didn't have to worry about Flint going to jail. He would never be traced here, Kate felt sure of it. Kate squinted up at the relentless sun, cicadas chorusing. They had left Oklahoma March 2. Nearly four months had passed and not a sign of being followed. Kate felt faint carrying Bo and moved him from her middle to her hip. This second son was such a big child and not yet two years old.

Kate trod along the trail, tired and anxious. "Your daddy will need to be leaving for supplies one of these days soon, but we're not scared, are we Napoleon Bonaparte?" she whispered to Bo, looking into his sky-blue eyes that reflected the exact color of her own. She touched his pug nose with the tip of her finger, and tickled his sunburned cheeks with the sprig of auburn hair that escaped from the bun placed at the nape of her neck. For a minute she placed her free hand on her belly where an infant lay curled inside. She fidgeted, turning to look all around her. Again, she waited for Rob to catch up.

Fortunately, Kate's heavy smock and oversized dungarees gave her some protection from the brush and blistering sun. Yet sweat dripped from her worried face and down between her breasts. She hoped Flint would notice how miserable she was and stop for a while, but she didn't dare ask him. He was eager to get where they were going. "We wouldn't want to hold your dad back, now would we boys. Let's try to keep up."

She felt eyes on her back and pressed onward. It would be a good idea to stay close to Flint and the rifle. With a furrowed, sunburned brow, she admonished herself for allowing the mountain lion to further taint an already uncomfortable day.

Rob's wagon bounced along behind him, heaped with enough cookware, clothing, and food to last a day or so until Flint could walk back to the Dodge parked at Gus' place. After several stops and tugs on the wagon, Rob stumbled and plopped down hard on the hot dry ground. His innocent blue eyes filled with tears as he looked up at Kate in desperation. Sweat dripped down the sides of his flushed face.

"Rob's getting' tired," Kate drawled, feeling protective of her son. "The side slats alone make that wagon much too heavy for that child." She marveled at Rob, her first born. Robert William Powell, only four years old but always helping like a little man, though he was slight of build and not much larger than Bo.

Fortunately, Flint saw that Rob was struggling and didn't scold the boy, but stopped to help. "Here you go, son." Flint swung Rob upon his back alongside the bedrolls slung over his shoulder. Kate pulled the wagon behind her as she continued to search the boulders that littered the mountainside and the canyon that beckoned beside them, where oaks, willows, and sycamores grew in abundance. "Why are you so fidgety, Katie?" he asked, calling Kate his pet name for her whenever he was teasing or in a better mood.

"Oh, I'm just looking at our homestead," Kate shuddered.

Warmth filled her heart as Kate watched Flint swab the sweat from his face and neck with his red bandana, raise his straw hat, and run his hand through his dark hair. He'd finally found them a home, and he carried his little son, although weary himself. And his plans were honorable for the homestead. She'd try to go along with all of it, despite the nagging worry that she'd never get to fulfill her dream of becoming a doctor. Flint placed his hat on his head. Rob's thin arms and legs clinched tightly around his father's neck and back.

They trudged on among sagebrush and other chaparral, sumac and rock. Bits of granite and sparse dry grass covered the hard brown earth. Grasshoppers with their monotonous hum, darted this way and that.

As she carried Bo along the uneven path, Kate kissed her son's ear and thought about the homestead. Surely Flint wouldn't want to raise hogs. She had slopped too many of the filthy things in Oklahoma. Cotton wouldn't grow here either. Thank God for that. There were better crops than cotton for this country, and for this mountain. And no more oil fields.

Kate stopped a moment to reposition Bo in her arms. She brushed blond-red hair back from his hot forehead. "We are goin' to farm dry-land melons. And you can help milk our good old Jersey cow that we left at Grandpop and Grandma's. Remember Bessie cow, Bo? Just think, chickens for eggs, and a rooster for the glorious sound of crowing in the early mornin'." Bo felt heavier. His eyes went closed and his mouth drooped open.

Flint talked of growing avocado trees, a good crop for this mountain, he had told her and the folks. She murmured thanks to God that at least here, her husband wouldn't have to look over his shoulder anymore and wonder if he'd killed a man, wonder if the law, or worse, some Indian hater trailed him. She glanced around again, as she had many times during her walk up the trail, but trembled when her eyes focused again on the rock. "There! There, Flint! It just leaped off that rock. Oh, no! I hope its den isn't nearby." Bo felt heavier in his deeper sleep, oblivious to her concerns.

Flint responded with a troubled groan but did nothing. Animals never seemed to concern him. He felt at home in the wild in a way that she never would. Pains shot through Kate's belly and were gone as quickly as they had come.

At last they stopped to rest and drink water in the shade of the giant granite boulder that Flint said marked the southwestern boundary of the homestead. Bo's bright blue eyes popped open and Kate planted his feet on the hard ground while she rummaged around in the wagon. "Come, boys, rest. Sit here and chew on these biscuits and jerky." Weary, she sat down clumsily on the ground, pulling the boys to her side.

Flint stood, looking around them. He scanned the ground and the gaping cracks in the bolder behind where Kate and the boys sat. "Keepin' my eye out for rattlers. They get near eight feet long in these hills, I hear. Keep awake." He drank from the canteen and passed it to Kate.

Their rest in the shade of the boulder was short. Too soon, they gathered their belongings and walked on.

The thought of an eight-foot rattlesnake continued to weigh on Kate's mind. She wasn't worried so much about the snake, but she didn't like it that Flint tried to scare her for no good reason. "You kinda stretchin' that snake, Flint? Eight feet? That doesn't seem possible."

Flint turned in his tracks and gave her his 'just you wait and see' look. "No matter, a two-footer can strike just as fast and furious as an eight-footer," he quipped.

She had learned long before that he didn't take kindly to her disagreeing with him or questioning him. It was a woman's place to let her man feel superior and, in turn, he was her protector. She had found that, when it suited Flint, he didn't go along with his Cherokee culture's belief that women were powerful, equal, and potentially dangerous because they knew how to bring about change through childbirth. It was apparent to Kate that Flint wasn't afraid of her.

In the brutal June sun, Flint's eagerness waned, and her own vision blurred, but she wasn't about to take her eyes off of the brush where a rattlesnake might crawl out or lay coiled, ready to strike. She knew that they were cautious creatures though, like Flint, hunted and hated. They usually didn't harm anything unless they were forced, same as some people. At least they shook their rattles to warn a person. More than some folks did. Still, she concentrated and listened intently for the sound of a rattler, while her eyes searched for other movement.

"Flint, how close do you have to be to a mountain lion to put him down with that Winchester?" Kate stuttered.

"He's harmless. Quit worrying and get up here." A stab of pain ran through Kate's chest. She tried to speak, but no words came from her mouth. Flint had lashed back at her with senseless aggravation and now she vowed to keep quiet and worry silently.

The walk up the mountain was supposed to be about a mile. At first the distance appeared short from where they had parked their Dodge at Gus Hay's, but it was turning out to be a nearly unbearable trek, one that she could endure for the paradise that lay ahead. But there was no house. To build a house would take weeks. And how would they get in and out of the homestead? What would they eat? It would take weeks to produce a vegetable garden. They would need to store potatoes and squash for winter. And winter on the mountain would be cold. Flint had better have the answers.

Kate felt tough as an old Tom and beyond her 25 years. She wore signs in her fine-featured face of too many days of toil in the sun and a life of struggle and disappointment. She wiped the sweat from her brow as she marched on under the merciless sun. Irish blood ran through her veins. She would keep her worries inside, waiting for eventual answers.

Kate clinched her jaw stubbornly and her eyes narrowed in defense of everything that went against her grain. Yes, patient with a stubborn streak. The stubborn streak Mom had always pinned on her. Kate considered it a positive trait, even if Mom thought otherwise.

Kate's thoughts reverted to Oklahoma. Although sad to have left her place and her life there, she wouldn't miss parts of Oklahoma, Tornados, for one thing. And it was hard to imagine any work as toilsome as picking cotton in those hot Oklahoma fields as Kate had done since she was old enough to crawl behind Mom and Pop along the dusty paths between the cotton rows. She'd even done some picking after Rob was born. How did her folks tolerate such slavery for so many years? She was glad now, especially for Pop, that they were in California.

There was the nursing school in San Diego, and of course, after that she'd go on to medical school and become a doctor like Dr. Dora. Kate shook her head recollecting Dr. Dora's words to her that she, Kate, could do anything she set out to do. And the Cherokee medicine man saw her future as a healer. It would happen, she knew. Kate smiled, determined to keep the dream alive inside. More than once since arriving in California, Kate had mentioned the possibility of school to Mom. Every time Kate was rebuked. And when Kate brought up the subject in front of the whole family, Flint raised his palm to her. Mom said San Diego was full of predators, meaning men. It would be unsafe for Kate. What difference did it make? She was Flint's woman, and Mom thought him a predator. Still, Kate ached to learn about nursing, now it was probably too late. Maybe she had asked for too much.

When she had become a mother right away, and then left her plans in Oklahoma, her lot in life was established. But it seemed that things were looking up now that they were heading for their own homestead. If only they could survive the worst of it. And if Flint would treat her in the same caring way Pop did Mom, they might stand a chance here.

A westerly breeze touched her warm skin, and a strange feeling overcame her. For a moment she forgot about the mountain lion and the rattlesnakes. Joy pulsed through her, a sort of liberation, an escape from a past that haunted her husband and gave them a new beginning. She jerked the wagon up the steep hill, reminding herself not to get hopeful just yet. Somebody would need to rid the mountain of that cougar, and then she would find a way to win her husband's love and respect.

CHAPTER—4

THE CAMP—JUNE 1929

Flint felt overwhelmed, almost delirious, from all the changes that had taken place in the last few days. So much work ahead of him that required immediate action. He focused on it now. A few days prior to signing the homestead papers, when he came to determine the boundaries of the claim, he knew that he had found a treasure here . . . a treasure in the soil, in the crystal sky, and in the crisp air. As he breathed in the fresh mountain air, he felt happier than he could ever remember. The Creator led him here, he knew for certain. He couldn't have planned it all or schemed it himself, but he'd have to break his neck to keep Kate from wanting more than he could provide.

Flint swabbed his face with the bandana. There was plenty of work on this homestead to keep Kate so busy she was likely to forget the notion of nursing the sick. And of course, there was the mountain lion to contend with. He pursed his lips and checked the flat rock.

Where a bank jutted out alongside the trail, Flint stopped. He laid the rifle against the bank and unfolded a map, pointing to a spot near the middle. "This is Mt. McGinny," he said.

Kate caught up with him and glanced at the map. Then he folded the map and stuck it in his shirt pocket next to his pipe and said, "It's rough farming, but ours to live on. The Creator brought us here. The Kumeyaay Indians lived here once. Course, like most tribes, they were either stuck together on some reservation or killed . . . probably killed." Flint knew that there had been bounties on the California Indians years before, and if it became known that he was Cherokee to any degree, he could be in danger. Best not to mention such a notion to Kate, he decided. He shook his head, ridding himself of a siege of memories and anger, but quickly turned his thoughts back to his life and what lay ahead. He couldn't get over the fact that so much could be theirs by just living here and doing what they loved to do anyway. Farming and hunting were in his blood. His ancestors were farmers and hunters. He was a farmer and would hunt the fallow deer on Mt. McGinny whenever his aching bones would allow. After his short stint in the Navy, he was sure that he wanted to farm more than ever. The Navy was the kind of regimented, structured life that he hated. For the life of him, he couldn't understand how those poor fools in the service stood it.

There was a parallel, he thought; good physical health depended on how happy one was with his life's work. As he struggled up the mountain, he prayed that his aches and pains would soon end. He planned to give thanks to the Great Spirit at the end of their journey up the mountain.

"The homestead agreement papers say we have lots of hard work ahead; a well to dig, fences to build, a shelter to erect. There are two creeks." He pointed in the direction of a group of oaks. "See those trees where the creeks come together in a Y? We'll set up camp there. Plenty of water. I'll start digging the well soon as we get settled. The spring is up the creek, comin' from the east. If the creeks dry up come late summer, why, spring water trickles right out the canyon wall." Flint smacked his lips. "Katie, you have to taste that sweet spring water. There's nothin' like it!"

"Yeah, a place has to have water," Kate responded apathetically.

"The shelter's got to go up first thing." Flint caught his breath. What could he say to Kate to make her see what he saw? He noticed her reluctance and he felt a spark of anger but tried to ignore it. Sweat eased down his face. He stopped to place his hand on Kate's shoulder for a moment. Guilt nagged at him for dragging her around from one place to another, running from trouble and constantly searching for what he needed. And he grew tired of her crying. He knew she cried. She tried to hide it from him but he had heard her. Especially at night when she thought everyone was sleeping. He clinched his fists, trying to curb his mounting frustration. For once he wished she could be happy for him. "We'll build a shelter before the baby comes," he assured her, but she wouldn't even look at him.

Wanting to avoid the glint of ice in her sharp blue eyes, he marched ahead. At 35, he was still seeking direction for his life, a way of life that would suit him, a place of solitude, a place to feel at home, something more than mere survival. He wanted something to fill the longing and emptiness inside, to end the feelings of discouragement, so he could feel proud.

As he listened to the cry of the hawk overhead, he thought of his Cherokee grandparents that he never knew. The government had forced them off their rich farmlands and driven them into Oklahoma, a wasteland by comparison. He wiped the sweat staining his brow. How he wished he could have known his father . . . he fought to remember details. His father never married his mother. Flint never knew why. It was common for white men to marry Cherokee women, though they would have experienced some bigotry. She'd married Turner, a white man, a few years later anyway. Flint spent time at the Reservation over the years, hoping to learn more about his white father, but no one knew anymore than he did.

He had lived around whites most of his life, since his mother married Turner, a wealthy tobacco farmer. Right away, envious of Flint's mother's attention to him, Turner hated him. Turner's ugly words echoed in Flint's brain over the years. If it hadn't been for his mother's love, he'd have gone to the reservation with the rest of the Cherokees. But they didn't fully accept him. To them he fit nowhere . . . not with whites, not with his Cherokee Clan.

And then, when he was fifteen years old, he returned home from school one day to find his mother laying on her bed in a pool of blood, her life drained from her. A bloody prod lay on the floor beside her bed. She'd used it to rid herself of the unwanted child inside her. Flint squinted his eyes, replaying the horror that had returned to his memory so many times over the years.

Sometimes he felt hollow, cheated, wanting them, his mother and father. Wanting a few more sweet childhood memories. Often, when he lay still at night before falling asleep, he could recall running barefoot through the pungent-smelling woods as a child. It was glorious freedom. Now he was pushed out of Oklahoma, more or less, but he was glad that everything happened the way it did. Heat rushed to Flint's face and he set his jaw. He pressed on with determination.

He had so much to say to Kate that he didn't say, nor could say. It seemed much easier just to walk, limping and plodding along in the heat of the day, suffering, if need be, with the affliction that robbed him of the robust man he was before the war. But there was no way to get the words out, no way to make Kate understand. His attempts to communicate with her felt crude, forced. She irritated him, hanging on him like an old heavy coat. But this homestead, this was something solid and sure, the one thing they could share. She would be here, and he could come and go as he pleased. Come back to her and the peaceful mountain to farm, when he was tired of talking politics in town and playing poker and swigging wine with his cohorts down in the valley. A glint of lightness filled him.

They topped the summit about mid-day where the terrain leveled out, greeting the shade and coolness of emerald-green willows alongside a fallow-deer trail. Flint turned around a moment to look back at the trail they had walked, then beyond to the valley below. A warm westerly breeze blew in his face. Bo fussed in his mother's arms and she cooed to him. Her soft gentle voice reached Flint's ears and he felt a pang of affection for her. Then he thought of his own mother and instantly felt a different pang . . . a pang of regret and anger. He felt angry at himself for not being able to help her and angry at her for leaving him to deal with life alone with Turner. A great heaviness came over him as they continued on. Once on the deer trail, Flint glanced up into the trees.

"These tall trees are a likely place for a mountain lion to perch, though usually they hunt at night." His grip tightened around the rifle.

Rob moaned again and scooted higher on Flint's back. His arms encircled Flint's neck and his little head lay tucked beneath the brim of the straw hat.

They hastened the last few yards to reach a cove of land, surrounded with willows, sycamores, and live oaks. There, a serene pool of water collected from the rocky creek coming down from the northeastern mountains. It was just as Flint remembered it. He was relieved it had not been a dream. Hurriedly, they splashed across the shallow, narrow creek to the shade of a vast oak tree, whooping, laughing, and running to the pool. Kate and Bo dropped to their knees at the pool's edge. Flint let the bedrolls fall from his shoulder while Rob slid off his back. Flint lined up with his wife and boys beside him on the silt at the pool edge, plunging their faces into the cool, sweet water, slurping and splashing until their thirsts were quenched, and crimson faces faded and cooled.

Kate helped the boys take off their heavy shoes and worn socks and then her own. Refreshed from splashing pond water on his face, Flint now stood and watched with amusement while his wife and boys stuck their feet in the water. Spring rains had been plentiful. A frog croaked and then another, echoing up and down the creek in the deeper canyon that ran from the southeast toward the west at the lower edge of the cove. A Thunderhead cloud, white as snow, billowed up behind the mountains to the east. The Thunderhead, an allusive sign of a summer rain.

Flint crouched, scanning all about him. Then he filled his pipe with Prince Albert tobacco and lit it. "Katie, listen to that. This place reminds me of back home, back in the hills." He puffed in the aromatic tobacco smoke. "Paradise." He spoke softly, rising from a crouch to stand, feeling like a sentinel guarding Eden, his eyes close to tears. "Listen, just listen to nature's marvelous song, like a flute."

A quail covey fluttered from a dense thicket nearby, and a hummingbird blurred as it moved backwards in flight. Kate and the boys reluctantly shook the water from their feet and pulled on their shoes and socks.

Not wanting to break the magic of the moment, Flint knocked the ashes from his pipe, stuck the pipe in his pocket, and spoke quietly. "Twilight soon to come, Rob. It's getting nippy." He motioned to Rob. "Let's gather these fallen oak branches and leaves. We'll need to keep a fire all night, every night. Keeps the puma away. He'll do his hunting at night." Under his breath, he whispered, "Course, we know that's not always the case."

When they finished piling the branches high, ready for the night fire, Flint pulled Rob's wagon across the creek to the campsite for Kate. He built a fire in a clearing at the edge of the vast oak and spread their bedrolls out underneath the ancient tree. After organizing the camp area, he poked at the fire with a sturdy limb, compacting the coals. With a heavy sigh, he leaned against the oak tree.

Exhausted, Flint felt the long, hot day suddenly take its toll on him, and he reached in his shirt pocket for his pipe. He watched Kate while she pulled the blue granite coffee pot from the wagon, filled it with stream water just above the pool, added coffee grounds, and placed it on a flat rock at the edge of the fire where orange coals sizzled. She seemed to move so easily, methodically almost, as if she was used to carrying extra, as if a protruding belly had always been there. *She is still beautiful.* He nodded to himself, feeling a tinge of pride. She seemed thin everywhere else on her body. Thin, but muscular. Flint tried in vain to remember Kate when she was not pregnant.

By the time the coffee began to boil, the pinto beans were steaming in a black cast-iron pot and Kate carefully turned sourdough biscuits in a cast-iron skillet. Rob sprawled out on the bedroll, watching his mother and jabbering to himself and to Bo, who slept beside him. Snoring softly, Bo still grasped his mustard-jar bottle with its black nipple that Kate had saved from Rob's babyhood, and had tied the nipple tightly to the top edge of the jar by a worn strip of rag. Flint held in a siege of laughter remembering how Kate had fashioned the darned thing together.

Droplets of milk escaped from the jar-bottle, making their way down Bo's chubby arm. Rob wiped them off with the edge of his blanket and covered his dozing brother.

Tomorrow couldn't come soon enough for Flint. But right now, he welcomed a good night's sleep. The aroma of freshly boiled coffee, beans, and biscuits mingled with crisp air. Now, with his wife and boys on their own homestead, Flint felt flooded inside with warmth that eased his weary bones.

When their bowls were empty, Kate washed the bowls and spoons in the creek above the pond and then puttered around the fire until sundown. Coyotes yelped. Whip-poor-wills began their night cry, as darkness surrounded them. In a moment, a billion stars found their place in the heavens above them. Flint watched his family while they relaxed by the fire. The moon, full and gold, peeked over the Cuyamaca mountain range behind Mt. McGinny, and his world filled with light. Tomorrow, Flint would begin building a new home on this mountain. And he finally had control of his life . . . he hoped.

CHAPTER—5

The Road In

After Flint settled his family in at the makeshift camp, he retraced his steps to get the Dodge from Gus' place. As he walked toward the worn house, Gus Hays stepped from his barn to holler at him. "Get settled already, Mr. Powell?" The Irishman's bib overall straps appeared ready to fall from his stooped shoulders. His tall, lean body wavered in the heat from too much drink. He held a bottle in his left hand and offered his right hand to Flint.

Leery of most men when first encountering them because of his Cherokee heritage, Flint stuck his hand out tentatively. But Gus made him feel more welcomed than he'd ever felt by anyone. "How do you manage here all alone, Gus?" Flint grabbed the huge bony hand to shake it.

Gus squinted and rubbed his stubble chin. "Well, animal friends live here too. Not alone a'tall. And me bottle, don't forget me bottle." He chuckled as he thrust his whiskey bottle in Flint's direction.

Flint accepted the bottle and tipped it to his lips. White lightening bolted and burned all the way to his fingertips. "Where in hell did you get this? This stuff's illegal. You make it?" Flint took a step to his side to keep his balance. After he wiping his mouth on his khaki shirtsleeve, he handed the bottle back to Gus.

"Aye, that I did. When ya' get settled, Mr. Powell . . . Flint, I'll show ya' where my still is. What'd ya' think the cornfield was for? My ol' cow, mule, horse, and chickens, all of 'em put together don't eat that much corn. Why, ya' know, Mr. Powell, Prohibition is gonna be the ruination of these here United States of America." Gus chuckled almost continuously, waving his arm toward several acres of healthy-looking, head-high corn stocks.

The two men stood in the dust and warmth of the morning sun, taking turns swigging the bottle. Gus' drab house and barn sat on flat terrain, surrounded by fields of corn, and without a single tree. Two fat puppies chased each other around Gus' dirty bare feet, nipping at his toes. He danced around to avoid their teeth. Finally, they scampered away, rolling in the dust.

"Got our campsite set up. Need to get my supplies in soon, Gus. You got any idea how I might get a road into my place?"

The older gentleman rubbed his salt-and-pepper whiskers and cocked his head. "Don't see how's you could get through from here with that one deep ravine in the way." Gus waved his bottle of corn liquor toward the ravine. "Government land on the outside of Widow Helm's place though, just south of you. 'Bout a mile of old wagon trail from Helm's on up. Might need to get an easement from the Widow to get from the highway to her place, which I reckon is 'bout another mile. One way or t'other that there is the closest route. Aye, Widow Helm sure is a pretty woman too. I hear she's an artist . . . paints real good." He grinned, but quickly added, "Not near as pretty as Mrs. Kate, I'd say."

Flint stood under the blazing heat wondering how he could enter his homestead should Mrs. Helm, the fine artist, not allow him to use her road. "Hope she's at home, Gus. Got to get supplies to my property soon. Winter's comin'." Flint frowned with curiosity about the lady. Would she be against him if she knew he was Cherokee? He could have a real problem on his hands.

"Oh say, Mr. Powell . . . Flint. I spotted the big king varmint top of those high rocks just above your place."

The big cat had shown himself several times already and Flint stiffened at the prospect.

"He's a young'un, but as big as they come." The Irishman's green eyes snapped wide open. "This here's his territory. He's been around for 'bout a year. Nearly scares the daylights out'a me every time I hear him scream. Wouldn't turn me back on the yeller beast." Gus grinned again. His sparkling eyes danced with excitement, reminding Flint of the young bronze Cherokees from his childhood visits to the Reservation. Their faces covered in spirit-world masks, bending and hopping around the campfire.

Nodding, Flint knew the mountain lion would warrant careful watching. He prayed that he would never have to destroy such a sacred animal. He feared he might have to eventually, especially since the kids would be roaming the homestead.

Leaving Gus, Flint drove the Dodge back to the main highway, headed east about half a mile, and then north toward Mt. McGinny. After another mile of rugged dirt road, following Gus's directions, he arrived at Widow Helm's. As he approached a huge house, he noticed her and caught his breath. A busty woman with loose, dark hair beneath a wide-brimmed hat strolled among a flower garden. She walked toward him, her long skirt flowing around bare ankles. Flint stopped the Dodge, his eyes never straying from her lovely form, as he stepped out of the truck.

She is more than pretty. A vexing grin spread across his clean-shaven face and, with a quick bow, he lifted his straw hat, offering his hand. "I'm Flint Powell, Mrs. Helm?" Flint wondered if he should spoil this neighborly visit with the request for an easement.

"What brings you here, Mr. Powell?" she responded in a deep vibrating voice.

Flint ran fingers through his thick, dark hair, and held his hat. "Homesteading just beyond those hills, near the bottom of Mt. McGinny. Thought maybe you could help with an easement." There! He said it and wanted to kick himself for fear of her response. She might refuse to help. "Gus Hays says there's an old wagon trail goes straight on from here, but from the highway to the wagon trail is your property." Words spilled out without much sense and sweat seeped through his khaki shirt. He stopped short of what he intended to say.

Mrs. Helm began strolling in her garden again and he stood there, watching her. He fingered his hat, not knowing what to do next. Either she needed time to mull his request over in her mind, or she didn't want a Cherokee using her land. He balled his hand in a fist as he waited for the verdict. He'd be in a real fix if there was no way to get up the mountain from here.

Reluctantly, Flint followed Mrs. Helm as she walked through her garden. He smelled jasmine. Together, they silently meandered along narrow paths between Iris, Lilies, and Sweet Alyssum for a few minutes before Mrs. Helm replied in her resonate and self-assured voice. "I see no problem with that. You'll not need an easement from me since my road has been through here for many years and runs right into the wagon trail. So, the road is yours, too. The same is true for the wagon trail from here on up the mountain. I believe legally it's called Easement by Prescription."

Flint took a deep breath, relieved and surprised that discussing the easement went so well. From what he had learned during his search for a home for his family, he should have rights to the road since there was no other way in. The wagon trail had been used off and on over the years, but he wanted to make sure that she knew it as well. After all, it was the gentlemanly thing to do.

"I heard of you folks at the Spring Valley Market earlier this week. Tell me about your family." Mrs. Helm flung her long dark hair away from her face.

Mrs. Helm, with eyes deep, dark brown, had an air about her of fine breeding, aristocratic ancestry. It was the way she held her head when she talked. She was straightforward. No hidden agenda, no forked tongue. He'd bet that she had never picked cotton in her life.

Flint told her about his family and of dreams for the homestead's future. Together, they walked and talked and breathed in the fragrances of Sweet Alyssum around them. Feeling he was saying too much, and wanting to listen to her lyrical voice, Flint held back so that she might talk more.

"I don't live here year round, Mr. Powell. When my husband's heart failed him and he died, I thought it important to take my two sons to an area where they would be exposed to the best education in music, so we live in Los Angeles most of the year." Mrs. Helm faced him and smiled, showing perfect bright teeth.

A strange tingling raced through Flint's heart. He returned her smile. Lightness filled him even though the heat bore down on his head, but guilt dampened his excitement when he thought of Kate, alone with the boys on the mountain.

"I come here to paint in the summer. It's peaceful here and, of course, these flowers need care. The Jasmine is my favorite. It grows everywhere, all over the banks and up the side of the house." She waved toward the house. The rough redwood siding hung in places on the ugly massive archaic structure, and dust covered the windows that were not completely broken out. The house's eves drooped, and the wide wooden porch that spanned the south end of the house, rippled with sways. An enormous contrast to the lovely flower garden where Flint stood mesmerized with Mrs. Helm.

If Mrs. Helm planned to continue owning this old place, surely it would need repairs over time, and maintenance too. Flint realized he had conjured a way to earn a living and to spend some time with Mrs. Helm. The guilt returned when he thought of his wife at the homestead, camping under the oaks, pregnant with his child.

Mrs. Helm was silent a moment, and then wrinkled her nose as if she read his thoughts. He looked down, hoping to hide the flush in his face. They meandered until they stood beneath the pungency of a Pepper tree. The sun filtered through the weeping branches of ugly green fern-like leaves. With turned-up chin, Mrs. Helm said, "The old house was built by Green's from Georgia in 1857. Then owned by Rutledge's. Later, it was a boys school, or orphanage really, before Martin and I bought it about four years ago to farm." Flint watched her and listened, intrigued, and taken in by her melodious voice. He followed her as she walked from beneath the Pepper tree, and stood again in the sunshine, closer to the house. "Martin died before we ever got a crop in," she said. "The house is scarcely livable but makes a wonderful studio and storage for my antiques and books. I use only a few rooms. This entire south end is closed off."

Her voice trailed. And then she shrugged her shoulders, as if to rid herself of something bothering her. In a more serious tone, she said, "I believe the house is haunted. Martin said I was silly, but I know that he wondered about it, too." She laughed as she had several times during their short visit, and the light returned to her face.

A flash of memory came to Flint. His mother's clan believed that human ghosts felt lonesome and wanted companionship. Sometimes they caused sickness so that the person might die and go to be with them. Of course, Flint, inundated by the Baptist Missionaries during his school years, had any such belief carried from his earlier years, banished during the course of his education. Flint quickly brought his thoughts back to the moment and to Mrs. Helm.

He could have stayed with the woman all day, but he thought of Kate, pregnant on the mountain. "Well, I expect to see you again, Mrs. Helm." Mrs. Helm flashed her white teeth and Flint smiled easily back at her, feeling young and vibrant again. Nodding farewell, Flint reached for her hand to shake it, but flushed when she didn't release his immediately. Mrs. Helm blushed and her freckled nose wrinkled. Flint tipped his straw hat and left without a limp.

After leaving Mrs. Helm's, Flint drove back to Gus' place, parked, and walked the mile home, following the rugged trail he and Kate had made with their children earlier in the week. He pictured Mrs. Helm; her face, her laugh. When he arrived back at camp by the pond, he realized that he had no memory of the mile walk on the rugged trail, no thought of the cougar roaming the mountain.

Early the next morning, while the little boys snoozed under their bedroll and after Flint had eaten the eggs Kate fried for him on the campfire, he walked back to Gus' and the Dodge and then drove to the wagon trail where it veered off at Widow Helm's. He began shoveling bits of granite rock and clay clods, soil dust and sagebrush, from high spot to low, from bank to rut. The road would be precarious in spots, where canyons loomed along the edge. He drove the Dodge a little further each day, as far as his improvements would allow. And at the end of each day, he laid the mattock and shovel in the truck bed and walked, following the wagon trail straight up the mountain before it leveled off, weaved around, and curved in and out of the hillsides before the wagon trail came to an end. Looking down into the oak-filled canyon, he trudged through sage a few yards before he heard the boys chattering. He saw them where they played in the cove and hurried to them.

"Just straight on up the mountain and around a bend or two and I'll be here with that old Dodge, Katie. A few more backbreaking days and it's all she wrote. Sure didn't look like there was so much sagebrush and so many rocks on that wagon trail. Some of it we'll just drive right over and wear down."

Flint's bones hurt and every muscle ached, but he loved to talk to Kate about any progress that he made on the road. He felt satisfied and laughed while he talked. He stripped his clothes off and then slipped naked into the pool of clear cool water. The boys copied him, and the three of them lolled in the pool, basking there until Kate had supper and coffee ready.

Two days later, as late afternoon approached, Flint drove the Dodge clattering down the last of the roughed-in road to a flat clearing a hundred yards or so up the hill above the cove. They would decide where to build the house before cutting in the last few yards of road. Flint whiffed smoke and coffee and hurried to camp, eager to lean against the oak tree and puff on his pipe.

CHAPTER—6

CAT TRACKS

Kate heard the rumbling of the Dodge, and felt an urge to run and meet Flint where he parked at the clearing above the cove. But on second thought, he might think her foolish. She held back, unable to run in her condition anyway. Rob scampered across the shallow creek and up the fern-covered bank to meet his father. Bo toddled behind Rob up to the edge of the creek but, unsteady on his feet, he unhappily turned back.

Now they could get their belongings and start living like decent folks. Making plans in her mind, Kate set to frowning. They'd need some farm equipment and supplies. And should be able to make ends meet with Flint's pension check, when and if it ever came, until they got a harvest of melons. She groaned at the thought of leaning over the campfire one more time.

As Kate looked up toward the clearing, she noticed Flint walking in stiff, jerking motions down the trail. Rheumatism acting up again, she guessed.

She flinched at the sight of her husband hobbling toward her. "You're hurtin' Flint. Why don't you take it easy for a few days now that the road's in?"

As usual, Flint laughed when he won her sympathy. Then he shuffled to the pool without answering her.

When the sun moved behind the trees in the cove, dimming their campsite, Kate served beans and biscuits to her family. She cleared and cleaned until she felt she must quit for the day. Then she tucked the boys in their bedroll where they slept side-by-side. Kate watched Flint as he stoked the campfire. Fiddling with his pipe, he finally lit the Prince Albert and relaxed against the oak. While she finished her coffee, Kate rested on her bedroll and they made plans.

Flint decided that the best location for the house was between the two creeks and back from the cove on higher ground. Kate agreed, though she hadn't even seen the rest of the land.

For a while, Kate vaguely listened as Flint rambled on about what he intended to do, mostly talking to himself. When he sat quietly by the fire, she crawled into her bedroll and listened to the crickets and night owl.

The next morning, Kate looked on as Flint shoveled in the last few yards of road. And in a few days, he left for Bonita to get supplies for the new house so they could begin building.

Excitement grew in Kate as the hours passed. She would soon have a little house of her own, and she was happy about it, for any kind of shelter. Upon returning to the homestead, Flint brought flour in muslin sacks, lard boxed in cardboard, canned milk, a 100-pound gunnysack of pinto beans, and dark ground coffee in squatty quart glass jars. To Kate's delight, he purchased several large, flat, wooden crates from a local lemon wholesale packinghouse. From other surplus outlets, a box of nails and used lumber.

The old wooden bridge in Spring Valley that crossed the Sweetwater River was being replaced with steel. The contractor, rather than trucking to a disposal area, offered Flint the wide oak planks that spanned the width of the bridge. There were enough planks to construct a good-sized floor and then some. With materials gathered, Flint began building their one-room house on a clearing a few steps above the cove and between the creeks, where they would have access to water.

Time whipped by, filled with building the house and planting, cultivating and watering the garden. They worked in haste since the baby was due near the end of summer.

On an afternoon in mid July, six weeks after they arrived at the homestead, and after Flint finished his bowl of beans, Kate sensed his edginess. He sipped the last of his coffee, then sat his mug beside the campfire and stood up. The boys played at the south edge of the cove, tossing pebbles into the shallow creek water. Kate noticed Flint's concerned glance their way.

Flint began carefully. "Kate, I've seen mountain lion tracks. Generally, I wouldn't be alarmed, but I've seen the cat on the flat rock and he looks lean. Keep the fire burning while I'm gone to Bonita."

At this, Kate stood stiffly when Flint faced her. He moved in front of her, brushed her hair back from her face, and kissed her forehead. "Well, time's waste'n. I'll check on the folks. Get what belongings I can haul. I need to buy another hammer and more nails. I'll be back before morning, if all goes well."

Kate's eyes opened wide at her husband's last words. To spring that on her just before nightfall didn't give her time to collect her nerves, to plan for the night alone. He didn't give her a chance to discuss it with him, to tell him that she was afraid in the middle of nowhere at night, pregnant, and with two innocent children. Despite what Flint thought, lean cat or otherwise, somewhere on this mountain, a treacherous animal hunted at night.

"Why do you need to go now? What's so important that it can't wait until after the baby?"

"What Kate? Wait to build the house? I need supplies, that's why."

"But, I . . . ."

Flint put his hand up, demanding her obedience.

Kate realized, that of all the nursing she had done, helping babies come into the world and endless cooking and caring for people, she didn't know the secret words or possible touch to administer to soften Flint toward her. She had a long night ahead of her to think about it and to weep inside for what she wanted most in life, for Flint to consider her most important.

Flint reached into his shirt pocket for his pipe. He hesitated a minute, bent down, and pulled back a corner of the tarp that covered the Winchester rifle and box of shells. He glanced at Kate. She already knew where the rifle and shells lay, but the possible need to use them went against her grain.

Kate decided that her husband really intended to leave her here alone with the children, possibly all night. Her stomach burned with disbelief. For a moment, Flint lightly touched her belly. Kate flinched. Flint stood frowning, and then poked the Prince Albert down into the bowl of his pipe. He knelt back down at the campfire, picked up a burning twig from the edge, and lit his pipe.

A twinge of anger flashed through Kate. "You can't just leave us here alone, Flint. You got a pregnant wife and two children to think of!" Her voice came out more demanding than she intended.

With equal wrath, Flint's teeth clamped down on the stem of his pipe and he left.

Kate stood watching him with regret that he left angry. Bonita was only 18 miles southwest from Mt. McGinny, on the outskirts of San Diego, but the road was rough and the truck old. It would take Flint time to get around to finding his supplies, and to visit awhile with Mom and Pop, giving them detailed plans for the homestead. Kate hoped that Flint would skip the part about the mountain lion. Afterward, Pop would load Flint down with plants and seeds for Kate's garden. Mom would send boxes of clothes and flour-sack dishtowels, hemmed, washed, and folded neatly, ready to use.

Kate began the laundry at the lower edge of the pool, furiously scrubbing dirty worn socks and Flint's extra set of khakis on her rub board. She wondered why she and the boys couldn't have gone along with Flint.

The boys scampered back and forth at the edge of the water. Kate finished the laundry, and afterward she laid the washed clothes over the brush to dry. She set the cast iron bean pot on the campfire rocks. Flint and Rob had gathered enough firewood to last the night, and had placed the firewood within easy reach at the end of the boys' bedroll. Gratefully, she wouldn't have to bend down many more times this day.

Kate had never been alone in the wilderness at night before. It was the mountain lion that made her feel uneasy. So far, camping here with Flint for nearly two months, the varmints were no more than a passing skunk, a possum family, and yelping coyotes a bit too near. The mountain lion, though, might sense Flint's absence and choose tonight to show up.

The baby pushed on her ribcage. "Confound it, you may be anxious to get out of there, but you hafta wait at least another month." The boys gathered around their mother placing their hands against her belly, laughing and giggling when a wave of movement protruded out against their hands. When Kate explained that the movement was the baby's foot kicking, the boys flopped over onto their bedroll, looking up at the sky in awe.

In awhile, Kate opened canned milk and fed the boys beans, biscuits, and milk. At dusk, she tucked the two towheads side by side in their cozy bedroll and gave Bo his last jar of milk with the black nipple, since the nipple was worn paper thin, and there wasn't another to replace it.

When Kate was through tucking the boys in, she washed the coffee pot in the creek and filled it with water, ready for early morning coffee. To keep skunks out of the bean pot at night, she hung the pot handle over the 16-penny nail that Flint hammered in the oak tree for that purpose. With a heavy sigh and everything in order around camp, Kate piled a few spindly oak branches and a large rotten log on the embers.

Exhausted, she eased down on her bedroll. Night arrived, moonless. Starlight sprinkled throughout the otherwise black sky. Sounds of crickets, a hoot owl, and a far-off band of coyotes wove a delicate melody. Relaxed, she leaned back. She almost laughed at her dilemma. A night alone in the wilderness, far away from any plan she ever made for herself.

A sudden harsh scream reverberated through the canyons and over the hillside. Instantly alert, Kate knew the horrifying noise. Like a tortured woman, the piercing cry of the big cat sent chills racing through her and she stifled a scream of her own. He was roaming nearby. Leaves rustled. *Must be that damned ol' skunk . . . not easy to see.* She quivered, unconvinced about the skunk. Her throat tightened. She focused on the faint crunching of oak leaves and branches.

Trembling, she reached for the Winchester, slipped a few shells in the chamber, and set the rifle on her bent knee. Aiming the rifle into the depths of the thicket across the pond and searching the darkness for movement, she waited for a pair of golden eyes . . . mountain lion eyes. She searched up into the large oak that grew beside her. No need to worry as long as the fire was bright, but when all the wood was gone, what then?

The rifle shook in her tired hands while her heartbeat drummed wildly inside her head. She might be in a better position if she stood. From where she sat, the cat could jump her from behind. But, then if she moved, whatever was out there might become startled and attack.

"Oh, my babies. I could kick myself for getting us into this predicament," she muttered.

What if a 44 bullet wouldn't stop a mountain lion even if she could hit it? "But the Winchester's automatic," her parched lips whispered. Kate's eyes pierced the pitch-black brush.

Oak leaves crackled above her in a slight breeze. Or *was* it oak leaves? Kate could no longer feel her trigger finger. The butt of the gun felt like a knife against her shoulder. Anguished, her body quaked at every thump of her heart. The once-thriving fire dwindled to a pile of embers. Dungeon darkness filled the cove.

Now there was no choice but to move to reach the firewood piled at the foot of the boys' bedroll. With her eyes fixed on the brush, she squirmed, stretching across her protruding belly to reach the wood with a shaky left hand. Not close enough. A choking sensation filled her throat. She moved to the right and scooted forward cautiously. Finally, she felt a limb under trembling fingers, then another.

The fire flamed again, and soon blazed high enough to brighten the edge of the brush. Again her eyes searched the thicket where the clothes lay drying. The campfire flung dancing images over the cove and into the oak tree where Kate scanned along each limb.

Her thoughts tumbled. That crunching, rustling noise was different than the sounds she'd heard on nights before. No doubt, the unwelcome guest had arrived. Now she wanted even her thoughts shut out in order to listen. Hair stood on the back of her stiff neck. The rifle weighed a ton, but she refused to move it one inch from her throbbing knee or pierced shoulder. The eerie night lingered long. Kate waited, fatigue overcoming her.

The shuffling of dried leaves startled Kate awake. She sat up, tightened the grip on the rifle that lay across her thighs, and instantly turned, rifle aimed. Her finger twitched on the trigger before she shrieked, dropping the rifle to her side.

"I could have shot your fool head off, Flint." Trembling, she flung the rifle to the ground. With a flash of fear, she scrambled on weak knees to the boys' bedroll, ripped the covers back, and took in a deep breath. Her boys were there, safely nestled together. Kate plopped down on bare ground beside their bedroll. The sun was breaking over the mountain and the campfire revealed only a wisp of smoke. Kate couldn't remember laying her head down succumbing to slumber.

Filled with self-reproach, Kate motioned toward the pond and the brush beyond. Shaking her finger, she jabbed the air in the direction of the pond. "Over there. A varmint, a big one, rustling around in the bushes! He was real close, Flint. All night long, right over there!"

Flint searched the area, eyes cast to the ground as he scanned the thicket. Frowning, he removed his hat and rubbed his wide fingers through his hair. "Yeah, yeah, Kate, I see, I see," he said in agreement. "Come over here. I don't want to scare the boys."

Kate struggled onto her knees from where she'd plopped beside the boy's bedroll. Flint motioned her toward the pond, away from the sleeping boys. As he pointed to several spots around the pond, he continued in a hushed voice. "Look here." He put his arm behind her back to steady her. Kate's eyes opened wide and her shaking hands covered her mouth to stifle a gasp. There, in the soft sand, were unmistakable paw prints. Kate's heart sank to her stomach as she whispered the words she dreaded most, "Cat tracks."

CHAPTER—7

GUS' VISIT

The homesteaders worked diligently on their shelter since Flint's trip to Bonita. It was imperative that four walls and a roof, at least, were completely constructed before time ran out, though Kate was careful not to push herself into labor early. The mountain lion incident was over, and Kate had no intention of ever being in camp at night again without Flint.

In the next few days, with Kate hanging on to the boys and Flint carrying the rifle, they walked the homestead property to see how the land lay and to make plans for it. Kate was astonished at the view from the slopes above the cove and the freedom she felt looking out to the valley and the faint slice of ocean beyond. "Flint, right here is a good spot for an adobe house, just like those down around San Diego. Cool in the summer."

"Good spot for the avocado trees, too, Kate!" he snapped. "I don't want to hear any more about any adobe house. Can't you be glad to have a house with access to water?"

"Never mind, Flint. I was just talkin'." Kate's heart sank. She only wished that sometimes Flint would listen to her dreams. Maybe want something she wanted, too. Besides, Flint would darned sure supply water to the avocado trees that he'd planned near the same spot, and soon. She knew that much.

Back at camp the following day, while Kate cleaned pots and dishes at the upper end of the pond, Flint and the boys tacked lemon boxes onto the framed-in room. Kate heard loud braying coming from the trail across the creek. She glanced up. In a moment, a gaunt man astride a huge black mule grinned back at her and chuckled as the mule's hooves clomped and clinked across the rocky shallow water.

"Gus Hays?" Kate stammered, raising both wet hands to her hair, pushing it back from her face. "Lordy, I must look quite a sight," she mumbled to herself. "Here I am with my hair a mess, round and pregnant, bending over scrubbing pots."

By the time she raised her knees from the sand, Gus had crossed the rocky creek. In his bony right hand, he clutched a gunnysack of clamorous chickens. A mongrel pup ran circles around the menagerie.

"How're you all, Ma'am? Brought you a start of Rhode Island Reds and, best of all, Brownie. Why, he's the best dern pup this side of the Pacific. German Shepherd, he is." The pup yipped, and when Rob and Bo ran up to him, they yelled and wrestled with the excited dog. Brownie chased his tail in circles and then scampered up the bank toward the house, the boys at his heels.

Hurrying from the house, Flint came to stand beside Gus. "Flint, here's my good neighbor offering," Gus said. Flint took the sack from him and set it on the ground as Gus slipped off the mule.

"Hope you all are ready for 'em. Thought I may as well bring them along since I was goin'ta come see how you all was doin' anyhow." Gus' beard was neat and trimmed, and his worn coveralls appeared clean enough. Kate wondered if the old man had family somewhere close.

"Doin' good, Gus. House is nearly ready for livin' in, I'd say. Got no floor yet, but still, walls and roof will help come winter. Kate nearly had a run-in with the mountain lion the other night when I was gone to Bonita for supplies. Saw tracks the next morning. Claw marks deep in that damp sand there by the pond."

Gus raised an eyebrow at Kate and scratched his whiskers. "Well, Ma'am, you don't want a run-in with that ol' king-o'-the-hills mountain lion. He's a big 'un. Brownie's mother goes crazy when that big cat's anywhere near. Why, his screechin' even scares me. Brownie'll do good for you all, watchin' out for your boys there. He's sure to be bigger'n they are in no time."

For a moment or two, Kate stood with her mouth open. After what that tough old geezer just said about the mountain lion, her fear jumped a few notches. Finally, curiosity getting the better of her, Kate opened the sack of chickens and peered in. "Gus, we're real glad to get nice hens. Sure need eggs. Say, you have a fine rooster here too. A family's got no farm till there's a rooster crowin'." Mostly she was glad for Brownie.

Gus helped Flint build a temporary makeshift wooden pen of lemon boxes for the six chickens and rooster, while Flint filled Gus in about his work on the road and his plans for the well. By mid-afternoon they said their farewell. Gus flung his spindly body upon the young docile mule and headed back toward his place.

As Kate moved around the camp, getting ready for supper, she thought about the last few days and nights. She mulled over what Gus said about the big cat. She felt humiliated and just plain scared, remembering how she actually fell asleep while that mountain lion crept around their camp a few feet away from her sleeping children. Flint gave her the impression though that the animal was sacred and usually harmless. Kate knew otherwise.

She rummaged in her supplies for flour and salt, and then stopped to watch her husband head back toward his nail pounding on the house.

"Flint," she called. "You're not likely to leave again when there's a chance that yellow menace might venture in, are you? I mean at night like that?"

He turned and yelled back to her. "I'd never leave you for the mountain lion again, Katie." He grinned back at her. He might have thought he was funny, but any humor intended fell on ungrateful ears, and he soon knew it from the scornful look she tossed back at him. He continued more seriously. "Might have to leave other nights after the room is built. But then you all would be safe inside cuddled up by the wood stove. The way I see it, we'll be sleeping inside by next week."

Kate wanted so much to walk up the hill to the knoll where she hoped Flint would build her an adobe house, though she loved the house he was building right now for her, regardless of what he thought. She felt stifled, closed in down here among the trees in the canyon. She yearned to see the Pacific, to see out and above everything. Up there, the sky was big and the breeze just whisked in and took her breath away. Living up on the knoll excited her the way the idea of nursing school had. With remorse, Kate knew that nursing school would have to wait awhile, but the adobe house? She would find the right moment to talk to Flint about it again. A foot kicked on Kate's belly from inside her and a twinge of pain reminded her that walking up to the knoll would have to wait until after the baby's birth.

As Kate became more and more uncomfortable, her burdensome body needed increased rest, but watching Flint struggle in his work around the homestead, Kate pushed herself even harder. Some days he dug on the well across the creek south of the cove just a few yards away from the garden area. He rigged a tripod with a pulley and bucket for lifting mud and water, rocks and slush out of the well hole. On opposite days, he built on the house, back and forth, digging mud one day, hammering nails the next. His choice of work depended on what supplies he had on hand, he said, and sometimes depended on which part of his body hurt the most. Kate wasn't worried about not having the kitchen floor down yet. Flint was burdened as it was, so they could move in the house before the floor was in place. Since she was nearly nine months along in her pregnancy, she felt about as useful to her husband as a dull axe.

Flint built a small chicken house with a larger chicken-wire run a few yards away on a knoll above the east side of the house. He complained of aching muscles during and after each completed project. However, Kate noticed a faint smile of satisfaction on his face along with the griping and groaning and her guilt lessened.

They were up against time with winter coming right on the heels of the baby's birth, so Flint wasn't wasting any time. The morning after the chickens were sheltered, he dug a hole behind the chicken run for the outhouse, and built it with boards and lemon boxes left over from the chicken house. Though he came in hungry and aching in every muscle, his face was animated with hope. Kate agreed with her husband; they were making progress. And she, as much as Flint, talked passionately about the day that the homestead would be legally theirs; lock, stock and barrel. Laying the planks for the kitchen floor would be the next project planned before winter, and Kate grew more anxious. A dirt floor during the winter was almost intolerable, especially with the children.

Finally, the day came when Flint left at daybreak for Bonita and returned in the late afternoon with most of their belongings. Kate and the boys hurriedly made their way from the cove garden to the yard.

"I'll set up the benches and table and hook up the stove," Flint stammered with excitement. "Why, I believe you can move camp inside before sundown. That'll be all she wrote. Just give me a hand here getting' the heavy stuff out of the truck, and then ya' all can get back to your garden."

Kate couldn't wait to see the room all finished, all set up and livable. A lump went to her throat and she wrung her hands, waiting for more to carry to the room. Rob rushed around, skidding here and there, helping Flint as reliably as any man. Bo screamed when he saw his bed, and he screamed louder when Flint tossed him his rag doll. Finally, after Kate and the boys gave Flint what help they could, they got out of his way and let him move about in the room alone.

Now, back in the garden, Bo whined. Kate pointed to his bedroll under the oak tree, and he obediently flopped down with his rag doll. While Rob struggled to carry water from the creek to the small garden, Kate finished pulling weeds and planted a few of the seeds Pop had sent with Flint. Rob huffed and puffed and grunted, but then filled his bucket with as much water as he could carry for the house.

The sun began to hide behind the oaks at the edge of the garden by the time Bo woke from his nap and sat up, rubbing his eyes. Unable to stay out of the house any longer, Kate grabbed the boys' hands, and the three of them hurried to their new house.

When Kate walked in, Flint had placed the large oak table that Mom and Pop had given them just inside the kitchen door in the southwest corner of the room underneath the bank of windows, just as Kate had envisioned. The cook stove set against the west wall between the built-in kitchen counter and the table. Kate looked around and wondered which box her canning equipment was in. She'd need it for canning her tomatoes if they ripened before the weather turned. If not, Pop would surely load Flint down with canning tomatoes during his next visit.

While Flint struggled with the chimney pipe, Kate hollered, "Come here boys. Now if this ain't fancy." She turned slowly around the room, showing it off to the boys. "It sure is gonna feel good standing up to cook." Kate patted her wood cook stove the way she would have touched a missed friend. Then she began placing their belongings where she thought they should go. Her large enameled bean pot was back in its rightful place. She clinked the side of it with her fingernail. No more blackened beans from that cast-iron pot. Kate smiled and looked up. Flint was standing with his hands on his hips, resting a moment, grinning at her. "No more black beans," she laughed, pointing to the pot, momentarily embarrassed.

Kate carried a stack of six heavy white plates and four mugs that matched the plates to the unpainted wooden counter Flint had built around the sink. They would need to visit the Bonita hog farm again one of these days soon, where the navy dumped kitchen refuse.

Heavy white dinnerware and stainless steel flatware had been thrown out accidentally with the refuse. The last time they visited the dump, Rob spied a large undamaged mixing bowl, and now it was stacked with two smaller mixing bowls on the counter.

At last, Flint carried in the box where she had packed her medical book, and placed it on the table. She pulled out the cookbook and canning books first and sat them aside. There, safely wrapped in a flour sack dishtowel, lay the magical book. Something happened inside Kate when she looked at that old book. She didn't know why it had that effect on her, but it did. It did. She carefully took the book out of the box and removed the towel. She touched the face of the book for a moment before she placed it on the highest shelf above the kitchen counter.

Pensive, Kate walked to the sink. There was no water pipe to the sink yet, of course, but Flint had placed a drainpipe from the sink, down through the floor, and across the path outside where the sink water drained into the canyon.

Kate opened the west window over the kitchen sink. The breeze circulated through and cooled the room. She breathed in as far as her protruding stomach would allow and got back to work. Digging around in an apple box, she gently brought out Grandma William's sugar and creamer, and placed them in the middle of the oak table.

Her heavy body moved slowly, but still she wanted to dance, to twirl, to jump up and down, but of course that was childish, so she decided to ignore the urge.

Bedrolls were laid out on the beds that Flint set up at the north end of the room. The double bed next to the wall would suit Flint and Kate, and the boy's would sleep together on their cot, a boy on each end. Between the beds, Kate fit a small, sturdy table. She sat a kerosene lamp on it, wound the alarm clock, set it according to Flint's pocket watch, and left the clock by the lamp.

Meanwhile, Flint placed a huge clothes chest on the east wall across from the square oak table. The morning sun would shine first in the window just above the chest. Beside the chest, Kate sat up a small crib, awaiting the arrival of the baby. Flint never said much about the baby, and Kate wondered if he was happy about another mouth to feed. She was afraid to ask.

By the time Kate made the beds, the chimney was ready for use, and Flint made a roaring fire in the stove. Rob ran for the pot of beans that hung on the oak. Kate shook with excitement, eager to try out the stove. She dipped water from the pail that Rob struggled to bring in from the creek for her earlier. Next she poured some of it into the blue granite coffee pot with a scoop of coffee grounds from one of the squatty glass jars Flint brought back from Bonita. Then she set the pot to the back of the stove. It sizzled the way pots did when water was left on the bottom. She closed her eyes momentarily then reopened them and felt the corners of her mouth curve up. In a trance, she stood tall with her arms folded above her protruding belly, staring at the water droplets jumping on the hot cast-iron stovetop.

Flint rubbed his hands together energetically and then scurried outside. He returned carrying the benches in that he had built of mill ends when they lived with her folks in Bonita. Kate leveled them the best she could on the dirt floor, one bench under the bank of windows on the west wall, and one on the other side of the table. Two single chairs sat at the opposite sides. The table was the one large thing they hauled from Oklahoma. Kate felt a pang of loneliness for Mom and Pop. She hadn't seen them since Flint brought her here to the homestead nearly two months earlier. It was the longest span of time that she had ever been away from either Mom or Pop. In some way, though, it seemed they were always near because of that table they had given to her and Flint in Oklahoma when Rob was born. Kate figured that giving the precious family treasure was Mom's idea, a late wedding present, a gesture indicating that she accepted their marriage, even if she didn't approve of Flint. Kate's melancholy mood left her when at last everything seemed livable.

Flint stood by the table. "Ah, nice, Katie. Won't get rained on come winter, either. No mountain lion can get in. A black widow . . . a snake maybe, nothing much bigger." He grinned at her and wrapped a strong arm around her slender shoulder. She didn't pull back, but leaned into his body, breathing in his smell of earth and sweat. "Let's get around that table and eat. I'm starved." Flint rubbed his hands together.

"I'll get the beans," she said, grateful that this would be the last pot of beans turned black and tasting like cast iron.

That first night in their new house, Kate slept like a baby snuggled beside her husband in their own bed. The next morning, she woke before daybreak while the moon was still aglow and a chill lingered in the room. Quietly, she moved from the bed, built a fire in the wood stove, and made coffee.

Sometime in the night, Bo had crawled from his end of the cot and lay snuggled beside Rob. When the coffee boiled, Kate poured herself a mug and scooted back on the bed at the end of Flint's feet while he slept. Sitting curled up against the rough board wall, she sipped the coffee. A warm, tingly feeling filled her. The sun peeked over Mt. McGinny and through the east window above the chest, scattering splinters of gold and silver on the large square oak table and over the dirt floor, transforming the room with lighted particles of shimmering dust. Birds' songs multiplied into a continuous melody.

The magic of the morning stayed with Kate. Hope stirred in her. Maybe everything would be all right after all. Nothing ever seemed this secure. Sure, she had been happy and in love since the day she knew Flint fancied her, but everything had gotten tougher after the boys were born. And then, her owns plans were dashed with Flint getting himself in trouble because of her. Momentarily, Kate felt a surge of fear that the law might find him here, but she shook the feeling away. There was no chance of that. This place was good, and Kate didn't ever want to leave it. She smiled to the new day, pressing her head against the rough wall behind her. This was what she dreamed of when she was a young girl and fell in love with Flint, before she decided to become a nurse and a midwife, before the Cherokee took her to their hearts to teach her the way of the medicine woman. All of what she had learned, loved, and fretted about, made her who she was now. A wave of contentment washed over her, like that of a starved animal that had finally feasted.

CHAPTER–8

SWEET BETTE

A few days later, on a crisp, August morning, Flint rose early to go to Bonita. "One more trip out to get the cow, now that the shelter is up, Katie. Got the side racks on the old Dodge ready to go. Before winter, we'll get those planks down for flooring in here. Meanwhile, sweep the walls down to keep out the black widows and sprinkle the ground to keep the dust down. I'll see you before dark with Bessie."

"Well, good. High time to get her. The folks don't need two cows and we sure do need the milk. Hear that, boys?"

"Did ya' hear that, Bo?" Rob said with a gleeful grin from where he laid on the cot, not quite awake, his small arms tucked behind his head for a pillow. His half-closed eyes followed Kate around the room. Bo moaned, rousing from sleep beside Rob.

"Give Mom and Pop my letter now, ya hear? And don't lollygag. Baby's due any day." She held her heavy belly and frowned, speaking nonchalantly since her husband didn't take kindly to actual demands from her, or warnings either. From the dull ache in her back, Kate knew that it wouldn't be long, maybe a few days, before labor would begin. But, she had no labor pains yet. Her water hadn't broken, and besides, Flint shouldn't be gone long.

"Well, now, I know you've had enough babies you all could deliver that young'un by yo' self." Flint copied her Oklahoma drawl when he teased. "I'll do ma' best to git back hea' in time, Katie." Then he left, leaving Kate to worry and wonder alone. Yes, she had given birth to babies enough to know how. But when Rob and Bo were born, Mom assisted Dr. Bonaparte, the old Frenchman, with the deliveries. And, yes, she had been a midwife herself. But she had never given birth with two small children watching and listening fearfully, and on a mountain with no grown person even remotely near. Surely

44

Flint knew that things could go wrong. Her baby could come with the cord wrapped around its neck, choking off its first breath outside the womb. Her little one might deliver feet first, or worse yet, one leg at a time, or face up instead of face down. Or, her placenta might simply not separate from the uterus. She would lose blood quickly. Oh, God!

Later that morning, pushing her fears aside, Kate filled the kerosene lamps as usual, and then headed for the garden. The boys fed the chickens a handful of corn and let them out of their pen to peck bugs and wild dried grass seed around the yard. Brownie watched the chickens as close as possible without losing sight of the boys. If the chickens ventured too far away from their pen, the pup nipped at their tail feathers and herded them back. Instinctively, the chickens would return to their pen to roost at the slightest indication of sundown.

The boys joined Kate in the garden. It was difficult for her to walk, her uterus tightening and cramping inside her for the last half hour. She refused to quit working until she was sure that labor had started and until she could no longer walk.

Pink-tinged mucus discharged at her last trip to the outhouse an hour before. Her time was near. She prayed that Flint would return soon to take her to Mercy Hospital in San Diego, where Doc Laraby would be called in for the delivery. She had made only two visits to Doc Laraby before they moved to the homestead, and had not left the mountain to see him since. She asked him to deliver her baby at the homestead, but he insisted that she get to the hospital. 'The rest will do you good,' he had told her. Even though Kate felt reluctant, she went along with his decision. Doc Laraby was a good doctor, a caring doctor, and he would be expecting the call from the hospital. Something told Kate she'd never make it there. She scanned the road and listened for signs of Flint. Nothing. She returned to her work, eager to take her mind off her fear.

Onions, carrots, and potatoes were growing fast in the lush soil of the cove, and the tomato plants Pop had started and sent home with Flint, now held a few blossoms and would produce before Fall. The small garden they planted would help keep food on the table for a while, but what about winter? Kate figured that there wasn't enough growing in the garden to store for the months ahead. They would need so much more, though Bessie gave her milk; the hens, their eggs. Flint worked some in town, doing a few odd jobs. He worked some in the hay fields, enough to buy a few staples such as pinto beans, coffee, flour and lard.

In a few years, when the truck farm produced melons and avocados, there would be more than enough food. Perhaps even extra money for a treadle Singer sewing machine and materials for making clothes and quilts.

Pop's garden was already laden with all kinds of vegetables, according to Flint. Kate hoped there was time for this garden to do the same. Though it was somewhat colder here on the mountain, it might stay warm enough until November. Kate knew to keep trying. She prayed for an Indian summer, long and warm, and she prayed for Flint to return home soon.

While Rob made several trips back and forth to the creek with his bucket to water the garden, Kate planted more of Pop's seeds. Bo crawled behind her on the ground.

The heat began to tire Kate, and even on hands and knees in the cool soil, the morning sun already felt near eighty degrees. It would reach near 100 before mid-afternoon, she feared. A butterfly lit on Bo's nose and he giggled. Kate laughed, but her laughter was cut short by a sharp contraction that spiraled through her like a bolt of lightening. With a yelp, she wrapped her arms around her swollen middle as she knelt there in the garden. A warm liquid gushed down her thighs and soaked her dungarees.

Rob sprinted to her, skidding to his knees. With his arm beneath hers, he helped her up. "It's all right boys," she assured them. "It's just time for the baby. Help me to the house, Rob." Her instincts told her this might happen, and sure enough it did. How could Flint do such a dreadful thing as to leave her alone when the baby was due? Getting the cow to the homestead could have waited a few more days!

Kate stooped as she walked, and hung onto Rob as they made their way up the narrow trail to the house. Bo and Brownie followed close behind. When Kate reached the stove, she poured the remainder of the water from the tin bucket that was kept on the counter into the kettle. There were coals left from the morning fire, enough to get some small logs burning. "Rob, you keep water in the bucket and logs by the stove. I'm goin' to need lots of boiling water. You hafta do what I tell you, son, and don't worry, ya' hear? Remember the way mama cows give birth to the calves, Rob?"

"Sure, Ma. But we're having a baby, right?" Confusion clouded his blue eyes.

"A baby that will be like you and Bo, only tiny." Kate patted Rob's towhead and touched the tip of his pug nose to reassure him. "But we hafta get ready first. Bring those clean flour sacks from the shelf right over yonder." With a groan, Kate crawled onto the bed.

After a twinge of pain, she rested a few minutes before changing her wet clothes for the dry nightshirt she had tucked away in the flour sack in preparation for her trip to Mercy hospital. She took a baby's gown out of the sack, along with a small blanket and several cotton flour sacks that she had cut into rectangle size, now washed and neatly folded for diapers. She set these on the counter by the sink near the end of the beds.

Bo sat quietly on his cot next to Kate's bed, short legs dangling over the edge. He watched his mother with round, somber blue eyes.

Kate wound the alarm clock and wondered what she would do if the birth didn't go as it should. But, she was more concerned about Rob and Bo. They were too young to understand.

Should she send Rob across the hillside for Gus? He was certain to have helped his animals deliver at one time or another. But, if Rob came upon a rattler, or the mountain lion . . . no, it was too far, nearly a mile. She grimaced as a flash of pain raced through her. Right about now, she could use some of Gus' corn liquor that Flint had told her about. But she and the boys would have to manage and hope for Flint to get on home.

Still, it was a real concern to Kate that she might have difficulties delivering. She covered her mouth to hold in another pain-driven scream. As her agony gradually subsided, she felt the infant kicking inside her. It was alive, but she had heard many stories told over the years of stillbirths or birth deformities. Or, she could hemorrhage and bleed to death, leaving the children alone here until Flint showed up. She called Rob and Bo to her side and held their hands.

"Remember boys, I am all right even if I holler. It hurts some when the baby is trying to be born. Sometimes it takes a few hours. Why, it may not get here till your Dad comes home," Kate said calmly, hoping to reassure them. She grimaced and waited for another contraction to pass. Rob went out with the bucket and struggled back in with another pail of water. Kate rose slowly from the bed and, bending to reach the sink, she poured cold water over a rag, then shuffled back to the bed.

"Bo, you hold this cold rag and wipe my face when I tell you." She laid the rag next to him. "Now I'm going to clean up real good and walk around a bit. That way our baby will come out easier." If she felt faint, or a contraction started to come, she could hurry to the bed and lay down until it passed.

Kate found Flint's old leather slippers and slid her feet into them. After moving around, and standing awhile on one slippered foot and then the other, she felt better. When she saw Rob rub his tummy, she remembered that the boys hadn't eaten since morning.

"Boys, I best get you a bowl of beans and a biscuit while I still can. Let's get around the table."

In the more comfortable bent position, Kate hurried as fast as she dared. She served the boys cold beans and the biscuits left over from breakfast. They ate unconcerned, for the moment, playing 'cowboys' with their biscuits. Kate shuffled around the room a while longer in the heavy slippers, leaving dusty trails in the dirt floor, the smell of beans and biscuits floating in the room along with her uneasiness.

Later, Kate sat on the edge of the rock-hard bench waiting for the boys to finish eating, mumbling to herself. "Think, think, what will I need beside me there on the bed to deliver this baby. Hafta make sure everything is ready. It won't be long." *Lord, I hope Bo goes to sleep before this gets awful,* she prayed silently. *I'd give my eyeteeth if this was done and over.*

Every few minutes, Kate moaned and groaned. In between contractions, she gathered her sewing scissors and a few inches of twine, placed them in a pan, and poured boiling water over them. Another contraction came . . . the excruciating splitting at her pelvis. When she was in one piece again, she folded and placed worn sheets on the bed to catch the blood and afterbirth that would soon flood from her, all the while wishing that this was the middle of the night so that the boys were asleep and not afraid. If Flint didn't show up soon, though, she would need Rob's help to get through this birth.

"Let's get down on the floor, boys. Rob, lay those gunny sacks over here closer to the bed." Kate motioned toward the pile of sacks by the front door. "I need to rock on hands and knees, it feels, oh, oh . . . ." She knelt down on a sack that Rob laid out for her. "It feels better like this. The Indians gave birth this way. Why, they just dropped their little papoose right out on a bear rug, or the forest floor." She tried to grin as she panted from the effort, managing only a grimace. Beside her on the cool dirt floor, Rob and Bo giggled, rolling like playful bears, back and forth, each on their own gunnysack.

Late afternoon came with Kate having contractions every five minutes. Soon there was no reprieve between them. She laid on her bed, fading in and out of consciousness, her pelvis splitting wider and sweat beading thicker on her forehead.

Bo hunkered at her side, touching her face tenderly with the cool rag. Now and then he grew tired of his chore, and escaped to roll on the gunnysacks. Rob threw a biscuit out the door to Brownie. A welcomed afternoon breeze wafted through the open window above the kitchen counter.

It was a good thing that Kate had filled the kerosene lamps earlier, as the canyons begin to darken now. She touched her lips with her fingertips. Flint should drive in with the cow any time now, she figured. Rob ran with Brownie to close the chicken pen and returned, leaving Brownie near the front step. He entered the kitchen and shut the door behind him.

Shaking, Kate lit the kerosene lamp beside her bed. Then she brought another from the kitchen table, set it on the sink counter, and lit it too.

Moving to the bed, she curled up in a fetal position. She groaned, knowing she was about to endure at least another hour of nearly constant excruciating pain. "That's it. That's all I can do. Rob, will you get me water? I'm so thirsty."

Rob dipped a mug of water from the tin bucket that sat on the sink counter and carried it to her. Water slopped from the mug forming small puddles in the dusty floor. Gently, he held the mug to her parched lips while she sipped the cool water and then lay her head down again. During a few minutes reprieve from agony, Kate dozed and woke as Bo patted her forehead with the nearly dry cloth. "Bo, you hafta' lay down now, and go to sleep. I'll be just fine. When you wake in the morning, you'll have a new sister or brother." Bo flopped over on the cot with his rag doll.

As the pangs continued, a strange power lifted Kate. Only the miracle of birth would be remembered after all the agony, which was a good thing, since Flint wouldn't leave her alone. If she refused to sleep with him, he might leave for good, or . . . oh, she prayed that he would return to the homestead to help her, at least to be near. He'd surely be home anytime now. Where would she put him tonight if he came home tired from his long day? There was no room on the bed with her there thrashing around in agony. If he showed up, maybe he would sit beside her and hold her hand.

Again vice-gripping pain enveloped her. She tried to relax and to breathe in wispy short breaths, but instead, primitive, animal-like grunting and groaning were the sounds that escaped from deep within her. The hands on the clock appeared blurry. Tears and sweat mixed on her face. In between pains, she heard the slow rhythmic sounds of Bo as he slept.

Rob lay at the end of his cot, watching his mother. "Bet that baby is a sister, Ma. I bet."

"Uh huh. A sister for you, Rob." Kate wiped the moisture from her face with the dry cloth Bo left beside her.

Suddenly, the urge to push her baby out grew intense. Kate was unable to resist the powerful sensation. Laying on her back, she reached up behind her, grabbed the iron bed railing, and yelled. "Oh, God, please," she pleaded. "Get this baby out of me!" Nothing happened except more excruciating pain, rising, rising, with no relief. Her screams woke Bo and he sat upright crying, his little round face red and sweaty. He reached his chubby arms out to Kate. She leaned toward him, wanting to get him there beside her, but instead curled back on her bed and wailed again. Pushing with every fiber of her being, sweat poured from her exhausted body, yet the baby didn't come.

Wide-eyed with terror, Rob stared at Kate. With Kate's energy drained, she feared she had no strength left to push again. The baby might die inside her. A minute passed. She wanted desperately to quell Rob's fears and to hold Bo, but instead, uncontrollable tears streamed down her face. Finally, another powerful sensation filled Kate, and with the next boisterous grunt and push, euphoria flooded her. In an instant, the baby slipped out.

Rob tumbled off his cot, mouth open, and eyes wild. Kate sat up, and leaned forward, gasping with relief. Covered with mucus and blood, the baby lie between her knees. She cried lustily. Kate lifted her and held her to her breast for a few minutes, nursing her. Rob watched with open mouth and blurry eyes. Then Kate deftly tied and cut the umbilical cord, and wrapped her baby in the soft pink blanket Mom had knitted and sent with the dishtowels. Kate lifted her dark-headed baby girl again and cradled her for Rob to see. Rob put his lips to his sister's forehead.

"She's perfect, Rob, and you bet right. She's a sister. Now I need to clean her and then feed this little Bette." Rob smiled, then yawned and crawled back in bed with Bo, who sat crying, his eyes swollen and red, his voice hoarse with fear. Rob hugged him. Soon Bo lay snuggled next to Rob with his thumb in his mouth, his eyes fluttering closed.

Kate wrapped the afterbirth in the sheets beneath her and placed the bundle in a gunnysack on the floor. It was another hour before she finished bathing herself and the baby. Then the olive-skinned baby girl nursed while she nestled against Kate.

The ordeal was over, the baby safe and healthy, and Kate didn't bleed excessively. She and her child both needed rest, but because Flint hadn't returned, Kate felt troubled, wondering if he ran off the steep, narrow road that wound its way up the mountain to the homestead.

Unexpectedly, Brownie began barking in the front yard. At the same time, a sudden piercing scream bolted Kate from her nestling. Shivering, Kate lay her baby down beside her, quickly slid her feet into the slippers she had tucked under the bed earlier, and crept to the front door to check the latch. The door was closed and latched, but she dragged the chairs from the ends of the table and boned them up against the door. Somewhere nearby the yellow beast roamed.

CHAPTER—9

MRS. HELM'S

Flint stalled for time. He visited the folks awhile, and then spent an hour prodding the cow into the back of the truck, hoping that his trip to get the cow was reason enough to be absent when his child was born. He couldn't bear to have Kate see him so weak, so afraid. She wouldn't understand, and he couldn't bring himself to talk to her about his mother.

Once on the road heading home, he stopped at the Junction for tobacco. "Arnie, I'll take a quart of Gallo and a can of Prince Albert."

Arnie asked Flint questions about his family and homestead and then said, "See you at . . . at . . . at the Junction Saloon, Flint? Got a good . . . good poker game already heatin' up." Arnie looked at the clock on the wall. "I'll head on . . . on . . . over there soon as I close up here."

Flint nodded to Arnie and frowned. He'd use the poker game as a reason to be away from the homestead. Kate wouldn't know about it, but a good poker game at the nearby watering hole would keep him sidetracked. The hoopla, the saloon girls, the whiskey, and the challenge to win some money, usually helped alleviate his guilty feelings for the time being. And then, after Kate gave birth, the memory of his mother would subside. And the memory of Turner calling him 'bastard' would fade, but only for a short while.

After Flint left Arnie's, he drove directly to the Saloon and joined the poker game, leaving his unopened bottle of Gallo on the truck seat. But, as he sat at the poker table, cards in hand, he couldn't focus on the game; couldn't bluff his usual, deceiving his cronies into believing that he had a winning hand. Because of it, he lost his last few dollars, earnings from Mrs. Helm the week before.

He'd taken a few sips of whiskey during the short time it took him to lose his money. Even with the whiskey in his veins, his heart felt heavy with guilt for losing his last dollar and for not getting home to Kate. But all he could see was his mother lying on the bed, blood pooling around her. He couldn't burn the image from his mind and he couldn't risk seeing Kate like that. Disgusted with himself, he pushed his chair back from the card table and stumbled out of the saloon to the Dodge.

While driving hesitantly along the road toward home, Flint eyed the bottle of Gallo in the seat beside him. He knew Mrs. Helm was at the big house, and when he reached her driveway, he slowed down. He dared to see if she was still awake. His hands burned hot on the steering wheel as he made the turn toward her house. With trembling knees, he parked by the front porch under a towering eucalyptus tree. The house lights were on. He broke the seal on the Gallo and took a swig.

Peering toward a lighted window, he saw Mrs. Helm watching him from where she held back the curtain. Flint slid out of the Dodge. She had opened her front door by the time he stepped up on the porch. Without a word, she motioned him inside. Her flowing gown, the same rosy color as her full lips, fluttered in the evening breeze.

"What are you doing here at this hour, Flint?"

"Kate's going to give birth."

"What? Why aren't you with her?" Mrs. Helm asked as she beckoned Flint to sit at the intimate table just inside the door.

He placed his hat on the table and stood there. Then he covered his face with his large hands. I can't . . . can't bear it."

"What are you talking about. The birth? You're afraid of a woman giving birth?"

Everything came flooding back, finding his mother's body, burying her on the hill, the loneliness afterward. His shoulders began to tremble and the words he'd been holding back came rushing out.

"She died. A wooden prod laying there in the blood . . . with the baby."

"Who, Flint? Who died? Mrs. Helm sat him down on the chair before he collapsed.

"My mother. Killed herself. Didn't want another bastard like me." He broke down sobbing. There! He'd finally said it. Finally got it out, but the pain stayed with him.

Mrs. Helm laid his head on her chest and rocked him, cooing. "There, there. It's okay. It wasn't your fault. It wasn't . . . ." She kissed him on the forehead, ruffling his hair. Then she kissed him on the eyes. He found solace in her warm embrace, solace that he could never find at home.

Tearfully, he cried out, "It was a secret, a . . . a shame. I was fifteen years old. Got home from school, looked in her room, there she lay . . . blood all around her." His voice broke. "Why would she risk an abortion, when she knew I'd be left with Turner?"

Mrs. Helm paused, the pain settling between them like an unwelcome visitor. "Maybe it was someone else . . . someone other than your step-father's child."

In defense of his mother, Flint struggled to say, "Mother wouldn't do that." But then he thought of the way Turner treated her, how lonely she seemed. "I've never thought of that before." But, of course, he had.

Flint jerked to attention; tried to get control of himself. He wanted to run, to get home to Kate and his children, to forget the past and all the pain it brought.

Mrs. Helm's delicate brown hand lay in the middle of the intimate table. "Flint, I didn't mean . . . ."

He patted her hand and then rose wearily from the table. "No, no, it's alright. I'll be around next week to get your windows repaired, after I get that plank floor down."

Mrs. Helm stood up from her chair and stepped close to Flint. Before he could will his feet toward the door, she leaned to him and gently kissed his cheek. Without forethought, he moved his head and was soon kissing her sweet-tasting lips.

For a moment, he allowed himself to forget, to stay lost in the longing. But all too soon, she pulled away.

"I'm sorry. I shouldn't have. It's just that you look so . . . forgive me."

"It's my fault. I shouldn't have . . . ."

"Kate's at home. She needs you."

Flint grabbed his hat. "I'd better go now." He rushed out, the wind howling. He could swear he saw the ghosts dancing on his mother's grave as he got into his truck and drove away. Probably the drink. It had to be the drink. Either that or he was going crazy. He knew they were trying to tell him something, to quit his drinking, to forgive the past, but the memories were waiting out there for him, ready to snatch him at any moment. He couldn't face the past, not now, not ever. He turned the truck toward home.

At the top of the mountain, where the terrain leveled off before dropping down into the oak-filled canyon and to his homestead, Flint stopped the Dodge, turned off the motor and set the brake. The alcohol and emotion left him exhausted and spent. There on the mountain, Flint fell asleep until early the next morning. And then he drove home.

CHAPTER – 10

CHANGE OF HEART

Kate woke when Brownie barked. She listened for sounds of the Dodge and heard it ease down the hill and into the yard. Remembering that the door was barred, she stumbled to the door and removed the chairs. She unlatched the door and hurried back to Bette to nestle beside her in bed. Bo and Rob snored gently, catching up on their sleep after the turbulent night of Bette's birth.

When Flint came through the door, he walked in timidly. With the door open, Kate heard Bessie mooing. At least Flint brought the cow home.

Kate rarely stayed in bed past sunrise, but now she lie still, watching Flint as he entered and walked toward her. He stood for a moment in the middle of the kitchen floor looking in her direction. And then, as if he finally figured out why she hadn't jumped up when he came in, he grinned and walked over to Kate. He carefully pulled the pink blanket back from Bette's face. "A girl, Katie? She's healthy."

"She's Betty Lee, a perfect Cherokee princess. Where you been, Flint? You smell like whiskey and . . . ."

The fragrance of perfume stung Kate's nostrils and hung there, turning to stone in her stomach.

"It got late," he murmured and backed away from her and the infant. "Decided to hold over in the valley. It wasn't time for the baby." Flint hobbled to the stove and started to build a fire.

"Why, I didn't expect labor for another week, but . . . ." Kate rose onto her elbow. "We sure could have used you here last night. The boys were darned scared. I couldn't help 'em. The baby comin' out and all," Kate snapped.

She wanted to say what really crowded her mind and what she felt in her heart, that regardless of the pending birth, Flint should have been home before nightfall. From the smell of him, he had done more than fetch Bessie.

Closing the firebox, Flint poured water in the coffee pot and then looked around for the jar of coffee grounds. Kate glared at him from tired eyes, thinking it was high time he learned where to find the coffee. Then she hid her head in the scant feather pillow beneath her head, feeling hurt and unloved.

CHAPTER—11

FLINT'S MEMORIES

Two days after Bette's birth, Flint rose early with Kate. While she began cooking breakfast and the children slept, he walked out to milk Bessie, now settled in her new surroundings next to the south slope trail. When he returned to the house, he sat the bucket on the kitchen counter. "Goin' to get materials, Kate," he said, peeking in Bette's crib and pulling back the pink blanket. She slept soundly, her tiny round olive-skinned face glowing. The child mesmerized him, this little girl. Obviously, Cherokee blood flowed through her veins.

"You comin' back tonight?" Kate snapped.

The little boys stirred on their cot, rubbing their eyes.

Flint dropped the edge of the pink blanket and faced Kate where she leaned against the counter, straining the milk. Her eyes, like two poisoned arrows, glared at him. Flint stood as straight as his wretched aching muscles would allow. "I'll be back to lay the planks." At that, he turned and walked out the door, not wanting to face her. She hated him, he decided, for not helping her give birth. He should have been there, at least to clean up the afterbirth, but he couldn't forget how he'd found his mother, dead in a pool of blood. He'd do without breakfast rather than feel the animosity between them. He hurried to get away, started the Dodge and drove up and out of the canyon.

He'd miss his usual time at the table with Rob and Bo after breakfast, smoking his pipe and planning his day while they snuggled up beside him on the bench, but Kate had snubbed him again, and he didn't want to be around her while guilt weighed heavy on his mind.

As he drove down the mountain too fast he thought of the previous days and the birth of his third child. The idea of the baby's birth without Doc Laraby there or Kate's mother as midwife terrorized him. Yet, he couldn't stand the sight of blood. He would have been no use to Kate during the birth.

Guilt spilling over into anger, he drove too fast and nearly lost control of the truck. He slowed down and tried to justify his feelings for Mrs. Helm. He'd spent an hour that night of Bette's birth telling Mrs. Helm about his mother and her mysterious death. Mrs. Helm had leaned across from him, listening intently, interested in his life, his past, his troubles. He'd needed more of her. She even reminded him of his mother. Refined, rich in education and high values.

But he had hurried out the door that night, while the turmoil of his wretched past continued to scream inside of him and before he gave in to more of Mrs. Helm. When he'd made it to a flat spot at the top of the mountain, instead of driving down to the oak-treed canyon to the homestead, he'd slept there on the mountain when Kate needed him.

Flint forced himself out of his troubled thoughts. When he got to the bottom of the mountain where the road veered, he gritted his teeth and drove slowly past Mrs. Helm's, not daring to stop there today. Still, he idled on the road, thinking of the repairs that needed to be done, not that he didn't have enough to do at home already. He planned to work on his own kitchen floor in the next few days. The planks would need to be cut to size. Not that it would please Kate to have a floor.

At times, Flint wondered if she might hate him for his Cherokee heritage, but then again, she'd always claimed to love his people. He had tried to fit into her life, even submitting at times to speak like a southern cotton farmer, drawl and all. It came to him easily. He tried to emulate Kate's father, knowing how much Kate respected and loved the old man. But Kate never responded to Flint's efforts the way Annie Rose, her mother, responded to her father. Annie Rose didn't expect more from life than doing as her husband wished. She was happy cleaning, ironing, and cooking. And she kept life in line for her husband like most white women. Kate was different. What *did* she want?

Flint pulled away from Helm's decrepit house and sped on down the dirt road, knowing he'd best get his mind on work and what Kate required of him. Engrossed in his thoughts, Flint hardly remembered the ride to town.

At the lumberyard, Flint's chest continued to burn as he absent-mindedly chose a saw and picked out large anchor nails for the planks. His thoughts tumbled from Kate, to work, and then to Mrs. Helm. Now as he left the lumberyard with his supplies, he needed a drink . . . a drink to stave off the memory of his mother . . . a drink to shed the pain of Turner's hateful words. But most of all, he needed a drink to forget that he'd failed his wife when she needed him most.

On the drive back to the mountain, Flint stopped at the Junction store where Arnie stuttered nonstop about the economy and the weather and invited Flint to take part in another poker game. Arnie plunked the gallon of sour wine down on the counter. Flint nodded, searching his Khaki pockets for the last of his change. He laid it on the counter and walked out with his bottle.

After Flint left Arnie's and drove on toward the homestead, he was ready for a smoke. While holding the steering wheel with his left hand, he clamped his pipe between his teeth, and poked Prince Albert tobacco in the bowl with his right thumb. Next, he struck the match with his thumbnail and lit the tobacco. As he left the main highway and started on the gravel road toward the homestead, he stopped and opened the Gallo.

Taking a swig, Flint frowned from the sour taste on his tongue. Soon, fire from the white lightening flamed in his chest. He chugged down a few more tips from the gallon and suddenly all his cares left him. He felt free of the burdens he harbored. He opened the truck window and knocked the ashes out of his pipe, stuck it in his shirt pocket, and started slowly down the road again.

When he reached the part of the road that veered from Mrs. Helm's, he stopped, hesitated, and turned into her driveway. His foot slipped off the gas petal and the Dodge jolted to a stop under the Eucalyptus tree. Mrs. Helm stood in the doorway. He looked her way. Mrs. Helm smiled, her dark hair glistening with the movement of her sensuous body. Gathering his courage, he wondered how she felt about him after his breakdown the other night. Whatever her feelings, he owed her an apology. He took a deep breath.

Meeting him at the Dodge, Mrs. Helm wrapped her arm around his. Together, they moved slowly into the ugly house where they stood across from each other next to the intimate table.

Confused, Flint felt a deep ache in his heart. For far too long, he'd kept silent, suffering alone. She was the first women he'd ever poured his heart out to.

A lump lodged in his throat when Mrs. Helm leaned toward him and in her deep, vibrating voice said, "Flint, what's the trouble? Drinking again and here you are with me while your family's up the mountain. Why?"

"Vi, I'm sorry for coming to you the other night crying like a baby." He gazed into her brown eyes.

"It's alright, Flint. I wanted to help you. You seemed so tormented," she said, taking his hand. She leaned toward him and he took her in his arms, searching for her lips, a need for understanding welling inside him.

For a moment, they both succumbed to the temptation. Then, as if they'd come to a mutual decision, they pulled away, each stumbling over words of regret and apology.

"Kate had a baby girl, without my help, Vi."

With his head spinning, Flint turned before Mrs. Helm could say more. He hobbled to the door, bracing himself at the threshold a moment before heading to the Dodge. He glanced around at Mrs. Helm. Disappointment filled her sensuous brown eyes as she sat down at the table. He didn't breath until he reached the Dodge. He would make it back to the homestead about the time Kate had the beans hot for the noon meal, and no doubt fresh biscuits or cornbread too. The swigs of Gallo had turned his empty stomach. As soon as he got home, he'd take bicarbonate of soda. Maybe Kate would be pleased that he'd found a good saw and that he intended to work on the flooring.

There were too many stirrings in him. For years, he'd worked hard to become educated, to prove he was just as good as any man, but the fact remained, he didn't know who he was. Too many problems, too many unanswered questions. He had complicated his life further when he had kissed Mrs. Helm. Guilt edged further into his conscience. At the top of the mountain, before heading down to the homestead, he stopped and took one more swig for courage.

CHAPTER—12

THE DEPRESSION

After Betty Lee was born in August, Kate was more determined than ever to become increasingly independent, to take care of herself and the children. She read her medical book while she nursed Bette. She sat in her rocker under the oak in the front yard and studied the book day after day. The feeling of lying stranded and helpless when she needed Flint didn't appeal to her. She wanted to make sure it never happened again, and if she had her own money, her own goals to follow, she wouldn't have to depend on Flint. Kate's dormant dreams stirred to life within her.

Meanwhile, Flint laid the discarded planks from the Sweetwater river bridge renewal down for the kitchen flooring. He had promised that his baby girl wasn't spending winter on a dirt floor. Occasionally, he held Bette and, with a smile, spoke a few Iroquoian words to her. He rarely showed the same adoration to the boys . . . or to Kate, especially since the fight following Bette's birth. No matter how hard she tried to ignore Flint, she cringed at the distance between them.

Winter on the mountain wasn't as cold as Kate had feared, and Flint and Rob had kept her supplied with oak limbs for the stove. She hadn't canned enough and the garden hadn't produced enough winter squash to last past the end of the year, but there was always a pot of beans on the stove, biscuits or cornbread, and Bessie's milk. She determined that next winter they would be better off.

By springtime, Flint had the well dug deep enough to satisfy him. An old car body with an engine served to pump water from the well. A pole barn with a scant tin roof kept rain off and served as a well house. Around and around a conveyor belt flapped, pumping water through galvanized pipe that led to the yard in front of the house. Kate looked forward to Flint spending more time at home now since he could listen to the radio he connected to the car battery, where he kept abreast of news about the government and the country's well being.

In time, Flint planned to bury galvanized water pipe in the ground a few hundred yards to reach the 36 avocado trees he'd planted. In two or three more years the trees would produce their first harvest. After that, perhaps Flint would consider building her the adobe house.

"Need to plow for melons, Katie, if I can find a work horse in time." Flint sipped the last of his morning coffee.

"Sure ain't gonna be easy farming up on those slopes like it is in the sandy cove. That ground up yonder is clay and granite." Kate looked to Flint for a response, hoping he would reassure her that the clay and granite soil on the slopes was good for farming. It was obvious that the cove would soon be too shady to grow even a small garden, the way the oaks towered nearby.

Kate strained the fresh milk that she and the boys brought in earlier from Bessie, wrapped a gallon jar full of sweet foamy milk in a gunnysack, and handed it to Rob. Bo stood beside him, pinching a corner of the sack with his chubby fingers. They knew to set the precious bundle in the cold spring water up the creek and cover it over with the metal tub that was left there for the purpose of keeping varmints out.

After the boys left with their bundle, Flint moved from the table and stood facing her. "Katie, once that ground is worked up, it'll grow anything. Lots of good in that hillside, especially the South Slope where the sun shines all day."

Kate stood looking out the kitchen window, rocking Bette in her arms and feeling reassured by Flint's faith in the mountain. She gazed at the cove where she'd planted lilies, myrtle, and blackberry starts in the lush soil. "Sure wish the cove was bigger."

"There's enough room on this side of the mountain," he answered tersely. "And, we're going to have plenty of help on this homestead one of these days, if you keep having kids, hey, Kate?"

When he called her 'Kate,' she knew she had said something wrong. What was it this time? She winced at his remark and wondered if he thought her day was any easier than his own. He didn't seem to appreciate how much Rob helped around the homestead, that he spent most of his day hauling buckets of water in that heavy wagon to the avocado trees.

If Flint noticed Kate's frown, he ignored it. He stood and headed for the door, smoothing down his newly grown mustache. "Time you come see the trees, Kate. They've matured some since you've been there."

Kate bundled Bette and carried her. It was good to get away from the kitchen. She hadn't taken in the view of the valley and the far-away ocean for some time. When the boys returned from the creek with Brownie trailing them, Flint ushered them all up the hillside to his avocado orchard.

"Trees are looking good, Flint," Kate said, when they reached the trees. She turned to the southwest beyond the house to see the distant faint blue line on the horizon. Flint's chest heaved with pride. He took the pipe out of his pocket, packed it with Prince

Albert, struck a wooden match with the edge of his thumbnail, and lit the tobacco. Kate could see how satisfied her husband was with his trees, but he never mentioned the adobe house that she had her heart set on nor would he listen to her ideas about becoming a nurse.

Disappointment and regret vying for her emotions, Kate straightened the blanket around her baby, hugging her closer. Then she kneeled down to feel the soil. Flint had hand-tilled with the mattock around the area, added oak leaf mold that he and the boys hauled from the canyon in the wagon, and planted the year-old trees. As dark and crumbly as coffee grounds and smelling rich with loam, the soil flowed through her fingers. Kate stood again and squared her shoulders. The truck farm was Flint's dream, but Kate decided to make her own dreams, even if she had to wait until the children were grown and gone. Resolved to the idea, Kate took in a deep breath of mountain air, and silently prayed that Flint's dream would never completely overshadow her own.

By late summer, Kate and the kids were alone much of the time. Since the birth of their last child, Flint had become distant, drinking more and coming home less often. She didn't know what set him off. She only knew she felt isolated and lonely when he was gone.

Flint needed materials to add a room onto the house, and to buy galvanized pipe to run water to the avocado trees. To make income from melons, Flint planned to farm dry-land melons on the forty south-sloped acres, but first he needed a workhorse for plowing and sled pulling.

Perhaps Flint was right about the work for extra income away from the homestead, but he was gone too much of the time. When he came home late smelling of whiskey this time, Kate's stomach ached with fear. She met him at the door. "Can't you stick around home like the rest of your family, Flint, and stay away from the whiskey?" He put his palm out to her to shut her up, but bravely, she said, "Flint, where you been drinking? Mrs. Helm staying at the old house?"

"Now Kate," Flint's dark steely eyes narrowed at her, and a nauseous whisky odor wafted through the room. "Mrs. Helm has nothing to do with anything except work and money, and you know damned well that she lives elsewhere most of the year." Flint loomed at Kate, and with one hand, grabbed her dress collar at the neck. He pulled her close to his reddened face, and then he let go of her collar with a quick jerk.

Off balanced and frightened, Kate stumbled back a step. She grasped at her neck where her husband's rough hand had twisted into her skin. Flint turned from her and plodded to the bed against the wall where he sat down hard and slid off his boots. He rolled under the covers with his clothes on. Kate stood in the middle of the kitchen for a few minutes. Hoping to stay calm and not wake the children, silent tears slid down her face and onto the hand that comforted her neck. This time, his uncalled-for roughness toward her put great distance between them. She pressed her hands against her face to iron out some of her sadness and then she went to the shelf and brought down the medical book. It would never be shelved again.

In October, Flint brought the San Diego Union Tribune Newspaper in and sat down at the bench. He was tired, but sober. Smoothing his chunk of dark mustache that covered the entire space from his nose to his thin lip, he opened the paper on the table. He skimmed the most important phrases to report to Kate. "Things have been good for the rich folks, but since the stock market crashed, it's lookin' damned rough. I saw it coming, just checking the stock market for the last few months. Some serious troubles ahead."

Kate didn't really understand about the stock market. Feeling ignorant, she shrugged and then nodded her head. It was unbelievable that so many people all over the country were out of work.

The entire country was in a 'Depression', Flint said.

To Kate, the newspaper was only good for reading comic strips to the kids or for starting the stove fire when Flint was through with it. And she needed the newspaper to wrap and protect her canning jars.

Kate stirred the beans while a pan of cornbread cooked in the woodstove oven. Cooking helped to keep her hands busy and her mind off the world's ills.

Even though Flint kept her more informed than she liked, she couldn't help taking some of it to heart, since this news caused her concern for Mom and Pop, and her brother Paul. Kate pulled the cornbread from the oven and sat it in the warming oven. She continued calculating. Mom, Pop, and Paul could come to live at the homestead. That idea eased her mind. Here there would always be vegetables from the garden, milk, and eggs. Flint had his work in the hayfields and the work Mrs. Helm provided. Kate prayed he would keep working.

She set the table around him and his newspaper and placed the pot of beans in front of him. She hurried the pan of cornbread to the table. It slipped from her hands and crashed beside the pot of beans. Flint glanced up from the newspaper, and riveted her a second with his steely dark eyes. She took a deep breath and then called the kids in for the noonday meal. Flint served himself beans and cornbread. He ate in silence as if his mind were elsewhere. Kate watched him as he finished his meal and pushed his plate back to move from the table. Without a word to her or the kids, he left in the Dodge. Kate stood a minute with her hands on her hips and shook her head. What if he completely abandoned her?

With a scant eighth grade education, a houseful of children, and more than a day's work each day, she could do any more than what she did already.

While she sat with the kids at the table, she glanced anxiously at the medical book that sat on her bedside table across the room. She planned to study it today during Flint's absence, just in case.

CHAPTER—13

OLD MAN WARNER

Late September brought cooler weather. The stock market problem continued; therefore, the Depression drug on for a year. With it, more and more people were out of work and in bread lines. It was a privilege to have a job of any kind. Flint continued to work at Mrs. Helm's and in the fields, and kept Kate informed of the news.

Haying was at its busiest time in the valley, so Flint planned to sleep in the hay barn and wasn't expected home until the next day. But sometime before dark, after the children ate their supper and were back playing in the yard, Kate was about ready to bring them inside for the night. When she heard the slow rumbling of the Dodge, she stepped out and stood by the kitchen door. Flint drove up to the edge of the front yard. The motor died abruptly as if a foot slipped off the pedal.

A frail figure moved slowly from the truck after Flint. At first glance, Kate thought the two men appeared hurt or, more likely, just tired. Flint staggered closer. Behind him, a bent old man with an unlit cigarette hanging from a slit of a mouth reached his hands out in front of himself for balance, striking the air.

Kate saw that the men were drunk. The boys and Bette were grouped closely by the front door playing marbles on the ground. She moved toward them to hide them from the appalling scene, but it was too late.

The wretched old man peered out at them from under a greasy brown hat, his eyes glazed. Brownie crouched near the children and, with a warning growl, tightened his upper lip, teeth showing, neck hairs stiffened.

Flint laughed nervously, directing a concerned glance toward Brownie. The stranger continued his jerky pace toward the front door behind Flint, shaggy hair hanging from beneath his tattered hat. A moment before the men reached the kitchen door, Kate grabbed Bette up into her arms and nudged the boys ahead of her into the house, where they scurried, diving headlong under their bed. Brownie growled and scooted back on his haunches in front of the men.

Flint stuttered, "K . . . Katie, this here's Warner. He and I are ready for some of your good beans. Why, Warner hasn't eaten all day. He needs fattening up to do you a good days work tomorrow." The men stumbled over each other through the door, falling onto the benches next to the table, snickering.

With Bette straddling her left hip, Kate pushed the bean pot toward the men, setting out a bowl and spoon for each afterward. The men's stench was unbearable. Kate whisked away from them and returned to sit on her bed next to the wall, laying Bette down beside her. The boys stayed underneath their bed but peered out, their eyes anxious.

With shaky hands, Kate lit the lamp on the small table that sat between the beds, while keeping a weary eye on the slovenly old man. He licked his bowl clean and then banged it down on the table. Slowly, he picked the cigarette from his grimy shirt pocket and lit it.

Flint shoved his side of the bench back, scraping the planked floor. He shuffled toward Kate and yanked an army blanket from the end of the bed where she sat huddled with Bette. Then he motioned to the old man to follow him as he stumbled across the room and out the front door.

The fiendish looking old man gave Kate a crafty look and tossed his lit cigarette in the leftover pot of beans. After a furtive glance at the Winchester rifle on its rack above the door, he followed Flint outside.

Kate slammed the door quickly behind the drunks and then peered into the bean pot. "It's good we had ours, kids." She tucked the children in their beds for the night. In a short time, Flint returned. Saying nothing, he fell asleep crosswise on the bed, leaving no room for Kate to sleep beside him.

Kate hurried to bar the door with a chair and then looked around the room, muttering, "Just where am I gonna sleep, Flint? Don't want to sleep with ya' anyway. You're a disgrace." Kate shook her head in disgust and tugged on a heavy quilt that lay under Flint. She rolled him back and forth, pulling on the quilt, finally jerking it from beneath his dead weight. He snorted and snored, but didn't wake. Kate placed the thick, warm quilt on the unforgiving, hardwood planks beside Bette's crib and wrapped one side of the quilt around her weary, bewildered body, falling asleep to the night cry of the whip-poor-will.

Before daylight, Kate woke from her bedroll on the floor when she heard Flint say, "Need some grub, Katie. Got work to do in the valley. Got you some help out yonder under the tree. The poor old bastard's been down on his luck, livin' in a reformatory of some kind."

Kate's right arm and ribs ached from sleeping on the hard floor. She felt injured . . . as though kicked by a horse. She snapped, "That damned old man can't be around here with these kids. He looks dangerous to me. You take him off this hill when you leave!" She straightened the clothes she slept in and jabbed her feet in her shoes. Then she hurried to make coffee and breakfast while her husband continued the argument, following her around, nipping at her heels, haranguing her.

"He needs work, Kate. He'll dig the ditch for the pipeline. You just show him what to do and feed him."

While Flint ate a quick breakfast, Kate filled a cloth sack with biscuits and dried venison, Flint's usual fare when he worked in the valley. Fuming, she shoved the sack at Flint. "Think what you're doin', leaving us alone here with that . . . that stranger."

Flint didn't respond to her pleas, not even with his usual raised palm, but took the sack from her and walked out. With a shrill whistle, he ordered Brownie into the front seat of the truck. Kate figured he needed him to watch for rattlers in the hayfield, but she needed Brownie much more than Flint did today. From the kitchen window by the table, she watched him drive from the yard as the first rays of sun splintered over Mt. McGinny. The withered old man still lay curled up under the small oak tree in the front yard, wrapped in the army blanket, his filthy hat pulled down over his ears.

The boys sat up on their cot and rubbed their eyes. "Flint ain't got a lick of sense. That old man could kill us all," she muttered to the kids until she saw Rob's wide eyes glistening with fear. "He might be different after he sleeps off his drunk." Still, Kate marched to the kitchen door, took the rifle off its rack, and leaned it against the wall, just in case.

Kate had the kids dressed and fed when she saw the old man peeking in the front window. With shaking hands, she opened the door a crack. "You stay right there and I'll bring your food, Mr. Warner."

He didn't respond, but when Kate returned to the door with the food, he took the tin plate of eggs and biscuits and the mug of coffee she offered, and then shuffled to a tree stump across the yard. As he slouched there, yolk dribbling down his chin, Kate saw him look toward the house ever so often, and she muttered to herself, "How can I get anything done today with you staring at me?"

When the old man's plate was licked clean, he returned to the front door where Kate stood, waiting. "Flint says to take that shovel and mattock there by the tree and dig a shallow ditch next to that galvanized pipe laying over yonder." Kate eyed the Winchester within her reach. With blank expression, the old man handed Kate the plate and mug, shaking his head that he understood her directions. He plodded over to the tree and, once there, he gripped the shovel in one hand and the mattock in the other, then ambled to the pipe.

As the day progressed, the old man looked weak and worn after chopping and shoveling the hard ground. He sat down on the ground now and then and drank water from the nearby faucet every half hour or so. Kate took the rifle and the youngsters with her to Bessie's stall, located half way to the avocado trees off the South Slope trail. After milking, they made their way to the outhouse, to the chicken yard, and back into the house. "I'd as soon watch for rattlesnakes as that old fool," she griped out loud to herself.

Fear of the old man was stealing her energy, and Rob became jittery as the hours passed. He'd been house bound too long. "You can go out and play in the front yard with your marbles, but stay away from the old man. Sure would give my eyeteeth to have Brownie here." Kate propped the front door open.

Squinting, Rob hopped out the door and stopped to look at the old man chopping at the ground across the yard. And then Rob got down on his knees on the hardened yard and, scooping up a handful of loose dirt, he carefully placed a marble on top of it.

Kate lay Bette down in her crib while she prepared a fresh pot of beans. Bo played with wooden blocks on the floor. After awhile, Kate looked out the door to make sure Rob was near. When she peered out, she saw the old man creeping toward Rob with shovel in hand, the boy still on his hands and knees in the dirt.

With a scream, Kate bolted out the door just as the derelict raised the shovel in the air over Rob's head.

Startled, the old man missed and fell backward. Kate jerked Rob from the ground and, half dragging, half carrying, she pulled him into the house, slamming the door behind them. Then she jammed the end of the bench under the doorknob for a barricade. She grabbed the Winchester and pointed it at the window. Warner wouldn't dare bother them now.

"Damned you, Flint," Kate hissed, as she watched the old man crawl toward the ditch and sit on a heap of loose dirt he had piled there from his feeble digging. He appeared to be in a trance.

When Flint pulled into the yard just before sundown, Warner still hadn't moved from his trance. Brownie jumped out of the truck and took his place on the front step. Kate saw that Flint was sober. Quickly, she removed the barricade and opened the door. Then she motioned Flint inside, shut the door, and leaned against it. She wasn't going to let Flint leave again before she had her say. Not this time.

"I've had it, Flint," Kate snapped, jabbing an angry finger at him. "The old man was ready to hit Rob over the head with the shovel when I yelled and ran out there, just in the nick of time. You get him out of here."

"Katie, Katie, slow down. I know, I know." He raised his hands in surrender. For once he agreed with her. "I didn't know that the old fella was off his rocker until I was telling the folks down at the Junction store that I got Warner for a farm hand. They know of him and tell me he's loony. Says he came from some crazy house or prison up north, so I got here as soon as I could. I'll get rid of him."

"Take him far, Flint."

"I will," he promised.

With relief, Kate watched Flint leave, slamming the door shut behind him and barricading it afterward. Moments later, she watched the men leave in the truck. "Thank God that's done." She closed her eyes and sighed with relief. "Kids, the old man is gone and Brownie is right outside. It's near dark, but we hafta milk the cow. Let's go, and when we get back we'll eat and get to bed."

The air was crisp by evening. Kate shivered and decided to build a fire in the wood stove. Then she made coffee. Soon, the children were asleep. It would be some time before

Flint returned, depending on where he left the old man. For once, Flint seemed humbled, as if he was genuinely sorry. Surely, he would take care of the old man.

Kate settled back on her bed, leaning against the wall with her coffee. How good it tasted after such a hectic day. Rob was on her mind. The thought of how close he had come to being maimed or killed brought tears to her eyes as she sipped her coffee. A whip-poor-will cried in the night. Finally, Kate felt snug and warm again.

Soon, much too soon, a low rumbling sound slowly intensified. She peered out to see that Flint was alone.

Moments later, Flint stalked in shaking his head, bewildered. "I'll be damned if that crazy old fool didn't get out and start running across the hill soon as I slowed down for a bad rut about half way down the mountain. Said he wanted out to go to his brother's place in Delzura. Hell, I would have taken him, but he just jumped out and took off on foot. Crazy ol' bastard." Flint scooped Kate close to him, squeezing her tightly and more passionately than she ever recalled. Stunned, she quietly swallowed.

"Let's go to bed," he said. "I'm too tuckered to eat."

Later, as Flint dozed, Kate lay beside him wide-eyed, her mind troubled. Always before, their homestead had a wonderful feeling of safety and security as if nothing could touch them. The little house was cozy and warm, and the Depression didn't even hit hard on Mt. McGinny.

It's too quiet. Kate laid still, her muscles tense. No coyotes, frogs, or crickets stirred. Brownie would let them know if anybody came around, and he was right there on the front step. It was well into the night before Kate finally laid her face against her husband's back and relaxed into sleep.

Up early the next morning, Kate fixed fried eggs, oatmeal, buttermilk biscuits, and coffee for breakfast. Still apprehensive, she pleaded with Flint. "I wish you wouldn't go today."

Flint put a hand on her shoulder to steady her. "Katie, we're gonna need a new room on this little house. As soon as we get a workhorse, we can start. I heard of an old building in the valley somebody needs torn down. That'd be enough wood for a room for sure. There's no call for wanting me to stick 'round here all the time. You got that rifle right there. Warner's gone. And Brownie . . . he's stayin'." Flint took his sack of biscuits and dried venison and left before sunrise.

It was true Kate was a good shot with a gun, probably better than most men. And the Winchester proved as straight and true as any rifle. No need to get all riled up. Just the same, she felt hurt and angry that Flint didn't have the backbone to stay and protect them. It wasn't that she couldn't protect herself and the children. It was that he didn't care; he didn't love her enough to hear that she was scared. In more ways than one, she was alone.

The boys rolled off their cot, rubbed their eyes, and dressed, mumbling something about their empty stomachs. They went right to the table where Kate had their breakfast warmed and ready. Kate lifted Bette from her crib and dressed her. The children ate every scrap of their breakfast before Kate said, "Didn't get much done yesterday, fellas. Let's go milk the cow, then see what we can find in the garden." It was a struggle to carry the rifle, the milk bucket, and Bette up the trail to Bessie and the milk stall. When the bucket was brimming with foaming white milk, they struggled back down the trail and set the bucket inside the house. The four moved toward the garden, hanging onto each other along the narrow path between the house and vine-covered bank that ascended to the creek, and down a few more steps to the cove garden.

Usually she refused to take the rifle to milk Bessie or to the garden, to protect against rattlers, but Kate worried that the old man might still be around with more skullduggery. The hair on her arms and on the back of her neck bristled. She thought it strange that Brownie never left the area when she and the kids were outdoors, but crouched nearby sniffing the air and watching the hillside, the creek, the bushes, and wild grapevines. Strange, too, that when they were all inside the house, Brownie lay near the front steps, alert and nervous. Before the old man came, Brownie chased rabbits on the hillside when he wasn't keeping the chickens at bay or guarding the boys.

Weeds needed pulling and the garden needed more water, but not today. Kate wanted back in the house, and soon. They dug a few potatoes, carrots, and green onions and put them in a basket for Rob to carry. Kate hurried to set Bette on her left hip, grasped the rifle in her right hand, and started for the house. Bo toddled slowly on the path in front of her. He would stumble if she hurried him, so biting her lip, she held herself back, gently coaxing him forward.

The bushes were full of eyes. Something or someone was watching them. She prodded the kids to move faster while she looked all around. When they finally reached the house, Kate rushed the children inside and barred the door, leaving Brownie out in the front yard. He growled nervously.

While Kate waited for her heart to stop hammering, she leaned the rifle against the wall. She had forgotten all about the chickens and young turkeys until now. If she let them out, they could at least forage, since the thought of getting corn scratch from the storage bin and then taking it to their pen turned her cold. No, the poultry would be all right. But the cow, what would she do about evening milking? And how could she explain to the youngsters what was happening without frightening them? Better not to mention the old man.

"Kids, I saw a big rattlesnake track out by the house. We're not going out until we're sure the snake has gone."

Her mind elsewhere, Kate set about feeding the children, and then tried to read the comic strips to them as Bette napped off and on, slumped on Kate's lap.

For much of the morning, Bo played on the floor stacking wooden blocks, and Rob stood on the bench looking out the windows along the wall above the table. "Ma," Rob yelled from his perch on the bench, "it's that mean old man with the hat." The excited boy jumped on one foot and then the other, pointing his finger toward the grapevines.

Kate grabbed Rob down from the window, her breathing shallow. "Are you sure he was out there?"

Rob shook his head, his eyes large.

Stay down here on the floor with Bo and play with the blocks." A tremor ran through Kate as she crept away from the window. She listened and hoped for the rumbling of the Dodge. Instead, Brownie began to growl just outside the door. Kate dared to check out the window nearest the door. She stifled a scream. The old man disappeared into the wild grape vines up the creek. Kate's hand flew to her mouth, and her eyes watered. She checked the rifle again. The shells were all there.

Suddenly, the room seemed cold and damp. She leaned the rifle against the wall and walked across the room to the wood stove. Brittle oak-branch kindling shook in her hands when she stuck them in the wood stove firebox on top of crumpled newspaper. She reached for a wooden match but it broke on the very first strike. The second match lit and the paper caught fire. She closed the firebox and crept to the window near the door, peering out. "Where is he now?" Kate whispered. Her eyes darted around. She jumped when something hit the opposite side of the house, the north side where there were no windows. "God help us!" Kate rolled her eyes, scanning all four directions.

"Ma, did you hear that?" Rob asked in a hoarse whisper.

Kate nodded. "Don't worry, Rob. Brownie is right at the front step." The old fool had thrown a rock and hit the side of the house, but why?

The children sat wide-eyed on the floor with their wood blocks. Rob peered up now and then, watching Kate as she moved nervously around the room, rubbing her hands up and down her arms.

Rob said, "Dad comin' home soon, Ma?"

Before Kate could answer, a second thud hit against the side of the house. It sounded louder, as though Warner had moved closer to the house. Brownie growled.

The day stretched on in an endless river of fear and apprehension. Shadows fell over the canyon. Kate lit the lamp on the table that sat between the beds and turned the flame low. Brownie stirred now and then, never leaving the front yard.

A low rumble alerted Kate. She jumped up from where she sat rocking Bette. It must be the Dodge. She walked the floor, Bette on her hip, wondering how she could convince Flint that the old man was out there.

Flint drove the Dodge into the yard. Kate looked out the window. The canyon grew dim, the nearly setting sun still lighting the top of Mt. McGinny. Brownie whined and wagged his tail. To Kate's immense relief, Flint was sober. Kate sat Bette on the floor with the boys, removed the barricade, and opened the door.

"Flint, he's out there. Rob saw him; I saw him. It's the old man, Flint, the old man." As soon as Flint walked through the doorway, Kate jammed the barricade in place behind him. She quickly explained what had happened. "We've been hiding in here all day . . . since this morning," Kate blurt out, as she grabbed Flint, pulling him to her, the tears she had been holding back all day long finally falling. This was so unlike her, but she didn't care. To Kate's uncharacteristic display of emotion, Flint said nothing. Instead, he just patted her on the shoulder and moved past her. Kate stiffened at his lack of compassion.

For several seconds, Flint looked thoughtfully at the children sitting quietly on the floor staring back at him. He stooped down, ruffling their hair, one child after another, and then stood. The room was silent with all eyes on Flint, standing in the middle of the room and still not saying a word.

Waiting for Flint to say something, anything, Kate began setting the table. It was later than usual for supper but, until Flint arrived, she had been afraid to walk in front of the windows. Finally Flint spoke, but only about his day, small talk, gossip from the junction. Despite his talk about the Depression and how hard times had befallen most folks, his presence relieved her. Although Kate knew he had a way of dismissing her troubles, which to him must seem small, she hoped he was thinking about what to do with the old man. Maybe he was afraid, too.

After the family ate quietly around the table, Flint grabbed the milk bucket and the rifle, and walked out to milk the cow. When he returned with the milk, he set the rifle against the wall, barred the door and said, "I'll take care of things in the morning, Katie. Let's get some sleep. It's too dark now to see anything out yonder anyway."

With supper over, Kate strained and jarred the milk, and left it on the counter. Throughout the night, she tossed and turned.

At daybreak, Flint woke when Kate set a mug of coffee next to him. He slurped it down, dressed, took the Winchester in his left hand, and removed the barricade from the door. "Kate, bar this door behind me, and don't open it until I come back." Kate held the door open, but her heart sank. He had called her Kate, and she saw the flash of fire in his steely eyes, the same fire that flashed in his eyes the day he put Schwartz down.

"What are you intend'n to do? Just get rid of him, Flint. Don't kill 'em." Kate grabbed her husband's sleeve. He turned to face her, an impatient expression flitting across his face. "We've finally made a life for ourselves, Flint. If you kill 'em, they'll find you and put you in jail. Just find him and take him away, you hear? Don't hurt him." Flint ignored her.

"Brownie, stay put," he commanded, yanking the door shut behind him.

Nothing could coax Brownie away from the house. The pup wouldn't budge until he sensed they were all safe.

Kate watched out the window and tried to follow Flint's whereabouts. She heard him call to Warner. Flint was a good tracker, so it wouldn't take him long to haul the old man to the truck and away, for the last time. She hoped that's all he had planned.

Kate felt uneasy when Flint hadn't returned right away. After about an hour, a shot rang out on the slope near the avocado trees. Kate jerked and her hands pressed against her throat.

"Dad must have seen a deer, kids," Kate murmured, yet she had trouble breathing. "Pretty soon Dad will be back and we can all go outside again." She read fear in Rob's face. His wide eyes darted around the room and back to Kate. His mouth gaped open and although he breathed sporadically, he said nothing.

Eventually, Kate saw Flint walk down the South Slope trail and on through the yard, scanning the ground where the road came down from the clearing above the cove. He walked on further, appearing to look for tracks. When he returned to the yard, he removed his shirt, turned the yard faucet on, and let the water rush over his head and arms.

Breakfast forgotten, Kate rushed to meet Flint as he came through the kitchen door. "The old man's gone. Walked on down the road," he said, his eyes averted. "Fresh tracks going that way. There's been nobody else walking on the road. Had to be him. I found the shovel lying by the pipeline ditch. I'll check down at the Junction, see if anybody's seen him." Flint poured hot water from the kettle into the wash pan, took it to the yard with a towel, and washed again before returning for a clean shirt and to relax at the bench for breakfast.

Kate thought it strange of Flint to wash twice, but then, he hadn't been to the pond for a while, and he had been working in the fields a lot. Still, something didn't quite add up. She felt edgy and wanted to confront Flint about the rifle shot, but stirred the oatmeal bubbling on the wood stove instead. Then she flipped the frying eggs over in the skillet and yanked the buttermilk biscuits from the oven. Shaking, she set Flint's coffee cup in front of him. She poured the coffee in, the pot rattling against the cup.

"Did you see a deer, Dad?" Rob climbed up next to Flint on the bench.

"I did, yep. Missed her. Too tuckered to go chasing after her."

Recalling the shot, Kate dropped the hot pan of biscuits that she carried to the table. The pan landed upright on the plank floor but some of the biscuits plopped out. She scooped them up quickly into the pan and set them on the table with the rest of breakfast.

"Let's eat, you all," Flint said tightly. Bo crawled up next to his father on the opposite end of the bench from Rob.

After breakfast, Flint lit his pipe, and leaned his elbows on the table while the sweet smell of Prince Albert puffed around him. The boys squeezed closer to their father, one on each side, and sat quietly, taking advantage of their father's solitude.

With a prickle of worry, Kate wondered why Flint looked so tuckered this early in the day. What really did happen up there on the side of the mountain?

CHAPTER—14

JACKSON THE MULE

The Depression continued to edge right along with Prohibition by the spring of '31. It was the consensus of most folks, though, that Prohibition was a joke and was about to be repealed, while the Depression was picking up steam. Still, Kate felt mostly unscathed by it all, especially since Flint's disability checks arrived at the first of every month for nearly a year now. A piddling amount, indeed, but likely to increase some as the years passed. But mostly, Kate was grateful that Flint had quit drinking after the incident with old man Warner. The fact that he'd quit at that time made Kate wonder even more what actually happened that morning. He might have killed Schwartz in Oklahoma, just because the man grabbed her shoulder. Warner threatened Flint's family in much the same way. Flint had a tendency to protect what was his with angry vengeance.

Now that Flint was sober day after day, Kate was more than glad to work with him until exhausted, making the required improvements for the homestead. The most recent involved laying pipe to the avocado trees. Easy enough except that the ground was rock-hard, and it would take many backbreaking hours to finish digging the ditch for the pipe. Old man Warner had dug only a few feet. After the ditch was dug and the pipe laid, hooking it all together and throwing the dirt back over it would be a cinch.

Soon after breakfast, Kate began cleaning the dishes in the kitchen sink. Rob and Bo took turns churning cream for buttermilk. As they churned, they chatted excitedly about the clump of yellow butter that balled up, rolling around inside the churn in plain milk. Both towheads squealed in glee at the sight of the yellow ball, and they rolled on the floor in awe, eyes staring up at the ceiling. Giggles lingered, but the boys were satisfied to leave the churn and tend to their other chore of carrying the heavy pots to the creek water that ran across the road beside the front yard. Dropping on their knees, their little hands rubbed the pots clean with sand.

Kate heard her husband across the creek at the pump house while she separated the butter from the buttermilk. She peered out the window above the sink. Earlier, he said that he planned to water the avocado trees using several leaky hoses that he had acquired for pennies. The trees had grown too large, and no amount of hauling water in buckets would do. Those leaky hoses were bound to bring on all sorts of vile language from Flint, though it would be quiet grumbling now that he was sober. He had been dry ever since his run-in with Warner. Kate squirmed at the memory of Warner and realized that she had never searched, as she had intended, for Warner's body in the canyon, or anywhere else on the mountain. She feared proving what she already knew.

Brownie barked somewhere by the pond. Kate set Bette on her hip and carried her to the creek, where she placed the child in the shallow water next to the boys. Since the run-in with Warner, she checked on Brownie anytime he barked. Brownie usually hung around the little guys and the chickens, and didn't bark unless there was good reason. "Brownie, I wish you'd be more careful with those rattlesnakes. You're gonna get fanged one of these days," Kate yelled a warning.

But it was Gus that Brownie welcomed with wagging tail. Gus rode Jackson, the young black mule, and led a drab old horse behind him. The animals' hooves clomped across the rocky creek that spilled into the pond. Something about that kind old gentleman warmed Kate's heart and brought a smile to her lips.

Leaving Bette at the creek with the boys, Kate made her way toward the pond to meet the menagerie.

"What have you got, Gus?"

"Heard you all were ready for a good work horse." Gus slipped off Jackson and landed spryly on the hard ground.

Kate looked dubiously at the old horse and walked up to her muzzle, reaching out to her. The nag nuzzled Kate's hand.

"Naw, not her, Mrs. Kate. Not old Sheba. She's my pet. But Jackson here, why he's able to pull any amount you put on him. He'll stand in the heat all day and not complain. As gentle as a lamb, eats dry grass or most anything that smells like it."

Flint left his work at the pump house and crossed the creek by the well, walking toward Gus and Kate. Kate noticed his jerky gait quicken when Gus mentioned using Jackson for a workhorse.

"What do ya' want for Jackson, Gus? He's as fine a mule as I've seen." He reached out to Gus and they shook hands briskly.

"Oh, I got no use for him anymore the way you all do. I just keep him around cause he's a friend." The lanky man rubbed his whiskers. "Suppose I could borrow him to plow the corn field and a few avocados now and then in exchange, Flint. Why, can't really sell a friend, now can I?" Gus patted the old mule on his back, raising dust. Jackson's tail swished and he nuzzled Gus' arched shoulder. Kate noticed a sudden cloud cover the old gentleman's green eyes, and she knew that Gus truly loved Jackson. His gift of the old mule was a sacrifice, any way she looked at it.

"You got a deal, Gus. We need Jackson real bad. I know just the spot to set up a corral for him. Say, how's the still down the creek?"

"Let's you and me go check it out later today, Flint. Prohibition is gonna be the ruination of these here United States, I tell ya'. 'Sides, I venture to say there's more liquor flowin' now than before the government stepped in. Prohibition, haw! What a joke." Gus slapped his knee bone. Kate grimaced at the mention of the still. She didn't like the sound of Flint's checking out the still later today or any time. For a few weeks, Flint had been sober and easier to live with. They finally were beginning to have a life together again. She prayed he wouldn't ruin it.

"What the hell do you care?" Flint questioned Gus. "You've made moonshine years before Prohibition."

"Well, now I feel obliged to share it with the whole derned country. Say, this new batch is made with my last crop of corn." Gus' voice became a whisper and his eyes rolled. "Corn liquor, she's gonna be mighty rich." He emphasized the 'rich.' Then he looked around the area and peered into the bushes nearby. A knot formed in Kate's stomach.

Gus looked at Kate, now holding the rope that hung loosely around Jackson. "You come down too, Kate. Have yourself a swig." He leaned forward and grinned at her, his green eyes snapping with mischief. "I got friends comin' up to check out the new batch tonight."

Kate glanced nervously at Flint, praying that he would say that he had too much work to do. Gus leaned forward, hugging his scrawny middle in the futile effort to control his merriment, unaware of Kate's concern. She bit her lip, fearing that a drink around the still would weaken Flint's resistance, and that he would start the habit again.

"Well," Flint said, "I think we'd best go down at night. Less likely one of those government agents sneaking around. Besides, we got lots of work to do while it's daylight."

Kate tried to conceal the ire in her words. "Just where is this still, Gus? I can hear you folks laughing and carryin' on when the wind is just right. Comin' from the creek a ways."

Gus answered by pointing down the creek that meandered toward his place. "Take that trail where my property links to yours. Right about there, by the creek." Gus grinned. "C'mon down. Right after sundown."

"No thank ya', Gus. That trip in the dark would be foolish for a woman with several kids, or a man with rheumatism, 'specially on the way back." Kate gnawed at her lip until it ached. She hoped that Flint would catch her meaning and agree to stay home.

"Well, I'll send a jigger home with yer man here," said Gus, ignoring her remark.

Gus left Jackson's rope in Kate's hand. He patted the fine young mule, and said goodbye, leading his horse, Sheba, back down the trail to his place.

Still holding Jackson's rope, Kate tapped her foot on the ground. With a clinched fist, she stiffened as she watched Flint return to the pump house, chuckling.

74

CHAPTER—15

THE FOUND HAT

After Gus' visit that spring day, Kate relaxed, since Flint never succumbed to Gus' invitation to meet at the still, but instead got busy making good use of Jackson. As spring and summer slipped by, Kate helped Flint as the kids sat beside the field, and day after day Flint hitched the old mule's harness to a rope and wrapped the rope around the sage. Together, they yanked clump after clump of sagebrush from the ground on the south slope. Flint told Kate that, after a few large rocks were removed, the following spring the field could be plowed and readied for melons.

November came and Flint continued to stay sober. He spent days at a time at the homestead without leaving. Old man Warner was nearly forgotten. Flint told Kate that folks at the Junction saw him leave on a bus. Someone must have gladly given him money to leave, even as difficult as it was to obtain. It was probably Flint, Kate figured, but she didn't mind, so long as he really did give him the money instead of killing him as she had supposed.

Every day, Flint brought home more dismal news of the country's economic plight, but Kate didn't care now that Flint was sober. After all, it didn't affect her except to give her the doldrums, and she couldn't do anything about it anyway. There was plenty to do without dwelling on other people's problems. Besides, Thanksgiving Day was near.

Flint finished piping water to the avocado trees the week before, and then began digging up the bank along the east side of the kitchen to make an area large enough to add on a bedroom. He was not in the frantic hurry to add the bedroom as he had been the kitchen. However, as soon as he noticed that Kate was pregnant again, or if she got the nerve to tell him before he noticed, he might be frantic about more than getting that bank dug down and the room built.

A warm Santa Ana wind had blown in since morning and would make working on the house difficult. But in a few days, the wind would be gone, leaving everything as dry as a bone and everyone relieved that it had finally ceased.

Before Kate left the house to milk the cow, she bundled Bette and set her in an apple box to watch the boys while Flint worked on the room. 'Princess on a pillow,' Kate called Bette every time she propped her up in the apple box.

Kate finished milking the Jersey, sat the milk bucket down, and covered it snuggly with her apron. Winter would be setting in after the wind quit, and it could be nasty weather for a spell. Rain was badly needed. But Kate hadn't taken a walk by herself for as long as she could remember. This was a good time to walk to the avocado trees and peer out toward the pale blue line of the Pacific Ocean. It felt good to move a bit, without carrying one child and hanging on to another. She hiked to the avocado trees. There she ran fingers over shiny fat leaves as they whipped in the gentle wind. Gentle, since the Santa Ana hadn't picked up to its normal lashing speed yet. Kate rubbed her hand up and down a rough scaly tree trunk. Turning to the west, she gazed long and far, and took in the Pacific with a deep breath. The Santa Ana blew at her back, coming from the Mohave Desert in the east, beyond several mountains.

It was lonely at the homestead sometimes, but Kate wouldn't trade it for anything. As she stood there, gazing out at the vastness before her and the faint blue line of the ocean, she wondered if folks in town and in other parts of the country really were having hard times.

Mom and Pop were expected to come for Thanksgiving. They would tell her the truth. She never knew when Flint was telling her the truth or just trying to rile her. And the newspapers, well, they made their living getting people all stirred up, buying bad news. God only knew how some folks loved to dwell on the misfortunes of others.

She walked on up the slope, not wanting to go back just yet. Something odd-looking lay under the sagebrush. The wind must have blown it in. Reaching down with unsure fingers, she nabbed the brown object, but quickly dropped it. *The old man's hat.* For what seemed a long time, Kate stood staring down at the tattered brown hat, her brow furrowed, and her mind a swirling whirlpool. Her hand felt contaminated from touching Warner's hat. She rubbed her hand hard against her dungarees.

Curious, she decided to look around the area to see what else she might find. A plate-sized rock, caked with dried blood, lay among a grouping of sagebrush a few yards from where she found the hat. She bent over, her spirit sickened and shaken.

It was clear now. There were never any tracks leading out of the yard and down the road. There never was anyone at the Junction who told Flint the old man left on a bus. Flint did what he had to do to protect his family, knowing they would never be safe as long as the old man was alive. It was the lesser evil, to protect them by putting an end to the old man. She rubbed her arms, her nerves raw. Flint must have shot him, dragged him over to the edge of the canyon, and threw him off.

"That's the skullduggery that took so long, and that's why he was doin' all that scrubbin'," Kate prattled to herself as she figured it all out. Then she looked toward the house. "Better get down there. Flint will be wondering why it's taking so long to milk."

Kate calmed herself and, lifting the edge of the bloodstained rock with the toe of her shoe, kicked the hat under the rock to hide it, then hurried down the slope to the milk bucket. The Santa Ana began to sting her feverish skin. Slowly, she walked back to the house, turning now and again to look behind her.

CHAPTER—16

THANKSGIVING

Kate worked hard the day before Thanksgiving, killing and cleaning the biggest gobbler. She placed it in the spring next to the milk and butter, weighing it down under a tub, where the cold, pure water kept it fresh, and where the animals couldn't disturb it.

The hike to the avocado trees and finding the bloody rock and the hat the week before still haunted her, but she determined not to let it spoil her Thanksgiving holiday.

At daybreak, Thanksgiving Day, Kate headed for the kitchen with Flint close behind her. "Got to get the turkey on early, Flint. We're goin' to eat soon as Mom and Pop get here. Wish Paul was comin' too, but I guess he's at that ornery independent age. He's gone off with his friends, accordin' to Mom's last letter."

Soon after the turkey was in the oven and breakfast over, the house smelled of sage and sweet spice. The boys drooled and rubbed their stomachs, eyeing their mother. She laid mincemeat tarts down on the edge of the table. The tarts disappeared as soon as Kate turned her back. Now at least, the boys would survive until the turkey was on the table. "Flint, that last deer you brought down made the best venison mincemeat ever," she said, as Flint passed through the kitchen and nabbed a tart. He too, moved as quickly as possible, hoping to get most of the chores finished before her parents arrived.

Today was special in so many ways. Flint was usually more cheerful on holidays and excitement filled the house, along with sweet spicy smells from every pie and tart Kate pulled from the oven. It had been several weeks since Mom and Pop drove up from Bonita to visit, and Kate longed to see them again. At their last visit, Pop was impressed with what she and Flint had accomplished and let them know in his quiet way. Mom, however, being a good southern Baptist, had not forgiven her for living in sin. Kate supposed Mom could never accept that Cherokee heathens dancing around a fire and singing some mumbo-jumbo was acceptable to God and ordained as a marriage. The fact that Flint provided no ring for her finger made him worse in Mom's eyes. Kate should never have told her mother about the ceremony. Probably no amount of doing was going to please her now.

Pop wasn't like Mom in that his love was unconditional, and whatever Kate wanted and saw fit to do, Pop accepted. Kate bit her lip as she poked at the potatoes, testing them to see if they were done.

The baked potatoes were nearly soft enough and the sage-savory turkey aroma floated throughout the house when Rob ran in breathless, skidding to a stop before her. He looked up at her with large eyes and his excited grin revealed a gap between his teeth.

"I was waitin' on the hill, Ma, when I heared somethin'. I put my ear down to the ground and I heard a mighty big roar like a car. Somebody's a' coming. Suppose its Grandpop and Grandma?"

Kate smiled at her excited son, and then touched his freckled, pug nose with the tip of her finger. "I reckon so, Rob. Let's get out yonder." She bit her lower lip and then held him back a moment. "Now, Rob, let's not worry your Grandpop and Grandma with stories of . . . of, well, the old man, okay? And better not mention that mountain lion either."

Rob frowned. Worry covered his innocent face. "No, Ma, I won't."

"Besides," Kate said, "the old man is gone."

"And we haven't seen no mountain lion, just heard him scream," said Rob, licking mincemeat off his fingers.

Kate grabbed his shoulder. "You heard him scream? When?"

Rob tugged away from his mother's grasp, anxious to get outside. "Oh, the other night. I think. Maybe I was dreamin'."

"Don't worry, Rob." Kate sagged relieved, praying that he was right. She patted her son's shoulder. "He can't come in the house. And Brownie will let us know if he comes close, ya hear?" *Lordy, Lordy, the mountain lion screamed and I was dead asleep.* She shook her head, dismayed, and followed her excited son out the door.

Pregnancy made her sleep heavier than normal. But, thankfully, there wasn't much morning sickness. She dreaded Mom and Pop learning the news again. She could just hear Mom. "How are ya' goin' to take care of another mouth to feed?" No, she wasn't planning to tell them. Not today anyway. And after Flint's reaction to the last birth, she feared telling him even more.

Waiting in the yard, Kate wrung her hands in her apron. Rob, Bette, and Bo hung back in the doorway. Kate hoped they wouldn't retreat beneath their bed as they had the last time Mom and Pop came, and as they always did when strangers arrived. From where she stood, Kate saw Flint making his way down from the avocado trees. The morning had gone well. Kate wanted it all to be ready so Mom would have nothing to do but sit and visit and hold Bette in the rocker.

A few minutes later, she heard the sounds of a car approaching. Before long, Mom and Pop stepped out of their decrepit Ford and a whir of excitement followed. Kate didn't remember Pop being so tall. Maybe it only seemed so because he was thinner now, his face prominent with high cheekbones. Mom's pulled-back flaming red hair had gray streaks running through it, and she looked a bit stooped. Time was slipping by. Kate noticed lines in her own face when she took time to look. Mostly though, she was too busy to care. It was how one felt inside that counted most. But Kate wasn't sure what she felt inside anymore. Suddenly, she realized how lonely she had been for Mom and Pop. Overjoyed, tears blurred her sight.

Pop wrapped his long arms about Kate. Rob, Bo, and Bette stood beside her, hiding behind her apron and hanging onto her trousers. By the time the huddled group got into the house, Kate's face was tear-stained.

It was a splendid day for Kate, with Mom and Pop and the whole family around the oak table. Thanksgiving dinner was delicious. It wasn't just that the meal tasted so good. It was a feeling of contentment because much of her dream had come true. They were all grouped together in one day.

After dinner, Rob and Bo jumped up and down, chattering. Kate stood back and watched as they grabbed their grandparents and led them around to see the hummingbird nest, a tiny felt-like cup hooked to the end of the oak branch that hung above the trail leading to the pump house. Grandpop said, "Well, Annie Rose, would you look at that?"

Grandma looked at the nest hanging on the oak branch in plain sight, and when the boys were sure that she was as impressed as Grandpop, they pulled both grandparents back again in the front yard, where the friendly long-legged granddaddy spider family lived, nestled in the crook of the oak tree trunk.

Later in the afternoon, Bo and Rob were content to play quietly in the front yard. They scooted around on the hard ground with the wooden toy cars that Pop carved out of mill ends with his pocketknife. Bette took a nap while Mom lay resting on the bed.

"I'm going down to check the pump," Flint said, as he knocked the ashes from his pipe. He rose from his respite after the ample meal and then headed for the pump house.

Seizing her opportunity, Kate asked Pop to walk with her up the hill to the avocado trees. Arm in arm they strolled. The weather was especially nice for late November, and she basked in the afternoon warmth.

Kate desperately wanted to tell Pop about Warner. Her stomach felt nauseous every time she thought about him. And where was the body? Tossed over into the canyon or thrown out into the brush where wild animals would have devoured him by this time. The whole affair lay dark and heavy upon her like a black cloud hovering over a thirsty mountain. She needed to tell someone, to seek absolution for her part in it.

Her steps felt weighted as she pondered the decision whether to tell Pop. It would mean Flint's neck if word ever got out. Kate opened her mouth, ready to confess what she knew.

"Pop?" Her father glanced down at her as they hiked. He nodded. She knew he was listening. He would love her no matter what awful secret she told him. "Nice day, huh?" Kate said, and for a few seconds, she stopped walking and looked down at her feet. She took a deep breath and hurried her step to meet Pop's stride. She couldn't do it, couldn't tell him. Best to keep her secret under wraps forever. She would forget all about the killing as time passed . . . she hoped.

As they reached their destination, Kate sensed the same wonder she felt when she came up here. "Pop, see this spot right here?" Kate pressed Pop's arm, guiding him westward. "No better spot for an adobe house. See that faint blue line? That is the ocean."

Pop squinted toward the west. "Why, if that don't beat all. I'll be darned if you ain't right, Kate. Shore enough, that is a wonder." Pop reached in the pocket of his coveralls and pulled out a plug of tobacco.

"Flint, he don't regard my idea of the adobe house," she said, shaking her head. Pop ripped off a piece of the stuff with his teeth as he listened to Kate.

"Maybe someday when he's satisfied with the rest of the homestead, he can think of something else. I've given up on the adobe house." Kate knew she really didn't mean what she said. She wanted that adobe house, just like she wanted to nurse the sick and doctor broken bones. Sometimes both dreams seemed impossible. Pop never discouraged her about anything, but he didn't encourage her to pursue her desires, either.

Kate straightened her back. There would be no help from Pop, she knew, just as there'd been no help from Flint. She realized that she didn't need help, not from anyone. She'd get what she wanted on her own.

Pop spat tobacco juice on the ground, leaving a brown trail of sweet smelling liquid. "You all have done real good, Kate. And it relieves me to know that this damned Depression hardly touches you. We're all are doing better than most. Poor folks that don't even have a garden spot. They's the one's hurtin'." Pop spoke with worry in his tone and sadness in his eyes. "Have a chaw of tobacco, Kate?"

"No, Pop." She tried to smile.

"Pop, is it really as bad as the newspapers say? Flint scares me with his talk. You know, none of it pertains to me. To us."

"You're wrong there," Pop said through the large lump in his cheek. "We're all in this together."

Pop suddenly appeared old. Kate hadn't thought much about it before. Pop would grow old and die someday. The thought of Pop gone from her life brought tears to her eyes, even though she believed that there was life in the hereafter.

"You won't have to worry, Kate, as long as you have this homestead. And don't fret about your Mom and me. We do all right."

"Its confusing, Pop. Sometimes my eyes tell me one thing and my insides tell me another." She frowned and shaded her eyes from the glaring vastness of the sky, from the ocean and the valley laid out before her. She was thinking how Mom and Pop seemed to like each other. They were such good friends. She and Flint didn't have that togetherness, the connection, the oneness that her parents had. Life was lonely. Often she grieved silently about Flint and about other things. She sensed Pop knew much about her and her grieving without the need for her to say a word.

"Kate, that's part of growin' up. But, that growin' up never ends, I guess, cause I do the same thing at my old age of 55." He grinned down at her, hugging her strong, slender shoulders. They stood watching the horizon together as the wind whipped up and the sun sank lower in the sky. Kate nestled into Pop's warm, embracing arms, sorry to see their time together about to run out. But she knew Pop would need to leave soon, to drive down the mountain before sundown.

As they began their descent down the trail, Kate glanced toward the sagebrush just up the slope beyond where she stood. Now would be the perfect moment to tell Pop about the blood, the rock, and the hat that lay among the brush. She opened her mouth but the words wouldn't come.

As Kate walked beside Pop, she kept her back straight and her head up.

When they were in sight of the house, Kate turned to Pop and said, "I have something to tell you."

"Oh?"

She knew Pop would understand if anyone could. "I'm pregnant," she blurted out, her shoulders slumped with relief to have finally told someone.

"I know," he said with a twinkle in his eyes. "Have you told Flint?"

"No," she admitted, training worried eyes on Flint who was still at the pump house, wrench in hand.

"You've got to tell him."

"I know," Kate said, but she wasn't sure how.

CHAPTER — 17

ANOTHER BOY

At the end of May, Donald Barkley Powell was born at the homestead. He came too fast for Kate to get to Mercy Hospital twenty miles away in San Diego. Because he was Kate's fourth childbirth, and because he was small, at least smaller at birth than the first three, he came easier. Kate reeled with relief when the ordeal was over so quickly. She even laughed with Rob, who was there beside her from start to finish.

Flint had driven to Doc Laraby's home in El Cajon to find him and, Kate had hoped, to get him to the homestead before the baby came. Kate realized that Flint escaped every time she was about to give birth, and for one reason or another had never made it back in time. She remembered how blood and birth had great significance to the Cherokee and wondered why such a belief would affect Flint to such a degree.

Kate had perfected tying and clipping her own umbilical cord after Bette's delivery. And then, after Donnie had rested on Kate's stomach for a few minutes, and the cord had ceased surging blood, she carefully went to work on the procedure.

Four hours after Donnie's birth, Flint returned with Doc Laraby. Doc examined Kate and Donnie and helped clean up. After Flint peeked at Donnie and forced a smile, he then stood in the middle of the kitchen holding his stomach. Sweat beaded on his forehead and then he walked out to the front yard.

Doc asked Kate questions about the birth. To her knowledgeable answers, he asked, "How did you learn about birthing in such detail, the technical terms and all, Kate?"

With her finger, Kate pecked the top of the Merck manual that sat on the stand beside her bed. Doc Laraby lifted the heavy book, opened it, and turned a few pages. "Now that's tough learning, Kate. You've had lots of earlier schooling? Pre-med or nursing?"

"No, Doc." Kate's eyebrows moved closer together, and then a pleasant feeling flowed over her and she giggled at the doctor. If a well-respected man like Doc Laraby could think her well schooled, why then, maybe he was right.

After awhile Flint came inside the kitchen and poured Doc and himself a mug of coffee. At the table, they drank from the hot mugs and chatted. Kate didn't pay much attention to their conversation. She lay with Donnie and basked in knowing that she, Kate, had somehow gone way beyond her formal eighth-grade education.

When it came time for Flint to drive Doc back to town, Doc ordered Kate to stay down for a week. She chuckled, but promised that she would try, knowing very well she'd be up and cooking breakfast for the kids as soon as he and Flint left the yard.

Fortunately, Bo and Bette slept through the ordeal of Donnie's birth, but since Rob was there with his small helping hands, Kate teased him that he had earned the title of 'midwife'.

Throughout the day, Rob skipped in from playing or from his chores to survey his new baby brother. Finally, with concern in his voice and a frown on his face, he asked, "Ma, why didn't Bette get a baby sister, like I got Bo for a brother?"

"I think God knows that we need more help in the melon field than here in the house."

Rob still looked worried and said, "Donnie sure is wrinkled and little, and he has no hair."

"Don't worry, Rob. Most babies are wrinkled," Kate laughed. "He'll come around. He's beautiful though, don't you think?"

Rob cocked his head, as if puzzled to see what his mother saw in this brand-new, wrinkled baby. Rob gently reached out and touched Donnie's hand. At once the infant wrapped his tiny fingers tightly around Rob's finger and hung on until Rob pulled away, astonished.

"Wow, Ma! Did you see that?" Rob smiled, flashing his large new teeth. "He sure is strong for such a little guy, and wrinkled and . . . and really funny lookin'." Finally, with bright, laughing eyes, Rob skipped across the kitchen floor and out the door.

Kate kept busy with the four children and the housework. Scrubbing diapers on the rub board seemed an endless chore. Since Donnie's birth the month before, the three older children spent most of the day in the front yard since the weather was warm and the one room shelter felt more closed in every day. Kate knew Flint had regressed to drinking again as soon as Donnie's birth was imminent, but he'd tried to hide it from her. He seemed uneasy when he was in the house around Kate and the children, and made himself scarce, either in the melon field or gone from the homestead.

When Kate's bitterness about his absence from the homestead returned, she reminded herself that every spare minute in the day would be spent studying the medical book, not fretting about Flint.

CHAPTER–18

FLINT'S ENLIGHTENMENT

This morning, since Flint had finished what he could around the homestead, it was time to check on Mrs. Helm's. He'd work there this week, catching up, and earn enough money for barbed wire to enlarge the cow's pasture. Although he'd determined to keep busy with the homestead, try to get the farm producing and food on the table, and build onto the house, he itched for a drink to quell the guilt he felt for fleeing his wife when she needed him most.

While Kate was busy with the children in the house, Flint stuck his head in the kitchen door. "Goin down the mountain, Katie. You need supplies for the house?" He stepped just inside the kitchen.

Kate looked up from nursing Donnie in the rocker while the older three children sat at the table looking at picture books. "Vanilla and coffee. Makin' bread pudding for supper. Bring the kids a stick of candy, will ya'?"

Bo slid off the bench and ran to his father, hugging his legs.

"I'll see about that candy." He ruffled Bo's hair and stepped back out the door, leaving Bo jumping up and down with excitement, chanting, "candy, candy."

He'd stop at Mrs. Helm's and find out if she needed any supplies before he headed to town. He'd missed visiting with her while she was away in Los Angeles for the winter months.

As much as he'd felt drawn to Mrs. Helm, he wanted her friendship more than anything, and was careful not to let passion destroy that. He drove slowly down the mountain this morning, mulling over the complications that tumbled in his head. In the end, he decided to by pass Mrs. Helm's place. Still, he looked forward to spending time with her again. Kate's lack of understanding increased. He could see it in her eyes, the anger and resentment fueling his own anger, but mostly his guilt.

He drove faster, anxious to reach the hardware store so he could purchase wire. While at the hardware, he figured the way he'd string the barbed wire so a corner of the cow's pen could reach the stream. He bought the wire, put on a pair of leather gloves, and hauled the prickly roll to the Dodge. Then he headed for the Spring Valley Grocery for Kate's supplies. While there, he shopped for the supplies but nearly forgot the peppermint sticks. He bought extra to appease his guilt for his thoughtlessness before heading east with the wire, peppermint sticks, and other supplies.

Nearing the Junction Store, he hesitated, but then pulled up in front and went in. Arnie sat Gallo on the counter and invited Flint to a poker game the following night. Flint shook his head that he would be there, but as much as he loved a good poker game and the fact that he usually won some extra money, he grew tired of the bosomed saloon women hanging over him, reeking of musk and cigarettes. He had more important things on his mind. He paid Arnie, and hurried out with the Gallo under his arm.

Leaving Arnie's, Flint drove in the direction of Mt. McGinny. After veering off the main highway, Flint pulled off at a wide spot in the road and opened the Gallo. After a few swigs, he was willing to face Mrs. Helm and his past. He heaved a sign of relief as the Gallo filled his veins and drove on.

Arriving at Mrs. Helm's, he parked in his usual spot under the eucalyptus. She met him at the door with vibrant red lips and bouncy hair and led him to the intimate table just inside. The late morning sun shone through the easterly windows, scattering a rainbow of color through the room.

After catching up on the local gossip and scheduling maintenance and repair plans for the summer months, Flint said, "Kate had another boy, born just last week at the homestead. Name's Donnie."

"I had forgotten she was due again. Were you there?" she asked, as she settled down in her chair.

Flint stared at Mrs. Helm as she nervously brushed at her wispy white gown. And then she looked directly at him, a hint of blush beneath her cheeks.

As radiant as a rose in the morning sunshine, she sat with accepting brown eyes, more beautiful than he'd remembered. He felt a connection, an understanding he'd never felt with Kate, and longed to pour out his pain to someone who would listen without judging him.

Embarrassed that he'd missed Mrs. Helm so much during her few month's absence, he turned his eyes away from her.

"Kate delivered the baby by herself . . . again. I went for Laraby. He checked her over afterward." Flint leaned his elbows on the table and cupped his head in his rough bronzed hands.

"What is it, Flint?"

"I let her down again." With his head still in his hands, he cried.

86

Mrs. Helm touched the top of Flint's head, patting him, soothing him. "Is that why you run away every time your wife needs you to help deliver a child?"

He grasped the hair that hung down near his hand. "I'm such a coward when I see blood!"

"It's trauma, Flint. You need to deal with it." Mrs. Helm's hand lay on Flint's shoulder now, warm and comforting.

"I've had too much wine, Vi. That's all. Got to get Kate's vanilla home."

"Listen, Flint. We're friends. Come talk with me again. It's good for the soul, you know." She placed her hand on the muscle of his upper arm and squeezed gently.

Flint left her and headed home, some of the tightness in his chest gone. He swabbed his face several times with his bandana before he got to the homestead, hoping to wipe away any signs of weakness. Kate hated weakness.

CHAPTER—19

The Authorities

Kate's energy rebounded, and after a month of strict attention to Donnie, she returned to every-day life, except with one more mouth to feed. Now and then Kate took a walk with the children just to smell the flowers, to gather bouquets for the table, and to get out of the one room that seemed to shrink as the weeks progressed.

The flowers hung over the banks along the road, covering meadows and coloring the usually barren ground. Their fragrance permeated the air, mingling with sagebrush and sumac. Yuccas, tall and stately and crowned with exotic white blooms, stood side-by-side with the rocks on the mountain, surviving the hard gravely earth from which they grew.

The beauty on the mountainside was such a contrast to the news on the pump-house radio where Kate heard one sad story after another about the Depression. It continued to take its toll across the United States. The newspapers, too, never ceased their tales of woe. The terrible state of the country was what drove Flint back to drinking, she figured. Kate kept as busy as she could, planning for winter, planning in case Flint drove off the road some night and killed himself, or if the authorities discovered his whereabouts and carried him off to prison for maiming Schwartz or killing Warner.

But as the year passed at the homestead, Kate worked with Flint and finished moving boulders from the east side of the house to the low area north and behind the kitchen. With pry bar, Flint loosened rocks of all sizes from the bank, hooked a rope around one rock after another, and then Jackson, with Kate leading him, pulled them in place. Donnie watched from the apple box nearby. By the end of day, he was as dusty and in need of a washtub bath as the rest of the family.

So, day after day, they shoveled dirt from the east bank and wheel barrowed it to the low end, then dumped it around the large boulders. Flint rarely left the homestead during this two months of arduous and back-breaking work, but when the fill-in was complete, he left for more building materials. And Kate, though weary of body, noticed that Flint returned sober.

Where the boulders were removed on the east side of the kitchen, with Rob and Bo's help, Flint built a front room. Kate kept food on the table and the chores done with one eye on their progress. A door now opened into the new room from the kitchen and another leading to the front yard. Flint framed in and put in place, two narrow paned windows, one on each end of the east side of the room, allowing the morning sun to shine in. Another window faced the front yard. Flint placed a chimney for a small pot-bellied wood stove between the paned windows. At last, the room felt cozy. Temporarily, beds lined two walls, so the new room served as a bedroom until additional rooms could be built. For the first time, the kitchen was open for its intended use.

Kate's back couldn't take much more house building. She hoped to see some of her family from Bonita any day now. Meanwhile, work didn't stop on the house, but in the weeks ahead, with Flint staying sober most of the time, Kate and the boys helped him add two small bedrooms on the north side of the house with a screened-in porch to the west of the middle bedroom.

Just before winter, the final nail was hammered into the metal roof over the new rooms. Kate stood out in the yard with Flint and the children. They looked at the larger house, complete with plenty of room. That was it. There was ample room, no matter how many more children came. A feeling of pride and relief came over Kate. Tears welled in her eyes. In a short time, beds were moved around to their appointed room.

The porch was where Flint slept now, a mutual unspoken agreement between him and Kate after she'd announced that she was once again pregnant. It was there he read the newspaper, smoked his pipe, and drank his coffee, and where he lay unconscious after coming home drunk.

Kate didn't mind about the porch. She was grateful that Flint left her untouched at night. She held her belly. Life wasn't getting any easier. Besides, Flint didn't help matters any when he never found time to pipe water into the house. After awhile Kate gave up any expectation of it ever happening. Permanently wounded by that one omission, she determined never to ask about the water pipe again.

Rob and Bo claimed the north end of the porch. A cot was set up for Bette in the little room at the far north end of the house, beyond the middle room where Kate slept. A cot sat in the corner across the room from Kate's bed. Donnie would sleep there when he outgrew the small crib he now slept in. Since Kate was expecting again, a new baby would need the crib before another year was out.

Then spring arrived. On one such cold morning, Flint returned from driving down the hill to get Rob to the bus that would take him 12 miles into the boxed-in town of El Cajon for school. It was the kind of morning when haze lay thick in the valley. Flint rested in his bed on the porch. Kate carried him coffee. He read the newspaper, moving at a snail's pace this early spring, since the wet cold aggravated his rheumatism.

Kate figured she'd have her turn in her bed as soon as labor started. She never stayed down as long as the doctor told her to, but then, she hadn't made it to the hospital either. She seemed to survive it, and even laughed when she'd heard of other women laying in bed a week or two after giving birth. Cherokee mothers would never pull such a stunt, and she found it disgraceful to pretend infirm when she was perfectly healthy and strong. Besides, Flint would not stick around to help her if she was down on her back; she knew that much.

A rumbling alerted Brownie. She heard a car coming up the mountain halfway up from the Helm's place. Kate hollered to Flint, "Car's comin'." She heard his feet hit the floor, and she peered excitedly out the window.

Kate wiped the counter quickly and gave the floor a few swipes with the broom, as Flint ambled through the house. He had brushed his hair and, smoothing down his mustache, he hurried to the front yard. He didn't like people finding him on his back, sick or otherwise. Besides, it wasn't that often they had company. A late model Ford with an official emblem on the side crept slowly into the yard. Kate stood in the kitchen door. Right off, she thought of Gus' still down the canyon. She clutched the edge of the door tightly, praying that they hadn't caught up with Flint after his run-in with Leonard Schwartz in Oklahoma. Kate figured they were probably here about Warner. Old Warner. Feeling faint, she leaned against the doorframe.

Two suited men got out of the car and Kate's throat filled with stones. The men took wallets out of their pockets and flipped their badges in Flint's face, then shook hands with him. The heavy-set man stood with his short legs spread apart, balancing himself on the rough ground. He spoke in a gruff, authoritative voice. "Are you Flint Everson Powell?"

Flint nodded.

"We're lookin' for Theodore Warner. His brother tells us that he hasn't seen him for some time and folks around the Junction haven't either."

The taller man stood like a guard to the fat one, with a gleam of righteousness on his raw-boned face. The gruff porcine man in charge eyed Flint accusingly. "Some folks seen him leave with you, heading out of town, and haven't seen him since. They say it was some time ago that he worked for you, Mr. Powell. Thought maybe he was here." The heavy man raised his fleshy chin, waiting for Flint's confession.

Horrified, Kate scrunched back into the kitchen out of sight and wiped her damp forehead with her apron. She could barely hear the conversation, but she didn't want them asking her questions. Her face would not lie about what she saw. It was vivid in her memory, even though it happened over two years before: the rifle shot, the old man's hat, the bloody rock. "Oh, Lord. Flint's telling them the same story he told me," she whispered softly.

90

The three men talked awhile about the homestead and the Depression. Kate could hear only an occasional word or sentence, but she didn't hear Warner's name mentioned again.

"Thank God," Kate whispered as if the walls could hear her. She peeked around the door but quickly pulled back out of sight. The air she'd held inside her lungs swished out. "They're leavin'."

Flint fixed his pipe and stood in the front yard until the Ford drove out of site. Kate heard him tromp back through the house to hole up on his porch, on his bed with his newspaper.

Kate wiped the beaded sweat from her forehead and heaved a deep sigh of relief that the authorities were gone without nosing around any further. Wondering how Flint could act nonchalant, she sat on the bench holding her nauseated stomach. She knew they'd be back. It was only a question of when.

CHAPTER—20

THE TRUTH ABOUT WARNER

For the remainder of spring and summer, Kate cringed every time she heard the rumbling of a vehicle, sure that any minute the authorities were coming to nab Flint away for the murder of Warner. Hatching a plan of how to make ends meet should that happen, she started searching for ideas, spending more time studying the medical book. Of course, she and the kids could always live with Mom and Pop, but Kate reeled at the thought. Any idea was better than depending on Mom and Pop. By the end of summer though, not a soul came to inquire about old man Warner. And as summer faded, Kate's fear diminished.

Winter came too soon again for Kate's liking. Abundant rains pelted down off and on, just as it had the winter before they arrived at the homestead. The north creek splashed high on the canyon banks, gushing over smooth granite rocks. The southeastern creek that ran over the road leading to the front yard flowed too high to drive or walk through. Just before winter set in, with Rob and Bo's help, Flint built a narrow wooden walking bridge spanning the creek a few feet up from a trickling rocky waterfall. Now they could walk from the front yard to the pump house trail without getting wet feet.

The heavy rain was a nice change except for traveling up and down the mountain, but the rain wouldn't last long, and when the sun came out again, the outdoors would reveal Mother Nature's finest, the fragrance of the earth. There was nothing like it. Kate figured that the slippery road and the need to shake mud from the gunnysack rugs at the front door for a few days was well worth the earthy aroma.

What was going on in the rest of the world seemed so far away, so unimportant to Kate. Making certain food was on this table was a world of worry in itself. She pondered these things as she tugged a box of empty jars out from under the kitchen counter. Another box held a stack of newspaper, which Kate kept for starting the wood stove, lining dresser drawers and shelves, and for wrapping canning jars, which she would do today. After the jars were wrapped in newspaper, they would be returned to the box and placed under the back of the house where the dirt was dug out, an area used also to over-winter potatoes, beets, onions, and squash.

A pot of beans simmered on the wood stove alongside a pot of boiled coffee. The morning chores were done. Kate wondered how she could continue to get everything accomplished with the addition of a new child to the family every other year. But she became more efficient and, fortunately, Rob, Bo, and Bette became more helpful as they grew.

With an air of arrogance, Flint said that the homestead could now be considered a truck farm. After all, it was producing a heap of dandy avocados and melons. Flint took a truck full of produce about once a week through most of the summer to sell at the Spring Valley Market or while parked at the junction, selling right out of the back of the truck. Kate thought about Flint and the way he drew people to him. No, folks were not strangers for long after meeting Flint, with his flair for flattery and his bent for social drinking. As an added benefit to buyers, Flint sold the produce at a very fair price. And because of Flint's generosity, it took little time to sell the entire load of produce. Folks had little money the summer before. Of course, they had little money prior to that and would have even less next season no doubt.

To Kate's disgust though, Prohibition was a joke, just as Gus had predicted. The whole thing had been repealed the previous year. Not that it mattered to most. Serious drinkers had their way of getting plenty of liquor to guzzle. But, as Flint and the newspaper reported, the Depression seemed to be gaining in heaps of sorrow for most people, giving them reason to drink. At least the United States had a decent President in Roosevelt. Roosevelt believed that relieving people from distress was more important than balancing the budget, so government projects were opened to employ some of the thousands of down-and-out folks.

Dale Andrew Powell was born without any complications in the middle of the winter. Doc Laraby even made it to the homestead in time for his birth, as the rain hadn't made the road impassable yet. Flint stuck around so that he could drive Doc back to town after the ordeal. And then, as it happened every time Kate gave birth, Flint disappeared afterward as if contaminated by the sight of blood. After all these years, Kate figured he'd return after drowning himself in a jug of Gallo.

Now, three months later, the little towheaded boy sat propped up like a prince on a pillow in an apple box that Kate placed strategically on the table. Dale watched the trees flitter in the rain out the bank of kitchen windows, while near him Kate wrapped jars in newspaper.

In the front room, Bo, Bette and Donnie played, chasing each other around in circles. Hopefully, the rain would stop. Since Flint had business in San Diego and would not return until late, she and the children would meet Rob today.

Since Rob had started school the September before, he had grown until his jeans were inches too short and his hair darkened auburn like Kate's. She hated that Rob had to ride the school bus so far into El Cajon, 12 long miles to and from, sometimes after walking the two miles to get to the bus in the first place. It made such a long day, and she worried about him the entire time. But, to Kate's relief, Flint usually needed to go out anyway, so most of the time he drove Rob to the bus and picked him up a few hours later. Bo would be old enough to start school the following year and then he and Rob could walk the distance together.

Kate placed a jar ring in each of Dale's hands. He champed onto them with his fists and banged them together again and again. Kate poured a mug of coffee and sipped it while she continued to wrap the canning jars and continued to think about survival and about Flint.

The rain stopped and Kate left her canning jars and newspaper on the table, wrapped Dale in a warmer blanket, and set him in the wagon. She and the children began their walk down the mountain to meet Rob. As they walked, they kept in the middle of the road to avoid rattlesnakes, and hoped that the mountain lion stayed closer to the top of Mt. McGinny.

Kate trudged along with Bo and Bette and Donnie rode in the wagon, squeezed in with Dale. It had rained just enough to dampen the top crust of the road, and as they walked, their shoes became heavier, laden with clay, and the air heavy with humidity as the early October day warmed.

Kate met Rob where the road veered off at Mrs. Helms. She leaned down, hugged Rob and kissed him on the cheek, just as she did every day when he returned from school.

Mrs. Helm was there, standing in her flower garden next to the road. Kate had often wondered about her, and wanted to meet her, but feared what she might find as Rob returned home from school.

She walked toward Kate and smiled. She was lovely. Kate pulled Bo close to her and stopped in the dusty road. "We've come down to meet Rob. Sometimes Flint can't get him from the bus." Kate said.

By this time, the sun had baked moisture from the road and the temperature began to rise. Sweat dripped from Kate.

Mrs. Helm said. "Kate, I planned to drive up that road to meet you one of these days, and here you are." She reached out to hold Kate's hand. Donnie and Bette tumbled out of the wagon and hung on Kate's leg, while Bo hid behind her. Mrs. Helm looked at the children and grinned. She wore a wide-brimmed straw hat and moving with grace, her heavy long hair bouncing in the afternoon sun.

Kate glanced down at her own simple cotton dress and worn brown oxfords with broken laces. Embarrassed, and filled with self-loathing, she removed her hand from Mrs. Helm's. How frumpy she must appear to the well-kept woman.

"Come over to the faucet and drink," Mrs. Helm invited.

Kate automatically followed the children, who scrambled on ahead, eager to quench their thirst at the faucet. She shivered at the sight of the huge old house, wondering how such a lovely person as Mrs. Helm, dressed in fine trappings, could stand living within its walls, electricity or not. But Mrs. Helm seemed delighted with life itself, and her smile stayed their entire visit.

"So glad we met before I head north for the winter," Mrs. Helm's friendly voice quivered with resonance.

Filling a tinge of guilt for distrusting Mrs. Helm and Flint, Kate mumbled, "We'll visit again, Mrs. Helm. I best get these youngsters on up the hill now." The children ran for another drink of water and then grabbed Kate's hands and legs, hanging onto her. She shook them off. Bette and Donnie climbed in the wagon while the sun beat down steadily, heading toward the western sky.

Mrs. Helm waved good-by, her beautiful teeth glistening through her open smile while Kate and the children started back up the mountain. Though envious of the lady, she was interested to learn how Mrs. Helm managed with no man of her own, but exuded confidence and pride in herself. She radiated beauty like a queen. Kate wanted that for herself but wondered how she could possibly gain independence with a passel of children still living at home.

An hour later, back at the homestead, Kate continued to wrap the jars, she thought about Mrs. Helm and her ugly old house. Even though the house was scary and dilapidated, it had electricity, and at least a quarter section of flat, silted bottomland surrounding it. It was perfect for farming, as Flint had mentioned more than once.

She wrapped her canning jars with the newspaper, not only to keep them from breaking while in storage, but also to keep the dust and spiders out. When it was time to use them again, the job of cleaning them would be much easier. "Nearly got all these jars wrapped, little guy," Kate said to Dale, who began to doze on his pillow inside the apple box.

She picked up another sheet of newspaper. A photograph on the page startled her. Unfolding the page completely, and with an involuntary shudder, she laid it down on the counter. Kate stared at the photograph. Theodore Warner. How could it be? But it was the same old man that Flint killed.

'Most people around Spring Valley were familiar with the old man,' the article said. 'Warner moved around the area for many years, not a criminal, but a fugitive from life itself. He was a hobo vagrant that came and went but didn't travel far from the area.' Shaking her head, she kept reading. 'Warner had a home with his brother in Delzura, and a room in the sanitarium up north where he recently spent time. Finally at rest, old Warner was found dead of pneumonia in Robinson's barn near the junction,' the article finished. It was dated a week earlier.

"But Flint shot the old fool," Kate murmured. "What happened up there that morning if it wasn't the old man's blood on that rock, and what about the hat?"

Because of the morning rain, Flint returned home early. He hobbled through the door. "Rheumatism actin' up."

Kate figured he planned to retreat to his bed on the porch, but she had a different plan for him. As soon as he sat down on the kitchen bench to untie his boots, she cornered him. "Flint, you see this newspaper?" She slapped the opened newspaper page down on the table. Flint kicked off his boots and turned on the bench, facing the newspaper. Kate continued. "The old man! He's dead! You read the paper every day, Flint! How come you didn't tell me? I worried you shot the old fool years ago. Why, I've been worried you'd get put away for killing him all this time." Kate leaned forward full of anger for her own mistrust of her husband, yet, frustrated that he hadn't told her about the article, which he'd surely read. "Don't you have any sense to tell me when you know damned well that, that . . . ." Kate stomped her foot and spun around with her back to her husband. Her face burned hot. She wrapped her arms tightly around herself. For years she had worried for no reason. Now she faced her husband again and snatched the page of newspaper from in front of him, waving it in the air. "How could I be such a fool?" she hissed.

"Katie, I don't know what you're talkin' about. I didn't see any article about any old man," Flint's voice sounded innocent enough. He grabbed the page of newspaper from Kate, reading it as he spoke. "Ah, old Warner. How'd I miss this? Why Katie, I've been at Helm's a lot working. I don't always get time to read the newspaper. Hell's fire, woman, you thought I killed that poor old bastard? I suppose you figure I purposely tried to do in Schwartz, too."

Flint's voice took on a sharp edge. "Are you actually accusing me of killing the old man? I told you that morning that I saw his footprints leading out of the yard."

Kate bit her lip, fighting back tears. "I saw it Flint, the old man's hat up yonder . . . the bloody rock. The gun fired when you were looking for him that morning. All this time, I thought . . . well, I don't really know." Kate plopped down in the hard wooden chair and put her head in her hands. "I figured you had no choice," she whispered.

Flint shook his head and became silent. He pulled his pipe from his pocket and filled it with Prince Albert. Taking his time poking the tobacco down, he finally struck a wooden match with the tip of his thumbnail and lit the tobacco. "I killed a deer, not Warner. Doe's head was down, grazin'. I aimed at the head, but her head jerked up." Flint's hand shook as he pulled on the pipe. "That little rascal of a fawn, no bigger than a pup, standin' right behind its mother's head. I didn't see it till I shot it. Made me sicker than a skunk. Drug it over to the cliff by the north trail there. Left it for the coyotes. Doe was long gone. I didn't want the kids to know." Flint sat hunched over with his pipe in hand. His mouth moved as if he tried to control the tears that filled his dark sad eyes, reminding Kate of the reason she loved him in the first place.

With remorse, Kate moved from her chair and sidled beside Flint on the bench, patting his arm. She turned her face from him, then got up and poured each of them a mug of coffee. As they sipped their coffee, Kate sat down across the table from Flint. Dale looked up from his apple box with big blue eyes. His tiny arms flailed the air in front of him, clanging the jar rings still clinched in his fists.

At last Kate could put the whole thing behind her . . . finally forget about the old man. Life was all right again for the most part. Unlike some folks in parts of the country right now, she and Flint were able to feed their children. Sometimes, Kate was on edge wondering what in the world would happen next. But, then the westerly breeze would calm her, or the coo of a mourning dove, or the children laughing. Life was mostly good and she was grateful. After all, the worse thing in the world hadn't actually happened. Flint hadn't shot and killed Old Man Warner.

A few days later, though, Flint came home from town and announced to Kate that the stock market crashed again and now, like it or not, they would be affected here on the mountain.

CHAPTER—21

FAMILY PICNIC

When Dale was nearly two years old, Benjamin Franklin was born with Kate acting as her own midwife again. Flint fetched Doc Laraby to check the baby and Kate. Flint wondered if the doc was actually serious when he advised Kate that she'd brought enough children into the world, and that her body wouldn't take much more. It seemed to Flint, though, that Kate grew tougher as the years went by. She'd already banished him from her bed some time ago, except for that one night. It only took one wrong move, one cold winter night beside his wife, he realized with resentment, to bring another child into the world, but that one night was worth it to Flint. Ben was two years old now and Flint still slept alone.

In April, with over a year to go in the decade, Flint wondered just how long the Depression could go on. It reminded him of the Potato Famine in Ireland and the Dust Bowl in Oklahoma, only on a bigger scale, affecting more people. At least there was hope. Things weren't quite as bad as earlier in the 30's, according to most folks. And at least the ones who could afford it could drown their sorrows in a bottle without being jailed for it.

The homestead thrived with the help of the older boys and Bette. Flint was grateful that Kate had stuck with him through the drinking, even though she treated him with resentment at times.

Some years the South Slope field resembled one huge clod if it didn't get plowed at just the right time. When it was time for plowing the south slope, it was also time to head over to Gus' to get his fields ready for corn, with Jackson pulling the plow, of course. Flint would plow one field and then the other. He smiled at the thought of Rob and Bo behind the plow in the next year or two. But timing the plowing was important . . . after a little rain and before too much sun. Flint glanced up at the sky. It was warm enough now, and after a short rain, he'd be ready to plow and plant for a solid month.

On this perfect day with the milking done, the gallon jar was sent to the spring for cooling with Dale and Ben since they had inherited the chore from Donnie and Bette.

Flint mulled over the idea during breakfast that he had better get the family on an outing before Kate became pregnant again some cold night. He knew it was bound to happen, as it did every time he managed to sneak back under her covers. Katie seemed inside her head lately anyway, and he didn't like it when she wouldn't talk. He figured she was worried about her father, who seemed to be growing more and more senile as the years progressed.

There was always so much work during the year. Because of it, Flint gauged the homestead a success. First came the planting of melons, then watering avocados every day. Next he prayed for rain for the dry-land melons. Afterward they harvested for months. When a little time off was in order, he figured he might as well take it, because there was no good time to leave the homestead. No good time except January, maybe February, but the road to the homestead was like a slippery mudslide of rained-on clay, and dangerous or impossible to go up or down in a vehicle. Flint had walked home many a time from the bottom of the mountain in January and February. And many a time, the four school children returned home after slipping and sliding, caked with mud from head to toe.

But during the month of April weather on Mt. McGinny was about perfect, as far as Flint was concerned. The month before, in March, he had brought home a 1928 Pontiac sedan, four doors with plenty of room. He bought it from a man, to whom the Depression had dealt a hard blow. So now that it was Sunday, he was anxious to try the car out on the family. He would take them to the beach, a place they had ventured only a couple of times since they moved to California, ten years before.

Kate had mentioned a picnic at the beach awhile back, and she might be thinking by this time that they were too tied to chores at the homestead to go that far for a whole day. Besides, with the trickle of war in Europe, Flint was burdened with thoughts of coming doom. He tried to talk to Kate about it, but she put him off with a scowl. He hoped to keep her in a good mood today. An outing might give her a different view on life, a change of heart. He wanted to make up to her. And he was damned tired of sleeping alone.

After breakfast, instead of heading to the pump house, Flint stood at the table. "Well, Katie, we haven't been on a picnic to the beach for many a moon, and you been a' sulkin', so we're going to get away from here for the day. Try out the sedan. See if we fit."

Kate squealed with excitement and the children raised their voices in chorus at the idea of seeing the ocean.

"The work will be here when we get home. We'll be back in time to milk. So, let's get dressed in our best and head out. We'll go by the folks, see if they can go, too. Brownie'll stand guard here." He watched his family hustle with excitement, bumping into each other as they passed through doors to get ready.

Kate hurried to gather all the ripe avocados off the counter. Then she peeled them and mashed them and sprinkled them with salt and pepper. She made sandwiches out of the mashed fruit. Breakfast milk was still out on the table, so she wrapped it in a dishtowel and stuck it in an apple box. The remainder of the picnic food went helter-skelter along with the milk and a jug of water, and a few cups and saucers. Rob and Bo struggled to carry the box to the Pontiac.

Flint quickly dressed in his best: a white shirt and black tie. Then he waited patiently, watching and listening while Kate gathered a pillow for Ben and a blanket for the picnic on the sand. Kate put on her only dress that fit and struggled to pull on stockings. She worked with her hair, braiding it and wrapping it in a bun on her head. Next she did the same for Bette's hair. She grabbed her Kodak box camera from the top dresser drawer and brushed past her husband. "Ready, Flint."

Flint poked the cherry tobacco he'd bought for this special occasion down in his pipe and ordered Brownie to guard the front door while the rest of the family climbed into the Pontiac.

Flint stood beside the car, waiting for his family to settle in. There was a scuffle in the back seat until Rob, in a threatening whisper, ordered Donnie to be quiet before Dad heard any fussing. He grinned outwardly when they were settled.

Flint eased in the driver's seat with his pipe lit, and they were off. Yes, it would be a good outing. Occasionally, Flint stopped at the dinky cottage that Mom, Pop, and Paul had moved to the year before. Paul hadn't moved away from the folks, even though he was well past the age to care for himself. He said that his Pop needed help, which was true. A day at the beach would do them all good.

When they all arrived at the beach and parked as close to the shore as safe, everyone piled out. Dale screamed at the sight of the ocean waves crashing loudly toward them. Bette and the boys ran fast to the edge of the water, Kate warning the whole time that they would drown. "Katie," Flint said, "Stop! You're a nervous wreck."

"Now, Flint, there are undertows." Kate ignored Flint and continued her tirade. "What about sharks? A big wave could knock one of these little kids down and carry them away."

Flint carried the apple box from the car and faced his wife again. "Katie, leave the poor kids alone. They can't drown in a foot of water."

"Dale, you don't go without holding Bette's hand, ya' hear? Mom, keep an eye on the kids while I get the picnic out on to the blanket? And Ben, you get to be prince on a pillow and sit in the apple box when it's empty." With joy, she barked orders. Flint laughed at her. It had been a long time since he'd seen her so happy. At least she was talking again, that was for sure.

Mom sat close to the water's edge on the cushion she carried everywhere these days. "Paul, don't go out so far," Mom yelled at Paul, and then, except for Ben who was now safely contained in the apple box, rattled off the names of her remaining grandchildren, though they had done nothing more than chase a wave out as it drew back from the shoreline, grab sea shells, and run back to safe ground.

Flint crouched down on the sand beside Pop and they talked politics and about how the Depression seemed to ease up now there was war abroad. "Jep, you got something festerin'. What's goin' on? Are you worried about the Depression? The war?"

"Old age creepin' up, I reckon, Flint." The old man's face looked like worn-out leather. Layers of wrinkles filled a sallow complexion. "Should have kept on farmin' instead of collectin' social security last year. Now, it's too late." Pop leaned his head against his curled-up knees as he sat there in the sand, but the gesture didn't seem to relieve his sadness. "Done sold the Bonita farm. Living in that little house down there in the middle of town with nothin' to do but sit. Can't drive anymore. Too many fast cars on the road, Flint, so I handed the reigns over to Paul, but he won't be hanging around forever." Pop looked to the sand. Despair dimmed his blue eyes. "Hardly enough yard to grow a tomato. Aint no good, Flint." Pop shook his head. "Why, I might just as well be dead."

Flint gazed out over the vast blue ocean and then to the pale gray waves crashing on the shore. He placed his hand on the old man's bony shoulder. "Jep, listen. Why don't you come on home with us for a while? The mountain air will do you good. You could work around as much as you see fit. Katie would love it. We'd all love it, Jep. Grow all the damned tomatoes you want. Don't worry about drivin'. When Paul can't haul you around anymore, I'll drive you. Think about it." Flint patted his father-in-law on the shoulder and walked over to Kate, allowing the old man time to consider it. "Let's eat."

Kate had already set out the avocado sandwiches made with white Langendorf bread. The avocado filling in the sandwiches had turned black but no one cared. It didn't change the taste. The milk was lukewarm but not sour yet. Mom brought two apple pies she had made the day before. "All in all," Flint said, "the picnic's damned good, except for the sand that Dale threw in."

In a short time, every crumb of picnic food was gone. Kate grabbed her Kodak box camera. The Kodak took good black and whites, and after each click, she wound and wound till the next number on top of the camera showed. She took a few shots of the family and then handed the camera to Bette and hollered, "Come on, Flint. Let's get down where the ocean is behind us and get our picture taken." With some effort, Flint raised himself and hobbled in the sand until he stood beside Kate.

They were dressed in their best today, knowing it might be many moons before it happened again. Flint watched Kate roll her stockings down to her ankles. Held up by garters, the whole affair looked thick and unbearably hot. But it was only proper for Kate to wear her dress out in public, and only if worn with long stockings. After a long pause, Bette took the picture.

Paul tried to sneak another swim in the ocean, but decided it wasn't worth worrying his sister and his mother over. He gave up the idea of swimming, raising his hands in desperation, and settled down to build an enormous sand castle with Rob and Bo's help. Beside the sand castle, Donnie dug a hole and got in. Bette and Dale packed sand over him until only his head stuck out.

When it looked as if everyone was safely away from the monster ocean, Flint took Kate's hand. They walked awhile down the beach, both laughing at doing such a silly thing as walking on the beach with the Pacific Ocean breeze blowing in their faces. He waited until they were out of her folk's earshot before broaching the subject of her father.

"Pop needs to come out to the homestead awhile, Katie. He's just feeling at odds with life, feels useless, I figure. Why don't you talk him into it. It would do him good."

"I'm worried sick about him too, Flint. His mind seems to be wandering. Let's take him home with us awhile."

Kate squeezed his hand hard and flashed him a grateful smile. The time had come for him to risk asking her the question. "How about letting me move back in with you, Katie, and move the little guys to the porch with their brothers?"

Flint couldn't tell if she was as excited about the idea as he and, for a moment, he grew hopeful. Yet when Kate looked at Flint, he felt as if he'd been fanged by a rattler.

"You know Flint, there's only one way that you'll ever get back under my covers. After I am too old to have another child again!"

"Hell, Katie, that could be another five or ten years."

"That's right, Flint." She let go of his hand, then turned and walked away.

CHAPTER—22

GRANDPA'S STRENGTH

The picnic at the beach was a day to remember, even though Kate felt some remorse for rebuking Flint about the bed and the porch. She just didn't have the strength to care for another child. Besides, one child after another would prolong her nursing goal. As far as Pop was concerned, the homestead would fix him soon enough.

The next day, Pop woke before daylight from the cot Kate set up in the front room especially for him. His movements awakened Kate from the middle room and they hustled to the kitchen where Kate lit a lamp and made coffee. The house was quiet. Birds were just waking and beginning their chatter at the first tinge of dawn. Father and daughter sat across from each other at the oak table, sipping hot mugs of coffee, while catching up on each other's lives.

"Your mom is proud of you, Kate. She says she doesn't know how you do what you do, up here on this mountain without friends and conveniences and all." Kate listened to the sweet sound of her father's slow drawl. "You know, she really isn't against Flint. It's his drinking that bothers her." Pop reached across the table and laid his hand over hers.

"She never told me that, Pop. She never tells me anything, just like Flint."

Pop's bright blue eyes twinkled and he tapped on the table with a crooked finger. "You remember us mentioning her father, your grandfather Williams? As ornery an Irishman as I ever did know. Course, from what your mom could gather, he had an awful life when he first came to this country, same as most Irish, so don't knows as we can blame him for some of his meanness."

Pop hesitated and pursed his lips. "Course, a fella' can face life with strength and kindness, hoping to make the world a better place, or he can become a victim full of self-pity and blame everyone for his sufferin', even blame his own family, and wallow in liquor." Pop shook his head, looking down as if shaking off some of the memory.

With a deep breath, Pop said, "You were too little then to remember that Grandpa Williams was a drunk."

"Grandpa Williams was a drunk?" Kate asked as she cupped her mug with both hands and sipped her coffee.

"Slammed Grandma Louisa around." Pop pursed his lips and frowned. "Flint's mild compared. Your Grandma Louisa would get her fill now and then and run off to some Indian reservation, leaving ever' thing including your mom behind for a spell. Returned when she got good and ready. Well, your mom couldn't take it anymore, seein' her mother mistreated and then disappearing for days at a time, and as soon as she saw a way out, she left home for good. She was only thirteen years old. Farmed herself out to one family then another, working in the cotton." Pop looked down, hesitating. Kate noticed a squelched tear, but waited for her father to go on with his story.

"When she got brave enough, went back home and tried to get her mother away, but your grandma wouldn't leave that ornery Irishman. The Baptist folks took your mom in. Helped her till she could stand on her own two feet." Pop stared out the window. Kate waited for him to go on with his story. "Then she ran into me," he continued. "Not a church man, but a family man, and she checked me out long enough to know I wasn't gonna be drinking and fighting. So, that was that. After your mom and me got hitched, why, we went back to check on her folks, still there fightin', and him drinkin'. That's it, Kate. She wants different for you. But she says it's your decision, and she knows you love Flint more'n anything. So she tolerates and bites her tongue for your sake."

"Why haven't I heard this before now, Pop?" Kate stood up from the table and placed her hands on her hips, her chin turned up in playful defiance.

"She's a proud woman, just like you. She wanted to forget her childhood and rarely speaks of it. And, she don't want to preach to ya'. Not much anyway." Pop grinned. "She preaches to me, but I don't mind. She's my friend; my Annie Rose."

Pop groaned while he eased himself from the table. Sunrays lit the oak tree in the front yard. "Reckon I'll go see what's going on in your garden, Kate. Need any help in here?"

"Nah, I'll call ya' when breakfast is ready." Kate was preoccupied with the thought of her mother having to live the way Pop described. Mom hardly knew her own mother and they were never as close as Kate and Bette.

In the past, her mom tried to speak to her but Kate resisted. Now it all made sense.

She wondered if she were passing on bits and pieces of wisdom to her own daughter. Would Bette learn by watching from example? Were the chats that drew her and Bette close while waiting for Flint to come home, enough to teach a young girl anything . . . enough to preserve the precious link between mother and daughter? For the first time, Kate blamed herself for the expanse, the absence of love and friendship between herself and her mother. Life had a way of turning on a person, even a person with good intentions. From now on, she would be more careful how she lived.

After a few days in the garden and taking walks with the youngsters, with many trips to check on the hummingbird nest and to count granddaddy spiders in the crook of the oak tree, Pop said that some of his stamina had returned. So when Rob and Bo begged him to venture to the crawdad pool by the spring with them, Pop didn't resist for more than a minute. Kate knew the boys were in good hands, and they would all watch out for each other. There wasn't much danger around the creek. The rattlers tended to stay on the hard dry hillsides, and the mountain lion had never been seen nor heard in the area of the spring since there were plenty of drinking holes further up the mountain.

Soon after breakfast, Flint drove to Spring Valley for supplies. "I'll expect Flint back when I see the whites of his eyes, and not a minute sooner," she told Pop as she finished up the morning dishes.

Flint took the old Dodge, since he needed more supplies than the car could hold. The Pontiac's brakes were going out and, according to Flint, it was a good plan to have both the car and the truck. He could keep at least one vehicle in working order and running. Time would tell.

Kate watched Pop's thin frame as he slowly followed the boys up the canyon. The barefooted boys grew impatient with him and hopped on ahead. Pop would need to step cautiously with his booted foot on rocks that littered the shallow creek bottom and where the creek water ran knee-deep. Rob and Bo jumped helter-skelter, mimicking the water skitters and pollywogs that swam to and fro between the rocks. Kate kept an eye on them until they were out of sight. She heard the echo of their laughter and chatter as they progressed up the creek through the fern-covered walls of the canyon, while frogs croaked their warnings. Kate smiled, imagining the three of them hovered together sipping ice-cold spring water that dripped from the pipe that had years before been rammed into the canyon wall. She almost wished she had joined them in their magical journey among the wet canyon walls, pretty green ferns, and drooping grape vines. But Kate figured it would do Pop good to spend time alone with the boys.

After a busy morning, Kate sat in the front yard with her medical book while Ben and Dale dug in the bank nearby, making roads for their wooden block cars. Over the years, Kate had read the medical book thoroughly, and later studied each section. With each episode of mumps, whooping cough, measles, or other ailment the children came down with, Kate relied on the book for advice. The knowledge was a lifesaver, along with the Cherokee remedies she had learned as a medicine woman in Oklahoma.

After a short while, Kate heard a yell coming from the creek where Pop and the boys had ventured. Kate craned her neck and glanced their direction, surprised their adventure ended so quickly. Instead, Bo ran toward her, arms flailing the air. Kate rose from the rocking chair, the book dropping to the ground.

Bo cried, his voice strained and excited. "Ma, Ma, Rob fell in the creek." Kate leapt up and raced toward the creek.

As Kate arrived panting and out of breath, Pop's lean, bowed figure came into view. Rob hung limp over his shoulder. Pop's knees wobbled as he struggled to walk over the last of the rocks where Kate met up with him. Running beside him, she said, "Bring him to the cot, Pop."

Breathless and his throat clouded with grief, Pop explained Rob's mishap. "I needed to rest. When I sat on the rock beside the creek, I must've dozed. The boys crawled the slippery bank above the creek and Rob lost his footing. He fell on the rocks just a few feet from where I was sittin'."

At the house, they lay Rob on the cot that sat in the front yard where Flint read his newspapers in the summer time. With ashen face, Bo stood close to the cot, shaking. "Ma, Rob ain't dead is he? Is he?"

Kate dared not answer, but focused on the exact moves to care for her motionless son. She breathed a sigh of relief that he was alive, unconscious, but alive. Kate turned Rob's head to the side in case he needed to drool. She proceeded to check through his blood-matted hair for the wound.

Pop kneeled down to Bo. "Just hold on, just hold on, Bo."

"Bo, run get your pillow for Rob's head." The frightened boy immediately ran in the house upon Kate's order.

"Kate," Pop said. "Let's get him in the car and go get help."

"Wait Pop. Let's stop the bleeding first." Bo quickly returned with the pillow and Kate placed it under Rob's head and neck, knowing to keep his spine as straight as possible. Then she ran in the kitchen and grabbed a stack of sterile feed-sack dishtowels that she kept handy for bandages. On her way back to the cot, she began ripping a towel into wide strips. With tears escaping, she worked carefully on her son. Wounds of the scalp, even if small, tended to bleed profusely. Kate found the wound but didn't attempt to cleanse it. From the medical book, she had learned that cleansing the wound might cause contaminants to enter the brain if the skull was fractured.

She gently placed a folded towel over Rob's wound and held it for a few minutes, careful not to use excessive pressure in case a fracture was present. Luckily, no fluids drained from his ears, nose, or mouth to indicate such a break.

The remaining children stood out of her way, looking helpless. "Pop, can you get the Pontiac warmed up?" Kate asked with trembling voice. "We'll likely use it soon as this bleeding stops." Pop did as she asked. Kate had learned that a wound such as Rob's could be deep, complicated by the skull's fracture or pieces of rock and gravel. He'd need a real doctor.

When Rob's wound stopped bleeding, Kate placed another sterile folded towel for a dressing over his wound and wrapped the strips of sterile cloth around his head, holding the dressing in place.

Kate prayed that Rob would wake, but he didn't, and now it was time to go. She'd done all she could and Pop stood waiting. Silent with grief, they carefully lifted Rob and placed him in the back seat of the Pontiac. Bo and the other kids stood motionless and white-faced in the yard. Kate yelled out, "Bo, you're in charge here, you and Bette. Rob'll be all right. You keep the kids inside 'til I get back." Tears fell in her mouth.

Turning to Pop, she sniffled, "He's still breathing, and it's even, not raspy. But he sure is pale. Best to see Doc Laraby. I know the way, but I don't know how to drive." Kate scooted into the back seat, maneuvering her way under Rob's limp body until she held his head on her lap. She gently tucked the small pillow under his neck. Pop sat in the driver's seat. Shaking like a leaf in a windstorm, she said, "Rob's got a little blood on his bandage, but I don't think he's bleedin' much."

"I'll drive, Kate. Let's get."

Kate knew Pop must be frightened to drive again, especially down that steep, crooked, ruddy road, but it had to be done. When life or death looms uncertain, a person always did what they had to do in an emergency. Pop drove out of the yard and steadily up the hill. Kate noticed that he gripped the steering wheel with both of his old white-knuckled hands.

The winding road leveled off at the top for a few hundred yards, and then dropped down the mountain, steeply. Grasping the armrest, Kate remembered what Flint said about the brakes. No need to remind Pop. The brakes would have to hold out. Besides, Pop already had the car in the lowest gear. Surely, they couldn't go very fast, even without brakes.

She grew more and more frightened. As Rob lay so helpless and pale in Kate's arms, the car jarred and rattled, forcing her attention on the rutted, winding road, with the steep canyon threatening to their left.

Without warning, the car sped faster and faster down the mountain even though Pop pressed hard on the brake. At the steepest part of the road, the Dodge headed for the bank on the right. Pop held the wheel, and hammered his boot down on the brake. "Can't stop the damned thing, Kate," he shouted. With a jerk and a crash, the car hit the bank and bounced. The steering wheel whipped around and around and back and forth in the grip of Pop's worn hands. The car careened toward the bank again. The car hit and scraped the bank the second time, bouncing back onto the road, heading straight down. Kate wailed each time the car hit the bank, and braced Rob in her arms.

Again, Pop steered into the bank, slicing rocks and clay, finally crashing to a grinding halt. The right wheel had crammed into the dirt bank, and the body of the car sat cockeyed and sideways in the middle of the road. Dust puffed up around the outside of the wreck.

"Oh, God!" Kate hollered.

Pop hit the steering wheel with the flat of both hands. "Son-of-a-bitch."

The ordeal was over, but nerves were shaken. "Now we're in a fix," Kate moaned. Then she bent her head and closed her eyes. In a whisper, she said, "Flint, where in hell are you when we need you the most?" He had never been there for them. Never.

Suddenly, Rob sat up. "What are we doing here, Ma?" He looked around with wonder on a bright face.

"Rob . . . Rob, you're all right?" Kate asked, checking him thoroughly for cuts and bruises. Then she hugged him tightly, a happy sob escaping her lips. "He's okay. I think he's going to be okay. Let's get this boy home, Pop, what do you think?"

"I think he looks hungry. Am I right, Rob?" Pop grinned and his chest heaved.

"Starved. Where're we goin' in the car?"

Pop leaned toward Kate and Rob. "Does yer head hurt, or anything else, Rob? Hope I didn't make things worse with my drivin'."

"Nah, nothing hurtin'. Well, my head feels a little sore." Rob reached up with both hands and patted his bandaged scalp. Except for a bit of dried blood on the bandage, he looked none the worse for wear. "What's this thing on my head, Ma? What happened to the car?"

"Fixin to see Doc Laraby, Rob. You fell on the rocks, knocked yourself silly. Grandpop carried you to the house. I bandaged your wound." Kate's tone turned serious. "Tomorrow we are goin' to have a little talk about that slippery bank, and how you and your brothers are staying to hell off it. Do you hear?"

"Ah Ma, we don't go there."

Pop craned his neck to look to the back seat and rolled his eyes at Rob. Grinning, he crawled stiffly out of the car.

When Pop opened her door, Kate scooted Rob out of the car. Rob stood up without trouble. He looked up at Pop, and then frowned. "Grandpop, I thought you weren't supposed to drive. You been pullin' our legs?"

Pop laughed. "Oh Rob, I guess you're right on that one. I was a doin' pretty good thar."

Later in the afternoon, Flint arrived home on foot. "What the hell happened, Kate? I couldn't get the Dodge around the Pontiac," he scowled. Removing his hat, he rubbed his hand through his hair.

"Rob fell from the creek bank and cracked his head on the rocks." Kate told Flint the jest of the story. In Kate's estimation, she had doctored Rob properly knowing it was imperative to stop the bleeding, and now that the crisis was over, she felt proud of her skill. And Pop was brave to drive down that mountain. Still, she felt edgy as Flint listened to the circumstances surrounding the accident, leery of his response. She looked at him, her eyebrows knitted together.

Flint shoved his hat back on his head and put his hands on his hips. "If you'd been watching the boys, that wouldn't have happened," he snapped.

Kate curled up inside. Instead of acknowledging her skill and the fact that she probably saved Rob's life, he'd admonished her. More than ever she wanted out. She racked her brain for a way to study medicine far away from Flint. She stuck her chin out in defiance. She'd find a way to get to Doc Laraby's in El Cajon, even if she had to walk.

CHAPTER—23

THE TURNING POINT

After Rob's accident on the rocks, Kate was grateful that he had no permanent damage. Blaming herself, she resolved to keep a closer eye on her children. Since his fall, she glanced his way often, checking the pupils of his eyes, hoping not to find delayed injury symptoms.

Flint's anger made Kate more and more uncomfortable. The morning after the accident, Flint said, "I'll walk down the hill and tow the car to a wide spot in the road." It looked in bad shape, and it wouldn't start up when he tried, so it would set there until he had time to work on it. Kate never heard Flint say a sharp word to Rob about falling from the bank, but noticed him watching their son over the next few days.

Pop spent most of the next few weeks in the garden. The huge plot was perfectly tilled and weeded while he was around. His mood seemed to improve, but he complained that he missed his Annie Rose. When mom and Paul came to visit the homestead the second time, and when they were settled down at the table to visit, Kate poured mugs of coffee and Pop told of Rob's topple down the incline. Then Kate raved of Pop's heroic efforts getting Rob to the house, driving without brakes, and finally the wreck. "Pop is doin' so well," she said. "All he needed was a little excitement."

Finally, Pop roused Paul from the table to see his handiwork in the garden, leaving Kate and her mother alone at the table.

"Mom, sit here." Kate pulled the chair back from the end of the table and Annie Rose sat down. Kate sat on the corner of the bench and faced her mother. Their knees touched. For the first time she felt a deep appreciation for the woman who raised her, who tended to her family with care, who led a narrow and simple life. "Mom, I love this big oak table. I don't know if I ever thanked you for it. Don't know what we'd do without it. Just about filled it with all the kids." Kate watched her mother closely, noticing the many fine lines around her eyes and brown spots dotting the back of her small leathered hands. It became obvious to Kate, too, that her mother was growing old. For a moment, Kate saw the old woman across from her not as her mother, but as another person.

"Yes, I believe you did thank us for it, Kate. And you shore do need it, that's for certain."

What Kate needed to say wouldn't come easy, but she knew she must say it. She steeled her resolve, took a deep breath and blurted out the words, "I wanted you to know how I appreciate that table, and everything you've done for me, for everyone. I love you, Mom." Kate stood and walked behind her mother, placing her arms around her shoulders.

As Kate's hands hung down in front of her mother, her mom took them in hers. The side of Kate's face touched her mother's as she stood leaning over her. Kate felt moisture on her cheek. She smiled, realizing that her mother felt moved to tears because of their conversation.

"Why, you've grown to be a good woman, Kate. Me and Pop are mighty proud of you." Mom smiled, but it was soon evident that her mother hurried to gather her composure. And it was difficult for either of them to show their true feelings for very long. But now, at least, there was no riff between them. They both knew they loved each other. Kate was content to leave it at that for now, and moved to the stove to refill their coffee mugs.

"Paul has a woman, Kate." Mom confessed out of the blue.

Kate jolted with surprise that her little brother finally had a girlfriend. She plopped back down in front of her mother and sat the coffee beside them on the table. "Is it a secret?"

"Nah, and don't let him get away without telling you all about her. She's quite a contrast in looks from Paul, but they're best friends, if you know what I mean." Mom raised an eyebrow.

"What does she look like?"

"Prettiest little Mexican girl I ever saw."

"Does that bother you? That she's Mexican, I mean."

"Why, Kate why would it bother me?" Mom's face wrinkled in surprise. "You know I'm not prejudice about that kind of thing. Look at our Irish blood, look at the Cherokee in Flint, and Choctaw in Pop. My own mother Louisa used to run off to the nearby reservation. To this day, I still wonder why. She was a tiny dark-haired thing . . . pure Indian. You can see that I took after my Irish father as far as looks go." Mom touched her graying red hair. "I'm proud of who we are, and I'm proud of Paul for choosing Maria. She's down to earth, not a prissy miss."

Kate sat quietly sipping her coffee, holding her mug with both hands. It took her a moment to ponder what Mom had just revealed; Pop, Choctaw? Kate shook her head, believing that she'd heard her wrong.

"Mom, you never told me that Pop was Choctaw. And Grandma Louisa, Indian?"

"That means you are too, Kate. What difference does it make? Besides, I figured you knew."

"You're full of surprises." Kate shook her head, feeling disturbed at some of the notions she held that now seemed questionable. She sat in silence across the table from her mother, sipping coffee.

"Mom, I'm fixin' to see Doc Laraby about medical training. Flint thinks I'm stupid, but I'm not, Mom." Kate was afraid that she might undo all the mending she'd accomplished today between her and her mother, but she decided to get things settled once and for all. Mom wiggled in her chair and nodded to Kate without a word.

"I've felt stupid sometimes. Got pulled out of school in the eighth grade, remember?" Kate glanced down at her work-worn hands, at her roughened nails, embarrassed to face her mother.

"Kate, you're smart as they come. Why, we couldn't have kept our cotton farm as long as we did if you hadn't pitched in when you did. Since then, you've educated yourself in lots of ways. Even life teaches more than fancy schoolin'." Mom looked at Kate with a smile and then clinked her fingernail against her mug. "Flint's life was complicated from the start. He's got internal struggles, the way I see it. Couldn't have been easy for him to grow up without his real Pa, and the one he did have callin' him names. Why, he don't know who he is." Tears of sympathy for Flint, filled her mother's eyes, Kate noticed with surprise. "And you, Kate . . . always expectin' the world. Go on, get your schoolin' and be satisfied with it. You may as well be satisfied with Flint too. He'll be happier if you are. Nothing wrong with it."

Mom had expressed acceptance of her complex son-in-law and had finally given her blessing to Kate's dreams. There was nothing to hold Kate back now. Life opened up for Kate to do as she pleased.

Now she needed a way off the mountain and into El Cajon.

CHAPTER—24

GOOD BYE BROWNIE

Brownie lay under the back of the house in the cool dirt during the heat of the mid-summer day, and then wandered out at dusk to take his usual place at the kitchen doorstep. He usually crawled out long enough to follow Rob as he milked Polly, morning and evening. This morning, however, he was nowhere to be seen. Rob stood in the front yard with the milk bucket. Even then Rob's familiar whistle didn't bring Brownie around. Kate dreaded the day that the old German shepherd died.

Bette had promised Dale and Ben that she'd walk them over to Gus's for the baby ducks he'd offered them, so she slung a gunny sack, with as many avocados as she could carry, over her shoulder for Gus. Bette would get the boys home before the sun burned them, and Dale and Ben would be ravenous by the time they returned for the noon meal. Kate could always count on hunger driving them home, so she planned to get the wash finished and the noon meal on the table before they got back.

After they left, Kate realized Bette had forgotten the Winchester, but they were all used to watching where they walked, and if a rattler crossed their path, they'd just wait until it passed. Although the mountain lion had not been seen nor heard lately, he had not been forgotten. Kate automatically looked in the oaks and sycamores and scanned the hillside with a shudder whenever she thought of the beast.

Flint and Bo had taken a delivery of melons and avocados to market and were expected back late that same afternoon. Bo had Shep with him. The little white shaggy dog had found Bo in the fields of hay and hadn't left his side. It was a good thing, since it had been some time since Brownie felt up to sniffing rattlers out of the hay.

"Where's Brownie this mornin', Ma?" Rob asked, swinging the bucket back and forth while he searched for the dog. "He sure is gettin' lazy in his old age, and grouchy. Have you noticed that? Sure isn't his self these days. Why, I haven't even heard him chasing rabbits since he tangled with some varmint a couple of weeks ago."

Kate pulled her washing machine to the middle of the yard and set the washtub on a sturdy stool beside it. She noticed a perplexed look cover Rob's handsome face.

"He's got fleas or something, too, Ma. Something's irritatin' the old mangy guy. I'll look for a burr or a tick on him tonight."

"Go ahead and milk, Rob. He'll be along behind you in a jiffy," Kate said, while she fetched a large kettle of hot water off the kitchen stove and poured it into the washing machine. She used the hose hooked to the faucet and added cold water to the hot water. Then filled the rinse tub with the hose water.

Just a few yards to the east of the front yard, Kate watched Donnie as he swung the mattock, chipping away at the clay bank. After a few strikes, he shoveled the loose pieces to a nearby heap, straightened his back, and leaned on his shovel, resting.

By the end of the summer, Donnie's work on the 10-by-12-foot notch in the slope would be complete, and with timbers laid across the top and a layer of sod over the timbers, the cave-like dugout would provide cool storage to keep the melons fresh until time for trucking them to market.

Donnie's thin arms were as hard as the clay he picked and shoveled. His bony back rippled with muscles, far too many for a nine year old, Kate noted with a frown. He liked this job to a point, he said. He wanted to be strong but found reading and learning even more important. He was a kid eager to tackle whatever was put before him. Kate admired him for it.

"Can I just quit when it gets too hot, Ma, and read?" His bright round eyes popped with question.

With one hand on her hip, Kate looked at him and laughed. "We're all gonna quit when it gets too hot, Donnie. That's why we start working so darned early in the day."

With effort, Kate started the gasoline-run washing machine and then gathered soiled Levis and khakis from the house. She brought them out to the yard, pushing them down in the washer's swishing water. Pop had found the old washer at an auction and surprised her by sending it with Paul and his new wife, Maria, during their last brief visit. Flint seemed as tickled as Kate about the washer, and he kept her supplied with fuel for it.

Kate pulled a chair close to the rinse tub and set a wicker basket on the seat. While the clothes washed, she grabbed the hose again and sprinkled the yard with a fine spray of water to keep the dust settled. Then, with the broom, she began sweeping the dampened dust off the hardened yard.

She had to do something to change her life. A plan culminated in her mind to fulfill her dream of doctoring the sick and infirm. Each day she thought of Dr. Dora and how she had encouraged Kate to practice, to use her natural ability to heal. She distinctly remembered too, that the Cherokee Medicine Man prophesied that she would become a healer. How and when that was supposed to come about, she didn't know. Kate stopped a minute with the broom, dreaming, remembering. Although she had overcome some of the obstacles that held her back, her plan wasn't perfect yet. She had no transportation and Flint wasn't likely to help her fulfill her dream. She needed to do something concrete soon.

Rob finished milking the cow and walked down the trail toward the house. Brownie, with stiff hind legs, wavered up from the canyon on the east side of the house. The old intelligent dog had grown thin and shaggy over the last year. "Hey, Brownie, there you are. Me and Polly cow missed you this mornin'." Rob yelled to the old dog as he carried the bucket of milk into the house.

By the time Kate looked up from sweeping the yard, Brownie lay close to the ground, pulling himself along as he scooted toward her. A rush of love and appreciation for the dog gripped her. "Poor dog, gettin' old and rusty. We'll get you some of that fresh warm milk, ol' boy." She looked at Brownie again, expecting him to hear and understand her as always.

But Kate didn't take her eyes from the dog this time. Froth fell from Brownie's mouth, his head hung low, and his muzzle swung back and forth slowly. His fur bristled as he continued to scoot closer, heading for Donnie. Terrified, Kate called to Donnie, in a voice just loud enough for him to hear over the noise of the washing machine. "Don! Turn around and stay where you are; don't move." Kate took her eyes from the dog to look at Donnie.

Donnie did as he was told, furrowing his brow at his mother. But when he faced Brownie, his jaw quivered open and he stared at the dog, bracing himself on the handle of the shovel that stuck in the ground in front of him. Kate's eyes darted back to the dog.

Disaster hung in the heat of the day as Kate faced the slobbering dog. Her mind drifted fuzzy with terror, but instinct took over. She reached for the chair that sat by the washing machine. Quickly, she nabbed the chair and pulled it in front of her. The wicker basket tumbled off the chair and rolled across the yard. Still gripping the broom in her right hand, Kate stepped sideways, now standing between Donnie and the dog. Two swift jumps were all that it would take and the rabid dog would be upon them.

Blazing insanity filled the old Shepherd's eyes. He growled deeply, shook his head low to the ground, and bared his teeth. This could not be their Brownie, their beloved faithful friend of so many years. He did not seem to recognize them, nor they him.

Donnie's mouth hung open and he breathed heavily. There was no need to wonder why. His life, as her own, hung by a thread.

Unaware of what was happening, Rob walked out the kitchen door and stood on the front step. He leaned back, bracing himself on the doorframe and froze. "What's the matter, Brownie, are ya' sick?"

"Rob, get the rifle. Hurry," Kate hissed.

Rob reached inside above the door, lifting the Winchester off the wall. "Ma, what are ya' doin'?"

"Shoot him, Rob!" she yelled. "He's got rabies."

"But, Ma, that's Brownie!"

"Now!" Kate screamed. "Rob, ya' hafta do it!"

Rob aimed at the dog's head. For an instant, he hesitated. The dog slunk forward. "Now, Rob. Now!"

Rob pulled the trigger just as the dog lunged, frothing at the mouth. Their life-long companion heaved into a lump, lying still in the dust in front of the chair Kate now bent over. Rob ran toward his dog.

"Don't touch him; don't touch him!" Kate screamed. "Let me have the rifle, Rob. We hafta make sure he's down for good," Kate's hands shook as she sniffed back her tears. She would rather have died than to give Rob the order to shoot his own dog.

As he handed Kate the rifle, Rob crumpled to his knees. He covered his face with his hands. "What have I done? What have I done?"

With the rifle raised to blurry eyes, Kate watched the motionless dog for a minute or two. Convinced that Brownie was dead, she leaned the rifle against the house and knelt beside Rob, now lying prone in the dust. She lifted his head in her arms and rocked him while he sobbed.

Except for tears that fell plinking upon the spade of the shovel and dried in the mid-morning sun, Donnie hadn't moved.

In the next few moments, a silent pool of sadness lay upon Kate and the boys. The canyon grew still, wildlife fell silent, and the oak tree's limbs hung in the gloom of the day.

Finally, Rob raised himself from the ground and stumbled to his bed on the porch. Donnie dropped the shovel and followed his brother.

Kate spread a canvas tarp over the dog and with heavy heart, walked toward Gus' to meet Bette and the boys.

After about half a mile walk, she heard her children coming closer. Excited and quacking like ducks, Dale and Ben carried their two new ducklings between them in a small wire pen.

Kate told them about Brownie. Bette cried the remainder of their walk home while Dale and Ben fell silent, their joy over their new pets gone.

For the rest of the day, Rob stayed on the porch until he dragged himself out when he heard Flint and Bo drive in. When Donnie didn't show up, Kate figured he'd remained on the porch, lost in his books.

Kate stepped out of the house to meet Flint and Bo, immediately giving them the dismal news about Brownie. In the front room, Rob stood with his head bowed. Bo seemed in shock about it all and, without a word, moved slowly to Rob. He placed his hand on Rob's shoulder and together they hung their heads. Kate's throat stuck with sorrow for them.

Before sundown, with Flint's directions not to touch the diseased dog with their hands, Rob, Bo, and Donnie gathered around their old friend, wrapped him in the tarp, and carried him to a large lilac bush that grew on the north slope. Dale struggled to carry the mattock and Ben, the shovel. They lagged behind their brothers and headed for the lilac bush. In the front yard, Kate stood with Bette and Flint, watching from a distance as the boys buried the dog beneath the lilac. Before the boys returned to the lamp-lit house for supper, a solitary coyote yelped a mournful howl on the north slope, echoing the sadness that filtered over Mt. McGinny.

Without Brownie, all their lives were in jeopardy on this mountain.

CHAPTER—25

THE VISITORS

After Brownie's death and the rabies scare, Flint ordered that everyone in the family be wary of any animal, wild or otherwise, be it rodent, coyotes, foxes, ground squirrels, rabbits, or bats. Brownie had probably been in a fight with a rabid animal and had been bit or scratched, no doubt, so there was danger lurking somewhere on the mountain. Flint could depend on Kate to keep the children close to the house for a while, and Bo said he'd watch Shep for any signs of disease.

The homestead was without a good dog, but Kate hoped for a quieter routine so that she could finally begin to apply some of her career plans. The Depression was losing its meanness, and Flint had mentioned that it was possible easier times were coming.

But just as Kate found a few minutes to sit down at the table with a pen and paper to write Doc Laraby a letter, havoc exploded somewhere in or around the chicken yard. She ran for the Winchester.

Just before reaching the chicken house with the rifle, a frisky red fox ran out from underneath the wire fence where he had recently dug a road for himself. Though he carried no chicken in his mouth, his belly was no doubt full of eggs. The fox looked at Kate with black beady eyes. He grinned as though begging for his life.

"You get out of here or I'll shoot you," she warned. He lumbered to the trail that veered up to the North Slope, his feathery red tail swinging. He stopped and turned his head to stare at Kate in defiance, as if he understood her when she said, "I'm countin' to ten, and you'd best be gone."

Her warning didn't faze the cunning fox. He continued to watch Kate with obsidian eyes and a foxy grin. When she lifted the Winchester to her shoulder, he turned tail and trotted off.

"You may be a cute little fox, but I'm keepin' an eye on you and you better not show up around here again," she shouted after him, loud and clear.

This would never have happened if Brownie had been around. Since Brownie died, several critters had snuck in the chicken house. And the deer ate the garden. Even an occasional rattlesnake wove its way into the front yard these days. Like a hawk watching for field mice, Kate watched for trouble.

It happened many times before. Flint hadn't gotten home yet and it was late evening. The little boys were long asleep on their cots and Donnie, Bo, and Rob read by the kerosene lamp that sat on their bedroom table. Kate finished the letter she'd started to Doc Laraby when Bette came to the kitchen. She sat across from Kate at the kitchen table, the lamp lit, waiting for Flint. Through the years Bette listened to Kate's troubles. She listened to her without complaint and without asking for much in return. Now that Bette had blossomed into a beautiful girl of twelve, Kate knew that she'd better warn her about men. Bette's dark eyes shone with the excitement and with the wonder that most girls feel on the verge of womanhood.

"We might as well call it a day, she said, folding the letter carefully and stuffing it in an envelope she kept in the drawer. "Funny how I've worried for years about your dad driving up that damned road in the middle of the night, drunk. But, he's done it for years now, and he always makes it home. No sense in worrying about him. He's playing poker somewhere, I figure. And you need your beauty sleep, Bette, especially now that you're growing up."

Kate licked the envelope and sealed it, deciding this was a good time to give Bette some advice. She quickly addressed the envelope and tucked it into her special drawer by the sink.

"Pop is a good man. The best there is, and your uncle Paul. Well, Doc Laraby, too," she said, looking at her drawer that held her hopes and her dreams. Bette pulled herself closer to Kate and placed her elbows on the table, listening intently. "You can tell after awhile if you can trust a man." Kate shook her head to enhance her warnings and clinked her nails against her mug. "But don't trust any of 'em 'til you get to know them."

Bette had a vague expression on her face, soaking in her mother's forewarnings a little at a time. When she wriggled on the bench, Kate figured she'd better let the embarrassing subject go.

"Can't you talk to Dad?" Bette cocked her head in question. "Would he come home at night if you asked?"

"He'd just get mad, Bette. Thinks I keep him down. Needs lots of socializing. You know, visiting with his friends, and I guess I'm not one of them." With saddened resignation, Kate pressed her face into her hands hoping to iron out the discontent. The simple gesture nurtured her and helped her acknowledge how she'd allowed life to treat her. She couldn't take it much longer.

Bette was about to leave the room when Flint drove into the yard. Kate heard voices. There were others with him. The sound of a child's cry grew louder as she opened the kitchen door. To Kate's dismay, Flint escorted a woman and child into the house. A tall, gaunt man staggered in behind Flint and quickly sat down on the bench.

"Katie, we're gonna put these folks up for the night," Flint ordered, as he turned to the woman. "Kate'll fix you up, Virginia." He had been drinking, Kate could tell, but he wasn't as drunk as usual when he came home this late.

The woman, Virginia, looked young but haggard. The stringy-headed child with a dirty face buried her head in the woman's dress and wiped her nose.

"I'll try to make some beds on the front room floor."

Bette stood in the doorway between the living room and kitchen, looking at the disheveled child. "Ma, could the girl sleep in my room with me?"

The haggard woman looked at the tall soused man seated on the bench. His head bent forward, as if he'd topple any minute. The woman turned to Bette. "It's okay, Elizabeth." She gave Bette a nod of approval for the girl to go with her.

Bette reached for the little girl who seemed eager to go along, and the two disappeared toward Bette's room at the back of the house.

Kate gathered up the ugly green Salvation Army blankets from the end of the boy's cot and some from the bedroom trunk. Since it was warm out, she had extra. She laid them on the rough front room floor. Virginia mumbled her gratitude, and without undressing, she helped the man onto the blankets, pulling one over them when they were settled.

Offering no explanation, Flint limped to his porch, and Kate into her middle room. The visitors seemed harmless enough to Kate, and probably after breakfast in the morning, Flint would take them back where he found them.

Flint hadn't mentioned the man's name, and probably didn't know the people before today. That was how he was, always doing things spur of the moment, offering strangers shelter for the night. Kate flung her nightgown onto the bed. It angered her that he'd bring home folks that he didn't know, especially after the incident with Warner. In some ways, Flint was so trusting, more trusting of strangers than he was of her. Blowing out the lamp, she dressed in the dark. She would never understand Flint.

In the night, Bette took the girl out to the outhouse in bare feet, but Kate trusted Bette to light the lantern that sat next to the front door and to watch for rattlesnakes.

Kate kept one eye open and wouldn't be able to sleep soundly, if at all, until the girls were settled in Bette's room again. After a few minutes, the girls returned to the front yard. One of the girls yelped. Kate thought for a second that one of them stepped on a stone or that the child was scared. But when she heard Bette scream, Kate jumped from her bed and dashed through the house. She called Flint, which she normally never did when he had been drinking, knowing the uselessness of it.

When Kate got to the front room door, she bolted out to the yard. In the dimness of the lantern light, she saw the silhouette of the tall man standing against the front of the truck with Bette, grabbing at her. Bette didn't move fast enough, and the man reached down to her nightshirt, ripping it open. With his other scrawny hand, he clenched her wrist. Bette struggled, but was unable to free herself. Elizabeth sat on the ground in the front yard beside the lantern, rocking back and forth, whining.

Kate yelled as she whizzed toward the drunken man. The memory of Warner standing over Rob with the shovel flooded her. Behind Kate, Flint let out a whoop of anger and darted past her. He reached the man first. The drunk let go of Bette when he saw Flint coming at him. Flint delivered a fist to the gaunt man's face. As unsteady as the tall man seemed, the blow easily knocked him to the ground. Plunging the man to the ground didn't satisfy Flint. He jumped on the rogue, straddling him. Flint hit the drunk, who squirmed underneath him on the hard ground. The drunk yelled in pain and swore obscenities.

A few times in her life, Kate had seen Flint move with extraordinary speed when angered or afraid, and getting past her in the yard to reach the swine mauling his girl was one of those times. The whole incident brought out the mother bear in Kate and, for the first time, she gave Flint real credit for his protection of her long ago in Poteau, when he'd risked his life to save her from Leonard Schwartz.

Flint was far from finished. "Why you pale-faced bastard. I'll kill ya' for touching my girl." Flint cracked his knuckles again and again against the man's jaw. Painful sounding groans and desperate grunts came from the two men, and their legs flopped and swiped the ground.

Kate grabbed Bette and then quickly swooped Elizabeth up from the ground and away from the violence, leaving the kerosene lantern there with the kicking drunks. Virginia had awakened from her bed on the floor and now stood at the front room door, a look of horror on her face. "Back to bed," Kate ordered. The woman seemed glad to oblige. Meanwhile, Kate rushed the girls to the kitchen. Kate lit a lamp and warmed a cloth from the leftover water on the stove. She didn't wait to see if the men were going to kill each other, or if Flint continued to beat on the man. "Bette, you alright?" She smoothed the cloth over Bette's face and hands.

"What'd I do, Ma? Why did he do that to me?" She asked, holding her nightshirt together. A pained, confused expression covered Bette's youthful face and tears welled in her eyes.

"Bette, drunk men don't care if they have a girl or a woman. He thought you'd be easy to maul, I suppose, 'cause you're young. Innocent. It wasn't your fault." As Kate washed Bette, Elizabeth sat on the floor, watching them in awe, her shabby brown dress covered with yard dust. Glancing at Elizabeth, Kate felt saddened at the poor child's neglect. Then Kate turned her attention to Bette, and said, "Remember what I told you last night about some men. Dogs, they are." Kate poured more warm water over the cloth and continued to wash Bette's hands and face, though by now there wasn't a bit of visible grime on her anywhere. "It was good that you hollered. But, don't worry. Your dad will make sure that drunk never tries it again . . . if he lives through tonight. Now, let's get this little girl washed too, and you girls get to bed. Don't worry about the man. He'll be sleeping outside the rest of tonight. We'll bar the doors and he'll be gone tomorrow."

By the time Bette headed back to bed with the child in tow, Flint came in and barred the kitchen door behind him. He looked at Kate. She handed him the wet cloth. He swabbed at his bloody hands and skinned face without a word before he stumbled in to lock the front room door. Worry and fatigue making her tired, Kate carried the lamp to her room. She and Flint went to their separate beds. His voice muffled, Flint explained the ruckus to the boys, ordering them to stay put. Kate blew out the lamp and then lay for a long time before falling asleep listening to the creaks and groans of the house.

In the morning, Bette and Elizabeth came to the table when breakfast was ready and retreated back to the bedroom when finished. Virginia stirred under her cover on the floor and Kate asked her to breakfast.

"Who is that man you were with, and why did Flint bring you here?"

"Victor wasn't able to drive. He was too drunk. Victor is my, well, my boyfriend. What was the fuss about out there last night?"

"Well, I'd get rid of Victor, if I were you," Kate warned, trying to sound as sympathetic as possible. "He tried to maul Bette last night when the girls went to the outhouse. Flint beat the tar out of him. I think he's sleeping in the truck."

Virginia began to cry. "I just wanted to help his little girl."

Kate flung herself onto the bench opposite Virginia. "Oh, Elizabeth is *his* girl? Does she have a mother?" Kate was surprised that this nurturing woman wasn't the girl's mother.

"I'm telling on Victor. I'm going to take Elizabeth to her mother. I think Victor might have run off with her without her mother knowing. He's going to kill me for it. I think Elizabeth knows how to find her mother; she's just scared."

Kate reached across the table to lay a comforting hand on the woman's shoulder. "Don't tell Victor what you're doing or where you're going. Get Elizabeth to her mother and leave the state. He can't find you if you go far enough," Kate advised, recalling the way Flint had escaped Oklahoma and Schwartz, and wondering herself how she would ever get away from Flint if she needed to. Flint might get aggravated if Kate said her piece, but this business with Elizabeth was serious.

Before Kate could get a bowl of oatmeal in front of Virginia, Victor came to the window. Dried blood covered his face, and Virginia gasped when she saw him there. To Kate's surprise, Virginia set her jaw, whipped off of the bench and marched staunchly to the door, unbarred it, and stomped outside. Kate took a deep breath. Trouble was just beginning.

Try as she might to mind her own business, she couldn't take her eyes off the two warriors. If there were more trouble, the boys could settle the fight. They would be in any minute to wash and eat. Flint would likely sleep awhile longer.

In the front yard, Virginia cried out. Kate hurried to the window. Victor had his girlfriend up against the truck, his long fingers wrapped around her neck. She leaned back against the hood, distress on her flushed face. When Kate opened the kitchen door and leaped out to defend the woman, Rob and Bo rushed out of the door ahead of her. With a yank, Bo flung the tall man to the ground. Bo loomed above Victor. At 15, Bo stood over six-feet tall and was broad in the shoulders, and now peered down at Victor with a grin on his handsome face that begged to have Victor challenge him, a chance to try his youthful courage, and to beat the hell out of a drunk, something he had not dared to try with his father yet, as far as Kate knew. One enormous boot could squash the stupid man lying on the ground.

In awe, Kate stood at the kitchen window watching the fight. Donnie ran out the front door with clinched fists, in time to see his brothers' gallantry. As Bo stood guard over Victor, Rob led the woman to the kitchen and then he went back to the yard.

The three brothers seemed disappointed that the fray was already over. They washed at the faucet before breakfast while Victor crawled back in the truck and sat hunched over. Virginia hunkered around the kitchen table with the boys while they ate. Kate carried a mug of coffee to the porch for Flint. When she entered, he sat up in his bed and rubbed his disheveled hair. Bluish scrapes and bruises covered his rugged face. Kate felt a pang of empathy for him.

"That woman you brought here last night needs help getting away from that fool out yonder, did you know that? He was hurtin' her out there this morning, mashing her against the truck, choking her. Bo jumped him."

"Hah! With Bo on him, you'd think he'd mind his manners, but he won't." With swollen knuckles, Flint cradled his coffee mug and took a long slurp. "I know the son-of-a-bitch. I'll get them down the mountain, Katie."

"Wish you wouldn't bring trouble here," she said, and pivoted away before her husband could snap at her in defense, or before he could quiet her with a raised hand.

As Kate passed Dale and Ben's cot in the middle room, they followed her to the kitchen. Kate thought it was good of Flint to help folks in need, but if he knew Victor was mean, drunk or not, it was ornery of him to bring him here. It jeopardized the family. That didn't sit well with Kate, and sooner or later, she and Flint were going to come to blows about his generous habit.

She thought about Elizabeth. When the poor child left here, God only knew what would happen to her. It weighed some on Kate's mind, and she went to a drawer in the kitchen and pulled out a clean piece of paper and a pencil. She wrote Doc Laraby's address on the paper and sat beside Virginia with it. "Take Elizabeth to this man." Kate poked at the paper with her pencil. "He's located a block west of the school in El Cajon. He'll know how to help."

Virginia looked around for Victor. He wasn't spying on her through the window this time. She took the paper from Kate, folded it quickly and stuck it in her pocket. "Thank God for you, Kate," she said. "I was beside myself not knowing what to do. I'll go there with Elizabeth tomorrow."

"Good. I'd appreciate it if you'd give Doc Laraby this letter I've written, too," Kate said, while she opened her kitchen drawer, pulled out the letter and handed it to Virginia. Without questioning, Virginia took Kate's letter and placed it with the other paper. Kate took a deep breath and smiled.

CHAPTER — 26

HELM'S LIBRARY

After the incident with Victor, Flint realized that Kate had good reason to be upset with him about taking strangers to the homestead. Of course, it was the child he'd been concerned about when he'd invited them home with him. No telling what would have happened to Virginia and Elizabeth had they gotten in the car with Victor that ominous night. In the future, though, he'd avoid hauling just anybody to the homestead. He'd mind his own business hoping to get on Kate's better side.

It was later that summer when Flint met with Mrs. Helm to once again discuss the necessary maintenance work around her huge ram-shackled house and yard during her absence. He enjoyed their friendship, but since the drinking incident, they'd agreed to keep their relationship on a friendship basis. She would be leaving for L.A. shortly and not return to the big house until the following summer. He would miss her.

"There are more loose boards," Mrs. Helm spoke, her resonate voice half-laughing as she took him around the side of the house. "The nails rust and just pop right out of that dry siding and the brush needs removal to keep possible fires from the house. Perennials could use some water when it's dry."

He thought he'd need to pull much of the Jasmine down from the side of the house to get to the loose siding. He had intended to take some starts of the fragrant plant to Kate, but so far hadn't got any home to her before the roots died in the heat.

Mrs. Helm shaded her eyes with her hands, "and, stop in now and then to make sure there are no squatters. You know, make the place look lived in." She flashed her white teeth in a smile. "I have the feeling sometimes that things aren't as I left them when I return here. It could be someone needing a place to get out of the weather now and then, Mexicans or transients of some kind."

When Flint first met Mrs. Helm, she mentioned her suspicion of ghosts in the gaunt old house and he wondered if she actually believed in ghosts. In his childhood, he'd heard of apparitions sent to act as guides. He'd seen strange omens, warnings, and wondered if a spirit was sent now to guide him out of the mess he'd made of his life. He didn't know how to broach the subject with Mrs. Helm without making them both feel foolish.

"Here is my address," she said, as she wrote on a small piece of paper and then gave it to Flint. She patted his hand. "Send me your hours and receipts for nails or other repair supplies. I'll mail your money so that you'll have it right away rather than wait until I return."

Flint took out his wallet, opened it, and placed the slip of paper with her neatly written address on it next to a few greenbacks.

Mrs. Helm was about to leave but added, "One more thing, Flint. You showed interest in the books on the table when you came by last week. While I'm gone, you're welcome to the library. Come see." She waved him in.

Flint followed Mrs. Helm through a door off the living room. A spacious room lined with shelves of books opened before him. He hadn't been in any library for some time, and had forgotten how much he loved them, wanted to read every last one of them from front to back. "Vi, I can't take any pay for the work I do around here if you plan to share your library with me. Reading these books would be pay enough."

"Nonsense, I won't hear of it."

He grinned at her and they walked out of the library. It was time to say good-by. Passing the intimate table where they had shared so much of themselves, Mrs. Helm touched Flint's shoulder as they walked. "By the way, Flint. I've been meaning to talk with you about . . . well, I believe we're close enough that you trust me by now."

Once they reached the front porch, Flint turned to her and nodded, hoping she would go ahead and say what she needed to say.

"Get help for your drinking before it's too late, as one friend to another." Flint listened, knowing she meant well.

Mrs. Helm clasped both of Flint's hands and held them. As she peered into his eyes, her expression begged for his favor, his willingness to take her advice. "Your mother's passing was traumatic. You need to deal with it before it destroys your life . . . your marriage."

Shaking, Flint's fingers pressed tighter around Mrs. Helm's brown delicate hands. He knew that facing his drinking, his mother's death, and his rocky relationship with Kate would be a huge challenge. He nodded to Mrs. Helm and averted his eyes from her, hoping to hold back threatening tears.

"I'll get it done, Vi. Before we meet again."

Mrs. Helm left for L.A. and Flint swabbed his face before he walked back into the house, peeked in the library and noticed several books there that he had always wanted to read. Great books, novels, history. He gathered three off the shelf. Shakespeare, Tennyson's English Poetry, and Tom Sawyer. Like a child, he wanted them all at the same time. He laughed at himself and the situation and recalled the Cherokee's motivation for becoming educated. It was their way of getting even, one way of getting back at whites. A room full of books; a dream come true.

Flint opened the window by the chair an inch or so. He thought how good it would be if Bette and the boys could read these books. But, Mrs. Helm hadn't mentioned that he could take any home. He eased down in the burgundy leather chair by the opened window and leafed through the books. "She must have read all of these. They smell like Jasmine." After reading a few pages of Tennyson's English poetry, Flint laid the book upon his chest. A slight breeze cooled him. He dozed.

By the time Flint woke, it was late afternoon and he had yet to go for supplies. He closed the window, left 'Tennyson' on a small table next to the cushy chair, shut the front door and locked it as he left. Perhaps tomorrow he would get some repairs done before he was drawn to the library where he could again explore. Life was rather dull without exploration, adventure, and new knowledge, and the books were overflowing with some of what Flint hungered for. He looked forward to that comfortable chair again.

In the next few days, Flint stopped at Helm's before heading for town. He wasn't in a hurry. There was plenty of time today, since he had few supplies to get, and the work at Helm's was mostly caught up.

Once there, Flint decided to check around the place, and then he would set the sprinkler before going inside. Looking around at the back of the house, he found the steps loose. He'd worked on them not long before, using new lumber for bracing and 16-penny nails. The steps were sturdy and tight when he'd finished. He moved back to get a different view of them, took off his straw hat. Running his hand through his hair, he squinted his eyes, unnerved to see the steps needing repair again so soon.

He worked on them awhile. With them sturdy once more, he changed the sprinkler on the perennials and then made a beeline to the library. Unlocking the front door, he went in. At the library door, he looked into the room. He whiffed the air. "I like the atmosphere in this room," he said in a whisper. "It's as if the musty old books speak." He entered the library leaving the door open. When he left the library the last time, he was certain that he'd closed the window tightly. Now it was raised an inch or two and a soft breeze moved the drapes. "The spring is probably loose on that ancient window sash," he whispered again. It would need to be looked at and adjusted. There was no end to the work on this old place.

He headed for the comfortable chair. The book, 'Tennyson', that he felt sure he'd left on the stand next to the chair, wasn't there. "I'm damned sure that I left the book there on the stand," he muttered. His brows wrinkled into a frown as he fumbled around on the floor. He found the book between the chair and table.

Flint decided that there had to have been someone sneaking in and out of the house. Possibly living in the one room that he found locked, or the back of the house that was closed off. His thoughts returned to 'Tennyson' and he resumed reading.

A movement by the opened library door caught his eye. He stood and hurried to the door. He found no one in the large front room and heard not a sound, neither of the doors opening or closing. Just a shadow, he decided. Maybe the breeze blew through the towering Eucalyptus tree that grew in the front yard. With the sun just right, it could have reflected on the large windows at the front of the house. When it came right down to it, though, he couldn't explain the movement. He flopped back down in the chair, leaned forward and listened intently, his eyes darting around the room. The imagination, he knew, had a way of making a person see things that weren't there. He'd seen it during and after the war, hallucinations and such. Trauma. A normal reaction to horror.

Feeling dizzy, Flint leaned back in the chair. In his mind's eye, he envisioned a pool of blood around his mother, and he wept.

After resting a while from his inner turmoil, Flint figured it was time to get back to work. The next time he came, he planned to check the house from stem to stern. There was a logical explanation for everything, even if it meant that his spirit guide was trying to tell him something.

Once again, he laid his book on the table, closed the window, and then the library door. When he went out the front door, he locked it and checked it, then headed for the faucet to turn off the sprinkler. As he passed the end of the house, the glass in the window that he had recently replaced appeared cracked again. He walked closer. A quick shiver ran through him. A crack ran across the window, just as the last time. It was this place, this old house. Something was amiss with it . . . or him.

CHAPTER—27

SOMEONE TO LOVE

It was early spring of '40 when Paul and Maria wrote, planning to visit the homestead soon. Flint had grown more and more sullen. Kate quit responding to him; quit wondering what she'd done to cause his withdrawal from her further. The kids were growing up, and Kate's future plans continued to cumulate in her head. Since she'd not received any answer from Doc Laraby about her letter, she figured that Virginia never delivered it. Or, if Doc did respond by mail, Flint might have intercepted his letter.

But for now, Kate looked forward to Maria and Paul's company. The two of them were so cheerful, full of life, and in love, just like Mom and Pop. Once into manhood, even with their mother's red hair, Paul had acquired a sweet disposition like Pop's. And petite, dark-skinned, good-natured Maria was a dear friend. Kate felt fortunate to have her for a sister-in-law.

Married a year, Maria and Paul, were still without child, but Maria was like a right arm when she came to visit, helping with every aspect of the homestead. She especially loved to play with the children. She helped Bette with her hairdo and brought her pretty trinkets and clothes from her own closet.

But it was Maria's friendship Kate craved mostly, since she rarely left the mountain and had few friends. She surely didn't care for most of the people Flint brought around who were either drunk or who acted with nonsense. Of course, once Flint became sober, these so-called friends didn't last as his friends. Thankfully, he didn't bring them home often.

Mom and Pop came on holidays now and then when Paul would bring them. Pop could drive if necessary. He learned that when Rob cracked his head on the rocks a few years back, but there wasn't much need to drive a car now, brakes or no brakes, barring another emergency. Mom and Pop were slowing down a bit, though Pop had been content ever since he took over his neighbors ten acres of land with its various produce that required his farming expertise.

But Kate, even with Maria's friendship, carried a lonely place within her heart, an empty spot that not even Flint could fill on the rare occasions that he tried. Perhaps Flint's coldness had something to do with the Jasmine scent on his clothes. Whether or not Flint chased skirts, as Kate suspected, her trust that he loved her had vanished long ago.

Flint had insinuated to her more than once that she held him back. As time went by, Kate began to understand more of what that meant, that she and the children were a burden to him. Over time he would discover that she wasn't stupid, just tolerant. So much time had passed though. So much time and love wasted. Sadness overcame her, knowing that her own husband didn't love her. She wept off and on, realizing the truth of it. Loneliness stole its way into her heart and, lately, anger stewed in her before she recognized it. Pleasing Flint was out of the question. Sleeping with him again would cause more trouble; she'd get pregnant and he'd turn further away. But she had other dreams to make come true. Dreams that Flint had prevented.

There would be an end to her patience, someday. Then she would confront her husband about the address she saw lying beside the greenbacks that he set out on the table the time he counted out a few dollars of spending money for the older boys. The handwriting was that of a woman's. The letters were worn and the paper wrinkled. It must have been in his wallet for a long time. Her husband's rejection of her didn't hurt so much any more. A steel rod hardened in her spine as time went by, but along with it, a sort of unidentified longing crept over her.

In a few days though, Paul and Maria would be at the homestead, and bring light to her life. When they left again, it would be much too soon.

It was just before noon two weeks after Paul and Maria's letter came, and Rob, Bo, and Flint were planting watermelon on the south forty. Dale and Ben played cowboys, clomping up and down the bank by the chicken house with willow-tree-branch horses between their legs.

Bette came running in the house. "I hear a car, Mama. Should I fetch Dad and the boys?" She ran outside before Kate could answer.

Kate followed Bette out to the front yard where Bette stood waiting to make a quick dash to the south forty. "You wait and see, Bette. It may be Paul and Maria. If it's strangers, you run fast and get your dad."

An up-to-date, fancy-looking black Buick pulled into the yard. "Bette, run quick. Tell Dad." Uniformed men sat with a woman between them in the front seat.

Kate trembled. All through the years, she was grateful that Flint had so far been safe out here on this mountainside full of rattlers and sagebrush. Still, the possibility often haunted her that the authorities would come for Flint sooner or later, just as they did when they came looking for old man Warner. She feared they would chase Flint down and take him away, leaving her alone with the kids and no way to support herself. Had the scuffle in Oklahoma with Leonard Schwartz, caught up with Flint after all this time? Of course, there was Gus' still. It might be illegal to make moonshine, even though Prohibition was long gone. The hair raised on Kate's skin. What could Flint have done this time?

Kate craned her neck to see the people in the car more clearly, and her fingers began to twitch. She rubbed her arms, feeling miserably tired. Of course, Gus' still wasn't any of Flint's doing, Kate tried to convince herself as her stomach churned. The people in the car were important, no doubt, and highfalutin' to boot. It might be wiser for Flint to stay at the south forty. What was she getting herself into, standing out in the yard like a target?

But before Bette got out of hearing range, Kate recognized Paul and Maria stepping out from the back seat of the car and she yelled, "Bette, it's Paul and Maria." Bette made a U-turn in the trail and ran back to the yard. Dale and Ben heard Kate yell, dropped their horses, and skidded to the front yard.

Kate swelled with emotion and clapped her hands, still uneasy about the uniformed men.

Moving quickly from the car, Paul yelled, "Hi'de Kate." He and Maria grabbed Kate and Bette, trading hugs. While embracing Paul and then Maria, Kate watched the driver over their shoulders, a husky, dark-haired man. He stepped out and faced her. He stood there, as if ready to salute her, holding a hat that matched his uniform. Navy, Kate thought. The taller man, not as significant looking as the stronger man, but important nonetheless, helped a slender blonde lady out on the opposite side of the sleek car.

Paul introduced the husky man. "Kate, this is Captain Wesley Garrison . . . and Wes' brother Jimmy, and Jimmy's wife Linda. Jimmy's a Navy pilot."

Kate nodded, twisting her fingers together with the corner of her apron. She couldn't take her eyes off the Captain.

"Hey, where're your boys, Rob and all of 'em . . . and that good-for-nothing man of yourn, Kate?" Paul shouted, as he lifted Ben and swung the boy around and around in their own private dance. Dale jumped up and down waiting for his turn, and finally Paul swung him around, set him down, and reached in his pocket. "Brought you boys each a fancy musical instrument." He pulled two harmonicas out and handed one to each boy. They whooped and smiled their thanks. Then both ran up the hill, blowing monotonous notes.

Paul eyed Kate and waited for an answer. She motioned up the hill and to the southeast. Bette answered for her. "Uncle Paul, Dad and the boys are planting melons on the south forty."

The friendly pilot and his pretty blonde wife reached for Kate and Bette's hands, and took turns greeting them.

"These folks are from Missouri," Paul said, as he grinned at Kate. "Wes and Jimmy are stationed in San Diego." He chatted on, explaining how he and Maria met their new friends.

"Actually," Wes finally spoke in his southern drawl, not moving from the side of the car. "We got homesick for cornbread and beans, and Paul told us where we could find the best. Right here. Is that so?"

Kate was shaking inside, riveted by the dark-haired, handsome stranger and his kind complement. She so seldom ever received a complement. She brushed her hair back with her hand and smoothed her apron down. How she wished that Paul hadn't brought such important people here. She'd like to skin her brother alive right now.

Kate wanted to run and hide . . . to rid herself of the light she knew must have shown from her face. It had been so long since a man had looked at her that way. She lowered her eyes and continued in the hypnotic trance she had been in since Wes Garrison stepped from his fancy car.

"Now Kate, we're not serious about putting you out for a good meal," Wes said as he approached her, his deep-brown eyes twinkling. Gently, he took her hand.

In a strange high-pitched voice, Kate blurted out, "No, no, we have plenty, and we're nearly ready for the noon meal. You all are welcome." Her eyes scanned the ground. She pulled her hand from his and took a step back. She glanced his way. He winked back at her, and her knees weakened. She'd better say or do something. "Bette, will you run and get the milk and butter from the creek? We'll see about those beans and corn bread. I hear Flint and the boys comin' down now."

After introductions and hand washing, everyone pressed in around the table. Ben mashed his corn bread the same way he mashed his biscuits, and would eat it with gusto as soon as he had it flattened it to his liking. The meal was devoured in no time, including avocados and fresh green onions from the garden. After the women cleared the table, Flint poked around in his pipe and chattered with the others about the homestead, avocados, cantaloupes, and watermelons.

Paul went to the Buick and returned with a guitar. He handed it to Wes. "Wes, I bet Kate would love to hear some of those old songs we sang when we got together last week. How about 'Down In The Valley', or 'You Are My Sunshine'?"

Good country music wasn't easy to find on the radio, and Kate and the kids had to stand down at the pump house to hear it, so when Rob and Bo saw the guitar, their approval sounded above the drone of farm talk and politics exchanged between Linda, Flint, and Jimmy.

Wes moved to a chair away from the table to accommodate the elbowroom he needed for the guitar. He began plinking the strings, singing 'You Are My Sunshine' with his deep and mellow voice. He deliberately looked at Kate, where she sat at the end of the bench directly across from him.

Kate continued to keep busy, even holding Ben half on her lap and then Dale, though they were too big to need it. Finally, she grew tired of the boys mauling her and pushed them away. They grabbed their harmonicas and made a beeline out the door. Kate made another pot of coffee. She sat down again when Wes finished singing and playing.

"What would you like to hear, Kate?" Wes asked her softly.

She stuttered and shrugged. He played a tune she didn't recognize.

Linda and Flint talked about farming awhile and then joined in on the more serious discussion between Paul, Jimmy, and Rob. "They always told us that war couldn't happen here," the pilot said, lighting a cigarette, "but you know, Flint, Hitler darned near has a hold on Europe. And we won't have a choice but to get in the middle of it soon. Staying out of it is damned near impossible."

Kate half listened to their comments. She had been so busy with her own life she hadn't realized that the far-off war could effect her.

"Yeah," Flint said in a worrisome tone. He took a puff from his pipe, "I've been frettin' about it for some time now."

When Kate heard Flint's worry, she wondered if the possibility of war could have caused some of his sullenness.

Bette and Maria vanished into the front room to look at the box of clothes Maria brought for Bette. Everyone seated around the table tapped a foot, or in some way joined in Wes' music, even those talking war. Dale and Ben finally returned to listen, squeezing in next to Paul at the table.

Kate was focused on Wes' every word. Had Flint caught the glance that passed between them? Kate wondered about it, thinking that surely everyone had. She looked down to hide the glow, the spark of life that flittered inside her, a part of herself that had died with Flint's drinking.

Flint hadn't said much to Kate or Wes through the entire meal. His attention was with Linda as they talked more about the homestead, and back again to the war abroad. Finally, Flint relit his pipe and then asked, "Wes, do you all have family? Other than Linda and Jimmy, that is?"

Wes stopped strumming his guitar and looked Flint's way. "Family's in Missouri. Two fine boys, Lawrence and Roy, near eight and ten years old now." Wes bowed his head for a minute, looking at his guitar. "Not sure if I still have a wife. Francie and I are, well, we're kind'a . . . kind'a . . . estranged you might say, not divorced yet. Not good being away from the family for years at a time with the Navy. Made it my life, you know."

Wes' account of his personal life answered questions that smoldered in Kate's mind. Not really married, not really. Kate jerked with excitement, and prayed that no one noticed her reaction or that she felt unsettled and guilty. She would have to be careful. Flint would wonder why she was red-faced, or worse, glowing. He might get mean if he knew his beloved servant, subdued and contained, escaped his wrath. Flint got a slap in the face without her raising a hand, and he could keep his Hitler mustache too, for all she cared. Feelings careened in Kate, confused and unnamed.

Eventually, those who had been planting seeds earlier, returned to the south forty to finish. Spring rains would get the melons sprouted and growing, so timing the seed planting was crucial.

Paul and Maria walked to the top of the mountain with Bette hanging on Maria's arm, while Jimmy and Linda walked behind. They were eager to see the homestead from the slopes. Dale and Ben trailed at the end of the group, making noise with their new toy instruments.

Kate offered to show Wes around the homestead, particularly her garden by the chicken pen that grew wider and longer each year. It was as good as the cove garden with all the chicken fertilizer and decomposed straw she piled on it, and the sun shined on it all day. No more carrying buckets of water from the creek. A hose was hooked to a faucet at the pipeline that ran up the hillside to the avocado trees.

"I don't know how you manage with all these youngsters, Kate. No electricity. No running water into your house. Still using the rub board to wash your clothes. Good Lord, you are one tough lady." Wes shook his head. His deep brown eyes smiled directly into her own.

"Have a gasoline washer. Have a wringer, too. Guess I wore it out. It quit on me. Rob tried fixin' it."

"Where? Let's have a look," he said enthusiastically.

Kate stood a minute staring at Wes, his hair, his eyes, the texture of his skin. Feeling guilty, she looked toward the South Slope trail. No sign of Flint. She took a deep breath and felt Wes' presence close to her. The way he looked at her made her smile. She led him to the dugout underneath the back of the house. He turned the washer over and looked underneath it. After a few minutes, he set it upright again. "I see what part the motor needs. I'll bring it next time I come."

Kate smiled to herself, her head down, she couldn't help gazing at Wes now and then, though she felt unfamiliar pangs inside herself doing so. He looked about her own age, thirty-five years old, or younger. Finally, she forced herself to look away as the two of them walked along the east side of the house toward the front yard.

"You know, Wes, I always hoped Flint would build me an adobe house by the avocado trees, with water piped into the kitchen. I'd love to look out over the valley below, where I can see to the Pacific Ocean on a clear day. Guess it doesn't matter any more." Kate bit her lip. She'd said it out loud. She'd given up on one dream . . . the adobe house, but she would never give up nursing. The Medicine Man had promised her she would become a healer some day and she counted on that promise like she did the sun rise over Mt. McGinny every day. "I wouldn't want to leave these oak trees anyway," she added, trying to convince herself it was for the best and that some dreams were best left forgotten before they ate at a person . . . ate 'em to death, "the oak trees don't grow up on the side of the hill, just in the canyon. And the creek, it sounds so good, especially at night. That little waterfall just barely trickles down." Kate made a trickle motion with her fingers. "Guess I'm used to things the way they are. It only bothers me that Flint, well, we don't get along, Paul or Maria probably told you."

Kate looked down wishing she hadn't said that, but she went on anyway. "I've learned to keep the peace when he is here. You know what I mean, don't start trouble by askin' for anything."

"Don't give up on your dreams, Kate," Wes said with concern. "Ask for what you want."

Kate surprised herself, telling a stranger her deepest dreams and hurts, and now she felt embarrassed. She quickly changed the subject.

"Wes, do you suppose I could learn how to play that guitar of yours?"

"I'd love to teach you, Kate. Let's go in and sit down with it."

The way Wes said her name sounded almost melodious. She listened for him to use her name again, hoping it would be often. On their way toward the front of the house, Wes picked a large blue morning glory from the vines that rambled up the lemon-box siding. He handed it to her. Their fingers touched and a gasp of surprise escaped Kate's lips.

She spent the next hour with Wes and his guitar in the two front room cushioned chairs. The morning glory lay on her lap. She kept her eyes from meeting Wes' while she focused on learning the guitar cords.

By the time the group returned from their walk up the mountain, Kate had learned some cords, and she and Wes were singing and laughing. Paul raised one eyebrow, cocked his head, and gave her his sideways grin, the same grin that Ben inherited. "Well, we hate to leave Kate, but Wes and Jimmy are due to check back in."

Reluctantly, Kate rose from her chair when Wes stood. Kate saw that Jimmy and Linda were getting in the car. Paul and Maria told the kids goodbye in the front yard.

Wes hadn't taken his eyes off her, but stood in the front room ready to leave. He held the guitar out to Kate. "I want you to have my guitar. Next time I see you, you'll know more about it than I do. You already got the knack of it. Sure will miss you, Kate."

Kate took the guitar. "Oh my, I don't know what to say." She looked down, holding the guitar, and walked into the kitchen. Wes followed. "Do you want us to come again," he asked shyly, "or are you going to break my heart?" He winked at her and grinned, his brown eyes gleaming.

She hid her flushed face again. Carefully choosing her words, she set the guitar against the wall. "This has been the best day, Wes. You're welcome to come anytime." She wanted to say how wonderful he made her feel, how alive and happy. "And I'll take good care of your guitar."

Swiftly, Kate moved to the yard and cooler air. Wes tagged along behind her. Jimmy and Linda were already waiting in the car as Paul and Maria hugged Kate in the yard. Kate reached in and touched Jimmy and Linda's hands in farewell. Before Wes got into the driver's seat, Kate stepped to his side. He leaned toward her and kissed her lightly on the cheek. Then he whispered something in her ear she couldn't quite hear. She decided he must have said, "Thank you."

After Wes drove away, Kate stood watching the puff of dust on the road that led out of the yard, up the hill, and away from her. He was gone. She wrung her hands on her apron. She prayed he'd come again. Often.

CHAPTER—28

ANTICIPATION OF WES

Kate was in a fog all week, and hardly responded to anything anyone said to her. Several times through the week, Bette had eyed her strangely and asked, "Are you alright, Ma?" But Kate answered her daughter vaguely. She couldn't bring herself back to the present moment.

Three weeks passed since Wes' first visit, and Kate slowly returned to the business of running her home. Only Flint never noticed that her thoughts were elsewhere. A misty rain came and went quickly in one day, but cleared the dusty air and added to the magic she felt in and around her.

As another weekend approached, Kate half expected Paul and Maria to drive in the yard anytime. They surprised her sometimes without writing first, and she held her breath, waiting with anticipation. On one hand, Kate hoped with all her might that Wes would be with them when they arrived, and on the other, she was scared to death of what her own reactions would be if he did come. Never in her life had she shook inside as she had when Wes was standing in front of her.

She had given up on Flint. Each day, he had sunk further into despair and he returned to drinking after only a few weeks of sobriety. She felt nothing for him anymore, neither joy nor fear. They were even now. He got what he wanted. Flint mattered to her as much as she mattered to him. He came; he went. And she continued to fantasize about Wes' return.

Kate felt drawn to Wes, but she wished she didn't desire him so much. The best part was that he cared about her. She was certain of it. That was the amazing thing.

Saturday arrived, and Kate kept busy cooking and cleaning and gathering vegetables from the garden. If company did arrive, she would be ready. It was a relief to Kate when

Flint decided to go to town. He had mentioned his reason for needing to go, but most of the conversation escaped her now.

Bette began setting the table for the noon meal. Rob and Bo tromped down the hill from the melon patch and washed up at the faucet in the front yard. Bette easily gathered up her younger brothers, their growling stomachs keeping them close to the kitchen. They clamored around the table when Kate placed the pot of pinto beans on. Bo served a ladle full of beans in each plate, while Bette forked tomatoes and onions onto Ben and Dale's plates, their little-boy energy clamorous.

When Kate reached into the oven for the cornbread, she heard a car easing down the gravel road and into the yard. The pan of cornbread shook violently in her hands. She whisked it to the table where it landed with a crash. Flint wasn't there to show his annoyance, so she ignored her own clumsiness and moved to the opened kitchen door.

"You're just in time," she hollered out the door toward Paul and Maria, who spilled out of the front seat before Wes. Reeling, Kate closed her eyes to ward off the dizziness. Wes and Paul wrestled something out of the back seat. They walked past her with some contraption, laughing and talking, and set the thing on the kitchen counter. Maria carried three or four records. Now Kate could see the contraption.

"A Victrola?" she squealed.

"Do you like it, Kate?" Wes asked.

Kate stared in amazement as Paul placed a record on the phonograph's turntable. He wound the handle and set the needle on the revolving record. Sweet country music filled the room during the meal. Kate invited each of them to join her at the table. The little boys giggled their excitement, the young men smiled while they ate with their eyes riveted on their food, and Bette watched Kate.

After the table was cleared, the little boys carried the milk and butter back to the creek. Rob persuaded Paul to go with him and his two brothers to see their dry-land melon patch on the south forty. After the last misty rain, sprigs of green from the seeds planted three weeks before had barely emerged. When the young men headed for the South Slope trail, Maria and Bette followed them.

In the kitchen, Wes wound the Victrola and started another round of music. Then he sat down close to Kate. She moved across the table from him. To be any closer was unbearable, especially now that they were alone. "Whose Victrola is that, Wes?"

"I brought it for you, Kate."

She lowered her moist eyes, hoping to conceal what the heat in her face must have revealed. "Thank you. I've missed music."

For several moments they sat in silence and began speaking at the same time, stuttering and then laughing. "You go first, Kate. I'd rather listen to you than to myself." They laughed again and Kate relaxed a little.

"Flint's gone to town. Might be back any time though."

"He won't hurt you if he finds me sittin' here talking to you, would he?"

"No, no. Huh, he hasn't slept . . . ." Kate gasped at her presumptuousness. Wes was just so easy to talk to.

Wes gazed at Kate, showing his understanding. "I heard about the porch," he interrupted. "Francie kept a separate room. She needed me for a meal ticket. I couldn't live like that."

He reached across the table toward her and placed his hand on hers. She jumped, but leaned into the table, closer to him. "It's okay, I won't touch you more than this." He smiled and his brown eyes twinkled. "I've missed you these last three weeks. Tried to stay away." Wes' voice turned to sadness. "We're probably going to war, Kate. Did you know that? That's why I had to act fast. I couldn't wait to tell you how I feel. I'm headed for Pearl Harbor."

Kate's smile disappeared and a feeling of loss filled her. "No, no, Wes. You've made me feel . . . feel so happy," she blurted out and felt immediately doused in shame. "I've been so empty." She placed her other hand over his.

"I know, Kate. I see the same emptiness in you that I've felt in my own marriage. It's hell."

Kate recognized honesty in Wes' face as he fought to keep his emotions in check. "It's strange to care about you so quickly. I liked you even before I met you three weeks ago, the minute your brother talked about you. You're more beautiful than I imagined. Wish I could have met you long ago. Now, it's too late."

"What are you saying, Wes? You're never coming back?" She felt a catch in her throat. He had said she was beautiful. She hadn't thought it possible anyone could think so, and now he was leaving.

"War time is inevitable. Who knows? Besides, there's Flint . . . and Francie, maybe." He shook his head at the futility of their situation.

Dale and Ben tromped from the canyon after their chore up the creek and scampered to the kitchen door. Kate pulled her hands away from the man who had stolen her heart. She needed air. Catching her breath, she walked out to the front yard. Wes followed her where they could take a walk and speak quietly, out of earshot of the children.

When they reached the garden, they stood in the sunshine, soaking in each other's gaze. The little boys heard their Uncle Paul and ran out to meet him and the others walking down the South-Slope trail.

"This is it, Kate. We're going to be leaving as soon as Paul gets down here. Let's just look forward to meeting again someday, shall we?"

"Yes, Wesley Garrison. Yes, let's do that. And write, will you?"

With a smile and a nod, Wes confirmed that he would write. Paul and Maria gave their usual warm hugs to Kate and all the children, and then they got in Wes' car.

Wes shook hands with the young men and the little boys, then kissed Bette on the forehead. "So long, you all. We'll try to come again in a week or so. That is unless I'm transferred." Gazing at Kate, Wes reached to her, pulling her close. Ignoring her children, Kate buried her face in his shoulder. Finally, Wes pulled away from her, got in the driver's seat and drove away.

CHAPTER—29

FLINT'S ADVERSARY

With his pipe in hand, Flint drove east toward the homestead. He had researched information on hospitals that specialized in helping people with alcohol addiction, and he hoped, help with gambling addiction too. He'd found a facility located further north, near Los Angeles, the closest and best. As a veteran, his therapy would be paid for.

His concern now was leaving the homestead for at least a month, the minimum time required for adequate therapy.

The last poker game he'd attended at the Junction Saloon with Arnie and the guys who hung around there, ended in his losing money, lots of it. At the thought of his losing money, Flint pulled hard on his pipe, sucking in the aroma of the Prince Albert. So far, Kate had no inkling of his gambling addiction, since she rarely left the homestead, and he'd been too cowardly to face her with one more reason to hate him.

He'd drunk too much, lost the money from the sale of an entire truckload of avocados, and wished he could talk to Mrs. Helm afterward. Instead, he'd gone home and slept. Kate ignored him. He tugged at his pipe, the red embers smoldering.

Wes had visited the homestead at least a half-dozen times that Flint knew of. Most of those times Flint hadn't been there. Kate seemed apathetic toward Flint, her mind elsewhere, on the Captain, no doubt.

Now, Flint needed to do something to right his life before he lost his Katie to Wesley Garrison, the married man, strutting around on Flint's turf.

As he maneuvered the truck along the highway, he planned to make up to Kate. After he'd sold another load of avocados today, he'd purchased everything on Kate's list, even remembering to get peppermint candy sticks for the kids from the Spring Valley Market. He bypassed Arnie's Junction Store where he usually stopped for Gallo and to discuss the upcoming poker game. Then he reached into his khaki shirt pocket for matches to relight his pipe. He struck his match with his thumbnail and lit the tobacco. Inhaling the smoke, he tried to relax.

Bypassing Mrs. Helm's place, he shifted the Dodge into low gear and started up the steep mountain road to the homestead. There were signs of unfamiliar tire tracks on the dusty road since he'd gone down this morning. Tracking was one skill he had acquired during his visits with the Cherokees throughout his younger years. Someone was at the homestead.

Just as Flint reached the top of the road, before it spilled down to the oaks in the canyon and the house, the Dodge sputtered. Flint stomped on the gas petal a couple of times to no avail. The motor died. "Oh Great God," Flint said aloud. "I forget to gas up at Arnie's."

He'd tried so hard to avoid the temptation at the Junction store that he'd even forgotten the necessities there.

Fortunately, he didn't have far to walk. There was a can of gas at the pump house.

The steep and gravely road down to the homestead caused him more pain than usual. From this higher elevation, Flint viewed the homestead before him. He felt proud of the cleared melon field and the avocado orchard. The oaks had grown so that he could no longer see the house from where he walked. It pleased him to see the land from here, even the wild roughness: the rocks and the yuccas. A movement on the flat rock beyond caught his eye. The mountain lion! A beautiful animal, he thought, a sacred spiritual animal, the wildest part of Mt. McGinny.

Just before the road swooped down into the yard, a steep narrow deer trail led off the road straight to the pump house. Flint decided he'd get the gas now and then check in at the house before heading to the Dodge with the gas.

A loud voice chattered on the hillside near the house. It was Paul. He had been correct about the tire marks on the dusty road. At the pump house, Flint picked up the can of gas and started back up the trail to the house. Glancing toward the house, he could clearly see Kate and Wes standing together by the shiny black Buick in the front yard.

Wes had come again. Flint knew that he came because of Kate. He'd seen it in their faces. Even a dense person could tell there were sparks between them. Flint set the gas can down on the trail and rushed to the house. In his hurry, he stumbled and fell beside the trail. Raising himself, his clumsy-booted feet sunk into the leaf mold beneath him. Tripping and scrambling, every bone in his body felt jagged inside him. He stepped to the worn trail that led from the pump to the house.

With so much chatter in the front yard, no one noticed him trudging closer and closer. Kate held Wes' hand as he leaned and kissed the side of her face. Suddenly, rage vibrated up Flint's spine. Every bloody scene from his memory flowed through him; the pool of blood around his mother when he'd found her dead; the pool of blood around Leonard Schwartz after he'd hit him with his fist; the pool of blood he'd imagined around Kate every time she gave birth; the pool of blood around the fawn that he'd shot.

"What the hell are you doin' with my wife, Wes?" Flint's hands went to his hips where he curled his fingers into a fist.

Wes jumped back from Kate, crimson faced. He took a deep breath and stuttered, "Just sayin' good-bye, Flint. Headin' to Pearl Harbor and might not get to see you all again."

Flint pushed his fists tighter into his hips. It was good effort on Wes' part to back out of his mistake. No sense in killing the captain, Flint decided. Let the war do it.

Paul spoke loud and clear. "Flint, we're running late. Hope to see you all soon." He said good-bye quickly before he helped Maria into the Buick.

Paul was trying his best to circumvent a bloody fight, Flint could tell.

Without so much as a wave to Paul, Flint stumbled in the house. To hell with the Dodge, he thought. He hoped that there was enough room beside the Dodge for the black Buick to get around it and to hell off his mountain.

No one followed Flint to the porch. When he reached his bed, he checked under it, searching for the last half-full bottle of sour Gallo he'd left there. After his last drunk, he swore he'd throw it out but had forgotten. He rolled the half-full gallon jug out from under the bed and swiftly yanked off the top. After he swigged down all that he could, he threw himself on the bed.

Wooziness overcame him by the time Kate entered the enclosed porch. She gathered the two kerosene lamps from the side tables. He knew she'd fill them with kerosene and replace them before evening. He watched her through scarcely opened eyes. She glanced at him, a disgusted look upon her face, and he sunk deeper in despair. A half-breed had no chance against a cocky military man. Even with the soul-numbing sour wine in him, he felt more alone than ever.

CHAPTER—30

RETURN OF THE MOUNTAIN LION

In the front yard, the small fire beneath the washtub had died out. The water felt hot on Kate's tanned skin as she rubbed a pair of Flint's socks up and down the washboard, occasionally sliding a bar of Fels Naphtha soap down them. After another rub or two, she threw the socks in a tub of cold water that sat on a stool next to the washtub.

She laughed sarcastically when she remembered what Flint had promised her years before when she stood under the sweet gum scrubbing Pop's dirty overalls. Flint hadn't meant what he promised. He had manipulated her into marrying him by saying that she'd never have to scrub the board after they married. Now, she felt fortunate if he even arrived home by sundown, and even more fortunate if he arrived sober.

Well, Kate felt cared about now. Her heart ached to see Wes again. He had told her that he loved her as he was leaving the last time, just as Flint came upon them. She didn't have the chance to respond to Wes, and she felt relieved that Flint kept his fists to himself. Kate knew what he was capable of.

But now that she and Wes had found each other, how unfair that he was forced to leave, maybe never to return. She figured she'd be heard all the way to the top of Mt. McGinny, if she were to yell out all the anguish she felt inside herself. Flint ruined her life at every turn.

Kate pushed Flint's khakis down in the hot soapy water. It didn't bother Kate that Flint ignored her for a while after his run-in with Wes. But, over the last month, Flint warmed up some when he was sure that Wes wouldn't be back, at least for a while. Kate slapped the khakis against the rub board and wiped sweat off her forehead with her bare forearm.

Dale and Ben ran in circles, playing nearby in the sunshine . . . sunshine so blazingly bright that it hurt to look up.

"Ma," Dale hollered. "We were trackin' the big lion this morning. We're the best trackers, cause we're Cherokees. Dad showed us how to spot those big cat prints, Ma." Dale crunched a green apple.

Ben chimed in, "No kiddin', Ma, big claws stuck in the dirt by the lemon and apple trees." The little boy danced around. One hand reached out mimicking a claw; the other clutched a half-eaten green apple. He slurped on the apple, growling at the same time.

Kate scrubbed her tender knuckles on the washboard. Her arms sloshed up and down in the hot water while she thought. How she wished Brownie was still here. For years he protected her kids, warned them of snakes, and probably kept them from dangers she didn't even know about. But the mountain lion hunted at night and there were deer aplenty.

She stopped momentarily to glance up in the trees and scan the brush and the hillside, then threw the khakis in the tub of cold rinse water. Course, Grover's baby was just toddling right out the front door in plain daylight, got grabbed right by the neck and drug off. Poor Grover and his wife had been crazy ever since, after watching that damned cat run off into the woods and leave forever with their little one. Kate shuddered. She would go see about those tracks tomorrow.

School was out for the summer. That was a relief in some ways. The boys needed more clothes before they could go to school again, and their shoes were falling apart, too. On the other hand, while here on the mountain and not busy with school, they tended to explore the way any normal boys would.

Kate pushed Flint's dirty khaki shirt down in the hot water. She rubbed down hard, wondering if Flint would ever get her gasoline washing machine back in working order.

The older and braver the boys got, and the longer the days, the further they roamed from the house. Still, she preferred having them as little boys amidst the lion, rattlesnakes, and rocky cliffs, than near-grown men like Rob and Bo, with war threatening.

Kate threw the khaki shirt in the rinse water as she listened to the boys' chomping.

Finally, it dawned on her what the boys were eating. "Confound it Dale, Ben, no more green apples. Throw those away! No more till they're ripe. You're going to have a bellyache. And don't go back up yonder. I don't want that big lion carrying you off."

The boys skipped up to Kate with their apples. Dale whined, "Okay, Ma, but I crave those apples. When can we eat 'em, Ma?"

"Not until they're ripe, and I'll tell ya' when."

Dale ran to the edge of the creek, looked longingly at his half-eaten green apple, and then threw it into the grapevines. Ben immediately copied his sidekick.

Dale pulled his harmonica from his jeans pocket and blew out and sucked in. After Dale's indiscriminate notes, Ben struggled to pull his own harmonica out from his back pocket, and then played the same tune. Hanging on to each other and their harmonicas, they scampered up the hill, their bare, leathered feet kicking up dust and gravel.

Now that the days were longer and more tiring, Kate made sure that the boys settled down in bed as soon as darkness filled the canyon. So when evening approached, supper was over and the kitchen cleaned, the little boys were finally quiet and the harmonicas laid to rest.

It felt good to have everyone at home and in bed. No haying for Bo and Flint, no school for the youngsters, no dates with the girls tonight for Bo and Rob. Except for worrying about Wes and pending war, there was no reason Kate couldn't get a good night's rest. She blew out the kerosene lamp, crawled in bed, and closed her eyes.

In the night, Dale's movements woke Kate when he got up for a trip to the outhouse with a bellyache. Ben whined for Dale to take him with him. Kate lit the lamp on the nightstand beside her bed and pulled dungarees on under her nightgown. After lighting a lantern by the front room door, she handed it to Dale. "With that full moon nearly straight up in the sky, and this lantern, you should see real good. Best get up there before you all need clean underwear." Kate walked out the door behind the boys and swatted them on their butts. She sat down on the front step.

The barefooted boys clung together, wearing only undershorts. They made their way out of the yard and up the bank toward the outhouse.

The moon hung in the clear sky, beautiful and bright. The boys chatted, while Kate watched them wobble together, the freckles of spangled light from the lantern moving along the ground with them. They made it around the chicken house and to the outhouse on the other side. As Kate sat on the step, she put her shoes on while she waited for them to rid their stomachs of green apples.

An owl hooted close by. Frogs croaked up and down the creek. Kate breathed in the warm night air, feeling like part of the landscape, with the moon her guardian. And then, the melodious night sounds that she felt such a kinship to suddenly deadened to complete silence.

Abruptly, chickens flapped their wings and squawked raucously, interrupting Kate's serene moonlit night. She jumped up and headed for the Winchester. "That darned fox," she hissed under her breath. "Sure do hate to shoot that cute little beady-eyed critter."

Kate grabbed the Winchester from its perch above the kitchen door and hurried toward the chicken house with the rifle. She expected to see the fox run out to tease her again as he had done not long before in plain daylight.

She stopped short at the edge of the yard.

"Oh, my God. Boys, stay in the outhouse," she commanded. Pulling the rifle quickly to her shoulder, she aimed it at the stealthy figure in the moonlight. The mountain lion stood on the chicken house roof, facing the trail where the boys would walk any minute.

Kate's trigger finger twitched. It might have been steady except for the vibration of her heartbeat.

The door of the outhouse slammed.

"Please be quiet," she whispered.

"Ma," Dale wailed. "We didn't mean to wake the chick . . . ."

The boys were in sight at the end of the chaotic chicken house, boggling along with the lantern between them.

Kate steadied her arm, her heart ticking off the seconds. The great beast crouched. Then it lunged down from the roof above the boys. Kate pulled the trigger twice. Bang! Bang! The shots rang out through the moonlit canyon and echoed over the hillside.

The lantern that the boys had been carrying between them dropped to the ground and rolled down the bank. Dale drug Ben by the arm, screaming down the bank after the tumbling lantern. The frantic boys stumbled toward Kate until they piled up against her frozen legs. She dropped the rifle and went to her knees before the boys, squeezing them to her.

The cacophony of squawking chickens and the rifle shots brought Flint and Rob to Kate's side.

"I think I got him, Flint. Oh God, oh God!" Kate blurted out a long, mournful, wailing cry. More horrified now, realizing what could have happened had she not seen the cat in the moonlight, she burst into tears and her arms surrounded the nearly naked boys, holding them close against her breast where she knelt.

Flint nabbed the rifle off the ground as Kate watched, still petrified. Rob found the lantern and relit it. The men walked cautiously to the prone cat. Using the end of his rifle, Flint poked him. No movement.

"Well, Katie," Flint yelled back to her. "If you aren't the damnedest sharp-shooter in the west. Either shot would have downed the yeller beast. Hey, boys, are you scratched at all? Bet you got the crap scared out 'a ya', heh?" Flint chuckled. The boy's bodies stayed glued against Kate.

Bo, who had grown quite large over the past year, stumbled out the front door, hopping on one foot and then the other, pulling on his Levis. Shep was at his heels.

Rubbing his eyes and clad only in undershorts, Donnie followed behind Bo. Wrapped in a blanket, Bette ran out in bare feet to hover over Kate and the frightened boys.

"Come see this, you all." Flint motioned in the moonlight to the late-night gathering, and then kneeled down closer to the mountain lion.

Kate took Bette's hand, and the boys, one on each side of Kate, hung on, clutching to her dungarees. They made their way to the end of the chicken house. Kate wanted to see for herself, to know that the menace would not threaten her children again.

Mouth ajar, the limp lion's white fangs gleamed in the moonlight. Flint pointed to a small dark spot oozing blood in the center of the big cat's head, behind his left eye. He pointed again to the dark hole near the heart of the dead animal. "I'm going to make a pelt of this animal," he said.

Kate stood over the mountain lion. "You son-of-a-gun. If you had grabbed my boys by their necks, I'd a spent the rest of my days huntin' you down."

"He was just doing what mountain lions do, Kate; hunting and eating." Flint said matter-of-factly.

"What is the matter with you, defending an animal that would have eaten our children?" She said with sarcasm, not waiting to hear his rebuttal. "Let's get to bed kids." Kate took her boys small hands in her own and led them back into the house. She helped them onto their cot. "I guess tomorrow, you'll just hafta track that little red fox, heh?" The boys hunkered down beside each other and closed their eyes. She left them to their dreams.

In the kitchen, Kate made coffee. Except for the two sleeping boys, the family sat around the table sipping on their hot mugs. After the excitement settled, the men yawned and headed for their porch. Bette sat with Kate a while and the story was told again, until Kate quit shaking. Later, they returned to their beds and things were once again peaceful over the homestead. The owl hooted close by. Frogs croaked up and down the creek.

The big cat had haunted the homestead for over a dozen years. Finally, he was dead. Tomorrow, the guys could bury the beast, or better yet, throw it in the field for the coyotes and buzzards. Gratitude seized Kate's soul. Wrapping a blanket tightly around her weary body, her ears still ringing from the rifle's blast, she allowed her heavy eyelids to close.

No doubt though there would be another mountain lion, a young one searching for its own territory. It would find its way to Mt. McGinny and establish itself here . . . sooner or later.

CHAPTER—31

RISING SUN

Even though nearly three months had passed since Wes' last visit to the homestead with Paul and Maria, that special day lingered in Kate's mind. In fact, she had been preoccupied with sweet memories and heady feelings while scrubbing the planked floor, and rubbing on the washboard. Many times she found herself standing in the middle of the room, staring into space. Only the worry of war and the memory of the mountain lion intervened in her thoughts of Wes. He had been transferred so far away, to Pearl Harbor, just as they both had feared.

Since Kate had met Wes, night after night had passed without her sleeping more than two or three hours. And the times she usually would have spent rocking in the front yard and reading the medical book or a Zane Grey pocket book, in which she vicariously lived a romantic life, were instead filled with plucking on the guitar that Wes had left for her when he came to visit the first time. She had nearly perfected what he taught her, and also taught herself some simple tunes.

The kitchen door was open this morning, fresh air wafting through. Kate cleaned up after breakfast and swept the kitchen floor. She could hardly wait to get out to the garden in the early morning sun when the day was actually pleasant. She learned from Pop exactly how to garden for plenty.

The Depression was mostly over, but there were more mouths to feed now, and growing boys needed more than beans and cornbread. During Wes' first visit, almost everyone around the table was preoccupied with the war abroad. The whole thing prickled Kate's skin, pecking at her like an old hen's sharp beak. She figured it best to remain as independent as possible, to keep the garden growing for as many months out of the year as the weather would allow.

Kate couldn't help noticing articles about the war abroad in the newspapers and in the Life magazines that Flint brought home. When her curiosity got the best of her, she read about the world beyond Mt. McGinny. Unlike her Zane Grey pocket books, this world, as the news presented it, was not romantic at all.

Worse was the dreadful realization that if the United States got involved in the war abroad, Rob and Bo would soon be called to serve. It was such a horrendous thought that Kate busied herself around the homestead, hoping to forget about war, hoping to forget about Hitler rolling over Europe. Even the worst years of the Depression here in the United States was child's play compared to what hell Hitler was said to have been causing elsewhere. But Europe and the war were a long way from Mt. McGinny, and a long way from Pearl Harbor.

Kate picked tiny weeds from between the shoots of corn and hoed weeds from the rows of green beans and small tomato plants. While she hoed, she chopped at Hitler, war, and anything else that created fear in her. When exhausted, some of the worry that muddled her mind vanished. The deer had visited the garden again and did some damage. It was time for a very high fence or another dog like Brownie, if there was such a dog.

It was mid-morning and Kate let the chickens out of their pen to pick bugs and grass. While at it, she stuck more straw in their nest boxes, gathered their eggs, and returned to the kitchen. An old hen had wandered through the opened kitchen door, and now she hopped out from under the counter onto Kate's swept floor. "Scoot! You'll make a mess on my clean floor, you biddy." The hen scurried outside.

Kate sat her basket of eggs from the hen house on the counter by the sink and peeked under the counter where she kept her box of stacked newspapers. That old hen had found herself a good nest. Kate laughed, and reached inside the box. She brought out a still-warm egg. She glanced at it and set it on top of the others but picked it up again, this time turning it over and over. *This is the strangest egg I ever laid eyes on. Looks like a picture drawn on it.* She held it to the light of the window. "Flint!" She yelled. She heard the thumping of the pump motor. He hadn't started the truck to leave yet, so he had to be somewhere close. She left the strange egg with the others and went looking for her husband.

She glanced up the creek, where she heard Ben playing by himself. Kate often found him on his stomach, his face close to the water watching water skitters kick around in the shallow pools of the creek. Her youngest child missed his sidekick so much, Kate wondered if she shouldn't have kept Dale home another year from school.

Kate found Flint at the pump. She hung on to the corner of her apron, pressing it between her fingers. She knew there was more to that mysteriously marked egg than met the eye, but she would not let on to Flint just yet.

He looked up from oiling the motor. "Katie, what's wrong?"

"Come to the house, Flint. You hafta see this." She turned to hurry back up the trail to the house, dodging the hummingbird nest that hung at the end of the oak limb.

"Can't ya' just tell me?" Flint yelled after her. "Oh hell, alright. I'm through here anyway."

Kate looked behind her to make certain that her husband followed. He plodded along, and after he stepped into the kitchen behind Kate, he scooted onto the bench at the table.

"Any coffee made, Katie?"

Kate gently picked up the unusual egg and held it in her shaking hand. Then she set it on the table in front of Flint. "Take a gander at that egg. What does it mean? The old hen just came right in the opened door and laid the egg in that box of newspapers under the counter. Can you see it, Flint? It's a picture, huh? A sunset? Never saw a red spot like that, not on the outside of an egg."

Kate poured Flint a hot mug of coffee and set it in front of him. He slurped his coffee holding the egg in his free hand. Kate watched him turn the egg over and over, looking closer and closer at it, and then he held it up to the window. When he held it up to the light, Kate saw not only the red spot, but muted spirals of pink and red shooting up from the red dot, and just at the bottom of the dot, a choppy horizon along the lower part of the egg.

Flint pushed his mug aside. His mouth moved but no words escaped. Finally, Flint blurted out impatiently, as if Kate should have known the significance of it all along, "The rising sun! Good God, Kate! It's a sign, an omen from the Great Spirit. That's a perfect red sunrise. Sun, horizon, it's all there . . . the sun, the Japanese national insignia. We're at war now, Kate. Mark my word!"

Kate scowled. That was not the explanation she'd hoped for, and Flint sounded scared. "Flint, maybe it's a sunset, not a sunrise, how do ya' know?" She took the egg from Flint, wondering why he always viewed things differently than she did. "I'm going to crack the darned thing, see what's on the inside."

"Wait! Crack it on the other side of the picture, maybe on the tip end," Flint cautioned.

Carefully, she cracked the egg, placing the yoke in a bowl. She swished the egg around, inspecting it. "Perfect, no blood spots. Just a regular hen's egg." Kate half expected more omens from the inside.

"Keep the shell; keep the shell! I'd like to show that to Arnie and the fellas around the Junction later."

Kate slid the eggshell into a canning jar and tightened the lid.

"We better get some work done, and quick." Flint spoke as if time was running out because of the omen. How could she do any more than she'd been doing all along? After another quick slurp of his coffee, Flint hurried back down the trail to the pump, leaving Kate's head buzzing.

As Kate regarded the egg one last time, she grew more concerned for Wes. He would be right in the midst of trouble. Jimmy, too. They told them as much when they visited. It didn't seem so real then, or even possible. Now it did.

One thing was sure in Kate's mind, every egg she collected from any hen was going to be looked over properly for other omens. She had seen pictures on eggs before, and even written words, but she had never paid them much heed. Just flukes, she thought. But this sunrise picture seemed too much of a coincidence. The Japanese were ready to attack any country in the Far East, according to the news reports. Though certainly not allies with the United States, Japan would be foolish to attack such a strong military; Kate knew that much. San Diego could be their next target, if they chose to be fools. No, America was safe. Still Kate's stomach turned sour and she pulled down the bicarbonate of soda to ease her discomfort.

CHAPTER—32

THE WAR

In the steel-cold daybreak of December 7, 1941, Flint slurped his mug of coffee before trudging down to the pole barn. He didn't usually get up so early, especially on a Sunday, but he was anxious to hear the latest news of impending war.

Now that there was the threat of war, Flint hesitated about leaving the homestead for any length of time. Even though he'd promised Mrs. Helm that he'd get professional help for his alcohol addiction and his past trauma, she'd certainly understand why his treatment would have to wait.

When he arrived at the pole barn, he turned on the radio that ran from the pump battery, and tuned in to listen to his usual station. He tinkered with oiling motor parts. An empty oil can lay on the ground. He picked it up and tossed it in the trash barrel.

As he did, the newscaster cried out in a voice filled with fear and anger, "Pearl Harbor bombed!"

"Pearl Harbor bombed! No, no," Flint whispered to himself, as if somehow whispering a denial might keep this life-spoiling news from being true. He shook in disbelief. The newscaster went on to say, "This was not expected, a complete surprise. Japan didn't have the military to do this awful thing, but it happened anyway."

Flint learned already that Germany had taken over Rhineland, Czechoslovakia, Austria, Denmark, Norway, the Netherlands, Belgium, and France. Poland was divided and Italy had taken Ethiopia and Albania. Britain was alone. Millions were dying in concentration camps and bombed cities. Americans were split, those who favored isolation from "foreign" wars and those who could remember their ancestors who came from across the ocean. And now this! "They're gonna blow up the whole damned world," Flint said out loud to the radio.

No need to be 'split' now. No choice left. Flint steadied himself against the pole barn. The egg omen was right.

Flint grew weary. His knees weakened and his face felt stiff and drawn from the unsettling news. His feet tired from walking the trail between the house and the pole barn, but he didn't wait to hear more. He must tell Kate right away. God! How he hated to tell Kate. She always prefered to hide the truth.

Flint stumbled through the kitchen doorway and sat down, hunched in his chair at the end of the table. His wide, rough hands covered his face, and he tried to speak without crying. "Kate, the bastards bombed Pearl Harbor." Tears seeped down his face and dropped through his fingers onto the table. Distress covered him with bodings of coming doom as he lifted his head to receive Kate's response.

Kate squinted at him as if she didn't believe him. Furrows rippled between her eyes and across her forehead. She grabbed the biscuits from the wood stove, quickly flipped them onto a platter, and hurried the platter of biscuits to the table. Then, as if the bad news had finally sunk in, she said, "Oh, no, Flint. Not . . . Pearl Harbor!" Kate stood red-faced by the table. She stared at Flint, and then covered her face in her apron.

Dale and Ben scrambled to the table as if they hadn't eaten in a week. Flint had never cried in front of them before, so when they looked up at him and saw tears, they quieted and crawled up on the bench close to his chair, peeking sheepishly at him ever so often. Kate moved to the stove. She held the end of her apron over her eyes, hiding them while she stirred the oatmeal.

Moments later, Rob walked in with the milk bucket. "Ma, here's your milk. The ol' gal did good." He scrubbed his feet on the gunnysack and walked across the room to the sink. "What's brewin', Dad?" Rob slumped and his face turned ashen when he looked at Flint. He set the bucket down.

Flint rose from his chair and placed a hand on Rob's shoulder. "Ah, son . . . the war's startin'. Pearl Harbor was bombed an hour ago. I just heard." He glanced sadly at the little boys, walked out the door, and trudged toward the pole barn. Rob followed him. Together they huddled around the radio as the frightening news continued, blasting out over the once-peaceful homestead.

"My God, Dad, I think Wes is in Pearl Harbor."

Flint nodded. "Better go get Bo. Get him down here. I'll wait here and listen. We got trouble a' plenty now."

Rob ran to the house and returned with Bo at his heels. The two boys, young men now, gathered with Flint at the radio.

Rob leaned over to look at his kneeling father. "Dad, Bo and I want to stay home and work. We've had enough of school. That alright with you?"

Flint didn't need to think it over. He wanted his sons at his side as long as possible. "Hell, why not? We've got plenty of work to keep you busy around here. And with the war, we need to get ourselves set up for a heap more trouble comin'."

Yet, even as he spoke these words, he knew how true his words might be.

CHAPTER—33

NEW NEIGHBORS

All thought of Doc Laraby vanished with the war. Why, Kate wondered, did the Japanese have to bomb right where the Navy transferred Wes? He had written a short letter the previous month and said he was settled in Pearl Harbor. She had read the letter to the family. Flint noticed her despondency and impatience and connected it to Wes. Now, Kate waited to hear from Wes in silent misery.

A few days passed before Flint brought more bad news. Germany declared war on the United States. It was as if there wasn't enough dead men and destruction in the war that Japan brought.

So Christmas came and went without much more celebration than baked turkey, mincemeat pie, and a simple tree. A group of Australian Pines grew at the side of the road just before the road swooped down into the canyon to the homestead. Rob and Bo climbed to the top of one of the pines and cut six feet off the top. Then they stuck the end of the pine in a five-gallon bucket of clay and set the tree up in the front room. Kate rolled out flour dough for tree decorations. The kids cut shapes in the dough with cookie cutters. Then they pressed in a loop of thread for hanging the shapes and used red holly berries for color. When dried, the shapes were ready to hang on the pine. Rob took charge and ordered the younger kids to place the decorations evenly over the tree. It lightened the mood for a day.

A few days after Christmas, another letter came from Wes. Flint brought the letter in to Kate and then sat alone at the table drinking coffee. As Kate read the letter to Flint, her hands shook and her lips trembled. Wes said that he had escaped injury from the bombing. Jimmy was out of the area and, as far as Wes knew, was all right, too.

Flint nodded, then took his pipe out and fixed it. He smoked without a word of response to her.

Why Flint usually brought the letters to her without opening them first, Kate didn't know. He certainly could read, but for some reason, he gave her the honor of opening and reading letters out loud to him or to the entire family.

Wes was alive and well. She held the letter tight. Unable to hold herself together any longer, she walked out to the yard, hiding her exuberance.

After that, a letter from Wes arrived one every other month or so to her and the family, and were sparse with news. Kate felt continually exhausted from worry, but at least she knew for the time being that Wes and Jimmy were alive. During this time, she'd written short letters to Wes in response, asking him not to mention them in his letters to the family. She sent them with Maria to mail for her.

A terrifying eleven months had passed since the Japanese bombed Pearl Harbor and, fear and confusion had spread like an epidemic thoughout the country.

Kate dreamed of Wes' return someday, and memories of their moments together flooded back when she picked up the guitar and began plucking the strings. She prayed for Wes to survive the war, and then her life could go on from there. Maybe then she'd find the courage to leave Flint. Wes would allow her to pursue her dreams. He would encourage it in fact. She smiled, eager for the day when Wes returned to the homestead.

After flying bombers in the middle of the war for months, Jimmy was sent home on leave. Linda would meet him in San Diego and then they would go to Missouri for a week or so, but he had a day free before Linda was to arrive, and so he planned to come with Paul and Maria to the homestead.

Paul had taken over Pop's old car and drove Mom and Pop wherever they needed to go, and since Paul was deaf in one ear, he would not be called to war. He and Maria came to visit Kate often. It was October and rain fell the night before. The earth smelled fresh and loamy from the warmth of the sun on the wet ground.

Since it was Saturday, and not a school day, Dale and Ben hurried the milk to the creek. Their plan for the day was to ride Jackson over every Mt. McGinny deer trail possible to keep the old mule in shape. Donnie finished his chores and piled up on his porch cot with his books. He probably wouldn't crawl out until the next meal. Kate figured that he was too young anyway to learn about the horrors of war. When Paul and Maria arrived with Jimmy, Kate gathered with the older boys along with Bette and Flint in the front yard, anxious to visit.

Jimmy was different now. In less than a year, the war aged him to a grievous, anxious person. Kate led him to a chair in the front yard. He sat there with his face in his hands. Kate watched Jimmy while the nervous grownups gathered around him. Finally he said, "Folks, I can't tell you the terror that is going on with this war. Why, I've seen men blown up in front of my face . . . oh God, many times. Their planes hit, blown up, full of fire, down they go, crashing into the ocean; my friends, good men, good people, some with young families. I just can't stand it."

Jimmy began to cry, his words jumbled from the effort to talk, and he looked at Kate. "Kate, you have to be tough. Rob and Bo are near old enough to get in this mess." Kate jerked when Jimmy talked of Rob and Bo, and she noticed a shadow cover Flint's face. As she listened to the frightened young pilot, he shuddered and lit a cigarette, inhaling it with a deep breath. "Me and Wes, well, we may not be back. Wes loves you all, you know, just as I do." Jimmy wiped the tears from his face with his sleeve and took another drag from his cigarette. Looking to the ground, he shook his head and went on. "You just have to be strong, that's all. There's not much chance for us. For a lot of us." Jimmy drummed his fingers against his knee, and said, "Linda and I wanted children." He stood and walked around the yard looking up into the sky and oak tree, blinking back tears, as if to rid himself of great suffering.

"Jimmy, come on in and eat. Come on," Kate led him by the arm, maneuvering him into the house and onto a chair. When everyone was gathered, she served the meal. Jimmy ate slowly while staring into his food.

Later in the afternoon, Paul and Linda left with Jimmy to drive him back to San Diego where he would meet Linda the following day.

Paul and Maria said they'd visit the homestead again soon. Kate loved her brother and she felt proud of him. He had grown to be a rather small man, strong though, and Kate was relieved that Flint honestly liked him. Flint told Kate that Paul wasn't cocky and that he listened to reason. Paul would be a good hand for the truck farm, he said, now that it was beginning to produce more than he and the boys could handle.

So when Paul and Maria returned to the homestead after a few days, Flint and Paul walked off together to work in the field and water the avocado trees while Kate and Maria stayed at the house for a visit.

Kate sat at the square table across from Maria. Sheepishly, Maria said, "Kate, guess what? I'm going to have a baby!"

Kate stood up and hugged Maria and laughed for Maria's sake, for Maria's joy, but she knew what lay ahead for her sister-in-law. With Paul not working, how would they take care of a baby? Of course, that's what Mom always said to her every time she became pregnant, and Kate wasn't going to start in on Maria the same way. Things would work out.

"And, Kate, what are you going to do about Wes?" Maria raised her eyebrow at Kate with a concerned half-smile. She reached for Kate's hands and held them for a moment. "I have eyes, you know. And Flint's . . . cold."

"Wes is a good friend. That's all." Kate averted her eyes. "I don't want Flint to know I write to Wes. You know Flint, he can get mean over nothing." Paul and Maria were bothered by Flint's drinking and that he neglected her, Kate knew. They might have said something to Wes about it. "And you know, Maria, Wes may not come back."

Maria gazed at her hands. An oily sheen glistened in her black, shoulder-length hair. A pensive expression covered Maria's face, her velvety olive skin beginning to show the first signs of motherhood. "Since he's still married, he sure can't help you out of your predicament here. But, looks as if he makes life happier for you. I can see it in your face, Kate. Love at first sight for you and Wes. It was the same for Paul and me, you know?"

Kate's face grew hot. "Yes Maria, but I don't want to think about it. It's trouble. I'm stuck here. Wes can't change that. We have youngsters to raise and Flint brings home supplies. He's made a farm out of this place." Kate searched her heart and mind, trying to justify life as it was, fearing the results should she make changes to it.

Kate's eyes flitted around the room, taking in everything around her, everything she and Flint had built together. Then she threw up her hands. "Oh, I know, Flint's a drunk and a bully, and sometimes I hate him. Chases skirts, too, I suspect. But, I'm not goin' anywhere. Wes is just a friend of the family, Maria. That's all he can be. But, Maria, I'd give my eye teeth to see him," Kate sniffed, covering her face with the corner of her apron to hide the turmoil inside her, turmoil that seemed to be building as the days passed.

About that time, Paul came thudding down the hill in a half-run, a grin on his face. When he got within hearing distance, he shouted, "How'd you two like to be neighbors?"

The women looked at each other and raced outside to meet Paul. Maria shrugged. "I'd love it, Paul. What do you mean?"

"Flint promised he'd help us build a shack on the North Slope, just off the trail yonder. I'd help with the truck farm. If things work out, why, we'd earn ten, maybe twenty acres of that slope. What do ya' think, Maria?" He had both a quizzical and guilty expression on his face.

With a grin, Kate realized that the men had already made their gentleman's agreement. Her heart jumped with anticipation of Maria living only a few yards away where they could visit everyday.

"Ah, Maria, I guess I should have talked with you women before sayin' yes to Flint's offer."

Marie's head tilted. "Would you mind having me for a neighbor, Kate?" she asked.

"Mind? Heck no, I wouldn't mind!"

Maria and Kate held hands and danced around in a circle, Paul looking pleased that his decision had been a good one.

The following week, Paul scouted around the valley for any old building that needed tearing down. To Kate's relief, he found a shed not far from the Junction, and better still, he could probably pull it to the site by the truck on a sled or trailer without tearing it apart and rebuilding. It would take less time and money in the long run to move it whole, since the farmer would give it to Paul if he moved it right away to make room for the new barn.

Within a month, the shed was in place off the north trail further up Mt. McGinny, and Kate felt immense joy. She and Maria were finally neighbors. Paul found wood pieces and scrap lumber to patch up loose boards, and he covered the sparse roof with tin. But, Kate knew that come winter, they'd need more than a campfire outside the door.

Paul worked for a few days, repairing a motor in town. Kate was glad to see that he bought a decent wood stove for the shack with his earnings. While down the mountain, he checked on the folks and took them to town for supplies. He stopped by Maria's relatives who sent her some other things for her little shack. Kate helped Maria make it homey, not wanting to see Maria start out with almost nothing, especially when pregnant.

After Kate did all she could to help Maria, she left Maria standing at her wood stove, cooking a venison stew for her husband. Kate started down the slope, heading back to her own place. She kicked up dust with her worn shoes and slipped now and then on spots of gravel that naturally covered the trail. She felt worried about Maria, but at least Maria wasn't sleeping on the ground, out in the open with a mountain lion roaming around. The memory of the mountain lion gave Kate a shiver and she was reminded of the night alone at the homestead campfire with the mountain lion creeping around. Now she lived in a real house with plenty of room. In a way, though, Paul and Maria were better off than she and Flint. They loved each other so much.

Kate reached her own yard, ready to get supper for her family. As she pulled a sack of cornmeal out from under the counter, she speculated on what the future might hold for her. Could she ever leave Flint for Wes? Whatever happened in the future, she'd try to face it with courage. But that old enemy self-doubt crept in and she wondered if she was up to the challenge.

CHAPTER—34

BABY TINA

By the next summer, the war was still raging. But the homestead continued to provide a sense of security. Kate worried about Rob having to enlist, but tried to keep her sanity when it came to Rob and to Wes.

Maria and Paul settled in. Paul worked hard in the melon fields alongside the other working hands. The homestead would produce good crops if the weather cooperated. Donnie hunted fallow deer on Mt. McGinny and trapped gophers, when he could tear himself away from his books that were scattered over and under his cot. Dale and Ben spent much of their time riding and taking care of Jackson, when he wasn't behind the sled or the plow. With Bette's help, the garden grew larger every year. The homestead flourished.

Now that early fall approached and the weather was warmer in the afternoon, the first thing Kate did this still-nippy morning was to build a fire in the stove to make coffee, then breakfast. While she always got out of bed at daybreak, before anyone else rose, as the years passed she seemed to need that special quiet time more and more: time to reflect on what she'd done with her life, time to plan for the future, time to pray.

With her mug of coffee in her hands, Kate stood at the stove, the feel of dawn seeping through her; the multitude of bird song; the crackling oak limbs flaming and snapping within the stove. She was glad to have Maria near. Even Bette cheered up with Maria around. And every few weeks, a short letter came to the family from Wes.

Maria had seen Doc Laraby a few times, and would go to Mercy Hospital for the birth of her baby, since it would be her first. But, should the need arise, should the baby come too fast, Kate stood ready to midwife.

Kate stirred the oatmeal and brought the basket of eggs closer to the stove. She'd cut open leftover biscuits and fry them in lard. The family would be rising soon, just about the time the sun peeked over Mt. McGinny.

Kate heard Paul and Maria's old car clanking over the rough road coming down from their place on the North Slope. Since it was so early in the morning, Kate figured it was Maria's time to head for the hospital. Excited, she wrapped a blanket around her shoulders and met them in the front yard.

Maria lay nearly prone in the seat, moaning and pushing against Paul while he shouted, "Today's the day!" Kate had always been tolerant of Paul's loud voice, a trait of his partial deafness. On Maria's side of the car the window was rolled down. Kate reached in to grab her sister-in-law's hands while she grinned across the cab at her brother.

Kate gripped the car door when she saw the pain on Maria's face. "Maria, you alright?"

"Oh, God. I'm all wet. My water broke!" Maria screamed.

"Get her in the house, Paul. You'll never make it to the hospital. She's having the baby right now."

Kate ran in the front room door and pulled the extra cot away from the wall. She found a clean sheet and quickly spread it over the blanket that covered the thin mattress. "Why did you wait so long, Paul?" She yelled in frustration while Paul struggled to hold Maria upright until he eased her down on the cot.

"She just started havin' pains an hour ago."

Wishing that she'd prepared more thoroughly for this emergency, Kate shook her head at her own omissions. She had instead, figured that since it was Maria's first time giving birth, she'd have plenty of time to get to Mercy Hospital after labor started. After all, she hadn't even taken any Blue Cohosh or other remedies that the Cherokees used for rapid delivery. Maria screamed again. Kate decided to follow the Cherokee's birthing method of keeping the patient upright during labor or the actual birth. "Help me, Paul. Let's get her in a kneeling position." Kate grabbed another blanket and folded it for Maria's knees to rest on.

Paul followed Kate's directions, but he shook violently and she worried that he'd drop Maria. "Take it easy, Paul. I'm a midwife, remember? Help her crouch there. I'll get hot water and the other stuff I'll need. Don't let the baby fall on the floor. Catch it, Paul, if it comes out."

"But Kate!"

"Just do it, Paul. I'll be right back," Kate said.

Bette woke and stood fully dressed in the middle room doorway, her eyes dancing wildly. When Kate saw her there, she said, "Bette, keep everybody out of here." Bette looked disappointed, but turned to leave. "Wait, Bette, come and help," Kate blurted out, mindful that Bette wasn't a child anymore; she could be of some use. "Keep hot water on. Pour some over these scissors and thread in this pan. Keep it boiling." Kate fumbled with the scissors and they dropped to the floor. She picked them up. Bette took them from her and then patted her on the shoulder.

In the front room, Maria moaned and then yelled. Dale stuck his head in from the middle room and Kate told him to keep everyone out until Maria had the baby. By the time Kate ran back to Paul and Maria, the baby's head showed. Kate slipped a towel under the tiny dark head and after another grunt from Maria the baby fell in the towel. After a second or two, the infant girl hadn't take her first breath yet and her skin began to turn blue. Frantically, Kate turned her upside down to get blood to her brain and then, with two fingers, swatted the infant's bottom. Instantly, the baby girl wailed loudly. Paul helped Maria onto the cot. Kate quickly tied and cut the cord, and with tears in her eyes, laid the newborn beside Maria. Paul hovered over them, singing to the child, "Tina . . . Tina."

Finally, while Maria nursed her infant daughter beside her on the cot, Paul left to fetch some clothes for Maria from their shack. The boys came out for the breakfast that Bette had put on the table. Flint meandered in from the back room. Looking at Maria cuddled with the babe, he asked. "What is it?"

"She's a girl." Kate said with satisfaction.

After a look of shock, Flint grinned and shuffled on through the room. Kate hadn't taken him his usual cup of coffee and he headed toward the kitchen. At that moment, Kate realized that she had forgotten to have Paul bury the afterbirth. "Flint, before you sit down to breakfast, will you bury this gunnysack of afterbirth?" Kate would have performed the deed herself, but she felt that she'd already done a day's work.

At the doorway to the kitchen, Flint glanced back at Kate with a frightened, gaunt look from his steely dark eyes. His reaction startled Kate. She knew such a request wasn't unreasonable. Flint stepped into the kitchen without a word or a nod. In a few minutes, she heard the truck start up and leave. "Now, what the heck?" Kate whispered. "Every time there's a little blood, Flint . . . ." That was it, Kate decided. She'd heard of people who couldn't stand the sight of blood for whatever reason. And the Cherokees believed that a woman's blood was powerful . . . and dangerous. She and Flint needed to have a talk one of these days soon. Today, she must take care of her two patients.

Kate would never forget the thrill that she experienced this day of helping a child into the world. She would never forget that she was on this earth to help, to heal, to doctor. She'd been so preoccupied with Wes and the war that she'd forgotten her true calling. With her hands and her heart, she was a healer.

Tina was small, but healthy. Maria would be a good mother for her baby. After all, she was a responsible and loving woman, but because the shack was so far away, Maria agreed to stay in the house with Kate for a few days.

After the first day, Kate became concerned when Maria seemed remote. This behavior wasn't at all like Maria, but it wasn't unusual for a new mother to get the 'blues'. Paul promised to get her to Doc Laraby for a checkup the following week. With time, Maria should be her happy self.

Finally, after Kate waited on Maria and the baby for three days, Maria said she felt able to care for the baby in her own little shack and Paul came to fetch her. Kate trudged up and down the north trail twice a day to carry fresh milk for Tina. Maria continued to be 'blue' and was unable to nurse her baby. Crisp autumn days were welcomed after the long summer. But nights turned nippy, too cold for a baby, so Kate made sure that Ben and Dale supplied Maria with plenty of dried oak limbs for her stove whenever Paul was absent.

A few days passed before Flint and Paul left again to purchase supplies in town and to deliver the last of the produce to the Spring Valley Market. Maria appeared happier and spent the day with Kate. Paul was tickled about Tina and, when not working, he stuck close to the two girls he obviously loved so much. Maria could always count on Paul to be home as soon as he could possibly get there. Paul wasn't a teetotaler when it came to drinking, but not apt to stay away from home for drinking, socializing, or gambling the way Flint did. Kate saw clearly that Paul loved Maria the way Pop loved Mom. It was the kind of love and respect that made Kate envious.

"Kate, Tina needs a bath. Can I do it in your kitchen?" Maria asked.

"Let's set up a pan on the kitchen table. It's warm in here," Kate responded. To keep the warmth in the room, she stuck another log into the stove.

Kate poured warm water in the pan and tested the temperature with her elbow. When the water felt right to Kate, Maria slowly and carefully bathed Tina. After laying a blanket and towels on the table for after the bath, Kate said, "Now, I've got to run in and hunt for that box of baby clothes. Mom and Pop and other folks keep expecting I'll have more and more kids. They've kept me supplied with all kinds of baby clothes, even now, and Ben's five years old." Kate laughed. "You can have the whole box. I suspect there's a decent outfit that might fit that little tiny girl."

Kate went to her bedroom and fished under her bed where she slid the cardboard box a few months earlier. When she brought out the box, she brushed the dust off and checked for spiders before heading back to the kitchen. Maria was sitting in the doorway of the front room. Tina lay in her mother's lap, uncovered by the scant blanket underneath her. Her bare head lay exposed to the afternoon breeze.

"My God, Maria, don't let that baby's wet head out in the breeze like that. She'll catch her death of pneumonia."

"The breeze feels good," Maria defended.

"Not warm enough for a baby!" Kate snapped.

Maria stood up and without a word, started up the North Slope with Tina in her arms, wrapped in the thin blanket.

Rob heard the disagreement while he stood in the yard with his hands on his hips. Watching Maria stomp away, he asked, "Shall I help her home, Ma?"

"Maria isn't herself, Rob. I don't know what's the matter with that girl. Yeah, you help her. I'll stay away from her awhile."

Flint and Paul didn't return for supper as expected. By the time Kate got the children fed and settled, the sun had gone down. She left Bette and Bo in charge. Despite her promise to stay away, her worry got the best of her. "Rob, let's check on Maria." Rob grabbed the Winchester, and Kate lit the lantern, since walking that far at night wasn't smart without either. Kate took the sack of food she had prepared earlier for the new mother. They headed toward the North Slope trail.

When they reached the shack, Kate and Rob opened the door. Maria stood in the middle of the room, her arms folded, as she gazed into space. Kate had given Maria Ben's old crib, and it just fit between the end of the bed and the wall, but the infant now lie in the middle of the larger bed that Maria and Paul shared.

"Maria, it's dark out there, and we nearly broke our necks getting here. We were worried about you since Paul hasn't come home."

Kate felt an even more immediate concern for Maria and the baby when she saw that Maria was so distant, a haunted look about her. Her usually bright eyes now shone as dark as shiny black pearls against her sallow skin. Her ebony hair hung like strings, even though she had always been so fastidious.

"You know Flint . . . probably in some darned poker game, or started drinking and talking, and he wouldn't care if Paul needed to come home." Kate set the sack on the table and opened it. "I suppose you haven't eaten. Come on over here, Maria. You've just got to eat to get better." Kate poured Maria a glass of milk and uncovered a small bowl of beans that she had heated before leaving the house.

Maria didn't say a word, but sulked to the table and slowly took a bite of the food that Kate set out for her.

It was chilly in the shack. Rob started a small fire in the wood stove and carried in an arm full of limbs and a log from just outside the shack door. "Well, that ought to do you till morning."

When Kate was satisfied that Maria could manage alone, she and Rob returned to the house. For a while, Bette sat up with Kate waiting for Flint. "Maria's got the blues, Bette. I don't know what to do. Paul needs to stay home for awhile, I think."

"Why did she get the 'blues', Ma?" Bette asked, squinting, her eyes dark.

"Changes in the body, I figure. It's from the baby. I had it a little, after Ben. But it went away. She'll be all right. But, I wish Paul would get home. Maybe I should have stayed with Maria until then."

After a couple of hours of mulling worries, Kate and Bette grew weary and went to bed.

In the middle of the night, the truck stopped in the front yard. Kate lay awake. The rusted cab door scraped open, then it slammed shut. In a couple of minutes, the truck continued up the North Slope trail. With Paul finally home to care for his family, Kate thought she might actually get some sleep once Flint was settled in.

Kate lay stiffly. The front door creaked open. Kate focused her eyes on the ceiling of her room while she listened intently. Flint staggered into the house and slammed the front door closed. Swearing obscenities under his breath, his off-balanced footsteps came down heavily and scraped the rough floor. "Son-of-a-bitch," he growled. Walls creaked as he leaned against them along his precarious walk through the dark house.

Kate hadn't moved but continued to listen. As she expected, he was drunk. She closed her eyes, breathing quietly so that her husband would think her asleep as he passed through her room. But he stopped and stood at the end of her bed, breathing laboriously. Sour-wine stench reached her nostrils, and she felt his eyes upon her. After the arduous day with Maria, Kate was in no mood to deal with Flint. Gratefully, he stumbled on his way to the screened-in porch where Rob, Bo, and Donnie slept at the opposite end of the room from their father's bed.

With a crash, Flint's bed plunged to the floor. Kate's eyes opened wide. Her heart hardened. She figured he threw himself upon the bed and passed out. No one got up from a pretentious sleep to find out.

The rooster's crow before dawn woke Kate as always. It was the time of day when no one bothered her. No one needed anything. It was her time. She loved the crack of dawn with the rooster welcoming a brand new day. Moving from bed, she pulled on the trousers and long-sleeved shirt she had worn the day before. Wide-awake by this time, she knew that Flint would be sleeping long into the day after his sousing the previous night.

Walking barefoot to the kitchen, she thought of Flint and the night before. It seemed to Kate that Mother Nature had more brains than humans. Everything had its place, its season, simple and straightforward, with rhyme and reason. Life for her, even up here on this mountain, away from the rest of the world, was complex, as unsure as a small boat without a sail on a large ocean of endless slapping waves. And that part of life, she blamed on Flint, his spitefulness and his drunkenness.

Kate crumpled a sheet of newspaper and, along with small oak limbs, lit a fire in the wood stove and made coffee. She stood watching the day begin, the sun edging ever so easy from behind Mt. McGinny. Thoughts of Wes filled her and warmed her. She felt God's nearness when morning dawned. That was when she asked for Wes' and Jimmy's safe return, gave thanks for all her children and the homestead, and asked for Rob's protection and that he wouldn't have to go to war.

At the end of each prayer, she asked for understanding of Flint, and a way to deal with his anger, his criticism, and his contempt toward her and sometimes toward the kids. She wanted to be happy and unafraid of him, but instead dreaded his every return to the homestead. What she really wished in her heart, but was afraid to ask God, was for Flint to go away and never again return to the homestead.

A vague noise filtered through the morning air, unlike the normal sounds that came from trees, creeks, and mountain. Perhaps it was a coyote. Kate squinted, turned around in the kitchen, and walked to the front room, trying to hear. She heard voices at a distance, yelling and screaming. Paul and Maria. Closer and closer, banging and bouncing, the truck clanked down the rutty road and, from it, an occasional scream ripped through the otherwise beautiful dawn.

In a tizzy to find her shoes and shove her feet into them, she hurriedly slipped them on, then ran out into the front yard. The truck careened around the last corner of the road and slid to a stop in the yard. Maria's head was bent over Tina's small body, wrapped in a blanket and held on the young mother's lap. Paul didn't get out of the driver's seat but from the opened truck window yelled to Kate through anguished cries. "Tina's not breathing. Kate, do something!"

"Get her in the kitchen, Paul, hurry." Kate ran ahead, grabbed a blanket from her bed and returned to the kitchen table. "Lay her here, Paul."

Paul reluctantly placed his infant daughter on the blanket. Maria eased down on the bench with her shoulders hunkered. Kate unwrapped Tina just enough to feel the pulse in her tiny neck. Cold and pale, there was no movement from the child. Perhaps all she needed was warmth. Wrapping Tina snuggly, Kate held her close to her body. "C . . . come to the front of the stove where it's warmer, Paul," Kate stuttered, searching her memory for any similar crisis in her nursing as midwife or medicine woman, anything to spark her memory for the right procedure, the magic touch to save the infant. "Hold her against you, Paul. I'll rub her feet through the blanket." Paul stumbled along much like a mummy with hollowed frightened eyes, fumbling for Tina. Shaking, Kate passed the bundle to him. Maria sat dull and crazed on the bench, her dark hair hung limp about her slumped shoulders.

Bette and Rob came out to the kitchen after hearing the pandemonium. Not knowing how to wake the infant child, Kate said, "We'd better take her in, Paul." And to Bette and Rob, "Something's wrong with Tina. I'll go with them." Paul carried Tina, now wrapped in the heavier blanket, and stood by the truck door. Maria followed him. Kate rushed behind them to the truck. She yanked open the rusted door, shoved Maria to the middle of the seat and Paul laid Tina on her lap. Kate squeezed herself in beside Maria before slamming the door.

Once on the road, Paul drove like a crazed man. Kate checked Tina as well as she could, without removing her from Maria's tight grasp. The baby was still cold. Her once pink-tinged cheeks faded ghostly white. Nothing Kate ever learned about nursing could have saved this dead baby. She couldn't bring back this infant child and it broke her heart.

As Paul pressed down harder and harder on the accelerator, Kate couldn't keep quiet any longer. "Paul, please slow down. It won't do a bit of good if we run off into the canyon. What happened to her? Did she smother? What?" Kate hated to ask, dreaded to say anything to either of these distraught parents. She felt woozy from sadness at the possibility of losing Tina.

Paul's response was not decipherable, but a jumble of words and pleas to God. His mind seemed to have been thrown into a deep well and was reaching for spindly threads to pull himself out. He prayed that he was having a nightmare that would bolt him out of bed and life would go on as it had been the day before. Then, between raspy sobs, he tried to explain to Kate what had happened to Tina.

"Tina just didn't wake up like she usually does about four o'clock. When I checked her just a few minutes ago, she was . . . she was cold, Kate," Paul cried shaking his head. "I picked her up. She didn't move, didn't wake up. Oh, God, don't let my Tina die." Somehow, her poor brother kept the truck on the road, wiping tears from his reddened face with his shirtsleeve as he carelessly maneuvered down the mountain.

It seemed to take forever to get to the hospital. When a sympathetic elderly doctor examined Tina, he informed Paul and Maria that their baby girl had died of pneumonia. Maria was traumatized into shock. The doctor gave Paul some pills for her.

"Be sure she doesn't have access to the bottle of pills. I'm afraid she might end her life in such a depressed state of mind," the doctor said. He placed his arm over Paul's slumped shoulders in a moment of silent compassion before leaving. The three of them waited, stunned, standing by the bed where Tina's small body lay. A stone-faced nurse came in after awhile and rolled the bed away. Tina was gone.

Paul tried desperately to think. He decided that after they returned home, Maria should stay the night with Kate. Tomorrow, Paul and Maria would leave for town, to tell Maria's family the dreadful news, and then Mom and Pop. He couldn't bear to tell them right now. How Kate felt for all of them. Together, Mom and Pop, Paul and Maria, and Maria's family, would arrange the infant's funeral.

When Kate walked into her house a few hours later, Bette had put the noon meal on for her brothers. They had eaten and the outdoor chores were done. Now they were waiting for the truck to leave in the afternoon for the supplies Flint didn't bring the day before. Darkness encircled Bette's eyes from crying throughout the day with sadness and worry for Tina. Bette took Maria's limp hand and led her to her small bedroom at the back of the house, and put her to bed.

Rob and Bo hugged Paul and cried with him. They walked, arms around shoulders, the three men, to Paul's shack. Rob would stay with Paul awhile. Bo and Donnie would drive in for supplies. Dale and Ben stood around, peering at the grown ups. Finally, they got on Jackson together and rode off toward the North Slope.

Kate peeked in on Flint, still an unconscious zombie lying cockeyed on the broken bed. A half-bottle of Gallo lay on the floor. Sneaking quietly, she took up the bottle, sat down on the floor at the end of Flint's bed and swigged on the sour wine until the bottle was nearly emptied. The brevity of Tina's precious life stunned her. Her grieving heart gave in to free-flowing tears.

Perhaps she had made a mistake during the birthing that caused injury to the baby. She should have insisted that Paul fetch Doc Laraby when Maria refused to go in for her checkup. Kneeling for the birth may have been the wrong procedure for Maria. She would have given birth just as quickly lying on the bed. Kate desperately wished she had kept Maria and Tina with her in the house a few days longer after the birth where it was warmer. Oh God, this shouldn't have happened. Kate's self-incrimination swirled in her head with the cheap wine. "What could I have done to save Tina? I don't know, I don't know," she cried.

Kate didn't give a damn if Flint woke to find her a useless servant. She couldn't have saved Tina any more than she could save her failing marriage. She wanted to beat Flint until he woke up and looked at her . . . really looked at her. Instead, she gulped down the rest of the cheap Gallo, leaned her head against the broken bed, wondering what she could do to make life right and where she should go from here.

CHAPTER—35

ROB THE MAN

Adding to Kate's grief about Tina, Kate had lost Maria, her only friend on the mountain. Soon after Tina's death, Paul and Maria decided it was best to move back to town, closer to her family. After another few weeks, Paul found work in the shipyard. Maria was pregnant again. They promised to visit the homestead often.

The war raged on for yet another fearful nine months. Since Rob had turned seventeen years old, Kate realized that her worst fears were about to materialize. Flint and Kate talked in private about Rob and war while everyone else slept. They sat at the square oak table late at night, lamp lit, to face the awful idea that Rob might have to go to war. They talked about it when they drove together to the market, leaving Bette in charge at the house. They talked about it standing in the yard under the shade of the oak. They talked about it until Kate grew sullen and refused to discuss it any more.

And now, it was such a hot sultry summer and Flint spent much of his days struggling to walk, rain or shine. It seemed that his condition worsened by the year. Kate felt empathy for him as he walked heavily from the radio under the pole barn, to the avocado trees where he irrigated, changing the hose from one tree to the next until all the trees were watered in one day. Flint seemed to have changed since the death of the baby. Kate couldn't put her finger on it, but something seemed different about him. She had an inkling that he blamed himself in some way for the baby's death just as she had blamed herself.

Dale and Ben were good help with watering. It was their chore now, but when Flint seemed thoroughly agitated, as lately, he worked hard, groaning and swearing, while he sent the two younger boys off to work the gopher traps. Lately, Rob, Bo, and Donnie often went to market for Flint, glad to get away from the homestead for a few hours.

But this day in particular, Flint seemed more agitated than usual, keeping himself constantly busy. Flint and Rob had some discussions over the last few days. Kate saw them together more than once, heads bent in serious talk. It was war talk, Kate figured. She'd noticed them in the yard together as she went about her chores. They never had much to say to each other until now. Over the years, Rob never took patience with Flint's snappish attitude, and he made it known that he believed that no one in the family, even if they did wrong, deserved to be yelled at or criticized, much less knocked down with a mean fist. Kate suspected her husband used his mean fist now and then. She had experienced some of his meanness herself. It was obvious to Kate that Rob and his father had never been close. She didn't blame Rob, but it was a shame that saddened her. Rob was a man now, and other than the discourse between he and his father, Kate couldn't have asked for more in a son. He had a mind of his own, but Kate sensed more.

Today, Rob hung around the house. Kate dreaded asking him what was on his mind for she figured that he was waiting for the right moment to tell her of his decision to enlist. She didn't want to hear about that nonsense. From a distance, Kate saw Rob and Bette talking grim-faced in the yard. She saw them concerned and sad, and she noticed Bette's moist face when she walked through the room.

Many of the young men in the valley had already gone into the military; Smith, Meza, Hallenbeck. As soon as they were of age, off they went. No, Kate didn't want to hear the inevitable, that her eldest, dearest child was ready to take the responsibility of a full-grown man at seventeen. It wouldn't surprise Kate if Rob enlisted, but she wondered how this great country could ask, or even allow, a seventeen year old to protect it.

Maybe Rob convinced somebody that he was eighteen years old, which was too young at that. This leaving at such an early age was just some crazy notion that the country demanded. Helpless to stop it, Kate stomped around, scowling.

How could she keep from going crazy; keep her heart beating if it happened? Kate stood at the sink. She gulped and pressed her hands against her rib cage, moved in front of the sink and began scrubbing on the oatmeal pot. She continued to question everything. War! There had always been some war somewhere in the world. She learned that over the years. But why?

In such a large world, surely there was enough of everything to go around. Work a little, farm, grow a little food, eat, raise children, love. What else could one want? Didn't everyone have at least what she had? Life seemed strange and cruel. And the longer Kate lived, the less she understood. No, she couldn't accept what was happening with Rob. Kate knew as well as everyone else, Rob had no choice. It just made everything seem more right if he was eager to jump into disaster. It just made those grown men in charge feel less guilty. Kate huffed out a breath of disgust, but it didn't rid her of the razor-sharp ache in her chest.

Bo and Donnie stood out in the front yard while Flint entered the kitchen behind Rob. Kate watched as he eyed Rob, who now stood with his hands on his hips, his head down. Rob must have known that he couldn't put it off any longer. Now he must say the most difficult thing of his life to her, and she was supposed to receive it with some kind of grace. Kate waited, numb with sorrow.

"Mom, I'll be leaving now. Don't really know how to say it, Ma. I wanted to tell you sooner, but just couldn't. My time's up." Rob's head stayed bent, his eyes down. "My bag is ready, not much I need to take." His magnificent blue eyes finally met Kate's. "Listen, Ma, I'll be goin' to school, radio school. I'll be safe and learning something new. It's okay, Ma. Dad's driving me in. I won't be back for awhile."

Kate crushed the tail of her apron with both hands, knuckles whitened. She reached at Rob, clutched him, touching his shirt, patting his arm. How to keep him, to make him stay . . . to hide him here in the mountains and pretend there was no war, or to make him see that it was all devil's work. Rob tried his best to sound convinced about radio school. Maybe he believed the cock-and-bull story the Navy tried to feed him. But there was no fooling Kate. She and most everyone else knew that he'd be in the middle of the war right after radio school. Foolishness! Just the same, she couldn't make him stay. No crying until later. She let go of his shirtsleeve. Rob already had the world on his shoulders, and she was exhausted from fighting the inevitable.

"Remember what I said, son," Flint reminded Rob gruffly. "What ever you do, don't let them put you on a submarine."

Rob nodded, holding Bette's hand as he led her to the yard. Kate followed behind Flint as he hobbled out the door behind Rob and Bette. Rob turned around in the yard to face his family. "Going to meet with Wes after radio school. He's put in a request for me. I'll tell him you said hello, and . . . and all."

"You take care of yourself, son. I know you have to go." Kate's voice quivered as Rob pulled her close to him and she leaned her head against his solid, comforting chest. A wave of desperation swept through her. Dale and Ben slipped quietly into the yard and stood sullen-faced behind their dad. They looked up with innocent eyes and fidgeted with their harmonicas. Bo seemed to have his eyes closed as he stood close to Donnie, his shoulders hunched, his arms folded. Donnie nervously looked to the ground while he made designs in the yard dust with the toes of his boots.

Rob kissed Dale and Ben on their ears. "I love you all. Now be good, and watch out for those gopher holes." He tousled the hair on Donnie's head and looked straight at him. Don't go stickin' your hands down in 'em. Rattlesnakes get down in there, remember?"

Rob faced Bette. "I'll miss you, Sis." They hugged each other's thin bodies for a minute before Rob let her go to grab Bo's hand and shake it. Bo cringed. How do brothers say good-by when they know they'll most likely never see each other again? Rob pulled Kate to him again, hugging her tightly. "I love you, Ma." He turned his wet eyes away from her, grabbed the satchel that sat on the ground, and got in the truck.

"He's just a kid," Kate whispered. She stood in the hard dirt yard with the remainder of her children. "We'll be right here, Rob," she said loudly before he shut the truck door. He nodded back to her. No one smiled as they stood waving while Rob drove away with Flint.

CHAPTER–36

LIGHTS OUT

Two months after Rob left, Flint came home from buying supplies at the Spring Valley market. When he was alone in the room with Kate he said, "Kate, I heard from Jake Anderson at the market that the Smith boy was killed somewhere on the Coral Sea." Flint wanted to cry, but decided to be brave for his wife and waited for her reaction.

Kate sat down weakly, bent over her lap, and put her paled face in her apron. "Oh, God, that poor family. He has a family, children. Flint, why don't you go see those folks?"

"I will Katie, I will." Flint placed his hand on Kate's shoulder, his voice husky. She stood and he pulled her close. "Rob'll be back. Life is rough for us right now, Katie, but I'll try to help you more. You know Rob had to go." Flint patted Kate gently on the back, still holding her close. "I would have gone in his place if they would've let me. I'm sorry, Kate."

Flint caught a flash of surprise on Kate's face as she looked at him. He realized it was the first time he'd ever told her that he was sorry about anything. He was sick that Rob had gone to war, and he knew she was at the edge of her endurance, numb with grief. They stood with their foreheads touching for a few minutes, mourning for the Smiths'. Mourning for the way life was right now.

In the days ahead, Flint figured that the family would simply go through the motions of surviving and wait. He made several trips each day to the pole barn and the radio to listen for any news about the war. When it was announced that there was a possibility of San Diego being bombed or invaded, he decided not to worry Kate about it. She was so irritable lately, he was sure to get his head bitten off. The Navy base would be the target, of course, but it was all too near Mt. McGinny, as far as Flint was concerned. These days, no good news ever came from the radio, and Flint wasn't naive enough to expect it for sometime down the road.

As Flint wondered how he should prepare for a possible invasion or bombing, the radio blared a warning to keep lights off so that any enemy plane that should sneak in during the night couldn't find its intended target. Flint could no longer avoid telling Kate. He clinched down on his pipe stem and took his time getting back to the house.

When he got to the door, Flint noticed Kate standing in front of the stove, spoon in hand. He grasped the edge of the door casing and pulled his aching body up from the step and into the room. "Katie, I sure as hell don't want to scare you, but it would be a good idea not to light the lamps at night. Just in case, you know."

"Just in case what? Flint, what are you talking about now?" Slamming her stirring spoon in the pot of beans, she whipped around from the stove. "Ain't much chance anybody comin' up on this hill."

"Now, Katie, don't get your dander up." Flint was already sorry that he said a word, but he had to tell her the urgent message. "The news just came that an enemy plane could sneak over to the coast some night, to the Navy base. If all lights are off, they can't spot us, now can they?"

"Well, I don't know how they could see the puny flicker from these kerosene lamps, Flint." With her hands on her hips for a time, Kate grew thoughtful. "Well, I suppose it's a good idea. But, I have to light the lamps. I'll just cover the windows with gunny sacks at night."

Flint spied Dale and Ben standing beside the open kitchen door. They had heard and stood looking at each other, fidgeting with their harmonicas. What hell for little children to live with. They were afraid because he and Kate were afraid. They were fearful because their brother left with tears in his eyes, and they knew he might never come home again. They were fearful because of the radio blasting news of ships being blown apart, of men dying. And now, invasion or bombs right in the nearby city. Flint didn't have any words of reassurance for the little boys. "God help us," Kate mumbled when she saw the boys standing there in the doorway. Flint nodded.

Lately, Flint noticed Kate looking at the newspaper and the gruesome photos in some of the magazines he had left laying around. What the news said was probably true, and Flint figured that Kate's common sense would tell her that if Pearl Harbor could be bombed or invaded without warning, San Diego could be invaded before anyone knew it, too. She looked toward the door where the boys stood. When they moved out of hearing range, she said, "Even up here on this mountain, twenty miles out of San Diego, we're not safe, Flint." Then she sat down on the bench, bent over, and sobbed into her apron. Flint placed his hand on her shoulder. "Now look here, Katie, we're gonna be safe and sound here. No call for worry." Flint hoped he sounded convincing, and was relieved when Kate shook her head in agreement.

A cargo plane roared overhead, the same time it did everyday. Flint watched helplessly as Dale and Ben ran through the house, heading for safety under their cots.

CHAPTER—37

MINCEMEAT

It was in the fall of '44 and the dreadful war raged on. Except for Rob and Bo, the other children were in school. It was their turn to trudge to the bus stop two miles down the mountain, and then take the twelve-mile bus ride to El Cajon and back every day, for the remainder of their school years.

Kate lifted the last batch of tomatoes from the canner and gently set them on the counter to cool, as she thought about the children.

Donnie was old enough now at thirteen years to do most of the hunting, and often took the Winchester rifle from its perch above the door. He walked up Mt. McGinny after school an hour earlier to hunt fallow deer, a chore that he had always loved. Some nice fat venison on the supper table would be a welcome change from beans. Kate hoped to make mincemeat, too.

Bo was usually with Flint, helping with haying, or marketing melons and avocados in Spring Valley, El Cajon, and at the nearby junction. They found a good buy on a Ford truck with a flatbed that would hold more produce, and Bo proudly drove the truck now himself. He had gone to school but quit when the war started, unable to justify being away from the truck farm even for school. Besides, as the report cards indicated, he could read faster and with more comprehension than any student in his grade. And now, Bo said that he was distracted anyway, worried about Rob's safety.

The last letter Rob wrote, he didn't have much to say. She intended to read his letter again after her canning equipment was put away. Life had to be dismal on a submarine with potential enemies hanging around overhead. For the life of her, Kate couldn't understand how Rob ended up on a submarine when Flint warned him against it. Kate and Bette talked about it into the night many times, and they agreed that Rob was telling his family, especially his father, in his own way, that he was a man now. He had a mind of his own and could make his own decisions. But still, Kate wondered, why place himself in so much danger. And why didn't Wes stop him? Maybe Rob felt safer with Wes, even on a submarine. As Kate wiped off the counter she tried not to think about how frightened Rob must be.

Bette helped Kate every day after school. In the fall, Kate was overwhelmed with canning the garden produce, venison, and mincemeat. And now, this late afternoon, Bette gathered potatoes, onions, and winter squash to dry in the sun for winter storage in the dugout behind the house.

Kate put away her canning equipment for the day and brought the pot of pinto beans to heat, made cornbread, sliced tomatoes and avocados, and set the table for supper.

She stood near the kitchen door when she heard Donnie holler to Bette as he trudged down from the north trail. "Got a doe, a nice one. Back strap for breakfast, Bette." Kate walked to the front yard. She watched as Bette dropped her vegetables on the ground to join Donnie as he strutted to the house. He carried the good-sized doe over his shoulder. Its hooves hung to the ground. Bette shouted, "Good work, Donnie. Didn't even take you an hour."

Since Flint and Bo had not yet returned from town, Kate helped Donnie and Bette hang the deer by the hind legs in a distant oak. Donnie skinned and cleaned it, with Dale and Ben beside him, helping to pull the furry skin off and watching their brother's every move.

"Lots of fat, Ma, good suet for mincemeat. Got any apples on hand?

"That's gonna hafta wait till morning. No school tomorrow, so Dale, you and Ben run up to the orchard in the morning. Right early. Fill up a bushel basket while Bette and I get the venison and jars ready. We'll start in the cool of the morning." Sweat beaded on Kate's forehead from the effort of helping hang the deer. "Then we'll grind the venison and suet, except the back strap . . . tomorrow though. Not up to starting now. Canning mincemeat takes a whole day. Gonna have supper and go to bed first."

After the deer was completely skinned and cleaned, Dale and Ben drug the skin, head, and innards up the North Slope trail and threw it in the canyon for hungry coyotes, buzzards, and other wild animals.

Flint brought a letter from Rob and Wes when he and Bo returned from town. There had been no letter for three weeks and Kate suffered with worry. She quickly read the letter aloud to Flint, and read it again as she stood before the family when they gathered around the table for supper.

The letter said that there were signs of an end to the war. Too bad, they said, that it couldn't end as WWI, with so many people in the entire world ill from influenza that there was no one left to fight. But, Kate knew it wasn't so for this war. There were plenty of soldiers left in the world, some to kill, some to be killed. Possibly her son and the man she loved.

In the letter, Wes asked about the guitar and Kate's learning. Rob sent his love. Kate dared to believe that they would come home soon. She laid the letter aside and they ate supper with little talk.

The next morning, Bo and Flint left with produce to sell at the junction. Bette and Kate each tied their hair back with a red bandana. Bette cleaned the morning dishes and hooked a grinder to the edge of the large oak table. Then she set a tub on the bench to catch the grindings. She began grinding the venison meat and suet that Kate had cooked and cooled earlier that morning. Next she ground a few tangy oranges with their peelings, while Kate chopped the apples that Dale and Ben brought in. Kate dumped them in with the raisins, oranges, spices, and the venison and suet, all tossed together in the tub.

Bette left the kitchen to water the garden as soon as she had finished her grinding chore.

Since sugar was rationed because of the war, Kate had saved some back for the mincemeat, and poured what sugar she had into the tub. She set the Brandy on the counter. Flint had brought it earlier that month, in anticipation of her next batch of mincemeat. She liked to use Brandy for preserving the mincemeat, but especially for the taste, and the sweet wine made up for the lack of sugar. Kate licked her lips. Brandy made it special for holidays, and this batch of mincemeat would be used for baking pies, tarts, and cookies for this next Thanksgiving and Christmas. The folks would come with Paul, Maria, and their beautiful daughter Libby, on Thanksgiving Day. Kate could hardly wait to see Libby again, already two years old. Kate took a whiff of the aroma of holidays; sweet apples and spicy cinnamon.

As Kate chopped apples, thoughts of Wes and Rob filled her heart and mind. A tear made its way to the corner of her eye. Weary of holding back the wailing that bubbled up inside her, years of accumulated frustration and anger, boiling to the surface, she allowed a single tear to fall. She was afraid though, if she let it out, she would sob uncontrollably and would never stop.

A full day of canning loomed ahead of her, and she felt edgy. Not that she minded canning, but she felt on edge and ragged because of the long, drawn-out, never-ending war.

The window above the sink counter was open. A westerly breeze filtered through and helped cool the room while she stood over the hot stove, sterilizing jars in the canner. Water boiled and bubbled in a small pan, plinking lids and rings together.

Kate mulled over Flint's idea that he could double or triple the produce and increase their income as much if he farmed more usable land, flat, bottomland, such as Mrs. Helm's. He and Mrs. Helm had talked of him leasing her land, moving the family to the big house, where there would be more room and the convenience of electricity. Life might be easier there. Flint hadn't insisted yet, and Kate struggled with the idea.

Any fears she might have had in the past about Flint and Mrs. Helm were gone. If Mrs. Helm was serious about leasing the house and land to Flint, she certainly wouldn't be staying there, even during the summer months . . . or would she? At that dubious thought, Kate sprinkled more cinnamon over the mixture.

Moving to and fro, she set up the clean jars on the counter. Her hands began to shake and she clumsily hit the bottle of Brandy, knocking it over. She opened it and sniffed the strong, sweet alcoholic wine. Tasting a bit with her tongue, it melted the hardness from her throat. She tasted it again. Then she chopped and stirred, adding just a bit of Brandy to the mixture in the tub. The concoction tasted tangy and sweet. After another sip of Brandy, Kate relaxed.

She loved to can mincemeat and began humming songs that she and Wes had sung. She hummed and chuckled, feeling dizzy. With measured slowness, she tipped the bottle again, holding it so that it dribbled into her mouth.

The jars were ready, sterilized and setting on a clean towel on the counter. Kate scooped the rings from the bubbling water with a long-handled spoon and laid them beside the jars.

She giggled, remembering how Wes gazed at her, his brown eyes twinkling. When Wes was with her, she thought about herself as a person; she felt important. And now, how she missed him, couldn't breath without him, felt dead without him. No, he was not just a family friend. Moisture seeped from her eyes. She thought she must be sick, oh God, not pregnant? No, that was impossible. It had to be the Brandy. It tasted good and she wanted to be free from worry.

Today was the first time since Pearl Harbor that she felt any happiness. She turned the bottle up to her lips. She chopped and stirred. Now she knew she wasn't following the recipe. She had lost her place and had forgotten just what she threw into the tub. So she added Brandy to the mixture, shaking the bottle until it was empty. When she was sure there wasn't a drop left, she flung the bottle across the room where it crashed against the pie cupboard and fell to the floor, still in one piece. Gritting her teeth, with trembling hands, she scooped another cup of raisins. She dumped the raisins over the mixture and then banged the cup several times against tub. It looked like enough mixture for several jars of mincemeat, enough for pies and tarts and cookies, enough to last the winter. She tested it with the tip of her tongue. Perfect.

The pressure cooker was ready for the jars as soon as they were filled. She stuck a few small logs in the stove. The room was hot, and sweat dripped down Kate's face. Feeling smothered, she nabbed a flour sack dishtowel off the counter and wiped her face. Wadding the towel tightly in her fist, she slammed it down on the counter. Nothing seemed right. Rob and Wes were gone. Flint didn't love her. She'd failed to achieve the career that the Medicine Man foretold. She was stuck on Mt. McGinny. She leaned against the counter for a moment to gather her wits. Now, the next step was to fill the jars. She pulled the spicy concoction closer to her.

As tears began to slide down her hot face, Kate began filling the jars by setting the funnel in a wide-mouth jar. A dipper of the mixture missed the jar and fell on the cast iron. Burned mincemeat filled her nostrils. Kate dropped the dipper in the tub of mincemeat and hurried, weaving, to lie down on the bench. Blackness surrounded her. She called out to Donnie and Bette.

Donnie jogged through the yard on his way to the pump. Thankfully, he heard her call, for although she heard him pass through the yard, soon after, he returned with thudding feet to the kitchen. Donnie stuck his head in the kitchen door. "What'd ya' need, Ma?"

Donnie was quick thinking and witty. Kate knew that he would soon figure out, from the sight of her laying face down on the bench and the smell of sweet liquor mingling with the spicy fragrance floating in the kitchen, what had happened.

"Damn it, Mom. Don't you know what that Brandy does to ya? Come on. Let me help you to bed."

Although Kate said she was willing to go, she hung there limp as a rag, arms hanging to the floor, ashamed but unable to move.

"No, no, Donnie. You go on. Leave me alone. I'm gonna finish canning in just a minute. I'm tired. I'm just tired," Kate slurred.

Donnie tromped to the stove where the tub of mincemeat sat. He then flashed back across the kitchen to the door and yelled out. "Bette! Bette! Hey, can you come down here?" Kate heard disgust in his young voice.

As Bette hurried in out of breath, Donnie yelled again. "Can you help me finish canning this mincemeat? Ma's been nipping on the Brandy and she's drunk on her ass."

Kate didn't feel much discomfort as she lay there face down on the bench, but Donnie gently lifted her head and slid a potholder under her cheek where her face mashed against the hard wood.

Bette scurried across the kitchen floor to the stove alongside Donnie. The kids had helped Kate can mincemeat before, and even in Kate's Brandy-soaked haze, she knew they could finish her job. Kate's eyes opened a slit, and she saw Bette peek around at her. Bette gave her a quizzical look. "Poor Ma," Bette said, and lifted a ladle of mincemeat to the funnel. "Donnie, look in that Kerr Canning Book there. We need to know how many minutes these jars stay in the pressure cooker."

"Says seventy five minutes at ten pounds pressure. Jeez, we're gonna be at this for days. Poor Ma, hell! Poor us, Bette."

The kids giggled as Kate watched them through the dim of her eyelashes, still unable to move her body.

"Have you touched that Brandy, Bette?" Donnie choked out." I told you not to. You see what happens? Look at you." Laughter contorted his face. He wasn't helping his sister much.

"Hush, Donnie, and get to work." Bette gave him the order with a serious face. Donnie leaned on the counter, giggling at his sister's act of dictatorship.

Sometime later, they got their outbursts of laughter under control. Kate hoped they might at least get serious enough about canning the mincemeat to check the pressure cooker gauge and regulate the heat beneath it. Otherwise, the cooker might blow up in their faces. They finished the sweltering job, leaving some of the cleanup work, and went outside. Kate forced herself up off the bench after lying dulled for over two hours. She washed her hands and face and then fixed the noon meal, not quite trusting what she might do next.

CHAPTER – 38

RUNNING SCARED

The day that Kate canned mincemeat, Flint and Bo drove to the market to sell produce. When they returned just before suppertime, Flint stepped from the truck and Dale ran up to him with wide blue eyes. "Dad, Ma got soused today. Ask Donnie and Bette. They know." And, as if afraid he'd be pinned down to tell more, Dale disappeared around the corner of the house as quickly as he'd arrived.

Flint was shocked to hear what Dale had said, and cocked his head to think more clearly. Soused, Dale had said. Only the one time, after the death of Tina, had he'd known of Kate drinking. He'd found her asleep on the floor by his bed with the empty wine bottle.

Flint moved away from the truck and noticed Donnie amble down the South Slope trail with the milk bucket, full and foamy. Limping quickly toward Donnie, Flint intended to talk with him before he got any closer to the house. Things were bad enough. Kate didn't need to know that he questioned the children about her.

When he reached Donnie, Flint said, "Set the bucket down a minute Donnie. We need to talk."

Donnie carefully set the milk bucket down on the sloping ground and looked at Flint. Apprehension flashed across Donnie's young face.

"Your Mom sick today, Don?"

Donnie rubbed his arms. "Well, Dad, she said she was tired."

"You all make mincemeat?"

"Yeah, me and Bette helped."

As they stood there in the early evening breeze, Flint figured that Donnie was the best person to talk to about Kate. He was not likely to hide the truth if pressed. Flint narrowed his eyes. "She drank that Brandy, Don?"

"Some, I guess," Donnie responded protectively. "Hell, Dad, she's worried to death about Rob. Got no friends, nothing pretty like I see other women wearing. I mean, that's not your fault . . . I guess." Donnie bit his lip and he looked down at his bare feet.

"Alright Don, let's get on down to the table."

At the supper table, Flint eyed Kate thoughtfully. Lately she hadn't prattled on with the children, as she used to do, about their school day or anything else. She simply went on about the business of getting food on the table. Bo ate quickly in silence and left the table after supper to clean out the truck. With few words, Kate methodically helped Bette clean up the dishes. Donnie sheepishly headed for the porch and his books while Flint sat at the table with his pipe. Dale and Ben sat beside him, unusually still. Whatever had been going on with Kate was affecting the children, too. He figured he'd better talk with Kate's folks about the change in her before anything else happened.

The next morning, lining up a day's work for Bo at the homestead, Flint left for a private talk with Kate's parents.

When he arrived at the folk's in Bonita, Mom was hanging clothes on the line at the back of their small cottage. When she saw Flint, she called to Pop in his garden where he knelt down on the ground inspecting a tomato plant. The elderly couple greeted Flint, guiding him to the porch, eager to hear the latest about the family.

Over the last two years, the folks had become completely white headed and now walked with bent backs. It was obvious to Flint that little Tina's death had nearly pushed them both over the edge, and now, with Rob at war, they seemed to have aged further.

The three of them settled down in wicker chairs under the shade of the neat back porch. Mom brought coffee and they sat together sipping on their mugs. Flint knew he had to dig up the courage to face the reprimand he had coming. "Kate's worn out, Jep. I'm worried that she's headed for a nervous breakdown." Flint waited for a response before he revealed more of his concern. Fear crossed Mom's face. She immediately glanced at Pop.

After a long silence, Pop was the first to speak. "We could bring her here for a spell, but I don't suppose she'd come."

"It'd be good if she could see Rob," Flint said, "but I'm not sure if she can hold out."

Mom, in her quiet but explicit way, said, "You all getting' along, Flint? Why, I mean, you all sleepin' in the same room yet?"

"No. No. She's got something else on her mind. She's afraid, I imagine. Can't take care of the youngsters she already has. Doc told her not to have any more."

Pop intervened. "Flint, it's yer' drinking that bothers her. She can't get close to you the way ya' are. You know . . . the inside of ya'. She wants yer heart." Pop's lip trembled. "Needs to know ya' love 'er, ya' know. Damned near all women need to know that. Got ta' mend the trust. You'll lose her for sure, Flint, if you don't get some help for your habit. Mark my word." Pop hunched his worn-thin shoulders.

Mom shook her head in agreement. That's just what she would have said, and Flint knew it. They were right. He'd have to get help. The thought of quitting alcohol made him physically ill. It wasn't a matter of just wanting to quit anymore. He was hooked. He was addicted to alcohol, alcohol of any kind.

Flint needed a smoke. Shaking, he clumsily fixed his pipe. He sat in silence with Mom and Pop for a few minutes, pulling on the pipe now and then, mulling over the facts. The people he trusted and respected most in the world, Pop, Mom, and Mrs. Helm, all told him the same thing. He'd have to face his problems or lose Kate. He'd lose Mom and Pop and Mrs. Helm, too, if he didn't get a grip on himself. Everyone he trusted and respected would give up on him. Suddenly, he grew frightened at the prospect.

Preoccupied, Flint had forgotten to puff and pull on the tobacco. The fire went out in his pipe and he frowned. "Well, folks, I know of a place," Flint finally admitted. "I've been doing some research. There's a hospital up north. Requires a month's stay. I've been puttin' off leaving home with all the work there is now, and the war . . . but the kids can take care of the homestead. I'll go soon. Rob might get home beforehand. Hate like hell leavin' Kate in her state of mind, but things aren't getting any better."

Flint rose from the wicker chair and placed his hand on Pop's shoulder. He patted the old man, and then dared to face his mother-in-law.

"Let us hear from ya' Flint," she said.

CHAPTER—39

An Intruder

Just as Kate might have expected, as soon as Flint got wind of her giving out on the bench during mincemeat canning, he drove down the mountain the next morning without telling her why. He was gone all day. He was up to something, but it didn't matter any longer. She had other plans.

In the last few weeks, Kate realized that her hands trembled, a constant slight shaking. She felt that if she didn't get the guts to follow at least one of her dreams, and if her son didn't come home from the war soon, she'd have a nervous breakdown.

Rob and Wes' letters arrived several days or weeks after they wrote. Sometimes two or three letters came on the same day. They never gave detail of what was happening. Kate and Flint agreed that Rob probably had orders not to give any information about the war, neither would he admit being petrified with fear. Wes probably couldn't say, or wouldn't say what he knew. They were still together on the same submarine, the 'Luzon', somewhere out there in the ocean. Knowing Wes was close to Rob provided some relief for Kate.

It was late fall and Kate worked from sunup until sun down just to keep busy. She went to sleep every night, exhausted from worry after two years of Rob at war. There was nothing to do but wait for letters and pray for the end of it. Thanksgiving wasn't far off, and she hoped to at least see the folks again on that day.

Flint worked off and on with Bo and Shep in the hay fields where they had gone to work early that morning. Shep was terrific at guarding for rattlers and even went searching the hay field for them. "Beyond the call of duty," Bo said of Shep. The three of them slept in a barn near the hay field, sometimes working a few days at a time before heading home during the slow season at the homestead.

Kate was grateful for the extra money that the work in the hay fields brought. It meant that Bette and the boys had shoes without holes. It meant that if a hole did appear, the shoes were replaced with brand new ones instead of homemade cardboard insoles.

Bette and Donnie were good help on the farm now, and there was nothing more than the usual to fear on the mountain while the men were away, but still it was a good idea to latch and push the table against the door, at least at night. It worried Kate, though, and she shuddered when Flint told her there was a German or Italian Prisoner of War Camp near the small town of Campo bordering Mexico, thirty miles southeast of Mt. McGinny.

It was silly to worry about it though, since she kept the Winchester just under the edge of her bed on the floor at night. The shells lay under her mattress, an arm's length away. Now at bedtime, she slipped her hand under the mattress and brought the shells out, laying them on the floor beside the rifle.

Kate was uneasy and anxious to get Rob and Wes home. Sometimes she felt Wes' kiss linger on her lips as she came up out of a sweet dream in the dawn's misty morning, a kiss that she could only imagine, a kiss that happened only in her dreams. She prayed for Wes, right along with her prayers for Rob, and waited for their letters. Worn from concerns for them, she felt old.

She lay wide-eyed, listening. Crickets and frogs sang their usual songs and, coyotes yelped their way across the hills, then were quiet once again. She wished for Shep, but Flint and Bo surely needed the dog in the hayfields more than she needed the dog at the homestead. Besides, Shep wasn't worth a darn without Bo. Flint hadn't found another dog to replace Brownie.

Kate mentally planned for the following day, dozed, with thoughts intruding again and again. Tossing restlessly, she questioned and wondered about things without needing or expecting answers. Her mind sometimes felt dusty as the fields in a hard summer wind. She needed deep sleep, a rest from the inner turmoil.

She dozed again, for a moment it seemed, before she startled. She'd heard a scraping noise. Perhaps she dreamt it. Maybe the wind was blowing a loose board somewhere on the house. She was awake now. The men must be back and trying to push the table away from the kitchen door. As always, the other entrance door for the front room was well secured at night.

Kate rose up on her elbow. The men knew to push hard on the kitchen door, push a flat stick through the crack and raise the latch before shoving the table back. Just the same, her heart quickened. "Flint, Bo, that you?" her voice choked out. The house fell silent. Something wasn't right. She hadn't heard the truck. And they always talked to each other or called out to her to let her know when they came home. "Oh, dear God!" her raspy whispers followed along with shallow breathing. Fear engulfed her, reminding her of the old man with the hat, years ago, who violated their peaceful homestead. By now, Kate's mouth was dry and blood pumped hard through her veins. She was fully awake and her throat tightened. The house creaked. She grappled to fill her lungs.

The table scraped along the floor a little bit more, a little further, far enough for a person to enter. Footsteps paced slowly and deliberately across the kitchen floor. Kate sat up on the edge of the bed, tense. She held her breath and, though trembling, she pulled the Winchester out from under the bed and fumbled for the shells she had placed on the floor earlier. Skillfully, she slipped a few shells in the chamber. The footsteps stopped. "Flint, damnit answer!" Kate yelled in the direction of the kitchen. Her voice crackled with uncertainty. The rifle was ready, lying across her lap, one hand on the stock, her finger twitching close to the trigger.

The house remained silent for some time. Whoever it was could be going around to the back window of the house, or maybe to climb up to the opened back porch, and then creep in toward her and the children. Absolute silence continued except the tick, tick, tick of her bedside clock. She strained to listen for any slight movement. What were they doing in there? And then a creaking door opened; the food storage cupboard. A few seconds passed. The cupboard door closed again. But what if it was Flint or Bo? What if they ran off the road and down into the canyon, and now one of them, injured and crazed, found his way back?

Her mind clouded. *There! There it is again.* She held her breath. Methodical footsteps walking, walking back the other way, the same measured stride in which the steps entered the house. Slowly, slowly then out the door, and a heavy footstep on the hard earth. *They're out. Maybe.* Again she gasped a few breaths of air into her lungs and pressed her fingertips to her mouth.

Kate figured whoever had entered the kitchen might come back. Who could have come in like that? Just tromp right in to somebody's house? Mexicans came across the mountain now and then, stopping in the yard for a drink of water and asking directions. The Mexicans were harmless and gentle folk. Kate sympathized with their plight and they were welcome to whatever they found in the cupboard. But if the person who walked in the house was from the Concentration Camp, they might decide to come back. To do harm, she was sure, though they couldn't know she held a rifle.

With ringing ears perked, she breathed quietly and kept alert through the night, glancing toward the one east window in her room where someone, anyone, could easily break it out and try to enter. The house creaked. But some creaking was usual, with the changes in temperature as the night cooled. Hours passed while Kate sat with the loaded Winchester in her lap, prepared. Her temples throbbed. She listened and waited.

Memories tumbled of that frightful night not long after they arrived at the homestead when she held the rifle for hours on bent knee, waiting for the mountain lion to leap out of the brush, or to drop down from the oak limb on her and her children. This time, though, she was determined not to fall asleep.

For several hours Kate heard no more footsteps, so she laid the rifle on the bed and got dressed. Then she waited.

The night was spent and day breaking when Flint and Bo came home and walked through the open door. Flint's voice reverberated through the house. "What's goin' on here, Katie?"

Kate walked heavily from her bedroom. Her face felt old and drawn. She hadn't bothered to brush her gray-streaked hair that fell around her slumped shoulders. When she reached the kitchen, she unloaded the Winchester and pushed it toward Flint, handing the shells to Bo. Flint took the rifle from her and placed it on the rack above the kitchen door. "Katie, you're scared white as ash. What the hell?"

He waited impatiently for her to explain, questions on his ruddy face. He and Bo moved the table from where it had been pushed away from the door back to its rightful corner with the benches.

"It was just after we all settled down last night." Kate's voice quivered like a wind-blown autumn leaf. "I wasn't asleep yet when somebody opened the door, and pushed that table back, walked across this floor." Kate waved her hand toward the door as she explained. "Sat there on the side of my bed with the rifle till I heard you all come in." Kate finished, at the edge of her endurance. "Who could have done such a thing, Flint?" She walked the kitchen floor, showing Flint and Bo where she thought the steps might have been taken. "Look here, a piece of biscuit on the floor. And a burned match! A Mexican lookin' for shelter, I suppose. Or one of them prisoners from the War Camp." Wearily, she sat down on the bench facing the table and smoothed her worn face with her trembling hands.

"Could have been, Katie," Flint said. He picked the burned match from off the floor in front of the cupboard. "Lit matches to see in the cupboard." Flint gave Kate a concerned glance and slowly walked to the stove. He built a fire and made coffee.

"Don't worry, Ma," Bo said. He sat down beside her on the bench, his long, strong arm encircling her shoulders. "I'm staying next time there's work to be done in the valley. At least until we find another good dog to stay here with you. If Brownie had been by that front step, nobody, I mean nobody, would have been fool enough to come through that door. Oh! Say Dad, we could fix a good lock on the kitchen door same as the one on the front room door, huh? That Concentration Camp is too close in my opinion."

Flint carried his wife and son mugs of coffee. His hands jerked with the rest of him as he moved across the room, but he got to the table without a spill.

Kate felt that she was in a dream, watching her husband wait on her. She saw real concern in his face. Concern for her. She must look as dreadful as she felt. Pressing her hands to her face, she ironed out some of the effects of sitting on the edge of the bed in fear and doing without an ounce of sleep all night.

Bo's eyes had followed his father's unsteady gait, and now he looked at him with a cocked head, "Are you alright, Dad? I don't believe I have ever seen you make coffee, and then to top it off, serve your wife." He grinned, showing his straight white teeth.

"Now, Bo, just cause you're way over six feet tall doesn't mean I can't still whip your ass."

Bo bent over in laughter, his handsome face reddened. "You're right about that, Dad. Thanks for that coffee, but you sit down with it. I'll get my own."

Flint obliged, and they sat around the table with Kate awhile, drinking coffee. For the first time in Kate's adult life, she felt like she might have the makings of a real family.

CHAPTER—40

THE STRIKE

The afternoon following the night of the intruder, Flint and Bo came home early in the afternoon. Immediately, they went to work on the kitchen door. Kate stood watching for a while. Her spirit lifted a bit. They'd lived in the house with that fragile door fastener for fifteen years, and now the men were fixing it with a sturdy store-bought handle and lock set.

When finished, the kitchen door opened and closed and locked properly. The men stood next to each other admiring their handiwork. Kate stepped in front of them and, without a word, she quickly hugged them both at the same time, then walked to the stove to stir the pot of beans.

At the supper table, Donnie told the family that he'd debated with his history class students earlier that day about Columbus discovering America in 1492. The history book was in error, he said, since America had been inhabited with many tribes of Native Americans for thousands of years before Columbus came.

Kate saw that Donnie stood up for what he believed. Flint had told him the truth about Indian heritage, a truth that apparently many young people in school knew nothing about. He had his father's will, certainly not hers.

Finally summer came and with it, youngsters home from school all day. With the fields producing abundantly, work was piled high from daylight to dark. Early in the day, Flint and Bo headed to the south forty to load melons on the sled, which Jackson pulled along at the edge of the field. Kate and Bette followed just to see the plump green watermelons and round golden cantaloupes lying over the field. When they arrived there,

Flint said that the gophers were taking over the melon field and hollered to Dale and Ben to fetch Donnie and his gopher traps.

Kate and Bette had a long, hot day of gathering and canning tomatoes ahead of them, so Kate was anxious to get back to the house. After whistling their amazement at the beautiful melons in the vast field, they tromped back across the dust and clods between the vines, following Dale and Ben.

Donnie let it be known that today he planned to settle down on the porch with the books he had borrowed for the summer, after his chores were done. But now, as Kate and Bette came upon the avocado orchard where Donnie bent over to check the gopher traps, Dale and Ben hopped around watching Donnie's every move. Nothing in the first, the trap was still not sprung. He stuck the trap back in the hole and moved to the next. He yelled out in excitement. "Hey, Ben, Dale, take a look. See guys, this is how it's done." Ben and Dale hunched over Donnie to see the catch.

Donnie emptied the trap of the mangled rodent, throwing it by the tail into the nearby sagebrush. He reset the trap, placing it carefully in the same hole and replaced the stake that kept the trap from being drug down. He sprinted to the next trap, Dale and Ben skipping behind, anxious to see the next mangled gopher. Kate smiled. They had forgotten all about their father's orders to get Donnie and his traps to the south forty.

"Now, wait, did this hole have a trap, or did the darned gopher drag it in? Where's the stake and wire? Maybe this wasn't the hole. Yeah, yeah." The three boys hovered together over the gopher hole. Kate would soon have to spoil their fun and remind them of their father's orders before she and Bette headed for the house. But meanwhile, she and Bette stood on the trail, laughing at the boy's excitement over the mangled gopher, and Donnie showing off his trapping talents. "I bet the stupid rodent got his tail in the trap and pulled it down in."

Kate gulped when she saw Donnie ram his hand deep into the hole. "Donnie, don't!" Donnie screamed, "What the . . . ." Jerking his hand from the hole, he flung himself on the ground away from the rattlesnake. He pressed his right hand between his left hand and his stomach, rolling back and forth on the rough ground. "Run guys, get back. It got me. Ma, Ma," he wailed.

"Donnie got fanged," Dale cried out, his sky-blue eyes round and frightened.

As Kate rushed to Donnie's side, she yelled, "Dale, run! Get Dad from the field. Hurry!" Dale, with Ben close on his heels, ran toward the south forty. Kate skidded, bare-kneed to the ground where Donnie lay shaking on his right side. His face appeared ghostly white and clammy. Bette hurried to the other side of him and kneeled.

Donnie whimpered. "Ma, Ma, that damned snake."

"Put pressure around his wrist, Bette. Here now, I'll take my apron, tie it around. Just a little tight now, so as not to cut his blood off completely," Kate said calmly.

"Am I gonna die, Bette?" Donnie cried.

"Be still, Donnie. Ma's a nurse. She'll fix ya'." Bette comforted him, holding his head up off the graveled ground protecting him from the sticker weeds.

Kate jumped up and headed for the house, then yelled back to Bette. "I'll get a knife. Keep his head up and keep him still."

A desperate wave crashed over Kate, but at least she didn't have to sit by helpless as she had when Tina died. Even though she had no herbs or concoctions used by the Cherokees for snakebites, she knew what to do. Still, Donnie's finger was blue and stiff and swollen.

Kate spied the paring knife on the counter where she had left it in the midst of her plans for canning tomatoes. She grabbed the knife, opened the firebox, and stuck the tip of the knife in the hot orange coals. When she returned to kneel next to Bette, she said, "Hold his hand steady."

Two crossed nicks with her knife on the swollen finger where the snake's fangs had jabbed produced a squirt of blood. Donnie cried out in pain. Kate leaned over the swollen finger and sucked on the tiny incisions, then spit out the venomous blood.

While Kate worked on Donnie, Bo sprinted toward her, shouting ahead, "Ma, do you need help? Should I get the truck ready?"

Kate stopped drawing blood and venom. "Just carry him down first, Bo. I'll work on him as we walk."

Flint and Dale ran side by side, Flint's face showing pain by the time he reached the rest of the tense-faced family. Bo carefully lifted Donnie from the ground and said, "Dad, he's alright, but we should get him to Doc Laraby to make sure."

Flint leaned over, resting his hands on his knees to catch his breath. "I'll get the truck started," he said, as an exhausted Ben reached the group and plopped down on the ground. Flint gave orders. "Bo, you go with me and keep him sittin' up. Dale, you and Ben get Jackson. Lead him down to the yard with the sled." Flint hurried sprite-like down the trail ahead of Kate and the family.

Kate thought that most of the venom was out, but Donnie's finger and hand were still an ugly, puffy blue. Kate kept up a swift pace beside long-legged Bo. She spit now and then, clearing some of the vile taste from her mouth. She sucked more blood and venom and spit again. "You'll be alright, Donnie. Lay still to keep your blood pressure down."

They reached the truck. Kate placed a hand on Bo's shoulder and he turned to her, his brackish teeth showing. "Bo, don't suck that blood out, ya' hear? If you have any decayed teeth, the venom could get in your blood stream and kill you." Kate prayed that Bo would heed her warning. She ran into the kitchen, grabbed two clean flour-sack towels, and ran back to the truck while Bo was getting Donnie settled in the middle of the seat. Shep leaped into the bed of the truck.

"You gonna be alright, Ma?" Bo asked. "You got any bad teeth?"

"No, no bad teeth."

Bo kept inquisitive eyes on Kate while she placed one towel under Donnie's hand, blood oozing from his finger. She handed the second towel to Bo. "Better tie another tourniquet on his upper arm. That swelling is worse. Leave the one on around his wrist. Loosen them one at a time, now and then. Keep his hand below his heart." Clumsily,

Bo tied the towel on Donnie's upper arm as Kate directed. She checked it. "That's just right, Bo."

Kate jumped back out of the way as Bo slammed the truck door shut. Flint shook his head that he was ready to leave. They sped away, out of the yard and up the dirt road, tires bouncing and spinning, gravel and dust flying.

Slowly, Kate limped back to the kitchen, raising her skirt above her knees, which were embedded with gravel and dirt and caked with blood. She poured water from the kettle into the wash pan. Bette followed her. "Oh, good Lord, Mom, you're hurt. Let me do that," she ordered. "Go and sit down."

"Bette, Donnie didn't look good. You saw him, white as a sheet." Kate moaned while she hobbled out of the house to the yard faucet, her daughter behind her.

"Mom, what are you doing? Sit down."

"Forgot to rinse my mouth, Bette. Snake venom." Kate turned the faucet on full force. She bent over and let the water gush in and out of her mouth for a few seconds before turning the faucet off. "Guess I got the most of it out."

Bette led her mother to the kitchen. Kate noticed her daughter's stern attitude. Her dark eyes snapped as her brows knitted together with grownup concern. With Bette's dark hair tied up in that bandana and that look about her, she was the essence of womanhood.

Suddenly, taking a more direct approach with Kate, Bette ordered, "Mom, sit down at the table. I'll fix your knees. Just take a gander at that, Mom, you poor thing. Your knees are caked with gravel, and blood's running down your legs. Hold still now, while I pour more hot water in your pan."

For the next few minutes, Bette gently soaked Kate's knees with a towel, dabbing until the gravel and blood washed away. Kate felt overcome with pride.

Carefully, Bette smoothed ointment on the gravel-pricked wounds, leaving them uncovered. "Mom, let's have coffee. You sit, I'll pour. Coffee's still hot." Bette poured them both a mug of coffee left over from the breakfast pot.

They sat at the table together in silence until Kate said, "Bette, you're a natural nurse. You've got the feel, the compassion."

Bette's eyebrows raised. "Me? You're the nurse, Ma. Or doctor. Just look how you took care of Donnie."

Kate reflected a moment on Bette's remark. Feeling a sense of pride, she realized that she had learned a thing or two, even without proper schooling.

Immediately after the noon meal, the three men drove in before the rest of the family left the kitchen. When Kate heard the truck, she sat a plate, spoon, and fork on the table for each of them, and then met Donnie at the door, leading him to the table.

While Donnie sat on the bench, grinning, Flint exclaimed, "Doc Laraby says we all are lucky. Donnie'll be well in no time. A bite on his face or close to his heart, probably would have been all she wrote." After a moment of silence, he said. "Bo, we better eat a bite and get Jackson unhitched from that sled." Flint eyes surveyed the yard. "Where is Jackson? And the sled?"

Kate watched and listened intently as Dale looked sheepishly at his dad. "Ben and me, we unloaded the sled into the dugout, didn't drop any melons, not a one, and took Jackson to his corral. Sled is over yonder by the dugout."

"Bo, we got ourselves two more damned-good farmhands." Flint patted the boys on their backs.

Listening to the conversation between Flint and Dale, Kate realized that Flint was changing. Changing for the better. She paused, then smiled as she filled their plates.

Bo looked at Kate, worry in his pale blue eyes. "Ma, sure am glad to see you're alright. We should have taken you in with us. You might have needed help too, suckin' all that venom."

"I'm okay. Anyway, we're gonna get a snake bite kit. I've heard there's such a thing."

"Got it right here, Ma. Doc Laraby sent it back with us," Bo said, and pulled the kit from his shirt pocket. He handed it to Kate. "Doc was pretty upset with you, Ma. He sent orders for you to never, never suck snake venom again! Course, Doc said you're a darned good nurse, Ma, and says he has a job for you whenever you're ready."

Kate smiled. Bette turned from the sink. She glanced at Kate with dark eyes that challenged Kate to do what she never had the guts to do. Yes, she had always wanted to be a nurse or doctor. Deep in her heart she knew she hadn't given up that dream. At every turn in her life, she had realized that dream in some way or another. And now that Bette had encouraged her, even challenged her, it was something to think about . . . seriously.

CHAPTER—41

WAR'S END

It was early summer of '45, and Kate hoped that Rob would get home from the war before his birthday. She walked out after breakfast, and stood under the oak in the cool of the morning gazing longingly toward the road. Waiting. Always waiting. Rob would be twenty years old in a couple of weeks. She placed her hands on her belly, remembering when she felt his first kick. Twenty years had gone swiftly.

The news everywhere reflected optimism for the end of the damnable war, and Wes and Rob's letters mentioned that there was hope too. Kate felt a stab of joy at their encouraging words. So Flint and Bo stayed by the radio as much as possible, giving it up only to Dale and Ben, the two cowboys in the family, who couldn't wait for their turn to ride the range with Red Ryder once a week. They made it known that this ritual was more important than any war. The cowboys, no matter where they were on the mountain, raced to the pole barn at the precise time the radio program came on, leaving Kate and the rest of the family mystified at their internal clocks. The boys lay barrels on their sides at the pump house radio, each straddling a barrel, and rolled back and forth on them until Red Ryder rode off into the sage.

The country was out of FDR's capable hands since his death in April, and according to Bo's report around the supper table, only God knew how things would go after the war, if ever there were an end to it.

It was as hot as hell on August 10, when the Ford truck rolled into the yard and Flint jumped out. Kate wondered why he'd come back so early. He entered the kitchen door quicker than usual. Bo was already home and followed in behind his father. Kate sat mugs of coffee on the table.

"Did you hear the news?" Flint asked, oozing excitement. At the same time, he and Bo sat down at the table in front of their coffee. Flint pulled his pipe and Prince Albert out of his khaki shirt pocket and set them on the table.

"Naw, Dad. What? I haven't taken time this morning to listen to the radio."

"Truman bombed the bastards, that's what! Christ. Day or two ago, hell, maybe a week ago, and nobody seemed to learn about it until yesterday, I reckon." Flint shook his head, slurped his coffee, and then he poked tobacco in his pipe.

"What does it mean, Dad? They bombed Japan? We should be seeing Rob any day then!" Bo jumped up glowing, deep laughter in his mature voice. "What do you think, Dad, huh?"

Kate stood with her hands on her hips, confused, but eager to hear Flint's answer to Bo's question. Bette walked in from the front room and sat down at the table with Bo and her father. Her dark eyes darted from her father to Kate, and then to her brother.

"Yeah, Truman bombed Japan. War is sure to be over soon. Rob should be home right afterward." Flint struck a match with his thumbnail and lit his pipe.

Kate frowned. "What are you sayin', Flint?" She sat down next to Bette and thrust her chin toward Flint. "Bombing seems like a way to make the war worse. What if they decide to do the same to us? It would be San Diego, wouldn't it, Flint? They'd bomb San Diego!" Kate's back stiffened.

In turn, Flint riveted a fearful glance Kate's way. "Bo, let's go to the radio."

Kate leaned into Bette, placing her head on her daughter's shoulder, and watched the men leave the room. "Rob's twenty years old tomorrow and already he's gone through hell. I'll tell you, Bette, when Rob gets home safe and sound, I'll never complain about anything again.

The bombing of Japan ended the war except for dignitaries gathering to draft final agreements. Kate shook her head as she rolled out dough for two mincemeat pies, amazed that a signature could make peace. The hearts of people made peace. Kate wondered why others, especially educated dignitaries, didn't know that. Of course, upon inspecting her own heart she could have sworn that she wanted peace in her life, her own little world, but there were too many longings stirring within. Peace hadn't come to her.

For days, she cried off and on with relief. It would be awhile before Rob would be sent home. He wrote that he was temporarily stationed in Texas. Why on earth, after all the hell for families and the service men especially, wouldn't the men be sent home right away, just for a few days? Kate banged the rolling pen down heavily on the dough and pushed hard starting from the middle of the ball of dough to the outside edge, over and over around the dough ball until the crust was the right size.

At least Rob was safe, and the family could look forward to all being together again, in awhile. And Wes? Where was he? Kate ached to see him. Each time she poured her wash water over the ground to water the morning glories that rambled up the lemon box siding, she thought of the day when, after he had checked her broken washer at the back of the house, they headed for the front room to play the guitar. As they walked beside the house, he handed her a large blue Morning Glory blossom and their fingers touched. The joy she felt at the touch of their fingers returned to her time and time again. It consoled and comforted her.

Kate thought of all the boys in the valley, three that she knew of, that would not be returning home now that the war was over. Hours of tears had already been shed for them and their families over the last four dreadful years.

Though Rob's letter said not to expect him for a few weeks, Kate still wore herself out each day preparing for his arrival, scrubbing the rough floors and weeding the garden. She scolded Dale and Ben until they had completely raked the chicken house clean of manure and decayed straw, and hauled it to the garden. A fresh pot of beans cooked on the wood stove, and Kate had her eye on the biggest turkey planned for that special day when Rob came home.

In between spurts of activity, Kate stopped in front of her bedroom dresser mirror to tuck in a sprig of her gray hair or to brush it back from her forehead. She listened for a low murmuring hum, the sound of a vehicle coming up the mountain, and she waited for a letter any day now telling the family when he would be waiting at the bus station for a ride home.

Rob would be tickled at how well the melon field was producing. As Kate marveled at the passing years, she moved to her rocking chair in the front yard and sat down to rest a spell. Rob would be surprised at how beautiful his sister had become. It had been over two years since Rob left, two frightening years. And Dale and Ben, how they'd grown. Kate turned her attention back to her mystery novel.

While Flint rested, holed up on his bed inside his screened-in porch reading the news and Life magazine, Bo went to water trees, and Donnie hunted fallow deer for venison. Dale and Ben played marbles nearby. Bette returned to her bed, where she sat brushing her long thick hair, 100 strokes, just as she did every day.

Except for Rob, the entire family was at the homestead today. They would all be hungry and gather at the house for the noon meal in another half hour or so. Thoughts of another meal interrupted Kate's mystery novel that Paul and Maria had brought her during their last visit. She had read many stories over the years. Mom and Pop or Maria and Paul brought her used pocketbooks nearly every visit. Except for strumming on Wes' guitar, reading was her only relief, and they all knew it. Even Flint left her alone when she escaped in these ways. Most of the stories she read, usually a romance western, ended on a happy note, with the hero winning the girl.

Kate could see Donnie in the distance carrying only the rifle. No deer today. The humming sound of a car turned Kate's attention away from her book. Probably just her imagination. She thought she'd heard the same sound multiple times over the last few days and decided to stop tormenting herself. Rob would get there when he got there. But soon the rumbling of a car grew louder. Finally, the noise stopped and then the sound grew louder again as though a vehicle were turning around up at the level spot above the cove. After a few minutes, the sound faded.

"That's strange," Kate thought. "Could be somebody got off on the wrong road and ended up here. It's happened before."

She leaned forward in her rocking chair, listening, and closed her book. She stood up in front of her rocker and turned, looking toward the hill, still wondering about the car or truck, and ready to give up her reading for now to prepare the noon meal. Donnie arrived and unloaded shells from the rifle. Kate heard Shep's excited bark echo from the South Slope trail. She figured Bo had finished watering the trees, no doubt starving by this time.

At the same time she heard a faint crunching of boots on gravel from the road that swooped down into the yard from the flat area above the cove.

"Boys, get Dad." Ben and Dale looked up from their marble game when they heard Kate's serious tone.

A tall slender man in a white hat came into view. He carried a duffle bag. Kate's paperback fell to the seat of the rocking chair and she began to run toward the figure in the white uniform. "Flint, Bo, Bette! It's Rob! It's Rob!"

Kate didn't stop at the nearly dry, rocky creek, but ran, arms lifted toward the sky. Her feet skimmed the creek, splattering water and little rocks against her legs, until she met her son on the other side of the creek where the creek met the bottom of the road. The duffle bag was left a few feet behind in the dust. Kate heard the thudding of Bo's heavy boots behind her, muffled with the excited yells from Bette and the other boys.

Rob's strong arms lifted Kate, swinging her around. As Kate's arms squeezed tightly around her son, Bette joined in before the four other boys piled on their brother, too. Within moments the four boys had engulfed the two women and Rob. They heaved him up on their shoulders and carried him toward the house. Flint ambled out the front room door with arms outstretched. Rob slid off his brothers and reached out to shake his father's hand. Flint grabbed his son, hugging him, and wept. "Happy Birthday, son. We're damned glad to see you."

CHAPTER—42

GOODBYE WES

Kate rejoiced at Rob's return, but noticed his reluctance to talk about his adventures on the ocean, or under it, even after two months back home. He appeared bothered if anyone pressed him about the war. Flint said he knew what Rob was going through and that the family might never learn about Rob's life on the sub. Kate wondered if Wes was going through the same kind of suffering as Rob. Wes had written the family that he would take a military leave in late August. September was now at hand. Wes had sounded ambiguous in the letter. Kate held her breath, afraid she'd never see him again.

Bette struggled through the tenth grade and now, the week before her eleventh grade, she informed Kate that she was not returning to school. They stood in front of the kitchen sink. Kate washed and rinsed the last pot and Bette slowly dried it.

"But what's there to do here, Bette? Nothing but scrubbing clothes and lifting melons to the sled. There must be something good at school. Isn't your heart set on anything? Maybe nursing. You have the nurture instinct, you know, Bette."

Kate remembered how she felt at sixteen, anxious to grow up yet afraid at the same time.

Bette seemed in the doldrums, and grumbled her answer. Kate realized that her daughter had no pretty things, not as nice as the other girls. "Bette, we can get you better clothes. I'll take the grocery money and do it." Bette didn't answer.

Bette was at a crossroads, Kate decided, as she dried the dishes with a damp towel. She worried that Bette was too much like herself. Her only daughter might allow her dreams to fall by the wayside as she had. Guilt engulfed Kate. What was to become of Bette if she stayed here all day and all night? Kate wanted to do something for her only daughter, something her own mother hadn't done for her, but what should she do, and what could she say to her daughter to keep from driving her further away?

"Bette, graduate! You have only two more years. Then you can go to nursing school, or do anything you want." Kate stacked the last pot on the counter. "Teaching maybe. I remember wanting to do nursing. I didn't know how to get it done without help. I'm telling you Bette, you hafta finish high school. Mom pulled me out of school in the eighth grade to pick cotton. Look at me Bette! Men can make a living with their muscles and their finagling and their conniving. We can't." Kate looked Bette in the face, hoping she'd see the truth of her words. "We end up being slaves to some ungrateful man, or working in a laundry somewhere for pennies." Kate spit out the harsh facts. She didn't want Bette to end up like her, stuck and without choices. But she had said enough, for now.

Fortunately, when school started the following week, Bette reluctantly agreed to try it again.

Donnie wouldn't want to miss the adventure that school provided, which, included the opportunity to debate. After the younger children left for school, Rob and Bo drove down the mountain in their recently purchased jalopy to visit friends in the valley and would bring home supplies on Kate's list. Flint said something about looking for farm equipment in San Diego, and left in the truck at daybreak.

Kate hardly remembered the last time that she'd had the place to herself. She placed the washtub next to the woodstove and filled it with tepid water. After a leisurely bath, she dressed in a worn but clean calico dress that Mom had sent to her. The dress felt cool on her skin in the warm September weather. She fumbled through her dresser and found hair clips. Pulling her shoulder-length hair back from her face, she placed the clips and then looked at herself in the mirror.

It had been a while since she'd taken the time to notice herself and she wasn't too happy about what she saw. It wasn't that she'd turned mostly gray or that her shoulders had rounded a bit. It was that the spark had gone from her eyes. The excitement of life, the hope she'd once had for her future had vanished. Wes hadn't shown up. Her children would be grown and gone in no time. And she and Flint were practically strangers. What was she to do?

Kate pinned the last sprig of her hair with a clip when she heard the familiar rumbling of a car or truck, but she figured the boys or Flint were returning earlier than expected. It was a rare event when anyone came just to visit. She thought back to the times when folks, strangers mostly, would come to the homestead with Flint. Gratefully, Flint had stopped the bad habit of dragging folks home with him.

An unfamiliar car crept down the road into the yard. Kate hurried to the kitchen door, throwing her apron over the bench on the way, and glanced up at the Winchester above the door. Finally, she stood on the step outside.

Recognizing the uniformed man stepping from the sleek car, the blood left Kate's head and she felt woozy. She grabbed the doorframe and hung on. Wes moved toward her.

"Kate, I had to come. How are you?"

She didn't move a muscle. "No one is here, Wes. I'm sorry you missed the family."

"You're here, aren't you Kate?" He laughed and reached for her hand.

She stepped toward him. "So thankful the war left you in one piece, Wes." She took his hand. It was hot to touch. "It was such a horrible time for you and Rob. For us, too. We expected to see you in late August."

Wes looked a bit thinner, but wonderful.

Suddenly, Kate was in Wes'arms. He held her tightly and the long awaited tears fell without shame, without holding back. He led her to the kitchen where she poured mugs of coffee.

Kate snatched her apron from the bench and pressed it to her eyes. "I figured you went to Missouri instead of coming here."

"Oh, no Kate. I had to see you." Before they sat at the table, Wes pulled Kate to him and kissed her forehead. "I've missed you night and day, Kate." Wes cupped her chin in his strong hand and kissed her gently on the mouth. Kate felt alive again as her heartbeat moved her body. This was what was missing in her life, a good man who truly loved her. Happiness overwhelmed Kate. Her spirit soared.

"Will you come with me to my place in San Diego, Kate?"

Kate shook her head that she'd go. She giggled and snuggled her head in Wes' chest. She felt the spark of youth return. They didn't sit with the coffee. Kate took Wes by the hand and led him to her room. She pulled a cardboard box from underneath her bed and began throwing a few clothes in it. There wasn't much to take. She would leave Bette a note. Bette could take over from here, and Kate would return now and then to help out. Besides, Kate knew that it wouldn't take Flint long to replace her.

Suddenly, Wes laid his land on Kate's as she threw her hairbrush in the box. "I need that cup of coffee. Let's talk in the kitchen."

Kate gulped at the hesitant tone of his voice. What was he thinking? She was ready to go, ready to spend the rest of her life with him. She'd get back to packing later.

When they sat at the table facing each other, Wes said, "Had to see you before I left for Missouri, Kate. I thought you might spend the night with me in San Diego before I left, that's all."

Kate refused to believe what she'd heard Wes say, but her blood began to boil inside her anyway and she spat out, "I figured as much. Will you come back?"

Wes frowned, his brown eyes guilty, but glanced at her and went on. "We'll see how things go. It's best I make sure about Francie. I mean, I need to know for certain that it's all over with her and me. At any rate, she's having a tough time with our two sons." He shrugged. "Wait for me, please, Kate?"

Instantly, Kate's spine stiffened as she jumped up from the table, knocking her coffee over. She bolted away from the spill, not bothering to grab a towel.

"You're leavin', and you're never comin' back," she said.

Kate hung her head, listening, hoping to understand, wishing she could agree with his plan, but cloaked in bitterness. Did he speak from his heart? Was he saying these things because he had changed his mind about her and needed an excuse to escape her? The war changed him. Yes, the war. Kate felt suddenly very old and she pressed her hands to her face, ironing out some of the sorrow.

Fear and death had brought Wes closer to his true feelings, and that was his love for his family. It didn't matter much about the truth now. He was leaving one way or the other. She gathered the strength within her, ready to say what she had to. She sat down across from Wes at the table again and looked in his face.

"Wes, if you must go, don't come back," she said sharply. "I'm not waiting another minute for you."

"I'm sorry, Kate."

Kate's heart filled with lead. That was it, the end of it. Wes had wooed her, seduced her, and filled her with love and desire. Kate glared at the spilled coffee on the table, unable to look at Wes after his final decision. Of course it was best for him to get back to his family, if that's what he really wanted. Kate's stomach was in need of a pinch of soda. They both had grown up since they first met before the war. She had to let him go. But more importantly, she had to get on with her life. Living her life for Flint and Wes . . . she'd let them rule her. She had given her life to others, but it was time that changed.

Rising from the bench was not easy. With a heavy sigh, she made her way to the guitar that sat against the middle room wall and gently held it. She returned it to Wes in the kitchen. "I sure enjoyed your guitar all this time, and taught myself some tunes on it," she said with a catch in her voice. He took it from her and leaned it against the wall.

"It's yours, Kate. Keep it to remember me by. We have a friendship, Kate. Let's remember it that way. I'd better go now, and not make things any more difficult for either of us."

Kate followed Wes to the yard, unable to believe that, after her heart had traveled with him through the treacherous war, after missing him every day and night and waiting for his safe return, he was leaving again, never to return. He turned and hugged her softly. She let him, stunned at the possibility that she'd never lay eyes on him again. Without another word, he kissed her hard on the mouth, just as he had in her sweet dreams of him during the war.

And then he left in his black Buick. Kate stood in the yard, her heart hanging precariously, her feet frozen to the ground, mummified. She listened until the sound of Wes' car had vanished.

When she turned, she saw Flint standing on the pump house trail in the shadows of the oak trees. She figured he must have left the truck on the flat above the cove to sneak up on her and Wes. The look on his face frightened her, not from the anger but from the hurt it expressed. He limped toward the house and past her, eyes straight ahead. Moments later, she heard him rummaging through drawers while she stood in the kitchen, wondering how to explain Wes' kiss. Flint returned with a bag in his hand and struggled up the hill. A few minutes later, she heard the truck leave from the flat. Like Wes, he drove down the mountain, leaving her alone, truly alone for the first time.

CHAPTER—43

FLINT'S AWAY

Late September arrived and Kate missed Flint more than she'd ever thought possible. He'd been away from home for nearly a month. The children were quiet about Flint's absence, as if they knew more than she did. She kept a pot of beans ready each night in case he returned. Now she'd baked cornbread after picking sweet tomatoes to slice for supper later. Kate found that she missed Flint coming to the kitchen for coffee; that his visits in and out of the house comforted her over the years. And if it weren't for his drinking, they might have developed a relationship built of trust, not anger.

Then again, there were times when weariness overtook her and she didn't give one iota about what Flint did or didn't do. For years she had scuttled her own wishes and needs in favor of Flint's and cringed at the possibility that it was too late to change that habit. She'd find out though, the following day, when she'd take the school bus with the kids to El Cajon and then walk to Doc Laraby's and they could talk about his offer for her to assist him in his work.

Kate stood from picking tomatoes and stretched her back. Her excitement grew as her plan that she had waited twenty years to implement, began to materialize. She grabbed her basket and headed for the house.

Donnie, Dale, and Ben hiked up on the mountain to hunt fallow deer, while Bo and Rob finished much of the work that needed doing on the homestead. Now, on Sunday, the two older boys left early to visit girlfriends in the valley. Kate knew there were girlfriends, but the boys hadn't brought them home to meet the family yet. Soon, Rob, Bo, and Donnie, maybe even Bette, would be gone from the homestead. After she set the basket down on the rough oak table, she ran her fingers across its pitted surface. She'd miss the talks she'd had with her children around this table. But it was time to move on, to start a new life.

Bette came in the kitchen. "Ma, I hear a car comin'. Seems too early for Rob and Bo. They shouldn't be back till nightfall, should they?"

For an instant, Kate felt a twinge of excitement, wondering if it might be Flint.

Kate and Bette hurried to the front yard. When the car came into view, Kate knew at once that it was Paul and Maria with their daughter, Libby. Disappointed that Flint hadn't returned after all, Kate determined not to let anything bring her down today. She lifted her shoulders and smiled. Mom and Pop were well, Paul and Maria said as they stepped out of the car. Kate grabbed Bette and Maria's hands, and with Libby on Maria's hip, following the ritual they held over the years, they danced around in a circle, celebrating in the front yard.

Inside the house, Kate made a pot of coffee and gathered with Paul, Maria, and Bette around the square oak table. Kate held Libby for a while until she fell asleep, and then Kate laid the red-haired girl on the couch in the front room. Kate poured fresh coffee all around, now ready for a good visit.

Paul looked at Kate and shook his head. "Heard about Flint's leaving. Sure surprised that Flint went to Pop and Mom for advice." Paul began awkwardly. "And then he finagled a way to get some help."

"Hush!" hissed Maria, dark eyes flashing.

"What are you talking about, Paul?" Kate snapped.

"You don't know, Kate?" Paul glanced at Maria who sat, arms crossed, glaring at him.

"What? Maria, what's he going on about? Will somebody tell us? Do you know, Bette?"

Bette shrugged, her frown mirroring Kate's own.

"Maybe I'm not supposed to let the cat out'a the bag, but too late now. He went to L.A."

Kate felt she'd been drenched in cold spring water coming right out of the side of the canyon wall. So he'd finally done it. He'd finally left her for Mrs. Helm. She sat back in her chair, blinking rapidly, trying to hold back tears.

He went to a hospital north of L.A."

Kate stared wide-eyed at Paul, not sure she was hearing correctly.

Paul got up from the table and walked around the kitchen, waving his arms. "To dry out, Kate! Flint was worried about you leavin'. Pop warned him if he wanted to keep you he'd better quit his drinkin'."

Relief flooded through Kate but it was quickly replaced by annoyance, and she narrowed her eyes. She looked at Bette. "I wish to hell Flint would talk to us. I wish he would be brave enough to speak his thoughts one of these days. Acts like nothin' is our business. I figure that everybody in the valley knows that man better than we do. That right, Bette?"

Bette acted timid as if she were afraid to speak her piece. Kate had an inkling of what Bette was itching to say, so she decided to say it for her. "Course, I haven't been easy on Flint. Haven't given him a chance lately, and he's mellowed some." Kate knew it was the truth, knew that she hadn't been forthright, especially with Flint or herself. She blamed him for causing her to lose her position as midwife, for moving them far away from her friends. She'd never given him a chance . . . made him feel inadequate. Frowning, she poured herself a cup of coffee.

"But this is good, Kate," Maria interrupted excitedly. "You should see a different man when Flint comes home. He wants to change. He loves you."

Kate shook her head, not trusting what she was hearing. "He said that?" she suddenly felt sorry for Flint, worried about him, all alone in some strange place. "He must've been scared. I wonder how long he'll be gone." Kate looked first at Paul, then Maria for an answer.

"I think it takes about a month, Kate." Paul frowned.

Kate opened her arms to Bette and pulled her close. Bette knew more about her than anyone. Her own husband didn't know her nearly as well. Bette was always the one who sat up with her when Flint was gone night after night. Bette was the one who comforted her when loneliness overwhelmed her. Bette needed something better out of life, something better than what Kate had. Kate wanted more for her daughter. She wanted her never to be afraid to follow her dreams.

The best way to assure that was to model those values. A peace settled over Kate as she hugged Bette tight. Tomorrow, she'd talk to Doc Laraby about making her job permanent. If Flint really wanted to keep her, he would pitch in with the rest of the family and help out in her absence.

CHAPTER—44

WIND AND FIRE

When Kate road the school bus on Monday morning to discuss her future career with Doc Laraby, she found him at his home office. He said that he was relieved to know she'd finally decided to use her skills. She would be in great demand and he'd take her with him on his rounds. She agreed to meet him December first at his office to begin work. She'd ride the school bus every morning and work until time for the kids to catch the bus again in the afternoon.

Flint returned home after the month's hospital stay. Kate watched him closely to see if he had actually improved. So far, he had not been explosive around the family, nor had he stayed out late to arrive home mean and drunk. For the first time in a long time, Kate's heart was at peace as she stood by the kitchen sink, gazing at the cove where the pink lilies bloomed again.

Flint was kinder, Bette had been dating a boy named Andrew, and Kate's thoughts of Wes had given way to her family, her homestead, and her new job with Doc Laraby that would begin shortly. Realizing that Wes was not going to be the one to make the connection with her, as Mom had with Pop, she looked for solace in her children. She realized that family and the homestead were her twin loves. They connected her to something greater than herself.

Standing at the sink, Kate dipped a ladle of cool water from the bucket and drank slowly. Even though she wasn't certain why the knots that used to bind her heart had lost their hold, she was grateful for their release. She breathed easier, and without fear.

A Santa Ana wind whipped up and over Mt. McGinny from the east. October winds right off the Mohave Desert could be expected off and on until February. The dry heat made folks wilt. Never lasting more than a few days, the departure of the Santa Ana would be more than welcome after this second day.

When Flint left for town early in the day, Kate put a pot of beans on the stove that would be done in time for the noon meal.

Rob and Donnie gathered watermelons from the south forty. Earlier, Kate had checked on them, and found that the sled Jackson waited patiently to haul to the dugout was already laden with the sweet dry-land melons.

Bo started the pump and planned to spend most of the day watering the avocado trees. Kate watched him for a minute on her way down from the melon field. He laid the end of the water hose beneath the tree, and Shep scurried around the basin, barking at the dried leaves as they rose with the level of the water. The avocados were practically a year-round crop with nearly a year-round income, and the trees had reached their full growth at about fifteen feet. Their fat leaves glimmered in the sun and rustled in the warm wind.

While the tree basin filled with water, Bo shoveled around the area for gopher holes and set traps. Gopher holes riddled the homestead grounds. But around the avocado trees, Flint demanded an effort from the boys to limit the critters. The avocado trees were precious to Kate too, and she was grateful that Flint had enough sense to plant the trees up on the slope where they received a little wind, where it never froze as it did occasionally at the house.

Kate became more and more unsettled after nearly two days of wind. She decided to get in the house and stay there until the Santa Ana died.

It would be lonely for the boys here on the mountain, with the older boys leaving soon and Kate going to work each day. At least they had each other. She brought a bowl from the cupboard and mixed cornmeal and a pinch of salt, thinking how good it was to have Bo home for the day. Usually, he spent his time with Flint, and was out and about, meeting people and friends daily when they went to market. Kate added two pinches of soda, two eggs and then poured buttermilk in the bowl, stirring the cornmeal mixture until she had the right consistency.

Rob and Donnie matched up well. Usually, Donnie talked philosophy and Rob listened. Rob didn't have much to say since the war, but he would listen with that far-away look in his winsome eyes, having never returned to the innocent person he was before the war. The war was too much trauma for any man, much less a young man.

While Kate began baking the cornbread for the noon meal, she heard the two harmonicas closing in on the smell of food. She saw Dale and Ben out the kitchen sink window. They were inseparable, and did their share of the work only when their older brothers used gruff voices, or when Flint gave them orders for the day, as he'd done today before leaving.

Otherwise, Dale and Ben ran the trails, hanging onto each other playing tunes with their harmonicas, which their Uncle Paul replaced with better and fancier ones as time went by. When their mouths tired from blowing and their feet hurt from running on the hard-as-rock trails, away they'd go, swinging across a too-deep part of the canyon down toward Gus' still on some spindly grape vines, or on their old tire swing that Donnie rigged up. Kate worried about them on the tire swing, but Flint said it was safe as long as they didn't let go when they swung out over the canyon.

As Kate watched the boys huddle together down in the cove, she saw little flashes of light. Upon closer inspection, she saw that they had the wooden matches she used to start the wood stove. "You boys put that out!" She commanded out the window. "Bring those matches here and stay out of trouble." She met them at the kitchen door where they hurriedly handed over the matches. "What's in your other hand, Dale?" Dale guiltily opened his fist where he held a short piece of grapevine. This wasn't the first time she'd caught the boys trying to smoke grapevine. Kate took the piece of grapevine and turned to Ben, her eyes demanding the goods he'd hidden behind him. He immediately gave Kate his contraband. When she was certain she'd temporarily warded off their mischief, she watched them as they returned to their swing, giggling and playing despite her bluster.

Kate wished Flint would stick around the homestead and help more with the little boys instead of simply giving them a few chores and leaving her to supervise. She couldn't keep up with Dale and Ben as she had with the first four children when they were their ages.

However, Flint's month-long stay in the hospital had helped him. Kate returned to the sink to wash pots and pans, but her mind was elsewhere.

Typically, Flint and the boys loaded melons or avocados early in the morning and he left, usually with Bo to help him unload at the market. Today however, he left Bo at home to water and said he had business about the homestead at the Department of Agriculture in San Diego.

With the new job at hand and Flint's return from the hospital, Kate's loneliness began to ease. Flint seemed to mellow as he grew older, or mellow because of the hospital treatment. Still, he would never tell her that he loved her. For a moment, Kate ceased her scrubbing on the blackened pot while she looked out at the cove and at the pond below the kitchen window, wondering where the little boys went.

When she was young and wanted to marry Flint, Kate expected that their lives would be like her folk's. But happiness had eluded her. Now, as she scrubbed roughly on the black pot, she knew that she would never have the marriage that she dreamed of. She tried to do most of what she thought pleased Flint, but he was unmoved by her efforts. Then over the years she'd grown hard and ceased trying. Now she would do what made her happy, and if he learned to love her, so be it, and if he couldn't, it was his loss. But either way, she would be happy with herself. She smiled at the thought and continued scrubbing.

Kate thought she smelled smoke and went outside to sniff the air. She was relieved to find the boys playing quietly with wood block cars on the dirt bank by the front yard. She looked at the sky with a tinge of worry but then returned to the kitchen and removed the cornbread from the oven. She figured the smoke must be from the wild fire that swarmed through Delzura a few days earlier but had since been quenched, according to Flint and the newspaper. Kate wondered what she would do should a fire ever start around the homestead, or sneak up over the mountain and down upon them.

Chards of sage, though, definitely blew in with the Santa Ana winds. Thankfully, the Delzura fire had been extinguished before this drying wind started.

With itching skin, Kate finished scrubbing the pots, set them aside, and dried her hands. She stirred the beans and then set the table for the noon meal.

Kate's worries about surviving the coming winter interrupted her concerns of fire. Dale and Ben needed good shoes before long. Most of the year they went barefooted, but when the temperature got down to forty degrees or below, they needed a coat and decent shoes. It seemed to Kate, that there should be more money for coats and shoes and even nicer things. The older boys got such a small share of spending money for all their work, but they didn't ask for more. Flint was in charge of the money, and it was difficult for anyone to ask for more than what he offered. The consequence was Flint's distain, his sullenness, which no one understood and rarely challenged.

When Kate wanted money for Bette's clothes, she had dared to challenge him though and won. So, there was hope that that aspect of Flint would change in time also. Kate was learning not to let Flint ruin her life, and if things didn't continue to get better, she had a choice. She would soon be assisting Doc Laraby. Most of the boys would be gone soon, and Bette wasn't far behind. She could move to town and live off the money she earned. Things would be tight at first, but she could make it if she was careful.

The wind had died down some by the middle of the day, and it was near time for the three older boys to come in to eat. Dale and Ben splashed their faces with water at the yard faucet. They slung the water off them, and rubbed their hands on each other's shirt backs before they ran in to the table. Wiggling on the bench, they watched Kate set out a bowl of beans, a hunk of cornbread with butter, and a cup of fresh milk.

A thudding of feet and a yell from one of the boys alarmed Kate. Donnie burst through the kitchen door out of breath. "Mom, Mom, fire's comin', hurry! You got to get out'a here! Rob and Bo say so, Mom! We're gonna hose down everything." Donnie stuttered in his effort to get Rob and Bo's instructions clear to her. "Bo's hosing down the avocado trees. I'm heading down to fill the tank with fuel for the pump, so Bo won't have to quit. Rob's unhooking Jackson from the sled for you all to haul yourselves out'a here."

When Donnie stopped shouting orders to Kate, she ran through the yard and up the bank past the chicken house, hoping to see the mountain more clearly. Faint streaks of flame flickered from the canyons that weaved down Mt. McGinny. The top of the mountain resembled a perilous dark cloud. The smell of burned sage filled her nostrils. *Oh, Flint. Please come home. We need you here.* She ran back to the yard where Donnie stomped back and forth, hands on his hips, looking more and more agitated with her. Dale, Ben, and Bette came from the house and stood in the yard, gawking at Donnie, boy turned dictator.

Knowing he was scared and needed reassurance, Kate clamped a calming hand on Donnie's shoulder. "Donnie, you boys can't stay here. That fire's too close."

"We aren't boys, Ma. Get Bette and the little guys on that mule and get to hell out'a here," Donnie ordered with indignation as he pointed to the road out. Then he turned from her. Quickly, he sprinted on slender legs toward the pump house.

Rob came down the trail, Jackson loping beside him. When he reached the yard, still holding the harness rope that hung around Jackson's neck, he yelled, "Hurry, Ma. This wind is fanning the fury."

Rob lifted Ben and then Dale up on Jackson's back. "Hang on tight boys. A puff of that wind could knock you right off that ole' mule. I'm goin' back now. Just get down the hill. Don't worry, Ma. We'll be okay."

Bette stood in the yard by Jackson. "Rob," she cried, "come with us."

"We'll be okay, Sis. Go on. Go on."

Rob handed Jackson's harness rope to Kate and ran back up the South Slope trail to begin the fight against the wind and fire, an impossible task. Kate shook her head.

Donnie sprinted back from the pump house and on through the yard. Without a word, he followed Rob.

Kate knew there was no use trying to convince her sons to leave the avocado trees and the homestead to go where it was safe. She didn't intend to leave either.

"Bette, you take care of the boys. I'm staying." Kate thrust Jackson's rope into Bette's hand as ash rained down on them. "The fire is coming down the mountain on all sides, so hurry."

"Ma, what are you doing?" Bette begged, her eyes wild with fear.

"Just get the boys to safety. Go on, there's no time to lose, Bette! Mrs. Helm may be at her house and can drive you out. If not, keep going."

Kate grabbed the hose hooked to the front yard faucet. She turned the faucet on full force and began spraying the lemon-box sides of the house, where blue Morning Glories still bloomed. Then she sprayed the front yard oak tree; the tree that had grown here on the mountain with her, the tree that was a part of her landscape. It was just a sapling when they came to the homestead in '29, and just as weak as she. Today, she'd surely need the strength of that mature oak.

Bette tugged on Jackson's rope, and he clomped on the dusty road behind her, carrying Dale and Ben. The boy's fingers clung to the old mule's black coat and they craned their necks in Kate's direction, their eyes wide with fright. "Ma, I can help, can't I?" Dale yelled.

"Yes, Dale. Take care of Ben. Now hurry. Get going."

Donnie thudded down the trail to the house again. "Ma, what are you doing here? Let me have that hose." He waved her on but without results. Finally, he stomped the ground and stood stubbornly with his hands rubbing his wind-whipped hair. "The guys don't need me up there. Rob has the hose and Bo is using the axe, choppin' sumac and sage as far away from the avocado trees as he can. I let the cow out. At least she can get away if the fire comes this far. We can find her later."

A covey of quail skittered through the yard and on up the road away from the fire that threatened them.

"Donnie, go see how much fuel we have for the pump. What are we to do if the pump won't pump water?"

"Ma, we have plenty of fuel. I checked already." Donnie grasped the shovel by the dugout and darted up the trail to the North Slope where he glanced up the mountain. Kate's eyes followed him as she sprayed water. Flames trickled down the North Slope toward where a portion of Paul and Maria's old shack still stood. Donnie yelled to Kate. "Ma, this ain't good." He ran back to her. Fear clouded over his dust-laden face.

"Donnie, you shovel that sage that's close to the back of the chicken house. I gotta do this." Water went everywhere, first the side of the house, where the Morning Glories bloomed, then the tin roof. "It's my home too, Donnie, and I need to protect it. Just can't leave it."

Donnie finally conceded. He started the dirty job of shoveling away the sagebrush that grew closest to the house and chicken house. They both knew they had to work like horses if they were going to save the homestead.

CHAPTER—45

TWIST OF FATE

Flint worked around Helm's after returning from the Department of Agriculture in San Diego earlier in the day. The hot wind made it difficult to repair siding on the house, so he irrigated the plants instead, since many were still in full bloom and would need extra water now with the drying wind. Mrs. Helm was expected to return to the house from town before noon that day. Usually gone to L.A. by this time of the year, she stayed to tend to some business. Flint hoped she wanted to talk about leasing her farmland to him, and of course, she'd want to know all about his month in the hospital, but first he needed to get to town. Mrs. Helm owed him some money and he had a secret plan to buy Kate a new washing machine.

As promised, Mrs. Helm arrived just before noon. They decided to get together later in the week to catch up on local gossip. Mostly, Flint was anxious to tell her of his hospital stay. Mrs. Helm paid Flint, and he left for Spring Valley to purchase Kate's washer. Once there, he spied a blue plaid dress in the window of a shop next to the hardware store. Smiling the entire time of the purchase, Flint bought the dress for Kate without much thought of the cost. She would be surprised and pleased too, if it wasn't too late to please her. She loved the color blue, he knew that much.

And as far as the washer, well, there was too much work around the homestead for Kate to be using a scrub board, even with Bette's help. Lord only knew how much Kate deserved the washing machine and that new dress. Regretfully, Flint was unable to remember Kate in anything but other's castoffs.

Flint purchased the washing machine and, with the help of the salesman, tied it securely in the bed of the Ford truck. He peered to the east, anticipating the look on Kate's face when she laid her eyes on her new washer. Flint smiled, feeling good about himself for a change. Kate hadn't asked for much over the years, and now with a little extra money, it wasn't necessary for her to do without so much. Time had gone by mighty quickly. The farm was about to make life easier for the family.

Flint checked the ropes one last time, shook hands with the salesman, and then got in the truck. He couldn't wait to get home with his treasures. The salesman standing beside the truck pointed to the east. Flint looked toward his homestead. The mountain appeared grayish, a remnant from the Delzura fires. Flint stuck his head out the truck window and spoke to the salesman. "Sure is spooky the way that Santa Ana wind brought down the ash from the other side of the mountain. I wonder if it could have started up again?"

"Sure could've I suppose, Mr. Powell."

By this time, Flint felt apprehensive and needed a smoke. He waved good-bye to the salesman and headed east. While he drove, he tried packing his pipe with tobacco. After dropping the pipe and tobacco in his lap again and again, it was finally packed and ready to light. Flint attempted to strike a match with one hand on the wheel, but one after another, the matches broke. His hands shook. He laid the unlit pipe on the truck seat beside him next to the package holding the blue dress. Something was amiss. He had a bad feeling, though he couldn't quite put his finger on it.

On the way home, he stopped at the Junction for Folgers coffee and Prince Albert. Leaving the truck running, Flint stepped out.

Arnie Stanton rushed out of his store toward Flint, but before Arnie spoke, Flint said, "Arnie, what's goin' on? Looks awfully damned smoky."

"Good . . . good God, Flint," Arnie stuttered and pointed eastward. "Your . . . your . . . mountain is on . . . on fire. Mrs. Helm was by lookin' for you. Had some of your kids, the two little guys, with her. Bette too. Why, yer . . . yer girl . . . she . . . she was cryin', says her ma and brothers wouldn't leave the homestead."

Before Arnie could add more to his garbled story, Flint jumped back in his truck. He slammed his boot down hard on the gas pedal. The tires spewed bits of gravel.

In back of the truck, Kate's new washing machine bounced around, but Flint didn't slow down. He had laid the washer down on its side and tied it securely. What good was a new washing machine anyway, if a man's house and family were burned up while he was gone?

"Katie," he muttered to himself. "You wouldn't leave that house to save your neck. Even if it killed you, you would stay and fight to the end." "I love you, Katie," he whispered. "I've been rough on you and the boys. What would I do without you all?"

Flint swabbed the dust and sweat from his flushed face.

Tears trickled from Flint's eyes, making tiny grooves in the dust and smoke that grayed over his tanned face. He loosened his grip on the steering wheel to find his handkerchief. He wiped away the anger and humiliation that rolled down his cheeks. Then, with great effort, he focused his energy on driving.

He pushed the truck as fast as possible, veering off at Helm's. As he headed up the steep, guttered road that led to the homestead, he prayed, *if Kate and the boys are all right, I swear I'll change.*

The month-long therapy in the hospital had helped him face his mother's death . . . the fact that she had given herself an abortion that caused her own demise. Flint gritted his teeth at the truth. She was probably afraid to tell Turner about the pregnancy, knowing he'd have killed her himself if another man was involved. It was a sad situation, but during therapy, Flint put the whole thing in perspective. He was not responsible for his mother's death, but he was responsible for Kate and the kids.

As he stepped down hard on the gas, the engine revving, Flint's thoughts drifted back to the time he met Kate. She was just a schoolgirl, but she rode a horse like a wild woman. When she was finally of age, he couldn't wait any longer, and took her to the closest Cherokee Medicine Man to make her his woman.

Smoke drifted down the canyon that ran along the right side of the rutted, steep, winding dirt road. The truck rattled, swaying now and then in a heavy puff of Santa Ana wind. It seemed though, that the wind had died down considerably since morning.

Rabbits jumped across the road in front of the bouncing truck. A quail covey skittered down the road toward him, scattering into the brush a moment before the truck would have hit them. A lone deer bounded in a zigzag frenzy down the hillside, smoky dust chasing its hooves. *It's gotta be real bad at the homestead, for the wildlife to be acting crazy this far down the mountain.*

Flint's mouth felt parched, his lips cracked from the dry heat. He hadn't been this scared since he thought he'd killed Leonard Schwartz. One thing was for certain, before Katie and his boys perished in this fire, he would die trying to save them.

The truck hit a large rut that Flint usually would have slowed down for. The tires bounced out of the rut and over to the side of the road. The motor died. This would be the worst time of his life to have the motor flood. He turned the key over. No luck. His lips pursed. Once again he pumped his foot up and down on the gas pedal. "Start, you son-of-a-bitch." The engine groaned twice, then let out a screech before dying. He slammed his fist on the dashboard. He pumped again. "Come on, damn it," he demanded, sweat dripping off his forehead. "Start!" Just then, the engine started and he revved it. Grateful, he took a deep breath.

Flint tried to keep his mind on getting home and off the hungry fire that swept down Mt. McGinny like a fierce eagle on innocent prey.

He needed desperately to focus on easing out of the gravel where the tires landed. If he didn't maneuver just right, the truck could slide further off the road and tumble down into the canyon below. This mistake was costing him time, maybe his life, and possibly the lives of his wife and boys.

Flint eased the gear in reverse, and carefully backed a few inches, figuring to steer out of the gravel and back onto hard ground. With a stroke of luck, it worked. He took a deep breath and grasped the wheel. The tires spun on the hard earth and the truck shimmied again on its way up the road. He had lost precious time but pushed on, holding the steering wheel tightly until his knuckles whitened and his palms blistered. He slowed down only for the larger ruts that might knock him off the road again.

At the top of the hill, before ascending down the last bit of road to the house, Flint scanned the blackened top of Mt. McGinny. Half way down the mountain, flames dotted the landscape. In the north canyon, a large bush exploded. Probably lilac or sumac, he figured. Many stately yuccas stood like torches. Flames jumped wildly high.

Flint's mouth gaped open at the horror of the mountain-eating fire. Tumbleweeds bounced with the wind, balls of fire lighting dried grass as they danced along like an old lamp lighter gleefully hopping from one lamppost to another, brightening an otherwise darkened street. His thoughts tormented him. This fire was unbelievably bad, the worst that he'd ever seen.

His wife and boys could be trying to save the avocados, but he couldn't see the trees through the gray din. Orange, red, and yellow flashes caught his eye, and he was sure the flames were right about where the avocado trees grew. Perhaps his precious trees had already been burned to the ground. Perhaps his family had already perished. Flint wiped sweat and tears from his face and eyes again with his shirtsleeve.

It was difficult to tell if the southeastern canyon below the melon field had caught fire yet, but if and when it did, that would be all she wrote. Because, if the huge oaks and willows up and down the canyon and in front of the house caught fire, Kate and the boys, and now he, would all be trapped; they couldn't get out if they wanted to.

"Thank God Bette and the little boys got out."

Tears and smoke blurred his sight. Flint swabbed his face again with his shirtsleeve. The house, the trees, nothing was worth sacrificing their lives for. "Why are you doing this, Kate?"

As the truck jostled down the last bit of road, Flint could see that the house was still standing. The cow lumbered through the front yard and stood sucking water from the shallow creek.

Flint could hear the pump motor thumping and the conveyor belt flapping around and around its track. The racket was a good sign. The truck jostled to a sudden stop beside the thirsty cow.

Suddenly, Flint spotted flames whipping up behind the house. He scrambled from the sweltering seat of the truck and ran around the east side of the house. Donnie held a wet shirt over his nose with one hand and held the hose in the other. He doused the flames from a small oak that grew beside the north creek. It was dangerously near the house. Flint grabbed wet gunnysacks that Donnie apparently had been using on the brush and hit at the nearest flames. Scanning the area dimmed with ash and smoke, Flint hoped to see Kate. There was no sight of her at the house. He figured she was at the avocado trees . . . on the hillside with the raging fire.

When it looked as though Donnie had the tree doused and the fire out, he turned the hose again on the side of the house and soaked the ground around it. But not too far from the house, past the area where Flint beat on the fire, there was a thicket of dried weeds and brush . . . lots of it.

"Donnie, Donnie, where's your mother?" yelled Flint. "Bo? Rob?"

"Ahh, Christ, Dad, they're at the avocados. Ma was worried Rob and Bo would get caught and surrounded. She's up there. Go ahead, I'm doin' okay here," Donnie shouted above the roar of the flames.

Flint ran, scarcely able to breathe. Smoke was thick and stuck to his throat and lungs. He was terrified that Kate and his two oldest sons were among it, surrounded by flames. He wouldn't be able to keep running this way for much longer. His lungs felt torched like the top of the mountain. While he ran, he struggled to grab the handkerchief from his back pocket, then held it over his nose.

Flames nipped at his boots and sizzled across the trail on sparse dried weeds. To his left, fire had snuck in from the North Slope trail, and the patch of sagebrush that grew below the avocado trees sprouted flames here and there. The chicken house was a few yards down the slope from those flames. Flint yelled to Kate but got no answer. He reached the avocado trees. The sled, heaped with melons, sat in the middle of the trail. Blackened sagebrush had burned itself out at the top edge of the avocado grove.

Newly tilled soil to the right of the grove posed no danger of burning. Flint yelled again, and ran down beside the trees toward the opposite end. Flames loomed larger at the northwestern end of the grove where he was headed.

With a jolt, a gopher hole swallowed Flint's foot to the top of his boot. "Son-of-a-bitch," he swore. Regaining his balance, he continued hobbling along. Fire crackled all around, pieces of sage floated on the Santa Ana wind through the heavy smoke-filled air.

Finally, Flint spotted three blackened figures, their faces unrecognizable. They worked with frenzy. Flint knew they couldn't have heard his calls to them over the roar and crackling of burning grass and brush all around them, along with an occasional whoop of wind. Water gushed out the hose that Kate held and sprayed over the nearby brush, the dead grass on the ground, and the avocado trees nearest the northwest end of the orchard.

Flailing his lean body, Rob shoveled dirt onto sagebrush and shoveled sagebrush back into burning sagebrush. Bo, his back bent as he swung the axe, chopped off sumac and lilac at their trunks, kicking them into the distant flames, making it impossible for the flames to reach and scorch the avocado trees.

"Katie!" Flint seized his wife in his hands and drew her close, squeezing her into his body. She buckled, dropping the hose, and Flint helped her set down in the shade of the end tree.

The boys coughed and took turns reaching for a drink of water from the hose. Sweat poured from their bodies and from underneath their straw hats, making streaks down their blackened faces. Bo called to Shep who crouched nearby, watching his master. The shaggy dog went to him and drank from the hose that Bo held for him.

Rob yelled, "Dad, Donnie's down at the house alone, I think one of us should get down there."

Flint saw that the boys were doing all that was possible here. He yelled over the swishing rapacious mountain on fire, "We'll take your mother down after awhile. I think it's safer for her to stay right where she is. We might have trouble at the house and chicken coop."

Bo axed down a too-close sumac. Then stood, stretching his back. Scanning the hellish fire over most of Mt. McGinny, he faced the North Slope. "Look! There goes the shack!" Paul and Maria's dilapidated, abandoned shelter, flamed wildly and crashed to the black earth.

Flint winced, remembering little Tina. Where was he when she died? Why hadn't he provided his brother-in-law and sister-in-law with better shelter? Was he drunk, curling up inside his own aching body, looking for something somewhere to ease his pain?

For a while, liquor took away the pain that he carried for his mother, took away the guilt for not being able to help her. The sour wine had helped deaden the fact that he was born a half-breed bastard.

But now, all that he ever needed was right here under his nose. It wasn't the still down in the canyon that he cared about, nor the poker games with the other drunks, nor the bosomed ladies that he charmed until they hung on him with their musky perfume. It wasn't the avocado trees or even the house. Without his family, those things meant nothing. Why hadn't he seen it before? His Katie, and his children meant everything to him. He would gladly die for them. From now on, things would be different. Now he saw things with new eyes. He would let them know how important they were to him, if it wasn't too late.

Flint left the three by the avocado trees and, in his jerky stride, hurried to check on Donnie. Flint wondered why he hadn't heard any sirens and doubted that the fire trucks could even maneuver up the narrow rutted road to the homestead.

When Flint got to the house, Donnie was nowhere to be seen. He followed the water hose to the end of the house where his son had stood earlier. Water gushed out the end of the hose and trickles of fire spurted through the dry grass on the bank behind the house. "Donnie?" Flint croaked out from a dry throat. No answer. Flint walked back and forth feeling like a worried old woman, and finally scooted down the short incline that veered off to the north creek. Donnie lay on the bank on his side, barely visible. Smoke poured around him from the burning thicket nearby. Flint lifted his son by his thin muscled arms and dragged him up the incline. Donnie was breathing. Flint figured he'd slipped and hit his head or inhaled too much smoke. Maybe he was just plain exhausted.

When they reached the water hose, Donnie moaned. Flint laid the boy on his side and washed his face with the bandana, dribbling a little water in his mouth. The distant burning brush might catch the house on fire, but Flint thought it would be a few minutes before it reached this distance. He hovered over Donnie and talked non-stop until Donnie tried to sit up.

"Thanks, Dad." Donnie laid his head down on the dirt again.

"Stay still, Donnie. You're tuckered."

At that moment, the pump motor stopped. Flint looked around. The thicket a short distance away flashed with flames. The house was in peril again. Flint was terrified to leave Donnie to get the pump going again, but he had no choice. If the house went up in flames, so would the big oaks all around, and even the pump house across the creek. The road would be cut off with those flaming oaks boiling up and down the canyon.

Flint scrambled up the bank and over to the pump house. He refueled and started the motor again. Watering the flames could resume now. Flint hurried back to the hose. With the thicket wet again, and after beating small fires with gunnysacks, the house was out of danger for the moment.

Flint took time to check on Donnie now and then as he gradually regained his strength. When he felt the urge to check on him one more time, Donnie came up beside him, beating the brush furiously with a wet gunnysack, as if he had never been overcome with exhaustion a few minutes before.

CHAPTER—46

Gus Is Gone

Kate struggled to raise her tired body. "I'm headin' down to see about Donnie. Maybe we should drag this hose to the back of the chicken house."

"We'll take it there, Ma. These trees are safe, and," Rob looked around as if to make certain he was right, "the wind stopped." He gathered the hose and dragged it along behind him. Bo grabbed the shovel and mattock. The three of them made their way down the trail.

Kate walked stiffly to the house, feeling every aching bone in her body. She could do no more and wondered if Flint's body felt this miserable all the time.

They were safe from the fire for now, except for the southeastern canyon that they could not possibly save from the fire by themselves. With luck, the melon field on the south slope would stop the fire there, since there was very little vegetation left on the field, and only soil at the edges. Above the field, dry sage and sumac grew abundantly in a jagged ravine. From there, the fire would surely seep down the canyon where the beautiful oaks grew. Soon, those trees, too, would be on fire.

A faint siren wafted through the smoke-filled air. At the same time, a powerless puff of Santa Ana wind scurried off. The last of it, Kate thought. Though the wind had ceased, it hadn't taken the ash with it, but left it to blanket the land, crusting the sycamores and oaks, and covering her face and the faces of her weary husband and sons. Kate's stomach churned.

Finally, the water trucks and bulldozers would arrive, cutting the fire away from the southeastern canyon. Another siren wailed from the direction of Gus' place. The thought had crossed Kate's mind, when she was spraying water on the fire near the avocado trees, that if they were able to save the homestead, they would go over to Gus' to help him. Now it sounded as if help was getting to him. Thank God.

The ordeal was nearly over. Kate was exhausted, but her heart felt huge and warm. No longer the same helpless child, ripped from school against her will to pick cotton, she had grown strong like the oak tree and proud of her children, Flint, and herself. Today they'd saved their home.

While Flint kept watch at the back of the house, beating fragments of flames here and there, Donnie relentlessly sprayed water into the oak tree at the front yard. The tree had grown over the years, now towering above the house. "A spark could set this thing off. It's mighty dry now. If it goes up, the house is gone."

Kate touched Donnie's shoulder. "The fire trucks are on their way. You can quit here real soon. I'm dead on my feet."

"Listen, Ma," Donnie said, peering at her through his gray mask of ash, "I think if Dad hadn't been here in time to pull me out of that burning brush where I passed out on the bank, I'd be fried right now."

Kate couldn't speak. She put her arms around Donnie and squeezed him with her last bit of energy. She held her son until he pulled away. "Your Dad is still beating brush, I see." Kate gasped with astonishment at what Flint showed today. Courage. He was there when she needed him most. She stepped into the kitchen, her feet too tired to do more than slide across the planked floor. Her filthy blackened shoes, soaked and worn, fell off. She kicked the shoes aside and placed the bucket of water from the counter on the floor, sat down in front of it, and washed herself.

Once the fire was out, she would heat the beans if they hadn't spoiled. Leftover cornbread from the noon meal grew stale and biscuits remained from breakfast. While Kate dried her feet and legs, she vowed to meet Flint halfway in their relationship. She'd learn to talk without blaming him or claming up. She'd tell him what she wanted and hopefully, he'd go along with some of her desires. It had been a long time since she'd really told him what she wanted. He'd changed a lot since then.

In sore bare feet, Kate hobbled to the stove. Grabbing a biscuit, she stuck half of it in her mouth. Famished, she could have eaten most anything.

Water trucks, bulldozers, and several men swarmed around the homestead, most of their manpower covering the canyon by the house. Men in hard hats hopped and ran, some with hoses, some with shovels. Kate watched them for a few trance-filled minutes, her hands clasped together against her chest and her eyes dimmed with teary gratitude. The firemen fought to extinguish every possible bit of the fire, finally leaving a truck and three firemen, including the fire chief, at the homestead.

The crisis was over. The ordeal left Kate with the realization that life could start anew; a life that she could have had all along. She hadn't known the secret until it all came together today.

CHAPTER—47

THE CLEANUP

Flint managed to hobble to the fire chief, though he had not been in such pain in his life. The fire chief said he was certain they could save the oak-filled canyon. Most of the fire was contained already.

"Helm's place has gone up in flames, no way of saving the dried-out old mansion," the fire chief said, shaking his head in disgust. "Seems the old place caught a spark. Nothing else burned around it, just the house. Strange. Your place would have been long gone too, if you hadn't been here. You're a brave bunch of folks, that's all I can say. We had to make sure that we stopped the fire before it got too close to those houses across the way before we came up the mountain. Couldn't have even gotten here without bulldozing your road. Mighty narrow in some spots, Mr. Powell. We straightened it some from where the road veers off at Helm's to the top where it levels out."

When the fire chief described Mrs. Helm's old house burning up the way it did, Flint thought of the warnings, the omens shown to him throughout that old house, signs to him that his life was falling apart along with his decrepit body. He had heard the message and began to straighten his life just in time. And if there were human ghosts in that old place, well, they weren't there any more, he felt sure.

"My kids are with Mrs. Helm. They weren't anywhere near Helm's place, I hope."

"No Sir, we checked. An old mule standing out in the field. Nothing else around there. No other animals that I could see. Place looked vacant. I didn't think Mrs. Helm or anybody lived there."

Flint heaved a sigh of relief that Jackson was all right, and he was certain that Mrs. Helm wouldn't have taken the children near the fire, even to check on her old house. But the house . . . the library. Oh, Lord. All those wonderful books. He shut his eyes, sad that the books had been destroyed.

Best not to say anything to Kate about Helm's until the kids showed up. She'd worry herself to death about them.

Kate began preparing food for the family. Every scrap of food she could find, she sat out on the table. Yet her family might be too tired, too famished to eat by this time.

Since the water trucks had contained the fire, and the chicken house was safe by this time, Bo and Rob threw down their tools and hose. When they got to the house, Kate said, "Gus' place looked like it was on fire from the ridge up yonder."

Bo and Rob shook their heads. "Oh, God, Rob, let's get over there. Gus wouldn't leave his animals. I know that. Oh, Christ, I'm give out."

"Let's go before it's too late, Bo," Rob said. "Tell Dad we're running over to Gus', will ya', Ma?" They left exhausted and black-faced with Shep at Bo's heels before Kate could warn them of further danger.

"Well, they're men now. They'll watch out after each other." But it worried her that they were already spent. No energy left to fight the fire.

Ten minutes later, Flint walked through the kitchen door holding his grayed straw hat. He had washed most of the black away from his hands and face at the faucet across the yard. "Katie, if you and the boys hadn't stayed here, the homestead would have burned to the ground." Flint didn't sit down at the table, but stood in the middle of the kitchen floor silently watching her. She waited for him to say something more.

Kate felt the blood rush to her face. She wasn't used to him eyeing her that way. After a moment of Flint's pensive silence, she hurried to change the subject. "I'm fixin' something to eat. Rob and Bo ran to Gus'. From the avocados, it looked like his place was surrounded by fire and smoke."

"Poor old bastard, all alone over there with no family, 'cept them damned animals. Well, I'll go check with the fire fighters. The Chief didn't say anything about Gus a while ago. I'll see if they know anything. They're spewing water down onto the oaks around the spring." Flint turned to walk out but stopped short at the door. "Kate?" he said hesitating awkwardly.

"Yeah, Flint?"

Donnie interrupted them when he popped through the door. "Never mind," Flint said, turning his hat around in his hands. "I'll be back." Then he walked out.

Kate placed food in front of Donnie when he came in. He ate and said, "I'm tuckered, Mom. Going to lay down."

Kate thought she heard more sirens to the west. *That must be Gus' place they were headin' to. Good.*

But in a while, Rob came in and slumped down at the table.

"Where's Bo?" Kate asked.

Rob didn't respond, but put his elbows on the table and his head in his hands.

"Rob, you tell me what's happened to Bo. Where is he?"

"He . . . he's staying.

"Why?"

Rob lifted his head with his eyes lowered. "To help the firemen that just got there when I was fixin' to leave. We got there too late, Ma. Gus is dead. Bo's giving the firemen some kind of report. Information on Gus." Rob shook his head in disbelief, and held his head in his hands again.

Kate stood behind Rob as he sat on the bench. She leaned against his back and hugged his shoulders. "Oh, no, Rob. That's terrible. Oh, poor old Gus. I'm sorry." She stayed there leaning against Rob. Tears welled in her tired eyes. She tried to hang on, not wanting to break down in front of Rob. Someone should have gone over to help Gus sooner. But there wasn't time. The boys had left for Gus' as soon as possible after the fire. She patted Rob on the shoulders and then set a plate and spoon in front of him. Rob's hands were black. But what difference did it make. It wouldn't make the beans and cornbread taste any different.

"Rob, eat and get washed up. You're tired. I'll get Dad." Barefooted, Kate went to find Flint. She didn't want to ask details from Rob. Rob had seen too much suffering and death in his young life. He didn't seem able to talk about Gus.

Kate found Flint standing by the fire truck.

"What's wrong, Katie?"

"Old Gus is dead." Kate couldn't hold her tears back any longer. They simply fell and she didn't bother to hide them. Let them fall. What difference did it make?

"Oh no. What happened? Did the boys get back?" Flint held his arms out to Kate, and with bent head, she burrowed her face in his chest.

"Rob came back. Don't know yet if Gus died from the fire or smoke inhalation. Guess he must have been near eighty years old." Kate cried while Flint held her tightly to him. Despite all that happened, this day was the best day of her life. She leaned her chin on his shoulder and sniffled. "Rob's too tired and weary to talk. You know how he is. I'm worried about him. Bo's giving the firemen a report over at Gus'. I'm gonna go to the house and make sure Rob eats. He needs to get to bed and rest." Kate patted Flint on the arm and stepped back. He glanced down at her bare feet. She left him there with a sorrowful look on his ash-covered face.

Kate limped back to the house to make sure that Rob had eaten and was resting. She heated the beans again. It was a sad day. Gus was gone. How strange life would be now. Even though they rarely saw him these days, except when Bo or some of the other kids rode Jackson over with a gunnysack of avocados, still, it was always a comfort just to know he was right over the hill, a mile away. Kate imagined that he would always be there with his gaunt, whiskered, grinning face, his snappy green eyes, and his heart of gold. It was a sad day indeed.

When Mrs. Helm brought Bette and Ben home just before sundown, she said that Dale and Jackson were not far behind. Jackson had been standing in the open field, far away from any danger, Mrs. Helm said, when they passed the burned house, and Dale begged for her to stop so that he could ride Jackson home.

"Oh, Flint, by the way," Mrs. Helm said in her deep vibrating voice, "After I saw flames on the mountain, I was in the process of getting the books out of the library, throwing them in the trunk of my car as fast as I could. I was worried about all of you." Mrs. Helm flashed her open smile. Kate felt a wave of jealousy but squelched it. After all, Mrs. Helm had rescued her children. Who was she to bear any ill will toward the woman? "I had decided to drive up here when I saw the kids coming on Jackson. Bette asked me to drive them down the road to safety like Kate wanted, so that's what we did.

Anyway, I need to get these books out of my car and wondered if I could leave them with you?" Mrs. Helm raised her eyebrows in question. "Don't have any room at my place in L.A. I want you to have them. Got most of the books out actually." Mrs. Helm laughed when Flint showed his approval. "Lost all those National Geographic magazines, though. A real shame." She shook her head and then motioned for Flint and Kate to follow her.

Mrs. Helm walked to her car, her skirt swaying, revealing bare ankles and sandaled, delicate feet. She opened the trunk of her car and showed Flint the books she had heaped there. Then the three of them hauled the books into the kitchen table, taking several trips back and forth. Kate grinned at Flint. Even with the pain on his face after the loss of Gus, he chuckled and handled the books as if they were valuable treasures.

All the while, Kate had been thinking about what Mrs. Helm said earlier. "L.A? Mrs. Helm. That's were you live?" No one seemed to hear Kate, there was so much commotion. Now Kate put two and two together. The address was Mrs. Helms, where Flint sent his hours from working at her old house. The sweet fragrance of Jasmine wafted from the books.

Mrs. Helm said in her resonate voice, "Flint, let me know if you decide to lease the farm land while it's up for sale. We can write the contract so that you can continue to lease the land until the crops are harvested, even if the land should sell."

Fire trucks remained down the mountain, Mrs. Helm told them. Though they couldn't have saved Mrs. Helm's old house, they hoped to stop the fire as it leaped over the hillsides and along the flatlands before it got to the Mexican neighbors further down the road.

Mrs. Helm added, "I'm not afraid to drive back down now. My sons are waiting for me in Spring Valley. By the way, nice smooth road you've made over that old wagon trail, Flint."

Kate frowned that Mrs. Helm's would consider that horrible mountain road nice and smooth.

Flint laughed. "Well, the bulldozers did a bit of work to make way for the fire trucks. I can't wait to try it out myself."

"Oh, I see," Mrs. Helm smiled again. "Remember Flint, consider my lease offer." They shook hands, and she drove down the hill toward the burned heap that was once a huge decrepit house.

Flint, with a grin on his ash-smudged face, hurried back and forth, carrying stacks of books from the kitchen table to the porch.

Rob came out of the bedroom and walked outside. He was gone a few minutes while Kate gathered dishes to wash at the sink. She was surprised to hear laughter moments later. It was Bo, and now Rob joined him. Bo had just returned from Gus', but what could possibly give them reason to laugh on a sad day like today? A bark, so familiar to Kate and so comforting, echoed along the west side of the house. Bette and the other boys heard the commotion and ran out. Kate followed them, chills running through her.

"Look here, Ma, one of Brownie's off-springs. He looks just like him. Take a gander!" Rob said. The dog's paws leaned against Rob's chest while Rob vigorously rubbed the dog's young coat. "Hey, ole boy. Good to have you back, Brownie."

Kate hadn't seen Rob so happy in a long time.

"A pal for Shep the mop," Bo said.

And a new pal for Rob, Kate smiled, her life finally feeling ordered.

CHAPTER—48

RENEWAL

Two days after the fire, the family sat around the old square oak table, slowly eating beans and biscuits in the soft light of the kerosene lamp. There were some late tomatoes and avocados, but Kate, too weary to prepare them, set them on the table with the salt, pepper, and a paring knife. A silent pall hung in the air for a while. The entire family seemed in shock and it would take some doing to get things back to normal. Shep and Brownie lay in the front yard napping.

Kate sat at the table in her blue plaid dress, counting her blessings. She wiggled her toes in the comfortable shoes that adorned her feet. Flint had gone to town the day after the fire and brought two pairs back to her, and one pair fit nicely. He asked her to plan a shopping day as soon as the homestead was back in order.

The memory of Flint grasping her closely with his rude strong hands during the fire flashed in Kate's mind, and she gazed at him at the opposite end of the table. He sat with his beans untouched, the full bowl in front of him, holding a biscuit in one hand. His eyes were upon her, his usual defiant expression gone. What was he feeling? Remorse, empathy, love? All seemed to be there, the hostility gone. He smiled at her, not the smile of a stranger, but of someone who recognized her. Without the whisky, the wine, the corn liquor, he was the man he used to be. He was the man who looked into her with passion from those darkest, steely blue eyes of long ago when they ran off to the Cherokee Reservation and they married, the Medicine Man performing the ceremony, young Indians chanting and dancing a wedding dance around a fire.

Suddenly, Kate realized something else. Flint had shaved his mustache. When, she didn't know. And that fancy washing machine with the wringer! And her new dress, how lovely it was. When Flint presented it to her, he said that it matched her eyes. He'd never done such thing for her before in his life. Kate laid her hands in her lap and lowered her eyes. The joy of knowing that her husband loved her flowed over her.

Even though the mountain stood laden with ash, ravished of its vegetation, everything around Kate sparkled. Flint had brought the blue dress home with the washer the day of the fire, and now, two days of turmoil since the fire, she realized the significance of it all. He had cared for her even before she and the boys risked their lives for the homestead.

It took the last two days to assess the damage from the fire. Surely the hillside, laid flat with black-charred sage and death-gray ash, would be ugly for months, but spring rains would eventually come and tiny spots of green grass and vivid wildflowers would pop up, bringing new life and color to the homestead. The sadness felt for the loss of Gus would go on for a long, long time however, and the memory of him would go on forever. In an effort to release some of her remorse, Kate pressed the tips of her fingers against her eyelids and then ironed her face with her hands.

Since the avocado trees were untouched by the fire, the homestead would continue to produce as usual. The few lemon, orange, and apple trees on the north slope were so badly scorched in the fire, there wasn't much hope for their survival. Dale and Ben were especially distraught about the apple trees. Flint promised to plant new fruit trees, closer to the house next time.

Flint finally took his gaze from Kate and ate his supper. Afterward he helped Kate clear the table. The family watched, perplexed. A second lamp was lit. Flint sat down again at the end of the table and announced, "Katie, I brought home water pipe." Immediately, Kate perked, uncertain that she'd heard correctly. "Donnie is goin' to get water to your kitchen sink. Don't know why we hadn't before. I can see how much easier that would make life for you and Bette. And the boys . . . they're the ones who haul the buckets in every day."

Flint had much on his mind, and he was letting it out. With flushed face, he stuttered now and then. "Katie, I could see you didn't want to move to Helm's, and now that the fire took that big old house, why, how about that adobe home you always wanted by the avocado trees? Bo and I can start building on it when I get the materials here this week. The little guys will like making adobe blocks."

"No, Flint, no! I'm not movin' anywhere." Kate stood. "Most of our kids were born right here in this house." Kate pointed to the floor. "We've been in here twenty years!"

"I thought you were always dreamin' of that adobe house where you can see out to the ocean."

A surge of surprise ran through Kate, realizing that Flint hadn't forgotten her dream of the adobe house, though she hadn't mentioned it for months if not years. She believed that it would be a terrible sacrifice for Flint to start rebuilding at his age. Besides, now she had everything, the love and togetherness she had yearned for all her life.

"I can walk up there on that slope and look out at that valley and that ocean anytime I want to," she said. "You're what's important . . . my family. I just can't leave this old house." Kate's eyes blurred. "I'm not about to leave that oak tree in the front yard either. I'm plannin' to set out under that tree when I'm old and can't move any longer." Kate sat down.

"Well, I'll be damned." Flint leaned back in his chair and pulled his pipe out of his shirt pocket. He filled it with Prince Albert, poking it down. Silence hung around the table for a spell before Flint found his voice again. "The fire did some good anyway. Much of the land that we needed to clear for more melon patch has been done for us. Just need to get Jackson behind the plow after a bit of rain come springtime, and it's ready for melon seeds." He lit the tobacco, took a few puffs, and leaned his elbows on the table.

"Bette, what do you have to say for yerself? Is your Andrew a decent man, or is he a mouse? He's sweet on you. Comes every weekend, don't he?"

"I love him, Dad," Bette said, crimsoned faced.

"Uh, huh." Silence again.

"Dad?" Bo spoke.

Flint answered with a nod.

"I figure to go into the army anytime now. No need to worry about it, Ma." He glanced at Kate. "There's no war. Not likely to be one either. It's just a two-year thing, Ma. I want to see other places. Maybe even another country."

Again, Flint nodded.

All eyes around the table focused on Bo. Even with Bo's explanation, fear spread over Bette's face and Kate felt a bit weak. Bette reached for Kate's hand.

Rob chuckled. "Hell, Bo, they won't let you in the army as soon as they find out that your name is Napolean Bonaparte!"

After an uproar of laughter around the table, Dale's sky-blue eyes squinted at Bo. "That's not your name, is it Bo?"

Bo's eyes opened wide and his white teeth gleamed. "Yeah, that's what Dad gets for giving the doc free reign to name his second kid after the doc, without first asking him his name. Now then, Dad wasn't one to go back on his word, so that's how I got stuck with that name. It means I'm a great leader, the emperor of France! Ya' hear that, Dale?"

After another burst of laughter, Dale, not daring to openly doubt anyone as big as Bo, wore an inquisitive smile for a while. Finally, Dale and Ben squirmed on the bench, both whining to hear more about the army. To Kate's amusement, they were ignored.

Donnie butted in. It was nearly impossible to ignore him. "I'm going into the service too, but the navy, not the army. Have to finish high school first. Only a two-year stint in the navy and they pay for college!"

Kate wasn't surprised that Donnie had researched and found enough answers to plan several years of his life ahead of schedule. That was his way of doing things.

Rob sat quietly, apparently listening to the chatter, chuckling now and then.

Kate knew that Rob was not the one to replace Bo as Flint's next sidekick. Dale and Ben together might fill those big shoes of Bo's. Flint seemed suddenly melancholy, and Kate wondered what he must think about losing Bo to the army. Although Flint no longer feared the war, Kate knew that Flint depended on the close friendship he enjoyed with his huge, capable, and handsome son. Bo's leaving would cause Flint considerable pain. No doubt, he would miss him sorely, the way she would if Rob or Bette left.

With turned-up freckled nose, Bette said teasingly, "Rob, what are you going to do with yourself, stay here and farm?"

It sounded to Kate that Bette was fishing to get Rob to open up. Maybe she knew something the rest of the family didn't. All eyes shifted to Rob. "Well, ya' all, I been meaning to tell you about Mae Smith. We're fixin' to high-tail it to Las Vegas and get married soon."

Dale and Ben looked at each other and snickered before Ben concentrated again on the flattened biscuit in front of him.

Flint said, "Be quiet, you two hooligans. Rob's got something important to say."

Every soul around the table watched Rob with anticipation and waited for him to spit out more news. Kate figured there were more secrets and he was forced to tell all or to flee. "Mae has a car and two kids, Nate and Ellen. Her husband got killed on the Coral Sea in '42."

Flint glanced at Kate. Kate was sure that Flint remembered, as she did, when Smith was killed, and that they mourned him the day Flint brought the bad news home.

Bette couldn't wait for Rob to finish. She jumped up and stood behind him, hugging his shoulders, her long dark hair flowing down across his face. Beneath his sister's hair, Rob smiled broadly, his eyes half closed and his face flushed. "I told you it would be alright, Rob," she said.

Kate laughed. "Well, wonders never cease. Better bring Mae home for a visit, Rob, before you get hitched. The youngsters, too. Guess I'm near a grandma, huh?" She raised an eyebrow. "Flint, are you feeling like a grandpa?"

Flint nodded, chuckled, and proceeded to fix his pipe. With a more serious tone, he said, "Rob, I visited Smiths' when their son was killed. Didn't see Mae. Is she pretty, Rob? Like Bette and your Ma?" Flint winked at Kate.

"Not nearly as pretty, I'd say, but she's good. Good, like Bette and Ma." Rob shook his head as he talked, as if to reassure his family.

"Any other surprises around this table?" Flint asked. He looked at Kate. "Kate, you hear from Wes lately?"

A tremor shocked through Kate. "Well, I guess you'd know if we got a letter. He said he'd write. Fixin' to stay in Missouri with his family according to Paul. He should. I figure it's about time he acted like a father to those boys, don't you think?"

The family was silent and Flint's expression asked for more from Kate. "What else do you want to know, Flint? I'll tell you anything you want to know," Kate said frankly. Her skin flared warm, her spine straightened. Maybe she left some doubt in Flint's mind about Wes and her intentions regarding him. She had learned that some men needed the challenge of competition, but the dishonesty of it galled her.

Flint heaved a heavy sigh. He knocked his pipe ashes into a gallon-jar lid. "Let's head for bed you all, soon as Ben gets his biscuit down. Got a busy day tomorrow. I'll help you with that water line to the kitchen sink, Donnie, since we got no adobe house to build. Dale, Ben, we got this farm goin' and I'll be looking for lots of help with lots of muscle . . . especially now, with Bo thinking about joining the army, Donnie heading off to the Navy, and Rob getting' himself a woman. We're not going to farm Helm's since most of the muscle has other plans. But, we'll be busy, real busy, and it'll make a man outa' ya'. We might have to retire old Jackson, you know, just ride around on him for fun. He's too damned old now. Done earned his keep. Anyway, I have my eye on a tractor. I saw how you two took hold and did as you needed to do when the fire came. I think you're good men, old enough and smart enough to drive a tractor. What do you whippersnappers' think? Can ya' take it?"

He looked straight at Dale and Ben, waiting for their answer.

The two good men were shaking their heads furiously up and down at each other and then at their father. Ben's mouth, full of biscuit, twisted in a crooked grin and his fist rotated in an effort to flatten another biscuit. Dale spoke for both of them. "You can count on us, Dad. We already know how to work this farm. Ask those bigger guys."

The bigger guys howled at their younger brothers' boasting. Bo's head leaned back in laughter. Donnie slapped his knee. Rob shook his head. "Yeah, yeah."

Flint grinned at his family around the table and continued. "Got more than enough work around here, so I figure it's all she wrote for haying in the valley. Mrs. Helm's too. Not sorry to be away from that damned ghost house. Mrs. Helm didn't seem too sorry that it burned to the ground." He laughed. Kate looked at her husband, wondering why he'd always called Mrs. Helm by her last name. Perhaps he never knew her first name.

"Besides," Flint said, "your mom is startin' a career. I believe she'll need some help getting back and forth to Doc Laraby's. Then he winked at Kate. "Until you learn to drive yourself, Katie."

Kate listened to Flint's every word as he continued. "Guess I'll be stickin' around here all day orderin' Dale and Ben around and reading on that pile of books, except for deliveries to the market."

Flint hesitated and then rose from the table and moved toward Kate. The family sat silent as their eyes followed his jerky stride. Flint reached Kate's end of the table and sat on the edge of the bench, facing her.

Dumbfounded, Kate peered up at him and wondered why he seemed so flustered. He carefully took her hand in his and spoke softly to her, almost in a whisper.

"Katie, I want to move back into your room. Can you stand me?"

Kate looked deeply into her husband's eyes. Then with her chin tilted up, she grinned. "That depends, Flint."

"I love ya' Katie."

"That's all I've ever wanted, Flint. You can move back in."

As they sat round the square table, Flint pulled Kate closer to him. Dale took his harmonica out of his pocket. Soon he and Ben were playing 'You Are My Sunshine'. Kate saw her image profile mirrored in the windowpane. She put a hand to her face. For the first time in years, she didn't need to iron out cares she found there. Suddenly, as the landscape brightened out the window, she remembered something the Medicine Man had promised her long ago and she knew that the Harvest Moon had risen over Mt. McGinny.

THE END.